SOLO COMMAND

SOLO COMMAND

BOOK 3 OF
THE WRAITH SQUADRON SERIES

AARON ALLSTON

RANDOM HOUSE WORLDS

NEW YORK

2024 Random House Worlds Trade Paperback Edition

Published in the United States by Random House Worlds,
an imprint of Random House, a division of
Penguin Random House LLC, New York.

RANDOM HOUSE is a registered trademark,
and RANDOM HOUSE WORLDS and colophon are trademarks of
Penguin Random House LLC.

Originally published in mass market paperback in
the United States by Bantam Spectra,
an imprint of Random House, a division of
Penguin Random House LLC, in 1999.

ISBN 978-0-593-72611-2
Ebook ISBN 978-0-307-79651-6

Printed in the United States of America on acid-free paper

randomhousebooks.com

1st Printing

Book design by Edwin A. Vazquez

THE ESSENTIAL
LEGENDS COLLECTION

For more than forty years, novels set in a galaxy far, far away have enriched the *Star Wars* experience for fans seeking to continue the adventure beyond the screen. When he created *Star Wars,* George Lucas built a universe that sparked the imagination and inspired others to create. He opened up that universe to be a creative space for other people to tell their own tales. This became known as the Expanded Universe, or EU, of novels, comics, video games, and more.

To this day, the EU remains an inspiration for *Star Wars* creators and is published under the label Legends. Ideas, characters, story elements, and more from new *Star Wars* entertainment trace their origins back to material from the Expanded Universe. This Essential Legends Collection curates some of the most treasured stories from that expansive legacy.

A long time ago in a galaxy far, far away. . . .

SOLO COMMAND

NAVAL LIEUTENANT JART EYAN looked rested and cheerful. The fact that he had only twelve minutes to live would have changed his disposition, but he did not possess that knowledge.

He descended the shuttle ramp to stand in the bay of the cruiser *Home One* and look around for a moment. When last he'd seen this part of the ship, many of the shuttles and utility vehicles within had borne the grime and combat scoring that were inevitable in any lengthy campaign. Now they were largely restored to shipshape state. The time *Home One* had spent in the repair yards of Coruscant had obviously been valuable.

Eyan was a Twi'lek, member of a humanoid species best known for the two fleshy appendages, called *lekku,* that hung from their heads where a human would have hair. Many humans forgot that *lekku,* more commonly referred to as brain tails, were sensory bundles, and often gave Twi'leks an edge in assessing their circumstances and possible threats being posed.

Eyan shivered. Ryloth, the Twi'lek home, was a hot world. On *Home One,* a ship engineered for a bridge crew of Mon Calamari, an aquatic species, the ambient temperature tended to be low enough to inconvenience him. The New Republic officer's uniform he wore was never quite sufficient to overcome this discomfort.

Still, he smiled, revealing a broad stretch of carnivore's teeth. It was good to be back.

An aide, a human female, approached him and saluted. "Welcome back, sir. I hope you enjoyed your leave."

"Oh, certainly." Eyan frowned for a moment, trying to remember just what he'd been up to on his leave, but the moment passed. His gesture took in the vehicle bay and indicated the vessel as a whole. "What sort of shape is she in?"

"One hundred percent, sir. All the admiral has to do is point, and we'll be on our way."

"Excellent."

"I wanted to let you know, you had a communication from your wife come in a few minutes ago. It was flagged as urgent."

"Is the captain on duty?"

"Not now, sir."

"Good. I can see to this message before I'm officially on duty again." Eyan nodded thanks to the aide and headed for his quarters.

What could be the trouble? He'd barely left her—as with many New Republic officers, he'd moved his family to Coruscant after being assigned to the former Imperial throneworld.

Barely left her after spending his entire leave with her, too. But he frowned, trying to recall just how they'd spent their time together. The memory wasn't coming in too clearly. He had the nagging feeling that something important was slipping by him.

At his quarters, he brought up his personal terminal and opened his mail. In addition to numerous messages related to his duties, there was the priority-flagged message from his wife. He brought it up.

There she sat, in the tacky red high-backed chair that sat before their terminal at home, and she looked distinctly unhappy, her greenish skin a little more pallid than it should have been. She glanced over to the side as though consulting with someone outside recording range. "Jart," she said, "those Wookiees are dancing in the parlor again."

Eyan switched off the message, not bothering to hear it in its entirety, and erased it. His fingers typed commands into the terminal keyboard. He watched the process, momentarily interested in how he could be so swift, so sure, and yet have no idea what he was doing. *Of course,* he thought. *How unpleasant. Those blasted Wookiees are dancing in the parlor again.* He retrieved his personal sidearm, a small but powerful blaster pistol, and checked it to make sure it was fully charged. He tucked it away in his pocket and departed, certain in what he needed to do to get rid of those dancing Wookiees.

"IN TERMS OF PURE STRATEGY, there was nothing of particular interest between the capital ships in the *Mon Remonda/ Iron Fist* fight." The speaker was a Gamorrean, one of the pig-snouted humanoids known for their warlike dispositions, but almost nothing but his appearance characterized him as a member of that species.

He was speaking Basic, which was beyond the capabilities of other Gamorreans. And his voice was not a natural one; his words emerged twice, once in a throaty babble that sounded like gibberish to most people, and once in a mechanical tone from an implant in his throat. Too, he was the only Gamorrean known to wear a New Republic Fleet Command uniform.

On the shoulder of his orange pilot's uniform he wore a unit patch that was much cleaner, much newer than the rest of the uniform. The main element of the design was a white circle, over which, in light gray, appeared the central symbol of the New Republic, a design like a stylized bird with upswept wings. Over that were twelve X-wing silhouettes, as if viewed from above, in black; one, in the lower left portion of the circle, was large, and the eleven arrayed around it were a third its size. All were oriented the same direction, from lower left to upper right, as though flying in tight, precise formation. Around the white circle was a broad blue ring bordered by two narrow gold rings. It was a brand-new unit patch for a nearly brand-new force, Wraith Squadron.

The being the Gamorrean addressed across the holotable was also unusual, though his kind was certainly well represented in the ranks of the New Republic military. Admiral Ackbar was a member of the Mon Calamari species, humanoids with fish-like features and rubbery skin. Though there were many Mon Calamari serving the New Republic, few had naval combat maneuvers named for him or had designed fighter craft as Ackbar had.

"Essentially," the Gamorrean continued, "we gave Zsinj only one course of action to take if he were to preserve the *Razor's Kiss*." He gestured at the replay of the deep-space naval battle being projected above the holotable. "You see his maneuvers to keep *Iron Fist* between us and *Razor's Kiss*. You see him slow his escape pace to stay with the crippled ship. All by the numbers, numbers our force dictated."

Admiral Ackbar's voice was low, gravelly, slightly more imposing than the standard for his species. "So you find nothing of interest in the engagement."

"If you will forgive me, I did not say that, sir." The Gamorrean manipulated the table controls to zoom the holoprojection view very close to the second of the two Super Star Destroyers. At this near distance, he and Ackbar could see that the mighty vessel was burning at innumerable points on the hull. They could also see swarms of starfighters, New Republic and Imperial, fighting above its surface.

"Mathematically speaking," the Gamorrean continued, "there is much of interest in the behavior of the One Eighty-first. In addition to the fact that a demonstrably loyal Imperial elite squadron should not be working hand in hand with a rogue warlord like Zsinj, there is something odd in the way they fight."

Ackbar's face suggested curiosity. "We detected no oddity in our analysis of the recordings. But, of course, you were there."

"If I may correct you, I actually was not. I was trapped on the hull of the *Iron Fist* for most of that fight, trying to persuade my starfighter to start up. No, it was after you showed me these recordings that I noticed it. Individual fighter pairs tend to respond with an interesting sameness to specific attack patterns. See here—" The Gamorrean pointed to a pair of TIE interceptors characterized by horizontal red stripes on their solar wing arrays. As a pair of X-wings approached from their rear, the TIEs broke off in a tight sweep to port and relative down, moving at an angle the X-wings couldn't match.

The Gamorrean stopped the holoprojection, scrolled the viewpoint over to the *Iron Fist,* and settled it on another pair of 181st interceptors. He advanced the recording as the interceptors cruised toward a pocket of combat, then set it to play at a normal rate. "Here, two A-wings from Polearm Squadron approach from the rear on the same vector. You see the interceptors break exactly the same way, the lead interceptor taking the higher position and the slightly shallower angle, the wingman going lower and taking a harder turn."

"A coincidence."

"No. The angle of attack dictates the way they break. Only with the One Eighty-first, however. I'm not sure what it means."

Ackbar leaned forward, his posture suggesting sudden interest. "Show me more."

LIEUTENANT EYAN MARCHED into the admiral's outer office with his broad, meat-eating smile fixed on his face.

The admiral's aide, seated at a desk outside the door to Ackbar's office, returned the smile. He was a human male who looked as though he thrived on naval food and could stand to thrive a little less. He stood and saluted. "Welcome back, sir. You look as though your leave suited you."

Eyan drew the blaster pistol from his pocket, thrust it into the man's stomach, and pulled the trigger. The blast slammed the man back into his chair but was not as loud as it could have been, muffled by contact with the victim's flesh. "It did," he said.

Eyan reached past the still-twitching corpse to press a button on the underside of the desk. The door into Ackbar's office opened.

THE ADMIRAL LOOKED up as the naval officer entered. "Ah, Lieutenant Eyan. Allow me to present Flight Officer Voort saBinring, also called Piggy. He is a pilot of Wraith Squadron and a mathematical prodigy. SaBinring, this is Lieutenant Jart Eyan, security detail."

Piggy rose to salute the naval officer. "Pleased to meet you, sir."

Eyan returned the salute. "Likewise." Then he pulled his blaster from behind his back, pressed it into Piggy's stomach, and pressed the trigger.

IT IS REMARKABLE, Piggy thought, *the suddenness of it. One moment, perfect health. The next moment, perfect agony.* He could not see, the pain in his gut was so great, like a bonfire lit upon his stomach and eating its way through him, and he could barely hear. He knew he lay upon his back but couldn't remember getting there.

I think I have only moments to live. Interesting.

But the science that had altered him, giving him control

over his emotions, giving him the mathematical acuity that had brought him to Admiral Ackbar's attention, had not done away with all of the biological imperatives that came with being Gamorrean. Another voice rose within him, growing louder: *Live, die, doesn't matter—kill him! Strike him until his bones are paste, rest your tusks upon the warm flesh of his throat, and tear it free! KILL HIM!*

Piggy's eyes snapped open. The assassin stood a couple of meters away, his weapon aimed at Ackbar, words forming in his mouth, words Piggy could not hear.

They didn't matter. The Twi'lek hadn't fired on Ackbar yet. Piggy reached beneath his left sleeve, and with a trembling hand drew forth a vibroblade like the ones most members of his squadron carried there. He thumbed its power on. Then he roared, a noise he knew humans to find intimidating, and threw the blade.

His target jerked at the sudden noise and spun to aim at Piggy. The vibroblade, instead of catching him in the chest, hit the blaster instead, shearing into the metal where barrel met trigger guard. There was a bright flash from the weapon and the assassin flung it away.

Piggy tried to stand but found that his shaky limbs were not making it an easy task. He saw Ackbar slam into the assassin from the side, the webbed hands of the Mon Calamari closing around the Twi'lek's throat . . . but Lieutenant Eyan effortlessly wrenched Ackbar's hands free and threw the admiral against the wall. Then, as deliberately as a diner sitting down to a meal, Eyan straddled Ackbar and closed his own hands over the admiral's throat.

Piggy forced himself to his feet. *Time left . . . estimated ten or twelve seconds. Kill him kill him kill him. Hard to see. Tunnel vision. A side effect of shock. Tear one arm free and beat him until he shrieks for death. He's strong, unnaturally strong.*

He walked, his feet unsteady, to Ackbar's desk, and got his

shoulder under the center portion. He heaved and it came up off the floor, though it nearly unbalanced him. *Good. I still have my strength. Hit him so hard members of his family light-years away cry out in pain and dread.*

He lurched into motion toward the assassin, lowering the edge of the desk as he built up speed, and was rewarded with his victim's sudden perception of him, a look of surprise on the Twi'lek's face.

Then he hit.

ON THE OTHER side of the joining wall, the ensign leaning against the wall of the lounge, a human female, was suddenly flung forward. She slammed onto the floor, her cup of caf splashing as far as the boots of the ensign halfway across the lounge, and she lay there unmoving.

The others in the lounge looked at the bowed-in portion of metal plate that had once been smooth wall. One knelt beside the injured woman. The rest scrambled for the door.

PIGGY DROPPED THE DESK so that it would not fall upon Admiral Ackbar. The motion was more languid than he liked. He didn't seem to have any energy left.

He regarded his handiwork. The Twi'lek's head was a quarter the width it should have been, a smashed mess that pleased one of the voices in Piggy's head even as it appalled the other.

Admiral Ackbar was struggling to rise. He was speaking. But suddenly Piggy couldn't understand the words.

The Gamorrean fell over backward as the heat and pain in his gut spread out to overwhelm him.

———

THE TWO TIE interceptors banked, maneuvering in a wide circle as they scanned for enemies, and the lunar surface sped by beneath them.

To someone seeing them for the first time, these starfighters might have seemed comical. Their cockpits were unaerodynamic-looking spheres taller than a human. Projecting from either side of the cockpits were thick posts, the wing pylons, each about the length of the cockpit's circumference. At the end of either pylon was a solar wing array, a curved, roughly oval wing with a deep notch cut out of the leading edge. Where normal TIE fighters were nicknamed eyeballs, for their spherical cockpits, in New Republic fighter slang, interceptors, with their narrower sight profiles, were called squints.

But no one seeing them maneuver or fight would continue to think them amusing. Agile and fast, armed with four lasers each capable of punching through starfighter armor, they were among the deadliest tools in the arsenal of the Empire.

Not that Imperial pilots flew these two.

"Rogue Two, this is Leader. Comm check."

"I read you."

"Two unknowns now showing on my sensor screen at two-eight-five. Follow me in."

"I'm your wing."

The lead interceptor veered toward the distant blip, the second following hard, their maneuvers tight and sure. Within moments, the enemy—two tiny bright spots near the horizon—came into view.

"Two, the computer gives a tentative ID as one interceptor, one X-wing."

"I read it that way. The X-wing is leading. Shall we get some separation, make them split up to cover us both?"

"Ehhh . . . not yet. Stay with standard Imperial protocols at first to make this a proper test."

"Right."

As the range meter numbers scrolled down to firing range, the oncoming starfighters opened fire. Curiously, the enemy TIE interceptor held in close behind the X-wing, dropping just beneath to fire, rising above to fire again.

The two interceptors bobbed and juked, ducking fire as they returned laser blasts. Their return shots slammed into the X-wing's forward shields, dissipating meters short of the X-wing fuselage.

"Hey, I get it," Two said. "You use the—"

Red laser fire from the X-wing hit him low on the circular transparisteel viewport. Two exploded in a bright flash, and Leader's interceptor rocked, hit by gases swelling from the detonation. The enemy interceptor and X-wing sped by.

Despite his demise, Two kept talking, his voice floating into his leader's comm unit like transmissions from a land of the dead. "Whoops, sorry, Wedge."

"No problem, Tycho." Wedge Antilles heeled hard to port, coming up behind the two attackers.

Instead of splitting up, with the faster interceptor trying to come up behind Wedge, the attackers had remained together, though they'd changed their formation: the X-wing was now in the rear, with the interceptor bobbing around just in front of it. It was tight, economical flying, and Wedge nodded. On their approach, the enemy interceptor had used the X-wing as a barricade, staying behind its shields except for the bare seconds necessary to line up a shot. The X-wing must have had most or all of its shield energy forward on the approach. Now, as they retreated, the interceptor was still enjoying the X-wing's protection, and that starfighter's shield energy would all be concentrated to the rear.

Wedge accelerated toward the pair, rising until he was slightly above their plane of flight. They knew he wouldn't overfly them; he'd tuck in behind and fire at their comparatively unprotected rears until they were destroyed. So their tactic had to be to break at some point. The X-wing wouldn't be able to outmaneuver him, so it would be the interceptor trying to get in behind him. That meant they'd wait until he was engaged with the X-wing before breaking.

The computer graphic representing the X-wing jittered within his sensor screen, announcing a laser lock. He ignored it and began a shallow dive, dipping down beneath the X-wing's flight plane as if to try a snap shot at the interceptor. But halfway into the maneuver he drew back on the yoke, sending him into a sudden climb.

And the enemy interceptor, rising past the X-wing's nose in an effort to keep the X-wing between itself and Wedge, suddenly jittered in the same sensor screen. Wedge fired and saw the green flashes of three of his lasers connect with the interceptor's engines. The squint blew out of the sky and Wedge jerked hard to port to avoid flying through the thickest part of the debris cloud.

The X-wing took advantage of his sudden dodge by peeling off to starboard, a hard turn—an obvious attempt to set up for another head-to-head pass. But Wedge switched his comm unit over to a general broadcast frequency and said, "Exercise terminated."

The voice of Garik "Face" Loran, onetime boy actor for the Empire and now New Republic flyer, came back. "But I'm not dead yet."

"You're protesting?"

"Not exactly. Just curious."

The vista of the lunar surface and the maneuvering X-wing faded abruptly to blackness. Wedge reached back to open the access hatch, situated where the twin ion engines were in a real TIE interceptor, and climbed out into overhead light.

The room was a large one, crowded with tables, chairs, and simulator units. Most were narrower units, the better to conform to the cockpit interiors of the X-wing, Y-wing, and A-wing starfighters used by the New Republic, but a few were spherical, such as the one Wedge had just vacated. The room was heavily trafficked by pilots, many of them in the New Republic's orange pilot's jumpsuits, and technicians in more somber colors. Most of the pilots were clustered around the various simulator units, monitoring the practicing pilots' efforts on overhead holo displays.

Across an aisle busy with human traffic, Face Loran dropped nimbly to the floor and looked curiously toward Wedge. Wedge saw a female pilot trainee glance at him, do a double take, then flutter her hand over her heart as she whispered into the ear of a confidant. Face, with his strikingly handsome features, intent green eyes, and somehow artfully mussed black hair, often had that effect on women. Wedge waved him over.

They were joined a moment later by two other pilots. Flight Officer Lara Notsil, a lightly built woman with downy blond hair, was possessed of a delicate beauty that belied her intensity and skill in starfighter combat. Captain Tycho Celchu, a fair-haired man with features that suggested he'd weathered a lot of turmoil in his life, spoke first. "Why'd you kill the sim, Commander?"

"We were here to test the youngsters' new combined-unit tactic," Wedge said. "As soon as you and Lara went out, it became just another X-wing versus TIE exercise. There's plenty of value in those, of course, but that's not what we came here for." He fixed his attention on Face. "What was your opinion of the effectiveness of your tactic?"

Face shrugged; he didn't look happy. "Nowhere near as effective as I'd hoped."

"You were presuming that experienced enemies would be so thrown off by the novelty of what you were doing that they'd be easy kills?"

"Presuming? No, sir. Just hoping."

"Lara, your thoughts?"

"Well, one exercise isn't statistically significant," she said.

"So anything I had to say would be premature. Irrelevant. But I think the tactic worked as it was supposed to. I received a lot of protection from Face's shields on both the incoming and outbound legs of the run, in spite of the fact that you flushed me out pretty easily. I'd say it was effective."

Tycho nodded. "I'd agree. But I think it's a one-shot tactic. Usable only in paired head-to-head runs or when you have an X-wing/TIE pair going after a single target. It would be best used at the start of any engagement, then abandoned."

"I'd say it's worth further practice and analysis," Wedge said. "Face, Lara, work up some automated exercises to give all the Wraiths the opportunity to play around with this." He checked the chrono strapped to his wrist. "Though not now. We have about ten minutes to get to our briefing. Dismissed."

The two younger pilots saluted and headed off into the stream of traffic.

Wedge called, "Hey."

The two turned, Face curious, Lara looking guilty, as if wondering if she'd forgotten to salute before leaving.

Wedge said, "Developing just this kind of tactic is one of the things I put Wraith Squadron together for. Good work. Keep at it."

They smiled and continued toward the room's main exit.

MOST OF THE MEMBERS of Rogue Squadron and Wraith Squadron were in their seats in the semicircular briefing amphitheater when Wedge and Tycho entered.

"Commander Antilles—draw!"

Wedge turned at the sound of Wes Janson's voice. The eternally youthful pilot, executive officer of Wraith Squadron, was on his feet, aiming a datapad as though it were a blaster pistol, thumbing the transmit button with manic intensity. Wedge sighed and brought out his own datapad to receive the transmitted file. But Janson's antics were a good sign. They suggested that the news Wedge was waiting for had arrived—and was good. En route to the main dais, he glanced at the Rogue Squadron executive officer, Nawara Ven, a distinguished-looking Twi'lek with brain tails arrayed artfully over his shoulders, and Wedge received a datafile from him as well. He glanced over the two officers' transmissions as he stepped up behind the lectern, then looked up at the pilots before him.

Two squadrons, nearly at full fighting strength, the best pilots he could assemble and train. He felt a rush of pride at what he'd managed to accomplish with these two units, at the level at which they'd managed to perform, but he kept it from his face. "I have mostly good news to bring to you today. First and foremost, Piggy saBinring is responding well to bacta treatment, he has regained consciousness, and all indications are that he'll enjoy a full recovery." That brought applause and exclamations of relief from the assembly. "Unfortunately, we still have no information about the assassin's motive in attacking Ackbar. When the admiral asked him why he was doing this, the assassin said he, Ackbar, knew why. You know the assassin died in the attempt. His wife and children are missing, and the investigation is continuing.

"Second, the *Mon Remonda* is within a day of leaving repair dock. By this time tomorrow, we'll be back in space and taking the fight back to Warlord Zsinj."

That brought more applause. *Mon Remonda*, the mighty Mon Calamari cruiser that was the flagship of the fleet commanded by Han Solo, had taken significant damage in its recent duel with the warlord Zsinj's own flagship, the Super Star Destroyer *Iron Fist*. But Zsinj's forces had suffered far more.

"Third, and directly as a result of this, you all have one last leave coming to you. Report to the shuttle bay at fifteen hundred tomorrow, with your bags packed and all your affairs settled; until then, you're on your own. Enjoy yourselves.

"However, we can't forget that the last time we had leave here on Coruscant, a covert unit probably belonging to Zsinj came close to assassinating the Wraiths. So we'll follow these protocols. Civilian dress only. I know you Wraiths have just gotten your unit patches, but you'll have to stow them during this leave. The more recognizable of you—you know who you are—should make some effort to conceal your features. Stay out of the bars pilots tend to frequent.

"Fourth, I have some changes to announce. The Wraiths have a new pilot for their roster—Targon, please stand."

At the back of the amphitheater, a pilot stood, and the Rogues and Wraiths twisted to see him.

The new pilot was a Devaronian—grayish-skinned, with diabolic horns protruding from his forehead and fanglike teeth that would only cause appreciation in the heart of a carnivorous predator. His voice, when he spoke, was surprisingly deep and resonant considering his apparent youth. "Flight Officer Elassar Targon reporting for duty, sir."

"Targon comes to us fresh from Fleet Command Academy; in addition to being a competent pilot, he's a medical corpsman. Once again we'll have a unit medic who can do more than put on pressure patches and make squealy noises. And unlike the rest of you, he hasn't yet had time to ruin his career or his mind."

"Then he won't do." That was Janson. "Send him home. Get us another lunatic."

"Excuse me!" The Devaronian pilot hopped up to stand in his seat, took a wide stance with one foot in the adjacent chair; he threw his arms back and chest out, posing like some super-human hero from the most ridiculous of Face Loran's holodramas. "Elassar Targon, master of the universe, reporting for duty!"

Wedge cocked an eyebrow at him. Interesting that a very junior officer would be willing to perform that sort of display in his first few moments with his new unit. Either the reputation of Wraith Squadron had convinced him that it was appropriate . . . or he was another complete maniac, and Fleet Command had found another mental case for his command. Despite the laughter erupting from the assembled pilots, Wedge clearly heard Janson speak again, "I withdraw my objection."

Wedge returned his attention to the pilots. "Targon, sit. Pipe down, everyone. Fifth, and last, there's going to be a little reorganizing to do within my squadrons.

"Until and unless we persuade Starfighter Command that we need to participate in another prolonged field mission, we'll be with *Mon Remonda* on active duty. I've been put in command of the ship's four fighter squadrons. I'm also transferring back to and assuming direct command of Rogue Squadron, effective immediately. I'll still fly with the Wraiths, as well as Nova and Polearm, when circumstances and opportunities warrant, but I'm relinquishing day-to-day command." He saw the Rogues' good cheer continue, but the Wraiths sobered with the realization that their very best pilot was leaving them. Wedge continued, "Lieutenant Loran, attention."

Face stood. Wedge saw a flicker of suspicion cross his face, but it disappeared quickly as the actor regained control of himself.

Wedge said, "This isn't a permanent promotion—yet—so we're not going to do anything to you that will leave permanent marks. However, it is my pleasure to confer upon you the rank of brevet captain, which entitles you to command a unit such as Wraith Squadron. Congratulations, Face." From a pocket he dug a semitransparent envelope, and this he tossed to the pilot. "Your new rank insignia."

As the other pilots applauded, Wedge glanced among the other ranking pilots of Wraith Squadron, gauging reactions.

Wes Janson, who was the senior lieutenant in the squadron, was applauding and smiling easily. No surprise, as he had no real interest in command or, ultimately, in remaining with the Wraiths; he preferred to be just one of the gang back in Rogue Squadron, so this promotion of Face over his head was not threatening to him.

Kell Tainer, the biggest human in Wraith Squadron and, after Face, the most hologenic, also looked as though he were comfortable with the choice. Perhaps he had ultimately realized that, though he was a brilliant flyer and very capable technician, he didn't have the temperament for or real interest in command.

The smile of Shalla Nelprin, the squadron's newest lieutenant, was broad and genuine.

That left Myn Donos, a lieutenant with more years and more experience than Face. He looked serious and contemplative. But then, serious was merely a step up from his usual expression, that of dour intensity. Still, he had to know that this promotion reflected a lack of trust in his command skills. Mere months ago, while wearing the rank of brevet captain himself, Donos had commanded an X-wing unit that had been slaughtered by a Zsinj ally, Admiral Apwar Trigit, and had suffered serious emotional trauma resulting from that event. He probably thought that Wedge still held no trust in him.

Which wasn't true. But Wedge Antilles's units were largely meritocracies. The most meritorious pilots were promoted fastest, and Face had demonstrated more tactical savvy and more command skills than Donos, even though Wedge felt Donos was probably reliable.

As the applause died, Wedge said, "That's it for now. Any questions?"

Face was first with a hand up. "If we're launching tomorrow, sir, when do we get Piggy back?"

"We never lose him. He has requested that he be trans-

ferred to the bacta treatment facility aboard *Mon Remonda*.
General Solo has approved the request. We'll haul him around
until he's ready to emerge, then put him back to work. Wes?"

The Wraiths' executive officer lowered his hand. "The
usual."

"The usual answer, too. We were lucky to get Face's
X-wing fully repaired. Wraith Squadron isn't getting any re-
placement X-wings anytime soon. The Wraiths will continue
flying mixed X-wings and TIE interceptors. Anything else?
No? Dismissed."

THIRTY MINUTES LATER, Wedge opened the door to leave his
quarters. He took an involuntary step back. There, shoulder
to shoulder, blocking the door, were Wes Janson and Rogue
Squadron pilot Derek "Hobbie" Klivian. Hobbie was struggling to keep his face straight; Janson's expression was merry.
Janson asked, "Going somewhere, Commander?"

Wedge shouldered his way between them. "We have leave,
remember? That's what you two should do. Leave."

They fell in beside him, one on either side. This corridor,
deep in the residential decks of Coruscant's Sivantlie Base, led
toward the turbolifts.

"Would you look at him?" Janson said. "Hair combed,
evening clothes immaculate."

Hobbie, his face as long and mournful as ever, said, "And
he smells like a fresh spring morning."

"I think our commander is going on a date."

"I think you're right."

"Meaning he really needs our help. How long has it been
since you've been on a date, Wedge? I don't think some of the
Wraiths were born then."

"We're your escort," Hobbie said. "We'll protect you from
yourself."

"So, who are you seeing?" Janson asked.

"What I'm seeing is kitchen duty in your immediate future," Wedge said. They reached the bank of turbolifts and waited for the lift to reach them.

Janson continued, "It's Iella, isn't it?"

Wedge scowled. "What makes you think that?"

"Oh, nothing. Just the way you look whenever her name is mentioned. Have you noticed that, Hobbie?"

"Oh, I've noticed. What do you think?"

"I haven't decided yet if she's right for our commander. And the rest of the squad hasn't voted yet."

The turbolift doors opened and they entered the shallow car, turning to face the hall. Wedge held his hand against the side of the entryway, preventing the doors from closing. "Roof," Wedge said.

Janson looked confused. "Roof? Not the personal vehicles hangar?"

"Roof." Then Wedge took a deep breath and bellowed, "About face! Forward march!"

By reflex, the two pilots spun. Wedge stepped back out into the hall and heard Janson and Hobbie thud into the wall at the rear of the turbolift. Then the turbolift doors closed and the car carried his pilots up and far away.

He smiled and summoned another turbolift.

TWO FLOORS DOWN, a quartet of Wraiths approached a door as anonymous as Wedge's.

Donos said, "He just received a promotion of sorts. We shouldn't present him with a mutiny first thing." He kept from his face the discomfort he was feeling.

Dia Passik, the female Twi'lek, said, "He insisted that he wasn't feeling well."

Lara Notsil smiled over her shoulder at them. "He lied. He lies all the time, you know."

"I know. But he seemed so genuine."

"He does that all the time, too. This is the right thing to do. Myn, Elassar, back me up."

The two men exchanged glances. "Absolutely," Donos said.

The Devaronian looked confused. "You change sides pretty fast, don't you, Lieutenant? I've barely met Captain Loran. I shouldn't have an opinion."

Lara scowled at him. "Wait a moment. A fellow Wraith says 'Back me up,' and you say 'I don't know'?"

The Devaronian straightened. His voice deepened. "My apologies. Absolutely. You're right. In fact, we shouldn't knock. We should just blast the door lock and kick the door in."

"We'll knock," Lara said. She rapped on the door.

There was no answer. She knocked again, more insistently.

From within came Face's voice. "Yes?"

"May we come in?"

"I'm not decent."

"When are you ever?" Lara opened the door and looked in. Donos could see over her shoulder; Face was lying on his bed, still in uniform, staring at the ceiling.

Lara pushed her way in and heard the others crowd in behind her. "What are you doing?"

"I'm learning to play a variety of musical instruments using only the power of my mind."

"That's what I thought. Now it's time to go out and enjoy yourself."

"Maybe you didn't hear the commander's orders about the more recognizable members of the squads?"

She snorted. "That was for Runt's sake most of all. When you're two meters tall, covered in fur, and the only member of your species in Starfighter Command, you have to lie low sometimes. But *you* can put on a disguise. I've often suspected that you sometimes put on disguises just to go to the refresher."

"Now, that's an idea." Face looked at her for the first time, gave her a smile that was meant to communicate cheer. "You go ahead. I'll be fine."

"Hey, I'm your wingman now. It's my job to keep you from making big mistakes. And it would be a big mistake not to enjoy the last leave you're likely to have for a while."

"Do I have to pull rank on you?"

"You only get to do that when it's appropriate. That's the unwritten law."

"Where'd you hear that?"

"I read it somewhere."

Face snorted. "All right. Give me five minutes to transform myself into something inconspicuous. Where are we going?"

Lara jerked a thumb back at her companions. "Since Elassar hasn't run up against Zsinj—or anyone but his instructors—before now, we're going to take him to the Galactic Museum's new display on Imperial Intelligence. Give him an idea what he's up against. Then we get a drink. Then you and Myn and Elassar give in to male biology and insult a bar full of soldiers, and Dia and I haul your battered bodies back to base."

Face looked helplessly at Donos and Elassar. "You see what happens when we don't get involved in the mission's planning stage?"

THE MUSEUM'S DISPLAYS on Imperial Intelligence were not, Donos decided, the one-sided history they could have been.

The first displays on the tour gave details of the Old Republic's Intelligence division, the secret police who were charged with protecting the Republic from subversion and treason. One display, a holoscreen within a container the size and approximate shape of a bacta tank, played a drama about Republic Intelligence commandos thwarting an assassination attempt made against members of the old Republican Senate. Another display was a transparisteel case holding a score of weapons and gadgets used by field agents; Donos recognized the technological ancestors of gear the Wraiths had carried in the field.

Another holoprojection showed a man in dark commando garments. He was dark-skinned, graying at the temples, intense interest in his eyes, his features just a little too diabolical to be beautiful. "I was Vyn Narcassan," he said. "In my twenty-year career with Republic Intelligence, I successfully completed over a hundred covert missions. I couldn't prevent Senator Palpatine's rise to power or his subsequent reign as Emperor. But I could, and did, engineer my disappearance. And despite Imperial Intelligence's burning need to silence me and extinguish all the secrets I learned"—the projection leaned forward as if to impart a confidence—"they never found me." He drew back, his smile creating deep dimples beside his mouth, his expression one of a satisfaction so immense that it bordered on arrogance.

Something about the projection jogged Donos's memory, but he couldn't figure out what it was. He filed it away for future reference. Someday, when he was trying to remember something else entirely, the answer would bubble up to the surface of his mind and annoy him intensely.

Farther along the series of black, ill-lit museum display halls—the decor an attempt, Donos thought, to edge visitors into the sort of paranoid mindset appropriate to subjects such as Imperial Intelligence—the displays became more unsettling. As Palpatine took power, the Intelligence Division became a tool of terror and retaliation. Displays chronicled assassinations, kidnappings of Old Republic loyalists, tortures, subversions. An interrogation chamber was shown in great detail, actual holographic footage of a subject being questioned about a rumored insurrection. The replay showed the subject, a man of Chandrila, dying during questioning. The narrator finishing up commentary on the event pointed out that the insurrection was entirely imaginary.

One display showed the longtime Intelligence head, Armand Isard, an aging man with an inhumanity to his eyes and features that were unsettlingly real even in holographic replay. Farther down the exhibition, another showed his daughter, Ysanne Isard, nicknamed Iceheart, a tall and elegant woman of formidable bearing, and told of her swift rise to power through two simple tactics: turning in her own father for treasonous thoughts and attracting the eye of the Emperor. After Palpatine's death, she had even managed secretly to gain control of the Empire itself for a time.

Face, his features buried under a wooly brown beard, lingered before the projection of Ysanne Isard for a long time, and Donos saw him shudder—a motion too slight for any but those who knew him best to notice. The Wraiths were aware that when Face was a boy star in holodramas, he'd actually met Iceheart, had even been invited to sit in her lap. Now Iceheart was dead, killed by Rogue Squadron's own Tycho Celchu, and Donos knew the universe was better off without her.

To some extent, Imperial Intelligence had died with her. To be sure, an organization with that name survived under the coalition that had replaced Iceheart, but it was not managed with the same inventive ruthlessness that had characterized Isard and her father. The organization was still a danger . . . but to fewer and fewer people as the years went by.

Instead of going out the exit at the end of the exhibition, the Wraiths turned about and went back the way they came, to give Targon a chance to view the displays again. As they passed the holo of Iceheart, Donos saw the Devaronian pilot pull up something held by a chain around his neck and press it to his forehead.

"A lucky charm?" Donos asked.

Targon nodded. "A coin of the Old Republic. It holds a lot of luck."

"How do you know?"

"My brother was never shot down while wearing it. It's better than anything else I have. He sent it to me when I joined the Academy. Better than my lucky carved bantha-bone. Better than my lucky belt buckle. Or my lucky gilding set. Or my—"

Face interrupted. "What's a gilding set?"

"Well, you know. For my horns."

"I don't know. What about your horns?"

Targon shrugged. "For special occasions, important festivals, we sometimes—Devaronians I mean—put gold leaf on our horns. For decoration."

"And this is just a device to help you do that?"

"That's right."

"What makes it lucky?"

"Well, the first time I used it, shortly before I entered the Academy, I attracted the eye of a certain young lady—"

"Never mind."

Donos and Face exchanged glances. The Wraiths and Rogues were light on pilots who put much stock in good-luck charms, but such pilots were common throughout the New Republic and the Empire. Donos saw Face's eyes light up, probably because of an idea for a prank.

"I was Vyn Narcassan. In my twenty-year career with Republic Intelligence, I successfully completed over a hundred covert missions." As they reached the display honoring the last of the Old Republic's Intelligence heroes, Donos gave the man one last look, took in his dimpling smile, then realized what it was the man reminded him of.

Not what—who. The man's skin tone, his dimples, his unusual physical beauty—they were all shared by another Wraith. Shalla Nelprin.

That rocked Donos back on his heels. But the physical resemblance was dramatic.

Donos smiled at the long-missing agent. "We'll just let that be our little secret, Narcassan," he said under his breath. "But I'm going to send Shalla a message and tell her to come visit this exhibit today. Not why. Just that she needs to. In case it means something to her."

"Who are you talking to?" That was Lara. Face and Dia were already a few steps ahead, arm in arm, with Targon trailing behind them.

"I'll tell you sometime."

"Edallia?" The voice, wavery and uncertain, came from behind them. "Edallia Monotheer, it's so good to see you!"

Donos glanced back. Approaching them was an old man, his hair a wispy white, his body so sparse of flesh that he seemed skeletal, but there was nothing menacing about the smile he was turning on Lara.

Behind him a dozen meters but coming at a trot was a middle-aged woman, overweight and matronly, her expression anxious. "Father," she called, and she sounded out of breath. "Not again."

The old man reached Lara, seized her hand, pumped it vigorously. "Edallia, it's been so long. Did you ever marry that boy? Did you graduate? What have you been doing?"

Lara tried unsuccessfully to extricate her thoroughly shaken hand. "Sir, I don't—I'm not—"

"I'm so sorry." That was the daughter. Reaching her father, she took his hand, forcing him to give up his grip on Lara's. "He's . . . confused. He doesn't always remember where he is. Or when."

"It's all right," Lara said, but she looked a little shaken.

The old man said, "Child, I must introduce Edallia Monotheer. One of my best pupils."

His daughter asked, "When?"

He looked confused. "What?"

"When was she one of your best pupils?"

The old man looked back at Lara, his eyes wavery, uncertain. "Why, it's been thirty, thirty-five years."

"Look at her, father. She's not thirty years old."

The old man leaned in close to Lara's face and peered. "Edallia?"

Lara shook her head, and though she maintained a cheerful smile, Donos decided that it was forced. "I'm sorry," she said. "I'm Lara."

"Oh." The old man drew back and looked around. "Where is she, then?"

"Maybe farther up the exhibition, Father. You go look. I'll be along."

With a courteous, if distracted, nod to the Wraiths, the old man began to walk back the way he'd come.

"I'm so sorry," the woman said. "He was once with Old Republic Intelligence, so he likes to come here day after day. He was shot on a mission shortly after the Emperor came to power." She indicated a place just in front of her temple. "He hasn't been the same since."

"It's not a problem," Lara said. "He was very nice."

"Thank you for understanding." The woman turned and trotted along in her father's wake.

Lara turned and bumped into Face and Dia, who had returned during the conversation. "Oops."

Face looked at her intently. "Gerwa Patunkin?"

"No."

"Totovia Lampray?"

"No." She smiled. "Stop it."

"Dipligonai Phreet?"

"Shut up." She pushed past him, laughing, and headed for the exit. "Let's get that drink. I need it."

"Moploogy Starco?"

"Face, I'm going to shoot you."

2

STARFIGHTERS SWARMED FROM the sides of the Mon Calamari cruiser *Mon Remonda* like insects from a deep-space nest. They formed up in four groups—two X-wing, one A-wing, one B-wing—and descended toward Levian Two, the world *Mon Remonda* now orbited. From this altitude, it seemed stony and orange and impossibly inhospitable, but the comm chatter the pilots were picking up suggested otherwise.

"Entering Delta Sector. More of the same. I'll map-flag locations of survivors." "Ravine Six here. Repulsorlift is out. I'm going to have to attempt a high-speed landing." "Ravine Six, switch to ten-oh-three. You've got your own controller standing by." "Beta Sector Base, this is Beta Ten. I read unknowns descending, four groups." "Beta Ten, this is Base. There are some TIEs in the unknowns but they're mostly friendlies."

Wedge sighed and activated his comm unit. "Beta Sector Base, this is Rogue Leader. You've got Rogue, Wraith, Polearm, and Nova Squadrons in descent to your position. Looks like we're a little late to the party."

" 'Fraid so, Rogue Leader. You've missed a Raptor raid. They blasted out of here half an hour ago. We've got settlements and facilities hit all over this hemisphere. Could we interest you in some search-and-rescue action?"

"Glad to oblige. Give us vectors for twenty search pairs and we'll get on it."

———

"SHIPS DROPPING OUT of hyperspace!" It was *Mon Remonda*'s sensor officer, Golorno, a human young enough not to be able to keep his voice level in times of stress. "I count four, five, six capital ships!"

Han Solo abandoned his armature-mounted chair and moved to stand behind Golorno. He turned to his communications officer. "Recall the starfighters now." Then he leaned over Golorno's shoulder. "Details, I need details," he said.

"Uh, uh, two Star Destroyers, one *Imperial*-class, one *Victory*-class. One heavy cruiser, a Dreadnaught, I think. Two light cruisers—telemetry says probably *Carrack*-class. At the back of the formation . . ." The young officer's voice dropped. "One *Super*-class Star Destroyer."

"*Iron Fist.*" Solo straightened and slapped his hands together. "He's finally decided to come in for a scrap."

He calculated unit strengths. His flagship was *Mon Remonda*, one of the most powerful of the Mon Calamari cruisers, and its pilot complement, led by Wedge Antilles, couldn't be better. Also in this portion of his fleet were *Mon Karren*, a Mon Cal cruiser of more normal strength, *Tedevium*, a frigate recently converted from a training ship back to a combat vessel, and *Etherhawk*, a *Marauder*-class corvette that was just one restoration job ahead of being dilapidated. Not nearly enough strength to handle the fleet Zsinj had assembled against him . . . but Zsinj didn't know that Solo's Group 2 was standing by outside the Levian system. One holocomm call and Solo's strength would be doubled, making this more of a fair slugging match. "Call in Group Two," he ordered. "How long before Zsinj's force reaches us?"

"Three minutes, sir."

"How long before the starfighters return?"

"They're grouping. Four or five minutes, sir."

Solo sighed. "Slugging match" was to be the correct phrase for it.

An impulse caused him to turn back to the door out of the bridge. As he'd suspected, Chewbacca was there, just outside, standing by. The Wookiee, who chose to have no official role in the anti-Zsinj group, but preferred to stay near the bridge and Solo, had come up as soon as the tenor of voices from the bridge sounded different. Solo gave him a confident grin.

"A second group is dropping out of hyperspace, sir!"

Solo whipped around to stare at the sensor screen again. It was broadening, updating—the data stream at the bottom indicated that the sensor screen was being supplemented by information from *Tedevium*.

It showed another force of capital ships appearing on the far side of Levian Two. Telemetry indicated that the new force included two Star Destroyers, two Dreadnaughts, a light cruiser, and a *Lancer*-class frigate—a vessel designed especially to assault swarms of starfighters.

"We're in trouble," Solo said.

Golorno turned to look up at Solo. He wasn't able to mask his fear.

Solo gave him a reassuring half grin. "Don't worry. I know when to dump my cargo and run." He turned to the navigator. "Set us a course out of here. What's the closest path to get us out of Levian Two's gravity well?"

The Mon Calamari navigator consulted his board. "Directly through the Super Star Destroyer's force, sir."

"Figures. Make that our primary course. Pass it on to our group."

"Done, sir."

"Communications, revise my order to Group Two. Tell them to be on course and ready for a jump at any second, but to stand by."

"Yes, sir."

He turned to Captain Onoma, a Mon Calamari male with salmon-colored skin. "Captain, take us out."

"Yes, sir."

"Third hostile group dropping out of hyperspace!"

Solo turned to look, disbelieving, at Golorno. "You have *got* to be kidding."

WEDGE ANTILLES STOOD his X-wing on its tail and blasted toward the sky.

He'd sent Polearm Squadron, the A-wing unit commanded by Captain Todra Mayn, on ahead. There was little tactical sense in keeping the faster craft back with the X-wings and B-wings. Now Wedge led Rogue Squadron and Wraith Squadron in escorting Nova Squadron, the B-wing unit.

Sensor data arriving from *Mon Remonda* showed Solo's group closing slowly on a unit of six capital ships. The Mon Cal cruiser was already swarming with enemy starfighters, and defenders from *Mon Karren* and *Tedevium*.

Wedge added up the numbers on that. Those two ships could field five squadrons of starfighters between them. The enemy force ahead could field nearly twenty-two squadrons. And then there were enemies coming up from behind—as Wedge's squadrons cleared the atmosphere, his sensors picked up two additional groups of capital ships chasing Solo's force.

This was not going to be good.

Wedge wondered if Baron Fel was among the starfighter pilots assaulting *Mon Remonda*. Soontir Fel was one of the greatest pilots ever to emerge from the Imperial Academy, one of the greatest to have flown with Rogue Squadron—and a man who shared a secret with Wedge Antilles.

They were brothers-in-law. Only they and a very few others knew that famous Imperial actress Wynssa Starflare was also Wedge's sister Syal Antilles. Since the disappearance of Fel and Syal several years ago, Wedge had had no news whatsoever of his sister. Now Fel was back, but flying for the wrong side, and there was still no word of Syal. It was a secret Wedge kept very close. One of his own pilots, Face Loran, had even starred in a holodrama with Wynssa Starflare, but Wedge had never confided the secret to him, even to obtain Face's reminiscences about his sister.

And now, once again, Wedge was rushing into battle with a force that might include Fel, leading to the grim possibility that he might have to shoot down his own brother-in-law . . . and perhaps lose any clue Fel might offer to Syal's fate.

Sensors showed that the *Iron Fist* force had, since the last communication from *Mon Remonda,* turned about and was now retreating before Han Solo's force. Wedge nodded. If Zsinj maintained a course toward the planet, his force and Solo's would blast past each other in a matter of split seconds, exchanging one low-accuracy barrage, and then Zsinj would have to turn his force around to pursue. By retreating before Solo on the shortest course to an area of space where the New Republic fleet could engage their hyperdrives, he prolonged the engagement.

Wedge's squadrons caught up to *Mon Remonda,* but circled around several kilometers from the Mon Cal cruiser. At this distance, the swarming dogfight between starfighters near the cruiser looked like twinkling stars. A grim simile—Wedge reminded himself that some of those twinkles were explosions that had once been friends and allies.

"S-foils to attack position," he ordered, and suited action to words by toggling the appropriate switch above his line of sight. His S-foils split and locked into the familiar profile that gave the X-wing its name. "B-wings, you may arm your weapons."

His sensors showed Zsinj's force spread out before the approaching *Mon Remonda.* Straightforward tactics; it meant *Mon Remonda* couldn't expect to make a minor course change to elude a tight group of ships even temporarily. Any minor course change would still send *Mon Remonda* into the umbrella of enemy ships; any major course change would allow the pursuit ships to catch up.

But this tactic was about to work in Wedge's favor.

They dove in toward *Iron Fist*'s stern. Sensors showed no starfighter response from the Super Star Destroyer—either the remaining squadrons were being slow to scramble, or all squadrons were engaged with *Mon Remonda*.

Then flashes of light emerged from the destroyer's stern, congregating on Wedge's force, and the ball-like detonations of concussion missiles began to fill the space around them. Wedge was rocked by a near miss. "Begin evasive maneuvers," he said. "X-wings, ready torpedoes. Remember, port engines only."

Pair by pair, his X-wings began a dance, juking and jinking to throw off the aim of the Imperial gunners they so rapidly approached. The B-wings hung back, allowing the X-wings to draw the initial fire.

Wedge's range meter scrolled down below two kilometers, the maximum effective range for his targeting computer. Enemy turbolaser fire increased in intensity—and proximity.

At fifteen hundred meters, he said, "Launch one, launch two." He fired, sending paired proton torpedoes toward one of *Iron Fist*'s stern engines. More blue streaks than he could count emerged from his X-wings, instantly crossing the distance to the destroyer, which was suddenly and brilliantly illuminated by their detonations against the port side of the stern.

He looped to port. "Novas, your turn."

"Acknowledged, and thanks, Rogue Leader." That was the voice of Nova One. "Novas, launch one and begin ion fire."

Blue streaks leaped from the B-wings. Then the ungainly-looking craft continued their dive toward *Iron Fist*'s engines, their ion cannons sustaining fire against the destroyer's stern.

Wedge wished them success. They were designed to hurt

capital ships; their pilots knew what they were doing. But if *Iron Fist* called back its starfighters and the Novas didn't notice in time, the entire squad could be lost.

Now it was time to meet the weak link of this force: Zsinj's light cruisers.

MON REMONDA RATTLED under blast after blast from the attacking starfighters. Solo ignored the vibrations. Shield integrity was good, the hull was holding up—they still had a chance.

His communications officer said, "Nova One reports damage to *Iron Fist*'s engines."

"How extensive?" Solo asked.

"Unknown."

Golorno spoke up, his voice now more nearly normal. "A lot of the starfighters on us are in retreat. They just broke off to head for *Iron Fist*."

"How many?"

"About half."

"Ah, good. Now they outnumber ours only two to one." Solo absently hammered the arm of his captain's chair. If only he were out there, in the *Millennium Falcon,* making a direct assault on the enemy . . . here, all he could do was issue orders and hope they were so good that not many of his people died.

They were never so good that none of his people died. Never.

"Message for General Solo," the comm officer announced. "From Warlord Zsinj!"

"Ignore it," Solo said. "I'll bet you a hundred Corellian credits he hates that. No, wait." He stood. "Chewie, get in here."

The Wookiee squeezed in through the bridge door, looking quizzical.

"Here, take my chair." Han helped his friend into the seat, which was far too small for him. "All right, put that message through."

The comm unit on the command chair lit up. Even from his angle off to the side, Solo could make out Zsinj's florid features, bald head, and exaggerated handlebar mustache. "General Solo," Zsinj said, "I'm calling to offer you an honorable—what is this?"

Chewbacca reached down and tilted the screen up so its built-in holocam would broadcast his face instead of just his chest. He grumbled something at the screen.

"It's, ah, Chewbacca, isn't it? Please put your owner on."

Chewbacca offered him an extended speech, nearly sub-sonic, bone-rattling. Solo smiled. It was an eloquent discourse on the ingredients that made up Zsinj, and not one of the ingredients was the sort that should be mentioned in polite company or during any meal.

"Wookiee is not among my many languages, you extruded fur thing. Where is Solo?"

Chewbacca returned to his discourse and Solo moved to stand beside Captain Onoma, taking in the officer's sensor readings, his mind once again fully engaged by the battle.

"THIS IS LEADER. Break by squadrons."

"Wraith One acknowledges," Face said. "Good luck, Rogues." He began a long curve relative up and to starboard, taking him and the Wraiths toward one of the two *Carrack*-class cruisers in Zsinj's group.

The Carracks were 350 meters long, looking like stubby metal bars with swells at bow and stern. Face knew them to be formidable opponents for capital ships; their batteries of ion cannons made it possible for them to disable much larger vessels. But the comparatively light number of turbolasers they carried gave the starfighters a chance at them.

The Wraiths approached their target from the stern. At Face's command, they split into two units, Wraiths One through Six going to starboard, Seven through Eleven going to port. Stern turbolasers opened up on them even before they were within range.

"Fire at will," Face said, "but make 'em count."

Runt and Donos were the first of his half squad to fire, the blue streaks of proton torpedoes drawing an instantaneous line from the X-wings to the flanks of the cruiser. Face watched their explosions balloon against the cruiser's side. He ignored the pure tone of his own target lock, twitched his pilot's yoke over so his targeting brackets fell within the center of one of the torpedo detonation clouds, and fired his own remaining torpedoes. Then he looped away from the cruiser's side, Lara tucked in behind him and to port. "Report," he said.

"One, this is Seven." It was Dia's voice, barely recognizable through the usual comm distortion. "We have port-side penetration."

"Ten is hit! Ten is hit!"

Face felt his gut go cold, and a quick check of his sensor screen showed that Janson, Wraith Ten, was no longer present. "Calm down, Eleven. Detail damage to Wraith Ten."

"He's not destroyed, One. An ion cannon hit him. He's got no power, he's ballistic."

Face sagged in relief. "Ballistic toward or away from the cruiser?"

"Away, One."

"Keep clear of him, Eleven. You're active, you'll draw fire toward him. Squad, continue report."

"One, Five." That was Kell; the sensor board showed him lurking closer to the cruiser than the rest of the squad. Face supposed that Kell, maneuvering in a captured TIE interceptor, considered himself harder to hit than the X-wings . . . and he was right. Too, the TIEs had no proton torpedoes, so

Kell had probably chosen the role of close observer in order to contribute to this battle. "Starboard impacts damaged the hull but did not, repeat, did not penetrate."

"All Wraith X-wings," Face said, "form up for a run on the starboard. TIEs, strafe the port side to keep their shields divided. Keep them honest." He toggled his comm unit to the fleet frequency. "*Mon Remonda*, Wraith One. Please dispatch a shuttle with a tractor for pickup of disabled snubfighter."

Face brought his X-wing around slowly, allowing the other pilots with functional X-wings to form up on him. Kell, Shalla, and Elassar, in their interceptors, were already beginning their strafing run against the port side. "Once more into the gauntlet, Wraiths," he said, and nudged his yoke forward.

They dove toward the cruiser in loose formation, X-wings spread far enough apart that their evasive juking didn't bring them in danger of collision. Streams of turbolasers and concussion missiles sought them, and Face heard a cry of surprise or pain from someone on his squadron channel.

Their proton torpedoes spent, at a half kilometer they opened fire with quad-linked lasers and continued firing and diving until the cruiser's flank was almost all of the sky. Face hauled up on his yoke, felt the high-performance turn drag him deeper into his chair despite the best efforts of the acceleration compensator to protect him from the consequences of his maneuver. He saw the cruiser's hull flash beneath him, saw columns of laser fire on either side—then he was clear and headed out to space again.

He spared a look at his sensor board. Ten Wraiths were still on the board. He breathed a sigh of relief—no additional losses. "Wraith One to squadron. Report damage. Ours and theirs."

"One, Five. Starboard side also breached. I think we've gotten both power generators and I think some of the reserve cells. Parts of the ship are going dark. They're not maneuvering."

"Thanks, Five. Now get your rear end away from that hulk before some gunner with a little power left decides to make fireworks out of you."

"Acknowledged, One."

"One, this is Four." Tyria's voice, level and calm. "I took a turbolaser hit, I think at maximum range. I have some wing damage."

Face checked her position on the sensor board, then maneuvered to sideslip past her. She was correct; her port S-foils both showed laser scoring on their trailing edges. "Any system failures, Four?"

"Not so far, chief."

"Keep me updated." He toggled over to fleet frequency. "Wraith One to Rogue Leader. Target secure."

Wedge's voice came back instantly. "Good work, Wraiths. Rogue target destroyed. *Iron Fist* showing difficulty maneuvering. Stand by."

"Acknowledged." He switched back to squadron frequency. "Wraiths, form up on me. We'll stay near Ten for the time being."

ON THE BRIDGE of *Iron Fist,* the Warlord Zsinj stood on the command walkway above the crew pit. He did not stare out the forward viewports, which showed only starfield along his enemy's exit vector, but down into the screens of his bridge crew.

He was not a tall man, nor was he physically impressive. He was as round as any merchant gourmand, and his exaggerated bandit-style mustachios suggested that his self-image was quite different from the image he projected. The white grand admiral's uniform he wore suggested a rank he'd never earned in service to the Empire, and those who knew that fact could not help but attribute to him the sins of pride and self-deception.

Only he knew how many of these attributes were affecta-
tions. False clues to persuade his enemies—and superiors,
and subordinates—to come to incorrect conclusions about
him. To underestimate him. Sometimes to overestimate him—
that could, on occasion, be as useful.

Beside him stood the man in charge of his ground troops
and starfighter support, General Melvar. Zsinj was lucky to
have found a kindred spirit in Melvar, a man who painted on
the face of a dedicated sadist when confronting the outer
world and then removed it, revealing features extraordinary
only in their blandness, in the warlord's company. Melvar
could blend with any crowd on any world with his natural
features, and probably had many more alternative identities
tucked away than the score or so Zsinj knew about.

"*Mon Remonda* and the rest of his fleet are still coming
on at full speed," Melvar said. "But even with the two *Carrack* cruisers out and our maneuverability impaired, we
should be able to give her a sustained broadside. If we concentrate on her power and engines, we'll trap her here. She'll
never get far enough away from Levian Two to make hyperspace."

Zsinj nodded absently. "Time until *Mon Remonda* is
under our guns?"

A crewman shouted up, "Ships appearing ahead, a drop
out of hyperspace. Three vessels, sir—a Mon Calamari
cruiser, an *Imperial*-class Star Destroyer, and a *Quasar Fire*-
class bulk cruiser."

Zsinj sighed, vexed. He looked forward through the viewports, but couldn't make out the new enemies. "I didn't realize Solo had more of his fleet within range. Not that it matters.
Enhance the view."

A hologram appeared before a portion of the main viewport. On it were the three vessels his crewman had described.
All three were turning to Zsinj's port, exposing their sides,
ready to fire on the oncoming Super Star Destroyer.

"They're angling toward the escape vector *Mon Remonda* will take," Zsinj said. "Toward our weak flank, where the *Carrack*-class cruisers have been knocked out. They're going to line up so that we'll walk into the worst of their damage if we adjust to continue our prosecution of *Mon Remonda.* But we're not going to play their game."

Melvar smiled. "I somehow doubted we were."

Zsinj called down to his communications officer, "Send *Red Gauntlet, Serpent's Smile,* and *Reprisal* on ahead. Punch a hole in the defensive screen they're throwing up. Bring the starfighters back to *Iron Fist* to act as our own screen." He turned to his weapons specialist. "Ready all guns. Tell them to fire on *Mon Remonda* as they bear."

"Yes, sir."

Zsinj straightened, smiling. "Solo really should have taken my call. He might even have survived for a while."

FACE SAW THE SHUTTLE towing Janson's X-wing disappear into one of *Mon Remonda*'s bays. The Wraiths' three TIE interceptor pilots followed him in. He knew from comm traffic that the group's A-wings were already aboard.

Then the leading edge of *Mon Remonda* came within gunnery range of *Iron Fist.* Turbolaser flashes by the hundreds lit space between the two capital ships. Far ahead, similar flashes illuminated the void between Solo's Group 2 and Zsinj's advance force.

Like a younger sea mammal sidling up beneath its mother, *Mon Karren* moved up below *Mon Remonda,* moving into the sea of turbolaser fire with her sister ship, her back to the larger vessel's belly.

ZSINJ FELT HIS shoulders sag as he witnessed *Mon Karren*'s maneuver. "We've lost *Mon Remonda,*" he said.

Melvar offered one of his rare frowns. "They've just barely moved into our range."

"Correct. But they're collaborating to absorb our battery assaults, dividing the damage between them. And since I was foolish enough to bring back our starfighters to protect our engines—"

"They can concentrate their shields against us. We have nothing to batter their topsides with to keep them honest."

"Correct." Zsinj shook his head. "This isn't going to go down in the history annals as a loss for me, Melvar, but it is a loss. One little mistake and Solo slips through my fingers."

"Still, you haven't lost anything but the ammunition and power you've expended."

"True." He leaned down to face his weapons officer. "Continue with the barrage until they make the jump to hyperspace. Not your fault, Major. Mine."

"Thank you, sir."

Still pensive, Zsinj turned away and headed out of the bridge. The rest of this battle was going to be mop-up; his subordinates could handle that. He needed to rest and prepare for the next engagement.

SOLO'S FLEET DROPPED out of hyperspace mere light-years from the Levian system and stayed in realspace just long enough to pick up the hyperspace-equipped starfighters and coordinate their next jump. Then they fled back into the comparative safety of faster-than-light speeds.

3

TIRED BUT ALL present and accounted for—a rarity in full-scale space-navy engagements—the pilots of Wedge's command gradually collected in the pilots' lounge of *Mon Remonda*.

It was a large chamber with rounded corners, all the walls in antiseptic glossy white, all the furniture in white or blue or green. A fully stocked bar dominated one wall of the chamber, but its cabinets were, while the ship remained on alert status, all locked down, with only nonalcoholic drinks available to the pilots. The air was drier here than in the rest of the ship; none of the pilots of *Mon Remonda*'s four fighter squadrons was a Mon Calamari or Quarren, so they tended to adjust the environment to be more comfortable to land dwellers.

Donos took a comfortable chair in one of the curves that served the lounge as corners and watched the other pilots with interest. The Wraith Squadron pilots were jubilant, especially with the scare involving Wes Janson, but those of the other squadrons exhibited less cheer.

One of the Rogues—a woman with long brown hair, a trim build, and an intense manner—sat in one of what the pilots called egg-chairs. These seats were shaped like white eggs a meter and a half tall, with one side scooped away so someone could sit within, mounted on a post next to a terminal niche in the wall so the pilot could turn his back to the room and do terminal work. Donos took a moment to recall her name: Inyri Forge.

The woman cupped her chin in her hand. Her brown eyes were glum. "He's changed the rules on us," she said. "We should have expected it."

Tyria said, "I'm not sure what you mean."

Forge gave her a look of evaluation, as though deciding whether to offer sarcasm or simple information, and settled on the latter course. "While you Wraiths were running around in disguise or doing your ground missions, we've been following Zsinj all over space. Into regions he controls, into New Republic regions he's assaulting, wherever we can find signs of his passage. We find little hints we can't afford to investigate, because many of them are false clues he's leaving to lead us into a trap or waste our time and resources. We also find the remains of full-scale assaults, where we always arrive too late—he's in and out before we can mount a response.

"But today, we get number two, and not only had he figured out our pattern of response times, but he was waiting around to hit us when we arrived."

"And," Hobbie said, "his fleet was huge. Something like twenty capital ships. More than we thought he could field. Our intelligence hasn't kept up with him."

"So," Forge concluded, "we have to change our tactics. To suit him. And that's not good."

Face Loran, from the little table he shared with Dia, said, "We don't need to alter our tactics. We need to alter *his*. It looks like he hasn't been bringing *Iron Fist* into gravity wells, probably because of the beating we gave him the last time he did, until today—when he had an overwhelming force. If he can keep doing that, he's going to beat us."

Elassar Targon stood at the bar, drumming on the bar top with his knuckles. "We need to follow all the leads we've been getting. Even if some of them *are* traps. What about the rumor of the bacta hijacking being planned?"

Shalla reached an oversized couch and twirled as she fell onto it so she lay face up. "Too obvious," she said. "Odds are a hundred to one that was one of Zsinj's planted leads. We follow that and we get ambushed again."

Elassar gave her a scornful look. "You've been doing all that analysis of leads, even before the Wraiths were back with *Mon Remonda*. Is that what you told the mission-planning staff?"

"It is."

"So you're the one who's keeping General Solo running scared."

Conversations subsided all over the pilots' lounge as fliers turned to follow this exchange.

Shalla pulled herself back and upright so that she leaned back against one of the couch arms. She did not look happy. "You know, you're wrong in so many ways it may take me a couple of days to straighten you out. First, I'm not the only one providing intelligence analysis to General Solo. I'm one of about thirty, and I'm a very distant link in that chain. Second, he's not running scared. He just has responsibilities to keep his subordinates alive long enough for them to get the job done, a concept that may be a little lofty for a school-aged thrillseeker like you."

Elassar's face set. "Are we still no decor?"

Pilot's parlance . . . by custom, only pilots were admitted to this lounge, and once inside, designations of rank, sometimes disparagingly referred to as "decor," were largely ignored. Even so, it was sometimes a strain to maintain this custom when the most senior officers were present, which is why their visits to this lounge were infrequent and short.

Shalla nodded.

Elassar took a deep breath, apparently considering his words. When they emerged, they were more reasoned than the Wraiths and Rogues were used to hearing from him. "I'm not going to pretend I know more about Zsinj or about intelligence operations than you. I don't. What I do know is that a pilot's job is to fly and to vape the enemy. The advice you and the others are giving to our superiors is keeping us from doing that."

"You're right," Shalla said. "But pilots have other jobs. Such as not flying straight into the ground, straight into a star, or straight into a battle situation chosen and lovingly set up by an enemy. I don't question that you're brave, Elassar. But are you so brave that you're happy to die pointlessly?"

"So what do we do?" That was Dorset Konnair, an A-wing pilot of Polearm Squadron. She was a small woman of very pale skin and very dark hair, with a blue star-flare tattoo around her right eye. Her flight suit concealed her other tattoos, all of them in shades of blue. She was also very limber, as evidenced by the ease with which she sat, legs folded tailor-style, in her chair. Donos knew she was from Coruscant, which probably explained why she was quiet so often in pilot gatherings; Donos knew the kind of suspicion with which some New Republic veterans viewed Coruscant natives. "Either we keep running around gathering Zsinj's crumbs and getting nowhere, or we bite on the bait he's deliberately leaving and let him draw us in."

Forge said, "We have to regain the initiative. Bait our own trap. Offer him something he can't afford to refuse."

Donos snorted. "Such as what? *Mon Remonda*? Have her limp through Zsinj-controlled space like a wounded avian and hope he comes swooping in to finish her off?"

"No," Elassar said. He struck another swashbuckling pose. "Offer him Elassar Targon, master of the uni—"

"Sithspit, you're obnoxious." Forge fixed Elassar with an amused glance. "But you're on the right track. I was thinking we ought to offer him General Han Solo."

"Don't do that," said Hobbie from his stool at the bar. His voice was more mournful than ever. "If Zsinj kills Solo, Wedge might be appointed to fill the vacancy."

"Good point," Forge said. "But bear with me a minute. Kell, didn't you say that General Solo had gone gallivanting around in the *Millennium Falcon* two, three months ago, delivering some high-security messages for the Inner Council?"

Kell, sharing a couch with Tyria, nodded. "That's right."

"There was no secret to the fact that he was moving about. And you used his trip to pull a fast one on Admiral Trigit. To distract him from his primary objective over Commenor's moon. You made him think Solo was still around, a viable target."

"Show due respect," said Runt. A member of a species whose representatives were usually too tall to fit in a starfighter cockpit, Runt was, by their standards, a midget, though he and Kell were the tallest of the Wraiths. His hairy body, his elongated face with flaring nostrils and large, square teeth, and his wide-eyed look all suggested that his kind were closer to being draft animals than intelligent humanoids, but his squadmates had found him to be a wise and capable being.

And somewhat odd. "You speak," he continued, "of the only flight of Dinner Squadron. The one X-wing squadron with an undefeated record and no losses."

"Oh, I forgot." Forge smiled. "But what I'm saying is that we have a track record of General Solo occasionally embarking on special missions even while commanding the Zsinj task force, and if there's anyone Zsinj might change his plans to nab, it's Han Solo. A chance for revenge is a powerful motivator."

"I like it." The voice came from another of the egg-chairs against the wall. It was turned away from the room, so the other pilots present had presumed it was unoccupied or that anyone there was engrossed in his terminal.

Now the chair turned around to face the room. Its occupant was Han Solo—not decked out in the uncomfortable-looking uniform that was apparently his bane, but wearing the comfortable trousers, shirt, and vest that were his preferred dress. His clothes were spotted with sweat stains; obviously he hadn't changed since his recent time on the bridge.

But his expression was amused. "But there are two problems with this plan."

Forge cleared her throat, concealing any surprise she might have felt. "And what are they, sir?"

"No 'sir.' No decor, remember? Problem number one is that the *Millennium Falcon* is currently stowed on Princess Leia's flagship, the *Rebel Dream,* and there's no telling when I'll see her again."

Donos privately wondered which "her" he was referring to.

"Problem number two," Solo continued, "is that we still don't know what Zsinj is up to. And you Wraiths are largely to blame for that."

The pilots under his command looked around for someone bearing a mark of guilt.

"By which I mean," Solo said, "since you figured out that he was planning to steal a second Super Star Destroyer, *Razor's Kiss,* from Kuat, and since you figured out how to determine where it would be so we could all blow it up, you've forced Zsinj to revert to his backup plan. Which is what?"

Forge shook her head. "We don't know."

Face said, "Though we have one lead. Saffalore."

That was an Imperial-held world in the Corporate Sector, home to a large corporation called Binring Biomedical. It was there that Piggy had been altered—had, in a sense, been created. A manufacturing facility owned by Zsinj on another world had fabricated the exact sort of transparisteel cages Piggy had been reared within, suggesting that Binring, too, might have a surreptitious relationship with the warlord.

"I'm as tired as you are of chasing down vague hints and leads and only dropping in after Zsinj is long gone," Solo said. "So *Mon Remonda* is leaving the fleet for a while. Saffalore is our next port of call." He rose and walked toward the lounge's exit. "Still, I sort of like your idea of luring Zsinj out to come after me. I wouldn't mind personally leading to

Zsinj's downfall." He offered a smile, almost sinister, back toward the assembled pilots. "Give that plan some more thought, too." Then he was gone.

"Never can tell when a Corellian will pop up," Donos said.

The pilots were diverted by a banging sound—Elassar hammering his head and horns against the top of the bar. His face a mask of tragedy, he suspended hammering to look at his fellow pilots. "Now I am done," he said. "I have performed the unluckiest deed possible. I've suggested that my commanding officer runs away from combat, and I've done so within his hearing."

"True," Shalla said. "To make it worse, you did it when we're still on alert status. Meaning you can't even blot out the memory with drink."

"Don't remind me. Shalla? Dear friend, kind lieutenant?"

"Yes?"

"Will you kill me? Please?"

"I don't think so."

"Runt. With your great strength, you could tear one of my arms off and say it was a handshaking accident."

Runt shook his head and offered up a human-style smile.

"Kell! You hate me, don't you? Well, I have an offer for you . . ."

"Not now, Elassar. We have more important people to kill."

Face perked up. "You know, Inyri, we could do what Kell and Runt did back in the raid on Folor Base."

Forge snorted. "Run a couple of X-wings along together with malfunctioning shields and just pretend we're the *Millennium Falcon?*"

"I didn't mean that specifically. But in a general sense, yes. What they did was to fake up a *Millennium Falcon*. With more time and more resources, we could do a better job."

Forge considered and looked among the other pilots.

Theirs were a mixed lot of dubious and approving expressions. "Maybe."

Face continued, "Don't you Rogues have the universe's best quartermaster?"

"Emtrey, yes." Forge nodded. M-3PO, called Emtrey, was a protocol droid attached to Rogue Squadron. He had a reputation for phenomenal skills at scrounging. "But he's not as good as he used to be. We had to throttle back some of his programming."

"Still . . ."

"Still, it's worth thinking about." Forge stood. "Let's find a conference room with a holotable and fire some ideas around."

The doors rose to admit Corran Horn. The former CorSec agent looked suspiciously at the pilots rising to their feet. "What did I miss?"

Some of the pilots laughed. In the months Rogue Squadron had been on *Mon Remonda*, Corran Horn and Han Solo had never been seen at the same place and time. It had spawned a running joke among the other pilots—the notion that, despite their disparate ages and personalities, they were the same person in disguise.

"We'll tell you in the conference room," Forge said. "You're late, so you get to take the notes."

Elassar fixed Horn with an imploring expression. "Lieutenant! With your skills, you could kill me and make it look like an accident. Please . . ."

HAN SOLO POKED his head into Wedge's office. "Got a minute?"

Wedge turned from his terminal and the report he was composing on the day's aborted mission. "Come on in. Distract me. Please."

The general seated himself with characteristic casualness

and grimaced at the work Wedge was doing. "I thought you ought to be aware of some scuttlebutt. I tried to catch you at the pilots' lounge, but you were hiding."

Wedge snorted. "I had to have some words in private with the squadron's executive officers. About pilot morale. What is it?"

Solo's face lost its usual cocky expression. Suddenly, alarmingly, he looked older and more tired. "It has nothing to do with Levian. This was relayed to me by some friends on Coruscant. The Intelligence investigation into the assassin who tried to kill Ackbar is looking into the possibility of a widespread Twi'lek conspiracy."

"Conspiracy to do what?"

"They have no idea. The Twi'lek planet Ryloth has always traded with anyone who had credits. Intelligence says there's a large warrior caste that resents the way the planet was dominated by humans for so long, and hates the way Ryloth is regarded as a merchant world—"

"That last part is true."

"Well, Intelligence wonders whether this action is part of some fanatical conspiracy designed to strike against humans. There's even talk of a conspiracy including several humanoid species, not just Twi'leks. And how such a group might want to eliminate Ackbar, who's known to be friendly to humans.

"Also"—Solo leaned closer and dropped his voice— "Cracken's people in Intelligence have tracked some interesting behavior among Twi'leks on Coruscant. Specifically, mid-level New Republic officers and advisors who have access to the powerful and the famous. Like the assassin, Jart Eyan. He was on leave just before his attempt to kill Ackbar. But apparently he and his family weren't on leave where they were supposed to be. They were out of sight for several days leading up to the murder attempt, though they'd set things up so their friends would believe they were at a resort. Where they were, what they were doing, nobody knows."

"You're leading up to something."

"You have several Twi'leks among your pilots."

"That's right. Tal'dira with the Rogues, Dia Passik with the Wraiths, Nuro Tualin with Polearm. My executive officer with the Rogues is Twi'lek, as is one of my mechanics, Koyi Komad, for the squadron."

"How sure are you of them?"

Wedge thought back. Tal'dira was a pride-filled warrior of the world of Ryloth. His word was his bond, and deception seemed like a talent beyond his capabilities. Dia was another matter; brought, like many Twi'lek females, as a slave off Ryloth, trained to be a dancer, she'd escaped and killed her owner. Or so her story went; it was true that elements of her background could not be confirmed. Nuro was a recent graduate of the New Republic's Fleet Command Academy and had trained with General Crespin in A-wings on Folor Base, as had several of his squadmates; he was largely an unknown factor. Wedge had known Nawara Ven since he re-formed Rogue Squadron, and Koyi Komad for years.

None of these Twi'leks had ever made him edgy when looking at him. None ever gave him the evaluative look that said, "I wonder what it would take to kill him?" His gut told him that they were dedicated pilots and technicians, not ringers for some power seeker. "I'm sure of them."

Solo's smile returned and the tiredness disappeared from his features. "Good." He rose. "I just wanted you to be aware of what was going on. Keep it to yourself, though, will you?"

"Certainly." As Solo opened the door to leave, Wedge said, "You know something? In spite of the way you seem to hate it, you're pretty good at this management stuff."

Solo lost his smile. "Don't ever, ever say that. Someone important might hear you. And then I'd be stuck with it." Then he was gone.

THE MAN WITH the impossibly bland features appeared before Warlord Zsinj's desk as though he were a holoprojection turned into flesh. "I have a present for you," said Melvar.

Zsinj managed to keep himself from jumping. Melvar, he knew, prided himself on his silent comings and goings, and the nervousness this induced in his subordinates—and even superiors—though he claimed that this was not the case. But Zsinj had recently spent considerable effort to train himself not to start. To cover for his momentary lapse, he twirled one of his mustachios in rakish fashion.

"How delightful," Zsinj said. "Have we instituted a new holiday, for which a gift is appropriate?" He waved his hands around to take in the lavish appointments of his office aboard his flagship, *Iron Fist*. "And wherever will I display your present?"

"I'm sure you'll find a place." Melvar smiled, the innocuous smile of a blameless financial officer, and snapped his fingers. A mere diversion; Zsinj knew that the man must have secretly thumbed the button on his comm unit with his other hand.

The door into Zsinj's office opened and a pair of guards escorted in two people. One was a man, lean, aging, graying—in fact, the man appeared to be growing older as Zsinj watched him, so great was the fellow's nervousness. The second was a woman, her companion's junior by twenty or thirty years; her hair and eyes were dark, her expression poised, perhaps resigned. Both were in civilian dress.

Melvar gave Zsinj a little theatrical bow. "Allow me to present Doctors Novin Bress and Edda Gast, from our special operations division of Binring Biomedical on Saffalore. After due investigation I decided to bring them to speak to you personally."

Zsinj folded his hands over the imposing swell of his stomach. He noted with satisfaction that his white Imperial grand admiral's jacket was spotless, nearly gleaming; it would be inappropriate to lead two doomed people before a shabby warlord. "Doctor, Doctor, delighted to meet you." He was charmed to see the first flicker of hope appear in the older man's eyes; this one would be fun to play with.

"Ask them," Melvar said, "about missing test subjects."

Zsinj gave him a blank look, as if struggling to recall something of little consequence, then said, "Oh, yes. Doctors, tell me where a Gamorrean and an Ewok might obtain the necessary skills—and temperament—to fly starfighters."

Dr. Bress, the male, tried to catch the eye of his younger colleague. Dr. Gast ignored his attempt; she kept her gaze on Zsinj.

"Well," Bress said, "they might have escaped from our facility."

"Ah," Zsinj said. He picked up a datapad and brought up his day's schedule. He'd have a massage in an hour, then sit down to a stimulating meal an hour after that. "It says here that I sent out a memorandum asking about possible test-subject escapes some time ago, and that you replied in the negative. Correct?"

Dr. Bress flinched. "Correct."

Zsinj slammed the datapad down on the edge of his desk, snapping the device in two. Bress jumped. Interestingly, Gast didn't. Zsinj modulated his voice to a snarl and allowed some color to creep into his face. "May I ask why didn't you tell me then, when I sent out the memorandum? Why do I learn about it now?"

"Because we weren't sure," Bress said. "We're not sure now."

Zsinj stared at him a long moment, then turned his attention to Gast. "I'm not sure I understand this man. Perhaps you could explain a little more clearly."

"I believe I can," she said. "Might I have a chair? We walked some considerable distance to get to your office."

Zsinj forced himself to mask the genuine surprise he felt.

It took a lot of nerve to make such a request when she should have been wondering how best to preserve her life. He took his first really good look at her. Adult human female in the prime of life, not beautiful but with cheekbones that made her striking and would do so throughout her life . . . and her eyes, dark, calm, unapologetic, were unsettling.

He forced a smile. "Of course. General Melvar, where are your manners? Give the doctor a chair."

Bress spoke up, his voice wavering: "I, too, uh, could use—"

"Do be quiet, Doctor Bress." Zsinj waited until Melvar situated a chair behind Gast. He gave her a moment to compose herself. "Now, you were saying?"

"My uncle, Doctor Tuzin Gast, was also on this project," she said. "He was the real pioneer on the cognitive-stimulation side of things. But he wasn't really suited to the project emotionally. He became rather too close to his test subjects. He developed real affection for them. Not a good idea, considering their intended use."

Zsinj nodded and gestured for her to continue.

"One day, a couple of years ago, there was a tremendous explosion in Epsilon Wing. My uncle and several test subjects were killed. Some were so close that their bodies were incinerated."

"I remember," Zsinj said. "It promised to be a tremendous loss until Doctor Bress told me that the dead doctor's assistant—and niece—was at the very least his intellectual peer and would be able to continue his work, without much loss of time. And he turned out to be right."

Gast nodded, acknowledging the compliment without smiling. "We reported the losses and continued as scheduled," she said. "Although we discovered some interesting things about the accident."

"Such as?"

She began counting items off on her fingers. "First, it was

suicide. My uncle mixed some volatile chemicals in a purification tank and set them off. His guilt apparently had eaten away at him until he could not stand to live any longer. Second, most of the test subjects that had died were those who were exhibiting the greatest aggressive reactions under our trigger treatments. In other words, they were the subjects who were most changed by our treatments, the most violent—"

"The most promising," Zsinj said.

"Yes. The most promising. He deliberately brought them together so they would die with him."

"You said *most* of the test subjects . . ."

"There was one exception. A Gamorrean. It had been through the intelligence series but not the aggression series."

"Its name?"

She shrugged. "I never met it. It was officially logged as Subject Gamma-Nine-One-Oh-Four."

"And this subject was supposed to have died in the explosion."

"Yes," she said. "But the only cellular material we found of it was blood plasma."

"Which your uncle could have extracted from the creature and distributed prior to the explosion."

"Yes."

"Was there only blood plasma found of your uncle?"

She shook her head. "We found his head and several other parts."

"How about Ewoks?"

"Two of the test subjects theoretically destroyed in the blast were Ewoks. They'd both been through intelligence and aggression treatments. We found body parts of two different Ewoks, so we had reason to believe both had perished."

Zsinj took a long breath. "Well. There's little doubt that Voort saBinring, a Rebel pilot of Wraith Squadron, is your uncle's pet Gamorrean. There is also reason to believe that

Lieutenant Kettch, a pilot with a pirate group called the Hawk-bats, is a similarly enhanced Ewok from the program. Tell me, why would both of them become pilots?"

Gast said, "We found fragmentary records indicating that my uncle had tested the Gamorrean on flight simulators as one way to measure his temperament and intelligence. He could have done so with an Ewok, too. I just don't see how an Ewok could have escaped . . . unless it was a test subject that he had never entered into the records."

He fixed her with an angry stare. "You could have told me all this back when I circulated my first query. It would have saved me a lot of difficulty."

"No, I couldn't." She returned his stare calmly, unapologetically. "I never saw your query. I have done my job satisfactorily."

"That's for me to decide."

"With apologies, warlord, but you're not qualified to evaluate my performance."

Zsinj stared at her a moment, then barked out a laugh. "Very good last words, Doctor Gast. But, now, it's time for a reckoning. Your division has failed me and blood must be shed if I'm to feel better."

He held out both hands and the guards leaned in to place a blaster pistol in each hand. These Zsinj set before the two doctors. "I'd be happy for you two to accomplish the task yourselves. That would save me some mental anguish, I assure you."

Bress looked with genuine fright at the weapons. "Sir, everything you've asked me I've done—"

"Yes. And now I'm asking you to do one final thing."

Gast picked up her pistol and checked its settings to make sure it was charged. Zsinj watched her with real interest. She was very cool and might decide to remove him from the universe to avenge her own death.

Bress, his voice climbing into a wail, said, "Please, sir, so much of the project's success is my doing, my mistakes have been so few—"

Gast set the barrel of her pistol against Bress's ribs and pulled the trigger. The sound of the blast filled the room, followed by the smell of seared flesh. Bress staggered sideways and fell against the office wall.

Gast held up her pistol and allowed Melvar to take it from her. "Now," she said, "will someone be killing me?"

Zsinj looked at her, forcing his expression into one of reasonability. "Shouldn't we? You've been part of a team that has covered up critical errors in judgment. Coming before me as a penitent, you've been insubordinate, even arrogant. You couldn't even carry out a simple request to kill yourself."

She shook her head. "Nobody asked me to kill myself. Your unstated request could have been that we kill each other."

"Nor did you show enough courage to try to kill me when you had the chance."

At last, she smiled—a lopsided smile full of sarcastic cheer. "Please don't insult me if you're going to kill me, too. I'll bet every credit I own, every one I've hidden away, that if I'd pointed that blaster at you and pulled the trigger, it would not have gone off." She leaned forward and her smile evened out, became more genuine. "Well?"

He regarded her steadily. "Well, you're correct in assuming that I didn't ask you to kill yourself. Why would I? You're blameless. Had you killed yourself, or allowed Doctor Bress to kill you, you would have proven yourself to be *stupid* and blameless, but fortunately that's not the case. How would you like to do me a favor?"

"I'd like that."

"Return to Saffalore. Dismantle the operation without letting anyone—and that means anyone at Binring—know you've done so. Send everything to *Iron Fist;* we'll consolidate the two laboratories. Set up the Binring facilities to detect and then annihilate anyone breaking in. Because at some point Voort saBinring's squadron mates are going to get permission to return to the land of his birth . . . and that will be a good time to eliminate them. Setting all this up guarantees your continued employment within my organization; each dead Wraith brings you a sizable bonus. Deal?"

"Deal." With her characteristic insolence, she extended him her hand to shake.

When she, the guards, and the still-smoking body were gone, Melvar returned to stand before his warlord. He looked curious.

"What?" Zsinj asked.

"You've instructed her to kill all the Wraiths. One of the Wraiths is an unknown quantity. Gara Petothel."

"I know. But since the mission to Aldivy went to pieces, she hasn't communicated. Our agent dead, her ersatz brother dead, and no word from her since then . . . I'd be happy to arrange for her protection. She has to give me a reason first."

"Understood."

"And how goes Blunted Razor?"

"The operation continues moving. Every day, we retrieve more tonnage of the wreck of *Razor's Kiss*." Melvar didn't add, "And only you know why we're wasting all this energy gathering up the wreckage of a destroyed Super Star Destroyer." He didn't have to. Both men knew he wanted to say it. Both men knew he wouldn't.

Zsinj smiled. "Dismissed."

4

FLIGHT OFFICER LARA NOTSIL leaned in close to hear every word of the briefing, to see everything that floated on the holoprojection.

She hadn't always been Lara Notsil. She'd been born with the name Gara Petothel, and had worn many others since her adolescent years.

She hadn't always had downy blond hair cut short, or a near-flawless complexion. Nature had provided her with dark hair and a beauty mark on her cheek. Makeup and trivial surgery performed when she'd created the Lara Notsil identity had rid her of them. The delicacy of her features and build remained from her true identity, but little else did.

She hadn't always been a pilot with the New Republic's Fleet Command. Since her earliest years, child of two of the Empire's loyal Intelligence officers, she'd been groomed to be an officer of Imperial Intelligence. In that role, she'd infiltrated the lower ranks of New Republic Fleet Command, had transmitted vital data back to her Imperial controllers and then to Admiral Apwar Trigit. She'd provided Trigit with information he'd later used to destroy Talon Squadron, an X-wing unit led by Myn Donos.

And now she fought beside the Rebel pilots who'd once been her enemies. It had originally been a deception, another infiltration, but was so no longer; it was where she wanted to be, what she wanted to do. But she also fought against the growing certainty that someday her fellows would learn her true identity, learn what she had done before she'd come to accept their outlook on the way the galaxy's sapient species should determine their destinies. When they learned who she was, they would reject her, and they would probably kill her.

Until then, she'd do whatever she could to keep them alive. To help them win. Soon, she'd confess all to her commander, Wedge Antilles, and he'd use her knowledge to help bring Zsinj to ruin.

Soon.

She shook away these distracting thoughts and forced herself to listen to her commander's words.

"Wraith Squadron," Wedge said, "has an admirable history of executing missions on its own, with minimal support . . . or no support at all. Let's assume that Zsinj has come to this realization. What we're going to do is change the rules on him. The Wraiths will be going in with their usual tactics . . . but they'll have a little support standing ready. By which I mean Rogue Squadron."

Several of the Wraiths made appreciative comments, but Gavin Darklighter of the Rogues made a face. "Now we're baby-sitters," he said.

Face shot him an amused look. "What if we light up a target for you baby-sitters to hit?"

"A real target," Gavin said. "Not just some defenseless motor pool or repair facility."

"A real target," Face said. "Something that shoots back."

Gavin schooled his face into an expression resembling dignity. "Then I'll be content to baby-sit. This time."

"Are you through?" Wedge asked. There was no censure in his voice, but side conversations quieted. Gavin nodded.

"Good," Wedge said. "Now, the Wraiths have a general agenda. Acquire information on what Zsinj might be doing at Binring Biomedical. We suspect a connection because his facility on Xartun was constructing the exact sort of cell Piggy essentially grew up in on Saffalore, at Binring. When Face, acting as Kargin of the Hawk-bats, had dinner with Zsinj, the warlord expressed considerable interest in the story of Lieutenant Kettch, a fictitious Ewok pilot with a story identical to Piggy's. This also suggests that the warlord has ties to facilities that perform modifications on humanoids. The Wraiths are to find out what they can about this modification program and Zsinj's ties to it.

"Piggy hasn't bothered to hide his background. Once he joined Starfighter Command, he became the most conspicuous Gamorrean serving the New Republic, and it became futile to hide where he came from. So our enemies may know we're coming. They probably don't know when. If there's anything left to find, it will probably be protected by standing defenses that have been geared for Piggy's squadmates. Which is one more reason to change tactics when appropriate. I'll hand this over to Wraith One."

He sat and Face stood. The younger pilot looked very sure of himself these days, Lara decided. Not arrogant, but at ease with what he was being called on to do. That was a good sign.

"We're going to take our mission in stages," Face said. "*Mon Remonda* support crews are going to make a visit to an asteroid belt around one of the planets in the Saffalore system and divert several waves of small and mid-sized asteroids toward Saffalore. These will simulate a series of natural meteor showers. The Rogues and Wraiths, in our respective starfighters, will be accompanying the third, largest, shower into the planet's atmosphere, which will hit—if our mathematicians get their numbers right—in their polar ice cap, where their sensors are less substantial. We'll fly in ground-following mode from our arrival point to a site near Lurark, the center of their planetary government. There the Rogues will set up base camp and the Wraiths will head on in to Lurark.

"Our initial goal is to find out where on Saffalore is the facility where Piggy was altered. The way Piggy has explained it, the circumstances under which he was smuggled out prevented him from knowing where he'd been held, though he suspected that it was within a few hundred kilometers of Lurark, if not in the city itself. A good guess would be the main Binring Biomedical facility in the city. But our first step there will be to try to find out what name Zsinj is using at the business end of Binring Biomedical. A simple check on their planetary net or a visit to whatever they use for a central business registry office ought to do it."

"No," Lara said.

Face looked at her expectantly.

"I mean, no, *sir*," she said, and was annoyed to feel herself blush. Genuine embarrassment—how long had it been since she'd felt that?

"Don't worry about it. Why no?"

She said, "You've suggested that we need to operate on principles of maximum paranoia. Well, you don't just march in to their records center—or access it via a terminal—and say, 'Who owns this company?' Let's assume they're as paranoid as we are. They might have set things up to flag queries like that."

"Well, I was thinking more about an anonymous check, or something using an intermediary. Are you recommending that we slice the network and try to steal the information?"

Lara shook her head. "No, save that tactic for critical information. What I'm suggesting is that we find out whether the information you're talking about is flagged; that fact itself would be valuable to know. We just lead with a safe question—from a different questioner—so we have a standard of comparison for behavior. For instance, let's say you, Face, decide to make the Binring query. Before you do, I go in, find out the name of a corporation we think is completely straight and above board, and ask the same question about *it*. I note what they do and how long it takes them to answer that question, and report that back to you. Then, when you go in—"

"I have a standard of comparison." Face nodded. "I get what you're saying. If they take a lot of extra time or vary their routine in some substantial way, we know they've been alerted."

"We also tail you on your exit, in case they decide to do the same thing. We can slip their tail or take him out, but we don't let him follow you."

"Right. You make a lot of sense. Anyone tell you you're a natural for intelligence work?"

Lara shook her head, not trusting herself to speak.

"All right," Face continued. "If we get that piece of information, we pursue it to see what else Zsinj might own on Saffalore—"

"No," Lara said. Then heads turned her way again and she felt herself flush red once more.

Face's voice remained calm. "Why not?"

"Well . . . on the Wraiths' other missions, we often found the name Zsinj was using on-planet, but never found any other major business enterprises owned by those names. Either he's investing in one business per planet, or he's using multiple names for multiple businesses. If history is any indication, there's no use in running down those names—not yet. If we ever want to try to mess with his accounts, his assets, using that name is good. For what we're doing with this mission, though, it's just a distraction. Something to cost us time his people may be using to hunt us down. In fact, I don't recommend that first bit, about finding the name he's using in his association with Binring, until *after* we've done our major raid, or maybe simultaneously. It may not be an important enough piece of information to risk anything on acquiring it."

Face considered. "Maybe you're right. Very well. Lara's

right. We will be staging a raid on their major fabrications facility, in the hope that he's following true to form and has a special Zsinj facility tucked away in there somewhere—or at the very least in the hope that we can figure out where the secret facility is from data in the public facility. So we'll follow our standard member assignments and protocols—"

"No," Lara said. Several Wraiths and Rogues laughed outright.

Face put his head down for a moment, then raised it, his expression one of long suffering, and turned to Wedge. "Is this what it's like for you?"

Wedge smiled. "You have no idea."

"From the bottom of my heart, I apologize, most sincerely, for every time I spoke up in a mission briefing. I mean it."

Wedge nodded. "I appreciate that, but I have to tell you: you've only just started to suffer."

"I believe you." Face turned back to Lara. "No, *what*?"

She gave him an apologetic look. "We've changed protocol already. We have Rogue Squadron on hand to look out for us. If we don't integrate this resource—this very, very dangerous and capable resource—"

Impassive, Tycho gestured, waving for her to keep the compliments coming.

"—from the very beginning, then there's no reason to have them along. We'd have to improvise their participation."

"She's right," Tycho said. "And I've had some thoughts about this. We could have the Wraiths, before or during their intrusion, get to certain key spots on the Binring buildings and plant targets there. Infrared markers, comm tracers, anything to give us an edge. Then if they needed to call an air strike, they could give us very precise data on where we needed to put our damage. 'Thirty-seven meters on heading two-five-five from Marker Number Three' is very precise, and our astromechs could integrate those instructions onto our heads-up displays on the fly."

"Good point," Wedge said. "Face, you haven't done enough work in figuring out how to exploit all your resources."

"I'm not used to *having* resources."

Wedge nodded. "Welcome to the real Starfighter Command. And having to think like a soldier instead of a pirate. All right, people, let's hear the rest of Face's plan. We're going to dissect it and reassemble it into something more likely to keep us all alive."

BRIGHTNESS—ILLUMINATION PIERCING the pinkness around him—awakened Piggy.

He could hear nothing, feel almost nothing—only the respirator adhering to his face, supplying him with air to breathe. It took him a split second to recall where he was, why most of his senses seemed to be failing him. Then he opened his eyes.

As with the last couple of times he'd awakened, he floated, suspended, in a bacta tank taller than a Wookiee. The bacta medium colored everything pink. He could see, beyond the confines of the tank, the antiseptic wardroom that was his temporary home. A medical technician, a dark-haired human female, waved at him, offering a smile that humans called "perky." He knew that human males could not help but be cheered by it. Nor was he entirely immune to it; the fact that she made the effort to reach him still lifted his spirits a notch. He waved in return, his motion slowed by the thick liquid.

Something was different. He ran through his checklist of surroundings, events, and circumstances to see what had been added. Nothing. He reversed it to look for what had been removed.

Pain. Ah, that was it. He didn't hurt anymore. He looked down at his stomach, which had not so long ago featured an injury that looked like a smoking crater, and saw only new flesh and some scar tissue.

Good. He would be leaving soon. He wasn't bored, was never bored—he could always work up problems of math, of navigation, of logic to keep himself occupied. But the lack of contact with others, the lack of activity that was useful, was beginning to annoy him.

There was motion outside his tank. He focused on several people walking with purpose into the wardroom, toward him, surrounding his tank—his fellow Wraiths. Their expressions were cheerful, and it was not the forced cheer that several had exhibited during previous visits.

The perky technician was waving at him, and when she had his attention, she gestured upward. He glanced up to see the top hatch opening. He kicked himself upward and moments later emerged into real air for the first time in many days.

When he once again had his feet on the ground, had a robe around him and a towel to mop away the remaining traces of bacta medium, he could begin to take in the words of his comrades.

Face said, "Forgive the intrusion, but we heard that the new vintage of Piggy was being decanted."

Lara said, "But it looks like it's turned to vinegar."

Dia said, "And it's corked."

A young Devaronian he did not know said, "I am pleased to meet you. I need you to kill me. Nobody else will."

The perky technician said, "You'll need as much as possible to avoid activities that put a strain on your stomach muscles."

Janson said, "To make sure you remember this little event, we've had some special things made up for you. Bacta-flavored candy. Bacta-flavored brandy. Bacta-flavored cheese."

Shalla said, "Kell and I worked up an instructional manual for you. It's called *How to Dodge*."

Piggy mopped away at his damp skin and allowed himself a slight smile. It was good to be home.

———

THE THIRD METEOR shower in as many days peppered the frozen arctic regions of Saffalore's northern hemisphere. Few of the meteors survived long enough to hammer the planet's surface; most burned up from the friction of their descent through the atmosphere, often leaving behind long trails to mark the fiery ends to their travels. A few had enough mass left to strike the ground as meteorites, often leaving deep craters in the hard, uncultivated ground.

And then there were the fabricated objects in their midst. Starfighters, almost two dozen, maneuvered away from the true meteorites and pulled up sharply from their descent, missing collisions with the ground sometimes by only a few dozen meters.

There were no rebukes for too-chancy flying over the comm waves. These pilots were keeping comm silence, staying in visual range of one another.

Three of the vehicles were TIE interceptors, the most lethal starfighters of the Empire. The remainder were X-wings, heavily laden with extra fuel pods under their S-foils.

The danger with an intrusion like this, Donos decided, *is that it's boring enough that you become distracted, and still dangerous enough to leave you dead.* Terrain-following flying was a tricky skill. Most of what they would be crossing tonight was tundra, hard-frozen ground and an ice sheet over it, offering little to endanger them. But there were occasional hilly regions and one mountain range to cross before they reached their objective. Under a comm blackout, each pilot had to keep a close eye on the sensors; he couldn't rely on the sharp sight of his fellows.

Donos kept his focus on the sensors. Focus was no problem for him. As a sniper for the Corellian armed forces, he'd learned to keep his attention unwavering on his target. Lives had depended on his ability to do so. He'd been good at it.

Of course, at a certain point, the suspicion that there was something wrong, something unfair, with what he was doing had begun to eat away at him. Yes, every target he had taken down as a sniper had been on the verge of killing an innocent . . . or many innocents. But the fact that he could never afford to give them a chance still nagged at him.

Enlistment in Starfighter Command had seemed the answer. He'd proven that he had the reflexes, the technical grounding necessary to become a pilot. There was never any moral quandary—everyone he brought down as a pilot had a chance to shoot back. He'd risen quickly and surely through the ranks, earning his lieutenancy within a year, being granted the temporary rank of brevet captain soon afterward.

His own command, Talon Squadron. Every member except Donos killed in the ambush on an uninhabited world no one wanted. Leaving him with a blot on his career he might never be able to erase. A blot on his mind he might not ever be able to heal.

He raised the visor on his helmet and pressed his hands to his eyes. His inclination was to steer away from these thoughts. He couldn't afford to do that. The emotions that rose—threatening to overwhelm him—whenever he sent his mind down this course were enemies he had to defeat. He had to hammer away at them until they left him alone forever. And he had to keep control of himself while doing it, so others would not see his weakness.

He'd lost eleven subordinates, fellow pilots, some of them friends. He'd lost his command; Talon Squadron had been decommissioned. He'd even lost his mind, or at least misplaced it, turning into an emotional wreck sometime later, when the loss of his astromech plunged him back into vivid memories of the destruction of Talon Squadron.

His new squadmates had lured him back to reality. Had forced him to look once again at life. To begin thinking again about his present, about his future.

He returned his attention to his sensors. There would be no future if he plowed into a hillside.

All right, then. There were two paths open to him . . . assuming he didn't get killed before he could begin to follow them.

First was the one that had dominated his thinking ever since Talon Squadron had died. For months, he'd considered putting in for a transfer to Intelligence, or resigning his commission altogether, so he could devote his life to tracking down the individuals who had destroyed Talon Squadron.

Inyri Forge had been right. Revenge was a powerful motivator. A desire for revenge, for justice, was always with Donos. It welcomed him to each new day when he awoke, lurked at the back of his mind as he did his work, made soothing promises to him every night when he drifted off to sleep. And sometimes it occupied his dreams. He knew, deep down, that if he were able to find the responsible parties under his snubfighter guns or in the sight of his laser rifle, he'd pull the trigger without hesitation, without qualm . . . regardless of what it cost him.

Of course, two of the most important conspirators behind the destruction of his squadron were already dead. Admiral Apwar Trigit had planned the ambush. Lieutenant Gara Petothel had provided Trigit with the data he needed for that operation. Petothel had died on Trigit's Star Destroyer, *Implacable*, and Trigit had died soon after, trying to escape in a TIE interceptor, brought down by Donos himself.

But others had to have been involved. Imperial Intelligence operatives had gotten Lieutenant Petothel her false identity and her posting with Fleet Command. They'd smuggled her from New Republic–controlled space to *Implacable*. Elements of the 181st Imperial Fighter Group now inexplicably helping Warlord Zsinj had participated in the ambush. There were plenty more conspirators who needed to die.

But part of him no longer wanted to be the instrument of

that death. An ever-growing part of him wanted to live a normal life. And that led to his second choice, the one he'd been toying with ever since he had recovered from his collapse: stay in Starfighter Command and try to rebuild his career, regain his respectability . . . renew his life.

A woman named Falynn Sandskimmer had loved him. He didn't know whether he'd loved her in return, whether he'd even been able to at the time. But he'd had affection for her, and what she'd felt for him had reminded him of what it was like to be a normal human. She, too, had died aboard *Implacable,* before he'd ever had the chance to sort out his feelings for her.

And now . . . he checked his sensor board for Wraith Two. There she was, toward the head of their formation, tucked in neatly behind Wraith One. Lara Notsil.

He'd exchanged so little with Notsil. Some advice. One ground mission in which he'd saved her from kidnapping at the hands of Zsinj agents. Conversation in pilots' lounges and during leave time.

But for the little amount of time they'd shared, she did occupy a lot of his thinking. Her intelligence and her beauty drew him. And her secrecy: she seemed to have no affection for the life she'd lost, the life of a farm girl from the world of Aldivy, and yet so much of her was private, locked behind doors that obviously led to her childhood.

And one other thing seemed so familiar to him: the way she seemed adrift, cut off from her past, yet having no apparent idea how to navigate toward her future. He understood that part of her, felt tremendous sympathy for her. They were so alike.

Yet that would mean nothing if neither one of them did anything about it. She might not even be aware of how he felt, of what he was thinking.

She isn't aware, an inner voice told him. *And she's not going to be. Don't foul up her life the way you've fouled up your own. Do something conclusive with your life. Resign your commission. Hunt down your enemies. Settle the accounts of your pilots.*

True. He shouldn't force his way into her life, only to abandon her when he went off on some justified spree of revenge. Better to leave her alone.

But what if he could offer her as much life, as much of a future, as he thought she could offer him?

Now you're using that misfiring hunk of erratic machinery you refer to as a brain.

That startled him. The words were in the voice of Ton Phanan, a fellow Wraith; they were typical of his ordinary conversation. Ton, who'd died mere weeks ago. Ton, who had also decided that he had no future, and perhaps had died because he couldn't bring himself to struggle for his life as hard as he should.

And there it was. Donos did have a future, as Ton did not. Donos could choose to abandon it and pursue his life of revenge, and then maybe . . . *maybe* . . . come back from it if he lived. Or he could just choose to live. Which meant doing something harder than he'd ever done before.

He might just have to forgive himself for letting his pilots die.

He might just have to initiate a conversation with a young woman who was suddenly important to him.

IT WAS A SPOT where the hillside leveled out in a treeless glade some seventy meters in diameter. Without repulsorlifts, they could never have all landed upon it, but Rogue Squadron and Wraith Squadron arrayed themselves precisely, in neat rows and columns.

As the pilots scrambled out of their cockpits under the sliver of a moon, Wedge said, "Get those camouflage covers out. Transfer any fuel remaining from the auxiliary tanks into the interceptors. Snap it up. I want us blanketed down and out of sight in ten minutes. We have dawn in less than an hour. Hobbie, Corran, Asyr, Tal'dira, I want you out on first watch. Everyone else, four hours' sleep. Face?" He crooked a finger.

He and Face took a few steps aside to be out of the bustle of pilot preparations. The ground underneath was covered by shin-high grasses that were too pale a green to be healthy-looking in Wedge's eyes. "We had a pretty good look at the northeast approaches to Lurark. Did you see anything to give us new problems?"

Face shook his head. "I don't think so. The big question is how to acquire transport—the city doesn't seem to be set up for pedestrian traffic."

"That's up to you. Sleep on it."

Face managed a rueful grin Wedge could barely see in the moonlight. "Oh, sure. As though I could sleep."

ONCE HE HAD the camo covers tied down over his X-wing and had made sure that his astromech, Clink, was settled in, Donos sought out Lara. He found her under her own camouflage cover, kneeling on the starboard S-foils of her snubfighter, whispering to her own R2, Tonin. He waited patiently until she emerged and extended a hand to help her down. "Could I have a word with you?" he asked, and was immediately annoyed with himself, at the formality of his voice.

"Of course."

He led her into the deeper shadow between her X-wing and Kell's TIE interceptor. "There's something I wanted you to think about." There, that was better—a more normal tone to his voice, in spite of the way his chest suddenly felt compressed. He was in full control again.

"What's that?"

"Me."

She looked at him, and one eyebrow went up, a mocking look. "Rebel pilots have the biggest egos in all the known universe . . ."

"Well, it's not like that. I'm asking out of a sense of fairness. Since I'm spending all this time thinking about you."

Her smile faded. "Myn, I'm not amused."

"Good. I'm not trying to amuse you. Look, I just spent a long time working up the nerve to bring this up with you at all. It was harder than almost anything I've done. So don't be amused. Take it seriously."

She took a step back from him, bringing her up against the wing array of Kell's interceptor. "No, no, no. Just turn around and go find someone else to be interested in. I'm not right for you."

He couldn't keep the smile from coming to his face. "Oh, that's a very good sign."

"*What* is?"

"You didn't say, 'Go away, I don't like you.' You started suggesting reasons that are theoretically in my best interest."

She wrapped her arms around herself, as though to protect herself from a chill, and glared. "I *don't* like you."

"Now you're lying. You do that a lot, just like Face. I'm getting better at figuring out when you're doing it." He stepped in close. "You can't get rid of me by lying to me."

"I'm a mess. I'm barely fit to fly."

"Me, too. We make a perfect couple."

"If I don't get killed, I'm sure my career is going to crater. I'm going to be a tremendous embarrassment to the Wraiths."

"How about that—me, too! Another thing we have in common."

"Stop it!" She looked surprised by the volume of her voice and looked around to see if anyone had noticed.

Donos looked, too, but the camp was still bustling with activity. No one stopped to peer at the source of the cry.

When he looked at Lara's face again, though, something

had changed. There was a stillness to her, a watchfulness that was almost reptilian. He suppressed an urge to step away from her.

"I could say twelve words," Lara said, "and when I was done, the very least you'd do is turn away and leave me alone forever."

He could tell that she was speaking the truth, and the fact that she had the power to do this, to send him away, dismayed him. "Then don't say them."

Donos had really only meant to let her know of his interest, perhaps to rattle her, but she now looked so distant and lost that he couldn't just let her be. He put his arms around her and drew her to him.

When her lips met his, they were clenched tight and she was shaking. But then she relaxed into the kiss. Her arms snaked up around his neck. She made a noise that was part wail, and only he could hear it.

There she was, suddenly part of him, and he wondered how he'd ever lived so long without her being there.

Then she drew back her head, her remoteness gone, her expression a little curious, a little anxious.

"That's more like it," he said. And realized immediately that it was the wrong thing to say.

She gave him a look he could only imagine her normally offering to someone pouring paint into her X-wing's engines. "Thanks," she said. "For reminding me what a gasbag of ego you are." She turned him around, trading places with him, and gave him a hard shove.

His head banged into the interceptor wing. "Ow," he said.

She spun and walked away from him at a fast stride. "Stay away from me, Lieutenant," she said. "Just keep away."

Oh, well. Considering how badly he usually did with people, that hadn't gone poorly at all. Donos sighed and headed back to his snubfighter, resisting the urge to whistle.

5

THE LANDSPEEDER SETEEM ERVIC drove along the old country road was old and slow, but it was still powerful enough to haul a several-ton load of grain cakes from his family business to his customers in Lurark.

He ran a hand through what was left of his hair. He could buy a newer, sportier speeder, of course. But he hadn't inherited the family's failing concern and then built it into a flourishing business by throwing money away on nonessentials. He was almost rich. He'd never be rich if he loaded up on luxuries.

True, it had taken him years. Cost him his first wife, who said he was boring, that they never had anything to talk about. Cost him his hair, which had fallen away as the seasons had passed. At least his hair was something to talk about. And, true, nothing ever really happened to him. But he was almost rich, and that was what counted. If his brightest daughter turned out the way he expected her to, she'd take his solid business and make a worldwide concern out of it. And she'd be rich for real.

He rounded a bend in the dusty road and something happened to him.

There, a hundred meters up, something lay in the road. As he got closer, in spite of the glare from the sun, he could see it was a body—a human body. He slowed, and when he was a mere handful of meters away, locked the landspeeder down in hover mode and hopped out to take a look.

Human female, dark-skinned, eyes closed, lying in the

dust as though she'd been thrown—from what? A speeder? There was no recent sign of repulsor traffic on this road. A riding animal? No hoof marks. In fact, there were no footprints around her.

She was wearing a black jumpsuit like a TIE fighter pilot's, and her pose—lying on her back, one arm behind her head—suggested she was sleeping rather than injured. There was no sign of gross injury. She wasn't even dusty.

He leaned closer. Maybe she wasn't hurt. Maybe he wouldn't have to interrupt his trip to the city. "Young lady?"

Her eyes popped open. She smiled, showing deep dimples, becoming insufferably cute. "Yes?"

"Are you hurt?"

"Oh, no. Just resting."

He straightened. "Ah. Well, good. Can I offer you a ride?"

She brought her hand from behind her head. In it was a snub-nosed blaster pistol. "Sure. In fact, you can offer me your whole landspeeder."

He turned to look back at his vehicle. A half dozen people were clustered around it, looking at the control board, peering under the reflective sheets tied down over the cargo bay. He hadn't heard them arrive; they might have materialized out of thin air.

He turned back to the young woman, who was on her feet. He offered her a weak smile and raised his hands. Well, at least this would be something to talk about.

BY MIDAFTERNOON, the human members of the Wraiths had been around Binring Biomedical several times and had spent long hours surveying the facility.

It was huge, easily two kilometers wide by one deep, most of that area taken up by fabrication plants. There were staging and loading areas for landspeeders and other transports. The place had its own light-rail depot.

Face, Lara, Donos, Tyria, Kell, Shalla, and Wes sat around a large circular table at an open-air café separated from the main Binring Biomedical entrance by a broad traffic thoroughfare. Speeder traffic was constant. Everyone on this world seemed to own a personal speeder, and the city was huge and sprawling, though not densely built up or occupied. Face estimated that he hadn't seen more than a half dozen buildings more than three stories in height. "All right, people," he said. "We have too much factory over there to search in one night. We need to have a good idea where Zsinj's special facilities are, or where we can find out that information, before we go in tonight. If the special facilities aren't at this site, we'll definitely need to get into their computer center. Any ideas?"

Lara said, "I see six likely places for a special facility, all connected to exterior docking areas. West Sixteen, Northwest Seven, Northwest Two, Northeast One, East Thirty, or East Thirty-One." Her designations referred to loading and unloading areas—West Sixteen, for instance, meant Western Quadrant, Loading Area Sixteen.

Wes said, "Just Northwest Two or East Thirty-One. We can eliminate the others."

Shalla said, "Just Northwest Two."

Tyria looked unhappy, but nodded. "Northwest Two."

Face sighed. He hadn't seen anything to suggest likely prospects, and their assessment baffled him. "Let's take that again, in the same order. Lara?"

"The places I noted lack power meters on the roof. Everywhere else in that complex, you get external power meters under lockdown cases. Backup meters for the city power managers to get their data, probably if the standard meter transmitters fail. I bet they're analog rather than digital and retain data even if their own power fails. Anyway, they're at regular intervals . . . except in those six places. This suggests that those zones have separate generators and don't depend on the city grid."

Face gave her a close look. "Lara, are you all right? You don't look too good."

He was right; she seemed paler than usual, with dark half circles under her eyes. She gave him a wan smile. "You always know the right thing to say. No, I just didn't sleep well. I'll be fit to go tonight."

"All right . . . Wes?"

The baby-faced lieutenant took a final sip of his caf and grimaced. "Cold. Um, it has to do with privacy and defensibility. Northwest Two and East Thirty-One have advantages that way. The loading-dock areas are down recessed alley accesses that can be closed, remotely or directly, by gates. Both have roof access for flying vehicles but mesh screens can be dragged across them, as well, to limit access. The alleys don't have doors or viewports, so the traffic down them can be private."

"Right. Shalla?"

She waved toward the east facing of the complex, which was around the corner to their right. "East Thirty-One had some vehicle traffic when we were looking at it. Really expensive landspeeders with reflective viewports. One of them was large enough to put a swimming tank in. I think that's the private entrance for corporate executives, board members, and so on. The really wealthy. Also, East Thirty-One opens onto one of the busy thoroughfares, while Northwest Two opens onto a back street with nothing but warehouse buildings facing it. Like Wes said, privacy issues."

"That makes sense. Tyria?"

She didn't meet his gaze. "I just know it." She seemed huddled in her chair. Kell reached over to take her hand, but she barely acknowledged him.

Face said, "That's not good enough, Tyria. What do you know? How do you know it?"

She shook her head hard, sending her blond ponytail flipping across the features of Donos beside her, and finally looked at Face directly. "I *felt* it. When we cruised past. There's something there. A residue of . . . pain. Of things so badly hurt that they desperately wanted to die. Not test animals, either. There was awareness there."

Face suppressed a shudder.

Kell said, "You felt something from the Force."

Tyria nodded. "I've been working so hard, to learn to relax into it, not to push at it . . . not to force the Force, as it were. Sometimes, now, I can put myself into a flow state where I'm almost not myself. I'm just reacting to what I'm feeling. I'd managed to do that when we cruised past. I almost wish I hadn't. I almost lost my last meal."

"Well, that's a good thing," Kell said. When Tyria looked at him, confused, he amended, "Not the throwing-up part. The flow-state part. That sounds like an improvement."

She managed a faint smile for him.

"Northwest Two," Face said. "That's our best entry."

"No," Lara said.

Face held up a hand. "Wait a second. Next to Northwest Two. Northwest One or Three. Where the security is likely to be less substantial."

"Yes," Lara said.

Face sagged in relief. "She said yes," he said. "You have no idea how long I've been waiting to hear her say yes."

Donos murmured something under his breath and Lara flushed red.

UNDER COVER OF DARKNESS, they emerged from beneath the sheeting covering the speeder's cargo bed. The speeder was parked between refuse containers in the parking area of a warehouse; across the thoroughfare was Binring's northwestern quadrant. This was the last the Wraiths would see of the speeder; at some point during the day its loss, and the disappearance of its owner, had to have been reported, and there was too much danger in piloting it around avenues of Lurark left almost deserted at nightfall. They'd acquire other transportation for their departure from the city.

Shalla, kneeling in the shadow of one of the refuse containers, scanned the empty street and darkened Binring buildings below through a set of holorecording macrobinoculars. "Downward-facing holocams with overlapping coverage," she said. "Standard placement. For Imperial forces, that is. Overkill for a pharmaceutical-fabrications plant. Wait a second."

Face knelt beside her. The second turned into several, then finally she spoke. "There's a gap in the coverage. The most northern holocam on the western wall is positioned so it can't really see around the corner. The most western holocam on the northern wall isn't far enough west to make up the gap . . . I don't think." She lowered the goggles and brought out a glow rod so she could look at the hand-drawn map they'd assembled that afternoon. "That's right. If we come in from the north, along this narrow approach, the holocams can't pick us up."

"It's a lie," Tyria said. Her voice was a whisper, a sad whisper.

Shalla shot her a look. "What do you mean?"

Tyria started as if out of some reverie and gave her a nervous smile. "I'm sorry, I didn't mean it that way. It's not your lie, Shalla. It's theirs." Her wave indicated the Binring building. "There's a big . . . watchfulness over there waiting for us. It's laughing."

Shalla said, "You're getting weird, Tyria."

"Yes, but let's take her at her word," Face said. "Shalla, could they have set up the mistake in coverage deliberately, as a lure?"

"Yes."

"What would they be doing?"

"They'd have a secondary set of holocams in a less obvious place." She brought up the macrobinoculars again. "I'd put them in those overhanging spotlights. There'd be no way to see them without getting right up to them . . . and turning the lights out, of course."

There was a whine of machinery behind them and their stolen speeder moved off into the avenue, Donos at the controls. His job was to pilot it some distance away, acquire another one, and return, then set himself up in a position to snipe if the Wraiths experienced pursuit when they departed. Face noted Lara staring after Donos long after the speeder was gone and wondered what was going on between them. Something cheerful, he hoped.

"All right," Face said. "We're going in by the high road."

Minutes later, the entire crew of black-clad Wraiths stood atop the near warehouse, one that was, mercifully, far less thoroughly defended than their target. It was also one story taller than the Binring building, which would work in their favor.

Kell spent a few minutes mounting a device at the edge of the roof. It looked something like a small projectile cannon on a swivel mount, but the repulsorlift-based clamping system at the base of the mount was like nothing seen on a normal cannon. "This had better work," Kell murmured.

"It'll work," Shalla said.

"How do you know?"

"My sister and I had one when we were little girls. They're very reliable. Proven technology."

"You and your sister come from an odd family, Shalla."

She smiled at him, teeth gleaming. "Don't be jealous."

Kell made a final adjustment to the weapon and peered through its scope. "Ready, Captain."

Face said, "Numbers only from now on, people. Five, fire at will."

Kell slowly squeezed the trigger. The device made a noise like a protracted sneeze and launched a missile across the street; the missile dragged a length of black fibra-rope behind it. There was the faintest sound of a metallic clank atop the Binring building; then a motor started up in the gun and drew the fibra-rope taut.

Shalla clipped two devices to the cable: sleeve housings with handlebars hanging from them. "Crawler ready to go."

"Go. Ten, cover her."

Janson drew his blaster pistol and aimed in at the far roof. For most people this would be considered a tricky shot with a pistol—thirty-five or more meters in darkness. But the other Wraiths knew Janson to be an expert pistol shot.

Shalla carefully gripped the handlebars of the lead crawler device and swung herself out over empty space. Nimbly, she brought her legs up so her knees were over the bars of the second device. Then she thumbed a control on the handles she gripped . . . and the crawler sped out along the fibra-rope, carrying her to the roof of the far building. A moment later, the two devices came back, the hand device pushing the knee device before it.

One after another, they took the crawler across, each Wraith settling in a crouch on the far roof. By the time Face arrived, halfway through the pack of Wraiths, Lara, Shalla, and Kell had already examined their surroundings for accesses and other sensors.

And found some. "Standard roof hatches at intervals," Kell said. "And infrared beams just over there." He pointed. "On the roof over Northwest Two."

"I find myself shocked," Face said. "No, really."

"We'll need to leave L—Two—one of the sets of infra-goggles so she can get through the beams."

"Give her yours. We'll rely on Four and her set when we're in."

Once they were assembled, Face directed Kell to disable security on the nearest roof access adjacent to Northwest Two. Within moments he had bypassed the basic security system there. Tyria led the descent down an access ladder, Face and Shalla close behind her.

And that was already a problem. Ever since Tyria had indicated that her fleeting control over the Force had given her some insight into what went on at Binring, Face knew he had to put her on the intrusion team. But she'd originally been assigned to planting tracers on the roof. Face had switched her duties with Lara's. But that cost the intrusion team some of its technical proficiency, Lara being more mechanically adept than Tyria. Kell, their demolitions expert, and Shalla, their intelligence expert, now had to share much of the security work Lara would have been handling.

The change also cost them some faith in their tracer team. Tyria was an old enough hand to have managed her temporary partner, Elassar, but Lara's abilities to handle an unknown quantity like the new pilot were unproven.

Face shrugged. It was done. It would do him no good to worry.

LARA PLACED THE FOURTH transmitter-marker against the knee-high barrier that served as inadequate warning to people that they should not go over the edge and fall off the roof. She activated it and watched it run through its self-test. Then she pulled back away from it in a crouch, making it more difficult for people at street level to see her.

Elassar was already four meters back from the edge, seated, popping something that looked suspiciously like candy into his mouth. "All done?" he asked.

"Not quite. I'm going to take a holo of the rooftop and surrounding area, then show on it where the markers are and transmit that to the Rogues. That'll give them a visual reference to go with their sensor readings. Why don't you make yourself useful? Or is that unlucky?"

He smiled at her, showing his fangs. "Not unlucky. I've

done everything I can for this mission in the field of luck. I've cast all the charms I could manage, and unlike the rest of you, I've refrained from doing anything unlucky. And I've made myself useful, too. I found something out."

Lara readied her holocam, held it steady before her eye, and began a slow, careful 360-degree turn. Once this special surveyor's holocam caught the panoramic image she wanted, she would be able to mark points on the image and type in numeric values related to their relative altitude and distance from one another. Then the gadget's internal computer would generate a proportionally correct image that any navigational computer, such as an astromech, could look at from any relative altitude. "What did you find out?"

"Well, that whole network of infrared beams over Northwest Two. I looked at it through your infra-goggles. The posts that the beams are coming out of are years old. They're well kept-up, but there's corrosion on them, and I can see where one of the posts has had to be straightened and realigned when it was knocked over or something."

"So?" Lara finished her turn and knelt with the holocam. On its built-in screen, she brought up the image she'd just taken. She slid a stylus from the side of the device and began marking her reference points.

"So the roof surface over there is brand-new. It's not brand-new here or on any of the places we've been walking, but it's brand-new there."

Lara looked up, suddenly disturbed. "Show me."

There was no marker to indicate the border between Northwest Two and Northwest Three, but they stopped a meter short of the first post that they knew held the infrared devices. Elassar knelt and Lara followed suit.

"See, here," Elassar said. He stretched a finger up almost to the point protected by the infrared. "A seam."

Lara couldn't see, so she risked a moment's illumination with her glow rod. Elassar was right: there was a score, straight as a laser beam, running along the roof between the two building sections. It was so thin as to be nearly invisible even in good light.

She switched the rod off. "So the roof material was laid down in sections. It looks just the same as the roof here."

"Yes, it does. It has been walked on and scuffed a lot, just like the roofing here. But it smells different. Much sharper. It's new."

Lara sighed. This had to be some new-pilot prank. But, obligingly, she leaned back and sniffed at the roofing they'd been walking on. It smelled faintly of industrial chemicals. Then she leaned forward and sniffed again at the other section.

The smell was stronger, crisper.

From her wrist sheath she pulled her vibroblade. She did not power it on. She dug at the seam between the two roof sections, prying the new section up. It was a gummy mass perhaps two centimeters deep and resisted her efforts, but finally she was able to turn up a flap of the material. Elassar obligingly pulled at the edge until half a square meter or so was revealed. The underside of the material was thick with tiny circular devices made of shiny metal. They were spaced at about eight-centimeter intervals and connected by thin silvery wires. "Pressure sensors," she said.

"Not a problem," said Elassar. "None of us walked on them. And we didn't apply pressure to pull them up."

"That's not the point. They've added a layer of security under the substantial security already in place, and it's a different type. If they've done that throughout the complex, the Wraiths might be dismantling one layer but not the new stuff."

"So give them a call."

"Which will probably give our presence away." She sighed and looked over the boulevard at the rooftop where

Donos was. She couldn't see him, but she'd heard his return with a new speeder a few minutes before. It was so hard, working with people; on her missions for Imperial Intelligence, she'd always been alone. No one else to be responsible for.

She brought up her comlink and thumbed on its scrambler mode. "Two to Six. Do not acknowledge. Additional security on roof suggests this site is prepared for your arrival. Check for new modifications to your surroundings. Two out." She grabbed up her holocam and rose. "Let's move out."

"COMM SIGNAL," a technician said. His voice was unnaturally shrill.

Dr. Gast blinked and looked around. She'd actually fallen asleep. *Boredom and lack of any decent occupation will do that to you,* she thought, her voice cranky even when expressed only in her own mind.

The control room was antiseptically white, except where the floor and walls were marked by black marks and scores resulting from the haste with which some of this equipment had been assembled. The four walls were occupied by banks of terminals, each dedicated to a different area of coverage or function. Six per wall, twenty-four in all, occupied every hour of the day, and never anything to report except the occasional repairman working on an adjacent roof section or an avian landing on the roof of the protected zone.

Until now, maybe.

Gast's own console was a nearly complete circle of terminals and controls, her chair in the center. She lazily swiveled until she could look at the back of the technician who'd spoken. "Let's hear it," she said.

"It's encrypted, Doctor."

"Decrypt it. Where's it coming from?"

"I have that." Another technician's voice. He didn't bother to wait for permission; he patched through his holocam view to one of Gast's terminals. She liked that. Initiative. Which one was this? It was Drufeys, the lean one with the lazy eye.

The holocam was an infrared unit. It was a static view of the roof, and showed two blurry red figures, one male and one female, creeping along the roof.

Away from the protected zone. Gast frowned. That was disappointing. Had they recognized the first line of security and decided to run away?

She turned to the console where her new intelligence specialist, a man on loan from Warlord Zsinj, sat. "Captain Netbers, what are they doing?"

Netbers rose and approached her. He was a huge man, easily two meters tall, with a musculature that suggested he spent more time improving it than he did sleeping. A pity he was so ugly—obviously a fighter, he looked as though he had fallen asleep in an automatic door and it had slammed shut on his face for an afternoon. But the eyes underneath his shaggy brown hair were dark and intelligent. When he spoke, his voice was deep and raspy. "They've seen the security perimeter."

"And it scared them off?"

He smiled. His teeth were regular. She somehow doubted they were original equipment. "No," he said. "That comm transmission was them informing the other members of their team. They're getting clear in case we caught the signal."

"We haven't seen any sign of other intruders."

"We will."

She turned back to Drufeys. "Monitor their progress. When they've settled in, have a squad of stormtroopers stand by within striking distance of them."

"Yes, Doctor."

She quelled an excitement rising within her and turned

back to Netbers. "I have a feeling this is going to be fun, Captain. Is it usually fun?"

He nodded.

KELL SWORE AND PUSHED his head deeper into the access hatch. He was hanging from sturdy metal rungs in the turbolift shaft, one floor below street level, illuminated only by the glow rod held by Shalla, who stood on the same rung he did and helped brace him as he worked. The panel Kell investigated opened into a maze of wires and circuitry, and his head was missing in that forest of equipment. "Give me more light."

Shalla leaned in closer to oblige, poking her hand and glow rod through the curtain of wiring. She could see his neck flex as he looked around.

Finally Kell withdrew—slowly, so as not to knock Shalla free of her perch. He twisted to look over his shoulder at the other Wraiths, clustered in the open turbolift door behind him. "Two was right. There's new wiring throughout. If we'd gone down and disabled the monitors on the panel between lift shafts, we would have set off another alarm."

Face asked, "Can you disable that alarm?"

Kell considered. Shalla knew this really wasn't his speciality. He'd said he was lucky to have done as well as he had on this mission. "Maybe," he said. "But I can't be sure I've identified all the security at that entry point. I think instead we need to go through a non-entry point."

"Like where?"

"Like here." He gestured at the curtain of wires. "Beyond this monkey-lizard nest, we have a riveted panel of metal between us and the Northwest Two lift shaft. But it's not armor quality. I vote we just cut through and descend."

"Do it."

Kell brought out his vibroblade and powered it on.

———

THEY WERE WITHIN three meters of the bottom of the shaft when Kell spotted the access hatch they would have used had they not changed plans. "Nine, the gauge again?"

He felt Shalla rummage around in the top pocket of his demolitions pack. Then she handed him the sensor device he'd had to use so many times tonight. It read electrical currents and was of vital use to mechanics and demolitions experts, two categories into which Kell fit.

He aimed the device at the panel and swept it all around the bottom of the shaft. It registered a considerable amount of electrical current flow beyond the panel, no surprise, and along the recessed slot used by turbolift cars of this sort to acquire their power.

There was also a suspicious spike of activity on the wall opposite the panel, just above the door out of the lift shaft. It took him a few moments to identify the hemispherical depression, not larger than the end of his thumb, in the metal just above the door. "Holocam recess," he said. "But it's set up to watch the panel. If we get across to the door side and drop beside it, it shouldn't spot us."

Face said, "There are no rungs over there, Five."

"Oh, well. Guess we go home instead." Kell had Shalla tuck the gauge back in his pack. He checked to make sure that his pack and other gear were secure.

Then he let go of the rung he was holding on to and leaped across the turbolift shaft, slapping into the far wall like a slapstick character from a holocomedy. He dropped the final three meters to the duracrete bottom of the shaft, his large frame easily handling the shock of landing. He gestured up at his comrades as though to say, "Simple."

He saw Face shake his head ruefully.

One by one they followed his lead. He half caught each of

them, fractionally slowing their descents, then got to work on the minimal security on the turbolift door.

THE HALLS WERE EMPTY, sanitary, still smelling faintly of something antiseptic. The lights were on at half intensity, making even the whiteness of the walls and floor seem dim. All the Wraiths could hear was the distant hum of air-moving machinery and their own faint footsteps.

Face didn't like it. It felt abandoned, and an empty facility would not yield them any secrets. It also felt somehow wrong. He glanced at Tyria to gauge her response—perhaps her abilities with the Force, however faint or erratic, would tell her something. But he could not read her face; at his own command, all the Wraiths, now that they were moving in what should have been populated areas, were wearing black cloth masks covering everything but their eyes and mouths.

All the Wraiths but Piggy, that is. No mask could conceal his species, and only one member of his species would travel with a commando unit this way.

"I know this floor," Piggy said. Both his real voice and his mechanical one were modulated so low that Face could barely hear them. "This was the third of four floors. We came down here only when we were injured. The bacta ward was right down—" He pointed his finger at a blank section of wall to his right and stopped.

Face asked, "Right down where, Eight?"

"Down this hall."

"That's a wall."

"I know." Piggy stepped up to the wall and looked at it very carefully. Then he bent to look at the flooring beneath it. When he turned to Kell, his expression, to the extent that Face could read Gamorrean expressions, was confused.

Kell obligingly aimed his electrical current detector at that section of wall, waving it about slowly. "Nothing to suggest any sort of door mechanism. There's some faint electrical activity beyond, but not immediately beyond. Several meters, I think, and no heavy electrical currents."

Tyria said, "The wear on the floor doesn't show that anything has turned down a hall here, Eight. And the floor looks as though it's been through several years of wear."

"Yes," Piggy said. But he still stared at the wall as if accusing it of lying. "They've taken up the floor from somewhere else and moved it here to conceal the deception."

"All right," Face said. "But even so, the only thing down this hall of yours was a bacta ward—correct?"

"Correct."

"We'll check it out if we don't find anything elsewhere. Let's look at what you never got to see before. All right?"

Piggy nodded.

They continued up the main hall, the only hall, to its end. On the left was a large double door leading into a circular chamber filled with equipment—panels, consoles, and terminals arrayed in a circle around some sort of large chair. The chair was obviously intended for medical usage; it featured brackets to fit around wrist and ankle, and was festooned with equipment on armatures—injectors, viewscreens, racks filled with bottles.

"I know that chair," Piggy said. "You got your shots there. And performed tests. But it was one floor up."

"Door's clear," Kell said. "No undue security. Do I open it up?"

Face said, "You said three of four. This was the third floor of four. You meant two above this one and one below?"

Piggy nodded.

"How did you get to the fourth floor?"

"By the turbolift." Then Piggy frowned and looked back down the hallway toward the distant turbolift door.

"But the turbolift ended at this floor," Face said. "There was duracrete below."

Shalla said, "It was very clean duracrete. No oil stains. I thought that was odd. But everything here has been so clean it seemed in keeping with the rest."

"Obviously, it was new," Face said. "They've blocked off the fourth floor. I wonder why?"

The others shrugged. Tyria merely gave him her I-have-a-bad-feeling-about-this look.

"We can leave now," Shalla said.

"There is no data without risk," Face said, "as one of my instructors used to say. We always wanted to shoot him for it. All right, Five, let's go in."

Kell triggered the door control. The double doors slid open and the Wraiths entered, blasters up, fanning to either side.

"DOCTOR?" SAID ANOTHER TECHNICIAN. "They're in the First Chamber." He put through the holocam feed to one of her terminals.

Gast looked at the screen and frowned. "They got through our outer perimeter."

Netbers leaned over her shoulder. "They're pretty good. But they're here. So they're dead."

"Alert your stormtroopers," Gast said, then issued commands to the others. "Prepare the Second Chamber. Activate comm jamming as soon as the door to the Second Chamber is opened. No, wait: Alert the other team of stormtroopers to take the intruders on the rooftop, *then* activate comm jamming as soon as the Second Chamber is opened." She frowned, angry with herself for her mistake.

"You're getting the hang of it," Netbers said.

———

KELL WAVED AN all-clear signal to the others. The walls and ceiling offered no circuitry suggesting additional security.

Dia and Shalla covered the door with their blasters. The others looked at the equipment in the room.

"I was never in here," Piggy said. "I don't know what the chamber was for. The chair wasn't here. The chair was one floor up, where they did a lot of testing. I solved math problems in that chair while drugged or while being electrocuted."

"Charming," Face said.

"There's something awful about this room," Tyria said. "Not in the room itself. Nearby."

"This is a game-table unit," Kell said. He was on one knee, looking intently at one of the pieces of equipment around the chair. "The table itself has been taken off and the unit repainted."

"So it broadcasts to the screen on the chair?" Face asked.

"Maybe." Kell looked over the unit, puzzled. "It doesn't seem to be fastened down, but it's powered."

"This machine washes clothes." Runt was staring with equal concentration at a silver-gray metal cube two-thirds the height of a human. "They had one like it on the ship *Sungrass*."

Kell waved his current detector at Runt's device, then at the floor around it. "It's self-powered. Like the game table. It's battery-powered or something."

"Why?" Face asked. He looked at Piggy, but the Gamorrean looked blankly back at him.

"TRANSFER CONTROL TO my terminal," Gast said.

Then she caught the hurt look on the face of Drufeys and she relented. "Oh, very well, you do it."

Drufeys brightened and pressed a button on his console.

———

FACE FELT THE FLOOR give way beneath him. All around him, Wraiths and equipment dropped. There was blackness and heat beneath him. When his feet hit he tried to roll and absorb some of the shock of impact, but he did a bad job of it and landed on his chest, the wind knocked out of him. He felt something heavy and sharp slam into his back and he grunted from the blow. There were cries and sounds of crashing all around him.

Awkwardly, he rolled to his back. The floor of the room above had split down the middle. Hinges to either side had allowed it to open like a door, dropping them what looked like a fall of six or seven meters.

And now stormtroopers were lining up at the edges of the room above. They aimed their blasters down at the Wraiths. One called out, "Throw up your demolitions gear or we open fire."

Face looked around. The Wraiths were in no position to resist. Only Kell and Shalla were already on their feet. Beyond Kell, Runt was unmoving, apparently unconscious. Beside him, a piece of machinery on her back, was another fallen Wraith—

"Dia!" Face was suddenly on his feet despite the pain. He knelt beside Dia, saw at once that she was unconscious, that her left arm lay at an angle that was not right. She was still breathing.

"Demolitions bag," the stormtrooper repeated. "Or you're all dead."

Face caught Kell's attention and nodded.

But Kell turned to Shalla, and said, "Do what they say, Demolitions."

Shalla didn't hesitate. She shucked off her own pack, which contained her infra-goggles, spare glow rods, and preserved food. She swung it around at the end of its straps and hurled it up to the stormtroopers above.

The speaker caught the bag. He and the others retreated. The ceiling began to close.

"What are you doing?" Face asked. "In thirty seconds they'll know we've lied. They'll open it up and start shooting."

"In thirty seconds we're supposed to be dead," Kell said. He pulled off his own pack and rummaged around in its contents. "Take a look around, One. You know what this place is?"

Face forced himself to look away from Dia.

The floor was some sort of grating. It seemed to be continuous, not made up in sections, and was sturdy enough not to flex beneath the weight of the Wraiths and all the equipment from the chamber above. The walls were heavy, dark metal with a tight grid of nozzles protruding from them.

As he looked, the floor grating beside the walls began glowing red. The redness spread toward the center of the room at a quick rate. Heat from the glowing portions of the grate swept across Face and the other Wraiths.

"They burn organic material here," Piggy said. He struggled to his feet, holding his side. "It's an incinerator."

LARA KNELT AND FRETTED. Still no communication of any sort from the team. Of course, they were supposed to keep comm transmissions to a minimum. But she wanted to know what was happening down below.

It didn't help that Elassar was so calm. The Devaronian junior pilot lay on his back, admiring the stars. "A shooting star!" he whispered. "That's good luck."

"Is it still lucky if it's one of the asteroids we shot into the atmosphere as cover?" Lara asked.

He frowned, considering. "I don't know."

Sixty meters away, there was a terrific metal crash and two hinged pieces of roof slammed open. An open-sided turbolift rose into view. The dozen stormtroopers within it jumped out, turning toward Lara and Elassar.

"I guess not," Elassar amended.

FACE LIFTED DIA, as mindful as he could be of her broken arm. "Sorry I said anything, Five. Blow us out of here."

Kell slipped his bag back over one shoulder. He held two charges, one in each hand. He tucked one charge into a pocket and tapped something into the keypad of the other.

Tyria hopped up on a boxy piece of metal equipment as the redness of the floor neared her feet. She peeled off her face mask. The other Wraiths began following suit. Face could see that they were already sweating heavily. So was he, but burdened as he was, he couldn't do anything about it. Tyria said, "What if the chamber is magnetically sealed?"

"It's not," Face said. "If it were, they wouldn't have bothered to demand our demolitions."

Kell said, "One?"

"What?"

"Where do I place this?"

"Your best guess. You're the demolitions expert. But this deep down, we may have stone and dirt on all sides."

"Imperial architecture is kind of conservative," Kell said. "One floor is often like another. Meaning that the main hall above may have a parallel on this floor. Which was—where?" He looked around blankly. In the fall and the Wraiths' subsequent disorientation, he'd lost track of directions.

Piggy pointed at one wall, then yanked Runt up before the heat in the floor grid reached him. The Thakwaash pilot looked groggy, but mobile.

Flame erupted from every nozzle along the chamber walls. The flames were no more than half a meter in length, but the temperature in the room rose instantly. Several Wraiths swore and all flinched away from the new heat.

"Three seconds," Kell said. "Find cover." He threw his package against the wall and moved to crouch behind one of the ruined metal cases of false lab equipment.

Face followed suit. He felt the floor grating begin to burn its way through his shoes the moment they made contact. He crouched and leaned back against the experiment chair, keeping it between him and the explosive charge, trying to keep Dia's limbs from trailing against the floor.

ONE FLOOR UP, a stormtrooper opened Shalla's pack and extracted a tube of processed nutrients. He pawed through the other contents of the pack, then held out the nutrient tube to his commander for inspection.

The commander said, "Uh-oh."

6

"I WASN'T TOO sure about this crematorium idea," Netbers said. "But I must admit it seems to have come off rather well. Though the warlord might have preferred a better souvenir than several kilograms of ashes."

Dr. Gast nodded. "But I think he'll be pleased that they didn't just die—that they died very, very painfully."

"True."

The building rocked and the sound of a muffled detonation reached them. Technicians jumped up and looked around as though deciding whether to situate themselves in doorways.

Netbers sighed. "Not good," he said. "I'm going to lead the stormtroopers down to the crematorium level."

Gast stood. "I'm going with you. You'll need me for access to all levels."

"Come along."

THE EXPLOSION HIT before Face heard it, before he comprehended it. All he knew is that something hard, the frame of the experiment chair, hit his back and propelled him forward— launching Dia toward the burning floor, the burning wall. He rolled with the impact, tumbling, trying to keep Dia from contacting the glowing floor grid.

He succeeded. His shoulder hit the grid and he felt the flooring burn through his light tunic, branding him. He continued the roll and the burning sensation tore down his back, across his buttocks.

There was a burning in his throat, too. It had to have been from his scream. He felt as though his back had been torn completely free, revealing bones and blood for all the world to see. He almost gave up then, as the pain told his body to tighten up into a tight ball and lie there until he died, but he felt his heels hit the floor and he rose, instinct and adrenaline giving him the energy to keep moving.

He turned back toward the source of the explosion. The flames on the walls were now growing, extending toward him, but in the center of them there was a different sort of light—whiteness, not redness. He lurched toward it, gaining speed.

There it was in his mind, an absurd image—his childhood visit to an arena on Coruscant where animals from all the planets of the galaxy did tricks for the entertainment of men. One of those tricks was leaping through fiery hoops and frameworks. Now he was doing it.

The floor grating disappeared two steps ahead, ending in a broken edge of red-glowing metal. He leaped over the edge into the white void beyond—

And hit something. White, cold hardness. He bounced off it and landed on his back.

And there the pain from his burns hit him. His back arched and he shrieked. His body would not obey him, would do nothing but writhe and shout.

He could not even look down to see if Dia was still with him, if he'd managed to carry the woman he loved out of that inferno.

LARA DREW HER blaster pistol and fired. Her first shot missed the leading wave of stormtroopers but checked their progress—most of them dropped to skid behind antennae, air-conditioning equipment, and other rooftop gear. The first of them returned fire and Lara realized rather belatedly that she had no cover before her.

Elassar had his blaster out in a two-handed grip. He fired, tearing uselessly into the side of the metal housing between him and his target. Lara grabbed his tunic at the shoulder and tugged him toward another metal housing.

They ducked down behind the landskimmer-sized equipment case and heard blaster shots hammer into the far side. "We're in trouble," Lara said.

"True. Should I charge them and wipe them out for you?"

"Oh, if you think you could, that'd be really decent of you." Lara popped up, took a quick shot, was rewarded with the image of a pair of stormtroopers ducking behind cover. "I'll help too," she said. "I'll call the troops."

"Deal."

Lara brought out her comlink. "Wraith Two to Rogue Leader. Emergency. Emergency. Do you read?"

The only answer was a hiss of static.

FACE FORCED HIMSELF to look around. He was in a hallway.

There, to his right, lay Dia. She was moving, her eyes half-open. Beyond her was a jagged hole in a once-pristine white wall. It was three or four meters in diameter, starting at knee height and continuing up into the ceiling and beyond, and it was lined in flames. Heat rolled out of it, a steady wind from a manmade hell.

Out from the fire shot Wes Janson, crashing into the same wall Face must have hit, but he kept his feet when he landed. His right shoulder and back were on fire. He dropped to the floor and rolled, swatting at the flame.

Then came Tyria. She landed short of the wall, her blaster

rifle in hand. Poised as a heroine from an action holodrama, she swept up and down the hall with the rifle. There was no sign of fire, even of burn upon her.

Four out. Four to go. Face heaved himself to his feet, leaving Dia where she lay for the moment. There was blood all over the flooring where he'd fallen. He decided not to think about that for the moment. Or about the pain—he swore and brought out his blaster pistol, then reached down and began dragging Dia out of the path of oncoming Wraiths.

Seconds later, Kell landed where she had just been. His hair was charred and his eyebrows were gone, singed away. There were burn stripes on his chest, stripes identical to the flooring in the crematorium—and not only on his chest. His palms and fingers were also black and red with the marks, and shook uncontrollably.

Piggy came flying out of the inferno and crashed into the wall. He bounced off and slammed to the floor atop Face's blood slick. A fraction of a second later, Shalla landed atop him. She was on fire and had burn stripes along her right side from armpit to knee, and she shrieked as she rolled to extinguish the flames. Piggy slapped at her, trying to help.

Seven of eight. The Wraiths looked at one another as, in their pained and distracted states, they tried to calculate who was missing.

"Oh, no," Kell said. "Runt—"

Then Runt was among them, his chest and left side fully engaged in flame, his fur blackening away as it fed the fire. He landed on his knees atop Piggy, howling in pain, swinging arms as though to strike the enemy burning away at him.

Kell leaped at Runt, a body check that took him from atop the Gamorrean. Piggy got up to his feet and fell atop Runt, hammering away at patches of flame his corpulent body didn't smother.

They just stood there breathing for a moment. Then Face straightened, despite what it cost him in agony to his back.

When he spoke, he found that his voice cracked with pain and exertion. "We're moving out," he said. "There have to be access panels or stairs near where the turbolift used to be. First, open communications with our other team and the Rogues."

Janson took the scorched comm pack from Runt's back. Fortunately the unit within, though blackened along one side, was functional.

Maybe.

Janson looked up from it. "I'm getting nothing but hiss. Some of it may be because we're too deep, but I think we're being jammed."

Face nodded. "That figures. All right, we go. Ten, you take point. Four, rear guard."

Janson and Tyria nodded to accept their respective tasks.

Shalla got Dia up to her feet and quickly rigged a sling for her arm. Dia still looked groggy, but she managed to catch Face's eye and gave him a look that said she was there, she was functional. There was no time for them to exchange anything else.

Piggy tried to haul Runt up to his feet, but the Thakwaash pilot shook off his hand and stood. He was a mess, much of his upper body marked by flame-blackened fur, and his eyes were wide, vibrating.

Face knew how he felt. It wasn't just pain. Anger blossomed within him like the explosive cloud from a proton torpedo. "Wraiths," he said, "no rules. No mercy. Take out anything that gets between us and home."

From the looks in their faces he knew they'd have accepted no other order.

LARA HAZARDED ANOTHER look over her shoulder. The nearest path to escape was the edge of the roof, some thirty meters back. But she was behind the last cover between this point and the edge. If she and Elassar got up to run, they'd be cut down. "I think we're done for," she said.

Elassar shook his head. "No. Today's a lucky day. I calculated it before we started on this mission."

"Ah. Did you remember to invite your luck? Or is it in its bunk on *Mon Remonda*?" Lara popped up to try another shot.

A laser blast, brilliant red, flashed out of the distance. It struck behind the equipment housing Lara had been firing at—and hit one of the stormtroopers there, blasting him sideways, leaving his charred and smoking body lying in plain sight on the rooftop.

Elassar gave her an infuriating grin. "My luck is your boyfriend. Excuse me." He leaned out to the right of the housing protecting him.

Lara and Elassar had enemies dead ahead, and Donos with his sniper rifle across the street to their left. That meant that stormtroopers close to the Wraiths could be protected from Lara and Elassar, or from Donos, but not both. Lara saw stormtroopers scramble to get their cover between them and Donos's more potent weapon . . . and as soon as they got around the side of their cover, Elassar opened fire, taking down one, two, three of them before the remainder realized the full extent of their predicament.

Lara prepared to pop up for another exchange of shots. The stormtroopers, she knew, had only a couple of options. They could retreat until they could get cover between them and both sets of Wraiths, or they could take out one of the directions of enemy fire . . . which probably meant charging her and Elassar.

They rose and charged, roaring as they came. Lara half rose and opened fire.

THE TECHNICIAN DRUFEYS, now in the command chair of the control room, watched events unfold on the rooftop. Of the eight stormtroopers who'd risen to charge the two visible Wraiths, four were now down, two felled by blaster pistols, two more by the laser sniper. The other four were in fast retreat. "This isn't going well," he said. "Call Argenhald Base and ask them to scramble a couple of TIE fighters. Give them the approximate position of the sniper."

The technician he had addressed, the communications specialist, said, "We're still jamming."

"Use a land line, stupid."

"You don't have to call me stupid."

"Yes, I actually do have to. Get to it." Drufeys settled back into the chair. He liked the feel of it. Too bad this facility was being shut down. But perhaps, if he displayed enough competence, he'd find some task with Warlord Zsinj. He smiled. He liked that idea.

THE WRAITHS WERE within sight of the old turbolift doors, were within thirty meters and could see how the doors had been laser-welded shut, when a side door slammed open and stormtroopers began pouring into the hall. Stormtroopers, an unarmored officer, a civilian woman.

"Get back!" Face shouted. "We have to—"

He was going to say "retreat." They had to get back and away from a numerically superior—and uninjured—enemy force.

But then it happened. Face recognized the big man in the Imperial captain's outfit. Weeks before, disguised as General Kargin of the Hawk-bats, Face had watched Shalla, in her own disguise of Qatya Nassin, bruise the big man in a test of martial arts skills.

And now he saw recognition in the captain's eyes.

The captain couldn't have recognized *him;* Face had been wearing burn-victim makeup designed to make stomachs turn. He must instead have seen Qatya Nassin in Shalla, recognizing her in spite of the makeup she'd worn at the time.

Shalla charged the big man and the dozen and more stormtroopers now crowding into the hall. Her intention was all too obvious: kill the big captain so he couldn't report that a member of Wraith Squadron was also with the Hawk-bats.

She's going to get herself killed, Face thought.

And us too.

He finished his command. "Charge!"

WES JANSON LURCHED into motion, charging in Shalla's wake, taking the left side of the hall where she ran along the right.

He had no wisecracks to offer now. He could only offer one of his other skills, one that might make him unfit for a normal life when this war was finally done. The skill that made him proficient at killing people.

In full stride, he raised his blaster pistol and fired, catching the lead stormtrooper in the chest. The man was thrown back into the arms of one of his companions, his armor now blackened and penetrated.

Janson didn't sight in—he aimed by instinct, by the natural point of his weapon, and fired again. The second stormtrooper took the shot in the dark visor material over his right eye.

Shalla wasn't firing—why not? Janson traversed right and shot at the lead stormtrooper on that side of the hall, catching him in the gut. Behind him was the big captain, now raising his own blaster. Janson fired again. His shot caught the man in the elbow, spinning him back into the wall, causing him to drop his weapon.

Janson traversed leftward again, targeting a stormtrooper with a blaster rifle, his shot catching the man in the throat.

Five steps. Five shots. Five hits. But the hallway was a natural channel for blaster bolts. Its straight lines would angle stray shots back into play. He'd never reach them—

He didn't. He felt fire again and suddenly the world was spinning, slamming into his head—

Dark.

NETBERS SAW THE DARK-SKINNED woman charge and for a moment was so surprised by this tactical insanity that he couldn't react. Then he shouted, "Fire!" and drew his own blaster pistol.

The woman's gaze was fixed on him. He knew he was her target. He knew why, too. And he couldn't get his blaster in line before she had hers aimed, before she pulled her trigger—

And the charred blaster in her hand failed to go off. He almost laughed. He aimed.

The stormtrooper in front of him was thrown back into him, jarring his aim. He shoved the man, probably already dead, aside.

A stray blaster beam slammed into his right arm. It spun him back and pain flashed through him.

That was all right. He knew pain. Pain was his friend.

When he looked up again, the dark woman was upon him, lashing out with a side kick meant to shatter his knee, to bring him to the floor. He twisted, took it as a graze against the side of his knee.

She was hurt. Burn marks all along her right side. Netbers swung at her flank, a left-handed slap that hit bare, burned flesh. The blow knocked her to the floor and she lay there, curled up, helpless.

Conditioning is a big part of it, Qatya, he thought. He

reached down and took a blaster pistol from the dead storm-trooper beside him. *You might beat me once, but never twice—*

Something loomed up before him and struck him across the face.

He crashed to the floor atop the body of a stormtrooper. The blow was incredible. He saw stars and his hearing failed. His body wouldn't respond.

His attacker bent over him. It was a nonhuman, a big hairy thing burned all over its upper body, with wide, staring eyes and lips drawn back over square teeth. It grabbed him by the collar and hauled him, all 130 kilograms of him, up into the air as though he weighed nothing.

Netbers lashed out at the alien, striking at one of its burned patches, but the creature grabbed his wrist with its free hand.

Then, as casually as though it were swinging a bag of grain, it slammed him into the wall. He felt his shoulder blade break under the impact, felt something grate in his neck as his head battered into the metal of the wall.

Where are my stormtroopers? But now there were black-clad, burned commandos charging past him, running toward the stairwell by which he and his men had descended. The commandos were firing blasters, shouting—Netbers could hear no noise.

The first wave of them passed and the burned alien swung him toward the opposite wall. Netbers felt himself hit, felt his right shoulder give way, felt something in his neck explode.

Then he felt no more.

"CALL IT OFF!" Face shouted. He was at the base of the stairs. Kell and Piggy were above, ahead of him, struggling across the bodies of fallen stormtroopers. Living stormtroopers were ahead of them, running for their lives. "Let's get out of here!"

"The woman." That was Piggy's mechanical voice, inflectionless in spite of the pain he must be feeling. "She is one of my creators. We need her." He fired up the stairs and continued his awkward run over the bodies of slain enemies. A moment later, he and Kell were out of sight, around a turn in the stairs, and all Face could hear was more blaster fire. He grimaced and moved up the stairs as fast as his tired legs and burned body would let him.

One landing up, the two Wraiths awaited him. Piggy had the human civilian in his grip. Kell waited, his blaster aimed up the stairs, for a counterattack.

In spite of her situation, the woman seemed calm. Face said, "Eight, when the next wave of stormtroopers comes, use her as a human shield. I'm curious to see how long it'll take blasters to burn through her."

"Yes, sir."

"I'm too valuable for that," she said.

"I doubt it," Face said. "But we'll see. If you want to live, you'll tell us a way out of here that doesn't involve more ambushes by your stormtroopers. If they do come at us, you'll be our first bit of cover. Well?"

"Access tunnels," she said. Her voice was cool.

"Show me."

She pointed down the stairs.

THEY GATHERED WHERE the big captain had died. Janson was on his feet, supported by Tyria, his right bicep wrapped in a thick bandage already stained through with blood, his arm hanging uselessly. There was blood spilling down his forehead, too, and a matching patch on the wall at head height. His face was already graying with shock. Shalla, too, was up. Runt was swaying and breathing hard where he stood; flecks of white spittle decorated the sides of his mouth. Seven stormtroopers and the big captain lay dead in the hall.

The female civilian, whom Piggy called Dr. Gast, led them

back toward the incinerator room. Fire from the chamber had spread out into the hall. The air was becoming smoky and flames licked along the ceiling at the far end. But halfway there, Gast turned a toward blank wall and said, "Gast access override one-one-one."

The wall section lifted like a high-speed doorway, revealing a small turbolift beyond. Gast gave Face a cool smile. "Down one level is an underground landspeeder channel with a utilities shaft running parallel to it."

Face boarded and the others followed. "You know what this means to you if this is a trick."

She shook her head. "No trick. Zsinj will have me killed for failure. So my survival means getting you to safety. Gast, descend to sub-five."

The turbolift descended for a few seconds. Then the door opened onto a dimly lit duracrete shelf. Beyond it was a drop-off; a few meters beyond that, a wall.

They exited cautiously, blasters raised right and left. This was a boarding platform for a railway of some sort, the drop-off being a low roadway.

"And may I say," she continued, "that I always enjoyed your holodramas?"

"You couldn't say anything that would nauseate me more."

She smiled, her expression still calm. "Though I liked Tetran Cowall more."

"That makes me feel better. He's a no-talent bag of bantha droppings." Face gestured right and left. "Which way?"

As THEY MOVED, fast as their ill-treated bodies would let them, they passed hatches allowing access into upper floors, tanks where water was stored and processed, power-cabling terminals, and equipment housings that were less easily identified.

Kell stopped beside a heavy metal beam running from the duracrete ceiling above into the duracrete shelf below. He tapped it with his forearm. His hand was still charred, twitching. "Hey," he said. "This is a main support beam, isn't it?"

Gast nodded. "I think so. Why?"

Face said, "Five, no. We can't bring down this whole building. There may be other innocents, other test subjects up there."

Kell offered him a smirk. "Boss, I don't want to blow *everything* up. Listen. We just passed a power station a few meters back."

"So?"

"So if we can adapt the power from that station to boost the signal strength of Runt's comm unit, *and* patch the unit's signal through this beam—"

"Then we use the whole building as an antenna." Face slapped his forehead and regretted it instantly as his palm encountered burned flesh. "Do it. Do it fast."

AT A DEAD RUN, Hobbie charged up to where Wedge and Tycho sat under their camouflage covers. "Signal from the Wraiths, Wedge. They need immediate air support."

LARA AND ELASSAR had circled around, maintaining fire against the now much more distant stormtroopers, reaching the point on the wall where their fibra-rope rig would give them access to Donos's roof, when they saw and heard the approaching TIE fighters. "Just what we need," she said.

She gauged the drop to the ground below. Not too far, she might land unhurt, but there was no place within a hundred meters to hide from a TIE. Likewise, the nearest roof hatch, its locks and security restored to keep guards and workers from noticing anything amiss, would take too long to open.

The pair of TIE fighters roared in from the south, decelerating as they came within easy firing range of the rooftop. They came to a complete halt, floating on repulsorlifts, when they were two hundred meters away. One was aimed directly at Lara and Elassar's position, the other at Donos.

Lara set her blaster pistol down and raised her hands. Elassar did the same. Across the street, they could dimly see Donos following suit.

They could hear the remaining stormtroopers approaching from behind—walking up at a casual pace, joking, their voices relieved.

Then one of the TIE fighters dropped as though it were a puppet with its strings suddenly cut. The other rose a few meters and aimed over Lara's head, off to the east—

There was a flash of blue light and the TIE fighter exploded.

The blast rained fiery bits of metal and transparisteel over the area. Lara felt a bite as a needle of glowing metal hit her forearm, then heat as the advance wave of the explosion reached her. She saw her Devaronian squadmate tumble to the ground, rolling across his dropped blaster as he did so, and come up on one knee already firing.

Lara dropped and scrambled for her blaster. As she swung it into line, she saw that one stormtrooper was already down, the other three aiming. Her shot took one of them in the knee, bringing him down flat on the roof, and her next shot hit the top of his head. He twitched for a moment.

She looked around. The other two stormtroopers were down. One had a burn mark on his gut. The other had a crater where his chest should be. And over on the roof across the street, Donos had his laser rifle in one hand and was waving with the other.

Lara heard the other TIE fighter zooming around out in the distance, but it had to be keeping nearly at street level. What had chased it off, destroyed the other? She looked to the east, but could see nothing in the darkness of the night sky.

"GOOD SHOT, LEADER."

"Thanks, Two," Wedge said. It had, in fact, been a proficient proton torpedo shot. He'd brought up his targeting computer, gotten a targeting lock on one of the enemy TIEs, and fired, all in less than two seconds. Then he led Rogue Squadron on a dive down almost to rooftop level over Lurark, vectoring so that they weren't aimed directly at the Binring complex. There was another TIE fighter out there, keeping buildings between it and the Rogues to stay off their sensor screens, and it didn't pay to be predictable.

In less than a minute, they'd have more than one TIE to deal with. He took another look at his sensor board. There, at its limits, he could see a cloud of red targets tentatively identified as TIEs coming in from the south. The local Imperial air base, seeing the launch of Wedge's X-wings, had dispatched at least a squadron to deal with them. This was going to be complicated.

"Leader, Seven." That was Ran Kether, the new pilot from Chandrila, handling comm duties. "Signal from the Wraiths. They want us to blow up a specific location so they can get out from a tunnel they're in. And to blow up the area bordered by the comm markers they've put up. They say it's a festering pit of evil."

Wedge laughed. "They shouldn't let Wraith One on the comm like that. His language is too florid. All right, break by flights. One Flight, Three Flight, vector to the south and prepare to engage the incoming eyeballs. Two Flight, blow some stuff up for the Wraiths and get them safely out of there."

He heard a groan, doubtless from Gavin Darklighter, who was part of Two Flight—and reduced to "baby-sitting," as Gavin had feared he would be.

——

"Shrike Four to Shrike Leader, I read two incoming targets, class X-wing. They're staying pretty close to building—top level. They're searching for a lock with sensors."

Shrike Leader, commander of the squad of TIE fighters defending Lurark, nodded. These were tactics he'd seen before. The incoming snubfighters had sent their squadmates on ahead, flanking right and left. The unseen X-wings would be coming back toward the center now, flying at street level to stay off the sensors, timing things so that just at the point the X-wings came within firing range, his TIEs would come within sight.

Shrike Leader knew better than to give them such an opportunity. "Reduce speed to two-thirds," he said. That would throw off the enemy's timing. The unseen X-wings would cross before them, having nothing to shoot at, and provide his TIEs with abundant shooting practice. Either that, or they'd break formation now, popping up out of the trenches of Lurark's streets, and the Shrikes could engage them immediately in dogfights.

But no X-wings came bouncing up out of the streets, and the two known targets came implacably on. Shrike Leader frowned at that. "Fire at will," he said.

A second later, one of the X-wings jittered within the brackets of his targeting computer—and dove, even as Shrike Leader fired. His linked laser shot superheated the air just above the enemy starfighter and hit what looked like a residential building.

His target was suddenly gone, down into the maze of streets below, as was the other oncoming X-wing—and just as suddenly, six more X-wings popped up from other streets, also on oncoming headings, and opened fire.

Shrike Leader banked hard, so sharply that his inertial compensator couldn't quite make up for the maneuver—he was thrown sideways into the netting of his pilot's couch.

Then he felt something like a hammerblow as his left wing was hit, penetrated—

Abruptly the world outside his viewport was spinning, starry sky, nighttime city lights, over and over, and he could see the laser-heated stump of his left wing falling mere meters away.

He felt a sickness rise in his stomach, but knew that his discomfort would last only for another fifteen hundred meters.

One thousand.

Five hundred.

WEDGE CHECKED HIS sensor board and smiled thinly at what he saw. The maneuver had been more successful than he'd hoped. Scotian of One Wing and Qyrgg of Three Wing had skimmed along at rooftop level, feeding their sensor data to the other Rogues, who had lined up their opening shots based solely on the transmitted data. As soon as Scotian and Qyrgg had detected targeting locks on them, they'd dived to cover among the streets, and the other six Rogues had jumped up and taken their shots. Suddenly the enemy squadron of TIEs had been reduced by five—three destroyed, two badly damaged and winging away—and the odds were now in the Rogues' favor.

The numerical odds, he told himself. *The odds were already in our favor.* "Break by pairs," he said. "Engage and eliminate. Keep your eyes open for additional incoming units." He arced to port, Tycho tucked in tight behind him.

LARA ACCEPTED A HAND from Donos and swung from the crawler to his rooftop. Elassar stood on guard, his back to them. "Thanks," she said.

"Welcome. Any word from the others?"

She shook her head.

A shrill whine rose behind them—and, like a landspeeder, an X-wing nosed around the building corner to their north, turning their way, riding on repulsorlifts. It climbed as it came until it was at rooftop level. The cowling rose and Rogue pilot Tal'dira nodded at them, his face serious as ever.

"That'll be the lunch I ordered," Lara said, under her breath. She heard Donos snort, saw him struggle to keep his face straight.

"Prepare to pick up your squadmates," Tal'dira shouted. "South face of the building complex. Don't get too near before we blow it."

"Understood," Donos said. "Thanks."

The Twi'lek grimaced, his expression speaking eloquently of how he'd prefer to be halfway across the city where starfighters were engaged in combat, rather than here chatting to ground-pounding commandos. He lowered his X-wing's cowling and goosed the snubfighter forward.

DIA LEANED IN close to Face, so that only he could hear, and asked, "Who is Terran Cowall?"

"What?"

"That Gast creature said she liked Terran Cowall more than you."

"Oh." He laughed. "She can have him. He's an actor from Coruscant. We're the same age. We competed for everything. Both wanted to be pilots. Tested for the same roles. Chased the same girls. He had no perceivable acting skills."

She managed a slight smile. "He was the one Ton Phanan was going to leave his money to. If you didn't get the operation to clear the scar from your face."

Face nodded, rueful.

"I haven't heard of him. Is he still making holodramas?"

"No." Face smiled. "That was one competition I definitely

won. He was a good-looking kid, but as he grew up he got sort of homely and couldn't find work. He hasn't made a holo in years."

The tunnel rocked and a section of it, seventy meters and more away, collapsed, sending dust and large chunks of duracrete rolling down the tunnel toward the Wraiths.

"I think," Face said, "that our ride has arrived."

The Wraiths rode out of Lurark in the back of Donos's new stolen flatbed speeder, lurking beneath blankets that smelled of feathers and avian manure. They lay as comfortably as they could—not comfortably at all for most of them, given the placement and severity of their burns. The city around them was alive with noises—distant explosions, occasional siren wails.

Lara, handling the comm unit while Elassar bandaged Runt, relayed information back. "Rogue Six and Rogue Five are riding guard over us, staying below sensor level. The commander and the rest of the Rogues are strafing the military base now. They're going to lead off pursuit from the next base out. That means we'll probably be able to climb out of the atmosphere at a fairly easy pace."

"Good," Face said. "Is everybody fit to fly?" He shined a glow rod from face to face to get responses.

Dia nodded. Her broken arm was now in a cast made of fast-hardening paste from Elassar's backpack.

Piggy said, "Ready to go home."

Shalla and Kell gave him tired nods.

"Fit to fly," Tyria affirmed. She wasn't kidding; when Face had gotten a good look at her, he found that the only damage she'd suffered was burns that hadn't quite penetrated her boot soles and some charring to the butt of her blaster rifle. When he asked how she'd gotten away unmarked, she'd merely shrugged.

Janson said, "Just try to stop me." He hadn't cracked a smile since the incinerator, and Face could finally see, in his grim expression and the anger deep in his eyes, the man Janson had to be when flying against an enemy.

Runt was slow to answer. Then he said, "We can fly. But we are groggy from what Eleven has given us."

"Just tuck in behind me," Kell said. "I'll get you there."

"We are your wing."

"All right, then," Face said. He didn't really believe they could all fly, but their experience and determination made it possible, and he didn't have much in the way of options. "We have one other problem. Cargo." He shined his light into the face of their prisoner, Dr. Edda Gast. She lay on her side, her arms bound behind her, expression perfectly serene.

"Put her in with me," Shalla said. "Beside me in my TIE. She's not big, I'm not big. We'll dump everything out of my cargo area to lighten up."

"And if she gets feisty?" Face waved his glow rod at Shalla's right side, which was decorated with bandages.

Shalla's face set. "Then I'll kill her."

"You have nothing to fear from me," Gast said. "The worst I plan to do to any of you is negotiate with you."

"*Negotiate?*" Face said.

"For what I know."

"I think I'll let Nine kill you now."

Gast shook her head, not apparently offended by his suggestion. "No, you won't. The Rebels—excuse me, the New Republic—doesn't do things that way. That's what I've always liked about you. And you do want to know where Voort saBinring came from. Why he exists at all. Don't you, Voort?" She twisted to look at the Gamorrean.

Piggy merely stared back at her, his expression unreadable.

"So start talking," Face said.

"No. You, personally, can't give me what I want. Elimination of any charges the New Republic might see fit to press against me. Enough money to start my life over again. Protection from Zsinj. I don't think I'm asking too much—"

"Gag her," Face said. He lay back against the side of the speeder's bed and tried to quell his stomach, which threatened to rise against him.

7

THEY RETURNED TO *Mon Remonda*'s X-wing bays, twenty-three starfighters. Some of them now showed new battle damage. Others were flown as though their pilots were drunk or worse. Medical crews were on station in the bays to help ease pilots out of cockpits and carry them on repulsorlift stretchers to the medical ward.

Two hours later, against his doctor's orders, with his back heavily swathed in bacta bandages underneath a white hospital shirt, Face returned to his quarters.

Solo quarters. A captain, even a brevet captain, warranted decent-sized accommodations all to himself. Face felt a tinge of the old guilt, the old feeling that he didn't deserve any such special consideration, given the good he'd done the Empire back when he was making holodramas . . . but he suppressed that feeling, burying it under a surge of anger. Ton Phanan had shown him that he needed to leave such thoughts behind. If only knowing what he needed to do were the same as doing it.

A *scritch-scritch-scritch* noise reminded him of duties he needed to perform. He took a pasteboard box from a drawer and moved to the table where the cages rested.

Two cages, each about knee height, each contained a translucent arthropod that stood and walked on two legs. The creatures were about finger height, with well-defined mandibles and compound eyes. Storini Glass Prowlers, they were called, from the Imperial world of Storinal. Ton Phanan and Grinder Thri'ag had each secretly come away from the Wraiths' Storinal mission with one of the creatures. Face had found Grinder's when it had been placed in his cockpit as a prank, and had given it to Phanan. Then Phanan, too, had died, and Face had inherited them. But both creatures were male, more likely to kill each other than coexist peaceably, and Face kept them in side-by-side cages.

He used a spoon to extract some of their food from the box. It was unappetizing-looking stuff, looking like little glass beads with green flecks at their centers. But when he poured a spoonful into each cage's feeder box, the Glass Prowlers fell upon the food as though it were the most wonderful of treats; the Prowlers' arms snapped out to scoop up each individual bead and their mandibles chewed away at the transparent coating and green flecks within. Face smiled at their voracity.

There was a knock at his door. "Come," he said.

It slid open and Wedge stepped in. "Am I intruding?"

"No. Just feeding my roommates. Have a seat." Face flicked a tunic from one of the room's chairs. He settled in the other, forgetting for a moment, flinching as his back came in contact with the chair.

Wedge said, "I just came in to see how you were doing. Well, more precisely, to see how you felt about today's mission."

"I figured you would. So I've been thinking about it."

"And?"

"And I feel pretty good about it."

That got him a raised eyebrow from his commander. "Can you explain that?"

"Well, I don't feel good about the casualty total, obviously. Sithspit. Janson and Runt in bacta tanks, everyone else bandaged and drugged up to the eyebrows . . . I have only four pilots fit to fly."

"So what makes you feel good about the mission?"

Face took a deep breath. "We had an objective. Get information. We succeeded, even if that information is going to be difficult to drag out of Doctor Gast. We got out of there with everyone more or less alive.

"Even more, it's obvious that they'd geared that whole facility to kill us, which is something we hadn't anticipated. We were channeled to the place they intended to kill us, and they threw everything they had at us—and we took it and got out anyway. That's a tremendous thing. When my pilots realize that, it's going to be harder than ever to stop them. To intimidate them.

"And then, again, there's the fact that the enemy went to such lengths to wipe out the Wraiths. They spent a tremendous amount of money and effort. They may want us dead, but they're showing us respect—which is something I need to point out to the other Wraiths." He shrugged, then winced again at the incautious move. "We all feel as though we've had the stuffing kicked out of us, then been fried up for someone else's meal—but we *won* this one, Commander."

Wedge nodded and rose. "I guess I don't have too much to tell you."

Face stood as well. "You came here to talk me out of a depressive state." He mimed drawing a blaster and placing it to his temple. "Good-bye, galaxy of cruelty. My pilots are all burned; I must kill myself out of shame."

"Something like that. But you're obviously too smart for that."

Face shook his head. "Too experienced. A year ago, I'd have felt like bantha slobber after something like this. Maybe even a month ago. Now, I just feel pride for my pilots . . . and a realization that I'm going to be sleeping on my stomach for a while. By the way, I'm putting in a commendation for Kell for his initiative, and one for Lieutenant Janson for bravery."

"Like he needs another one."

"Maybe he can build a little fort out of them."

Wedge smiled and departed.

There was another knock at his door.

"Come."

Dia almost flew through the door. She wrapped her arms around his neck, high so as to avoid his bandages, and drew his face to hers for a kiss.

A long one. He held her to him, the two of them able, at long last, to be clear of the military traditions that made it inappropriate for them to embrace before the other pilots, to be able simply to appreciate that they were both still alive.

When she finally released him, it took him a moment to remember what he'd been up to recently. "I sure am glad you two arrived in the right order."

She looked confused. "What do you mean?"

"I'd have hated to have offered you the chair and given the commander the kiss."

She gave him a smile, the one she'd never displayed before the two of them became a couple, the smile that was only for him. "Let's see what we can do so you'll always remember to keep the order straight."

DONOS SETTLED ONTO the stool next to Lara's and looked across the bar. "Fruit fizz, double, no ice," he said.

Lara looked curiously at him. "You know there's no one tending bar."

"Sure, but some of the old formalities have to be maintained." Donos looked around. The two of them were the only people in the pilots' lounge—not unusual, considering the lateness of the hour, and the way no one much felt like celebrating. "I was wondering if you'd thought about what I asked you to."

"You, you mean."

"Well, us, really."

"Sure, I had plenty of time, when I wasn't planting comm markers, shooting at stormtroopers, and tending the injured."

"That's what I thought."

She gave him an exasperated look. "Lieutenant, will you give me an absolutely honest answer?"

"Call me Myn. Sure."

"What do you want from me?"

He took a deep breath, stalling as he composed his answer. "I want to get to know you better. What I do know, what I've seen, suggests that we'd be good together. I want you to stop saying it can't ever be—stop throwing that up as a theory and let us accumulate some evidence. I want to make you smile with something other than a wisecrack. I want to know who you really are."

Her laugh, sudden and hard, startled him. "Oh, no, you don't."

"Try me. Lara, does *anyone* know who you really are?"

That put a stop to her hard-edged amusement. She had to take a moment to consider. "No."

"Even yourself?"

"Least of all me."

"So how do you know no one can love you for what you are? Until you know, you can't have friends, you can't even really have family—you have to be absolutely alone in the universe." He took a moment to settle his thoughts. "Lara, I just want you to give me a chance. But even more, even if it's not with me, I'd really like to see you give *yourself* a chance."

She looked away from him, studying the gleaming brown surface of the bar top. Real wood, protected by so many coats of clear sealant that it shone like glass. He could see thoughts maneuvering behind her eyes, could see her examining them as if measuring and weighing trade goods. But her expression wasn't clinical; it was sad.

Finally, her voice quiet, she said, "All right."

"All right, meaning exactly what?"

"All right, I'll stop avoiding you. All right, let's get to know each other."

"All right, let's find out if we have some chance of a future together?"

She looked back up at him. "I'm pretty sure I'm going to break your heart."

"Well, that's a step in the right direction. Can I break yours, too?"

She didn't smile. "Maybe you already have."

NORMALLY, TAKING NEWS to the warlord didn't cause General Melvar's stomach to host some sort of internal dogfight. But sometimes the news was bad. Such as when he'd had to tell Zsinj how much they'd lost in the *Razor's Kiss* battle with General Solo's fleet.

Such as now.

Approaching the door to the warlord's office, he nodded at the two guards on duty, two handpicked fighting men of Coruscant, and activated one of the many comlinks he carried on his person. This one signaled a very special set of hydraulics he'd had installed in the doors to most of Zsinj's private quarters and retreats. They opened the door at a fraction of the speed and with almost none of the noise of most door mechanisms. Silently, he stepped inside, waited for the door to slide shut behind him, then stood before his warlord.

Zsinj looked up. He hardly ever jumped anymore. So disappointing. "What is it?" he asked.

"Word from Saffalore." He set a datapad before the warlord. "Here's the full report."

"From Doctor Gast?"

"Not quite."

Warned by something in Melvar's tone, Zsinj sat back and laced his hands together over his prominent stomach. "Give me the short version."

"There was a raid on Binring Biomedical about thirteen hours ago. As far as we can determine, it was by the Wraiths."

"Were they killed?"

"No."

"Were *any* of them killed?"

"We don't think so. Survivors on the site think some of them were injured."

Zsinj's jaw clenched, then he forced himself to relax. "Go on."

"They killed Captain Netbers."

Zsinj sighed. "That's a blow. Netbers was loyal and proficient. Is that it?"

Melvar shook his head. "They had Rogue Squadron with them, apparently flying support. Early reports indicate that Wedge Antilles was back flying with the Rogues, as our man on *Mon Remonda* suspected, so he was never in any real danger at the Binring site. They blew up the research center and apparently strafed one of the nearby air bases for fun."

"And what does Doctor Gast have to say for herself?"

"They took her."

Zsinj went absolutely still. Melvar waited, watching, but the man did not blink for long moments, and Melvar knew this was going to be a bad one.

Zsinj rose, slamming his chair into the wall behind him. "They took her alive?"

"Apparently. One of three stormtroopers who survived the bombing witnessed the Gamorrean pilot capturing her. Her body hasn't been found."

Zsinj made an inarticulate noise of anger. He twisted and seized one of the chamber's decorations, a flagpole bearing a banner in the Raptors' colors, red and black and yellow, and slammed its base onto the top of the desk, obliterating the datapad. "They took her? She knows all about Chubar! She knows all too much about Minefield!"

Melvar heard the door behind him hiss open. He heard it hiss shut almost instantly. The guards outside must be peeking in, and, seeing that the warlord was in no danger—only the general was—they'd returned to their posts.

Zsinj swung the flagpole laterally, narrowly missing Melvar, and slammed its base into a trophy case full of memorabilia from his many military campaigns. The case bounced off the wall and toppled forward, crashing onto the floor beside Zsinj's desk.

Zsinj glared at the fallen case as though it were a new enemy. He threw the flagpole aside and, from a hidden pocket at his waist, drew a small but very powerful blaster pistol. He fired at the back of the trophy case once, twice, three times, blasting a crater into the expensive wood with each shot.

The room filled with smoke from the blaster emissions. The door slid open behind Melvar and then shut again.

Zsinj stood, shaking, glaring at the damage he'd done, then tucked the blaster away and sat heavily back in his chair. Melvar let out the breath he'd been holding.

"Well, we can't have this," Zsinj said. His voice was raw and sweat beaded his forehead. Sweat was also beginning to stain his white grand admiral's uniform at his armpits and chest. "Activate our man on *Mon Remonda*. Tell him to kill Doctor Gast if he sees her. Whether or not she's there, tell him to kill his primary targets. We'll need to sacrifice some units as bait for Solo's fleet if we're to mop up the rest of them. And put Project Funeral on full speed ahead." He held up a hand as if to curtail an argument, though Melvar did not feel like offering one. "I know, it's a little premature, but all these Ranats biting at my heels are going to ruin my entire plan if we don't do something about it now."

"Understood, sir." Melvar saluted. "Do you want your office restored, or will you be wanting to redecorate?"

Zsinj looked at him, puzzled, then glanced around at the damage he'd wrought. He managed a bark of laughter. "I'll redecorate. Thank you, General. Dismissed."

———

ON FARAWAY CORUSCANT, in one of the tallest of the planet's towers at the heart of the old Imperial governmental district— a district as large, geographically, as mighty nations on other planets—Mon Mothma rose from the chair before her makeup table.

Not that the Chief Councilor of the New Republic's Inner Council was overly fond of makeup. She made no effort to hide the gray creeping inexorably through her brown hair. She went to no particular lengths to hide her age—she'd earned every one of those years and would not insult others of her generation by suggesting that there was some shame in the accumulation of time.

Still, she needed a little matte to make sure that her face was not too shiny when the holocams caught her under bright lights, and these days she was a little too pallid to suit herself—a bit of color, even artificial color, suggested that she possessed more vigor and health than she actually felt.

She gave herself one last look in the mirror, adjusted the hem of her white gown, and marched with simulated energy to the door of her quarters.

They opened to admit her into the hall, and there waiting, as she knew they would be, were two members of her retinue.

The smaller was Malan Tugrina, a man of Alderaan— a man who'd lost his world long before Alderaan was destroyed, as he'd attached himself to Mon Mothma's retinue in the earliest days of her work with the Rebellion. He was of average height, with features that would have been vaguely homely if not covered by a natty black beard and mustache, and the only thing striking about him were his eyes, which suggested intelligence and deep-buried loss. There was little striking about his abilities, too, except for his unwavering loyalty to Mon Mothma and the New Republic, and his skill at memory retention—everything said to him, everything that passed before his eyes, was burned into his memory as though he had a computer between his ears. He handled many of her secretarial duties with both the efficiency and the pedantic manner of a 3PO unit. "Good morning," he said. "In half an hour, you have—"

"Wait," she said. "I haven't had any caf this morning. Can you expect me to face the horrors of my schedule when I'm not fully awake?" She swept toward the nearest turbolift. "Good morning, Tolokai."

The other individual said, "Good morning, Councilor," in his usual monotone. He was a Gotal, a humanoid whose roundish face was adorned with a heavy beard, a broad, flattened nose, and, most dramatically, two conelike horns rising from his head. The horns, Mon Mothma well knew, were sensory apparatus that made Gotals some of the most capable hunters and reconnaissance experts in the galaxy—not to mention bodyguards. With Tolokai beside her, she knew she'd always have warning of an impending attack, no matter how well prepared. It gave her an edge she needed in these dangerous times.

Mon Mothma summoned the turbolift as her companions stepped into place behind her.

Tolokai said, "If I may, Councilor, there was something I wished to show you."

"It's nothing I have to remember for too long, is it?"

"No, not too long. I do this in the name of all Gotals everywhere." From beneath his tunic, he brought out a long, curved vibroblade and drew it back.

The world seemed to shift into a sort of slow motion, like a holocomedy slowed so everyone could see each twitch, each gesture. The vibroblade darted forward. There was a roar of noise, a voice, from beside Tolokai. Then Malan, arm outstretched, moving in a bizarre sort of flight, drifted into the path of the weapon. The blade point touched his chest and drove slowly in; then Malan's momentum carried Tolokai's arm out of line, bearing the Gotal into the wall.

Malan, the vibroblade buried to its hilt in his chest, his face turning ashen, wrapped his arms around Tolokai's and turned to Mon Mothma. He spoke slow words she couldn't grasp. Tolokai yanked in slow-motion frenzy at the weapon he'd driven into his friend's chest.

Mon Mothma turned and found herself able to move at a normal rate. Her hearing returned to normal. Malan screamed, "Run, run!" Tolokai's words made less sense: "Stay, and accept the death you know you deserve!"

She reached the door to the nearest stairwell. She heard a thump and a gasp from behind; she hazarded a look and saw Malan sliding across the floor, Tolokai advancing menacingly toward her. She ran down the stairs as fast as she could.

Not fast enough. As she reached the first landing she felt something yank the back of her hair, and suddenly she was flying down the next flight of stairs—

Flying halfway down. She hit the stairs, pain cracking through her rib cage and chest, and rolled to a stop at the bottom of that flight.

Her wind gone, her energy gone, she could only stare up the steps to where Tolokai stood. His expression was as reasonable, as emotionless as ever—as it was with every Gotal. She tried to ask him why, but could only mouth the word; she had no breath with which to expel it.

But he understood. A Gotal would. "For my people," he said. "To rid the universe of the scourge you call humankind. I'm sorry." He descended the steps with meticulous care.

When he was halfway down, Malan, his tunic drenched with blood, came toppling over the rail from the first flight of steps and fell full upon Tolokai. Then the two males were falling and rolling, to the accompanying sound of cracking bones.

Mon Mothma tried to get clear, succeeded in rolling partway aside, and the two men landed across her legs, pinning her in place.

The men lay still, their eyes closed. Tolokai's head was bent at an angle that was not survivable. Malan had frothy blood on his lips. Mon Mothma looked at them, trying to grasp what had gone so wrong in Tolokai's mind . . . trying to understand how Malan had managed to surprise him with his attack. It shouldn't have been possible.

Then Malan's eyes opened. "Iwo," he said. "Iwo, Iwo . . ." His words were mere whispers, barely audible.

Mon Mothma leaned closer to hear him.

"Iwo, I won't be getting you that caf." His eyes closed and his head fell back. But his chest still rose and fell, though there was a rattle in his breathing.

And once again, Mon Mothma had work to do. She brought out her personal comlink and thumbed it on. "Emergency," she said. "Councilors' Floors, Stairwell One. Emergency."

Liquid rolled down her face. She wiped at it with her free hand and looked at it, expecting to see more of Malan's blood, but her own tears glistened in her palm.

GALEY WAS A MASSIVE MAN, all chest and muscle, with legs that were short enough to keep his height in the average range, though no one dared tell him he wasn't proportioned like a holodrama idol. His hair was red and shaggy and his expression perpetually quizzical, as though he didn't ever quite understand what was going on around him.

Which wasn't the case. He understood his job well enough—programming menus for the cafeteria and officers' dinners on *Mon Remonda,* making sure there was hot, fresh caf available at all the conferences and meetings and briefings, making special arrangements for dinners for important visitors.

This was an important job. He knew it to be at least as significant as any piloting position. A military force ran on its stomach, after all.

But the job didn't pay well, and offered little respect, and so he was very attentive on his last leave on Coruscant when the men with intelligent eyes came to him and offered him a lot of money.

And now he was supposed to kill somebody. Somebody important. It would take precise timing and careful arrangement. It would take skill and knowledge.

So it pleased him that he had figured out just what the various requests for refreshments actually meant. They were like a code, and he had cracked it.

A request for one large pot of caf and a tray of sweet pastries for the captain's conference room, for instance. That meant an unscheduled but routine staff meeting led by Han Solo, not by Captain Onoma. Onoma's meetings were always smaller and didn't call for quite so much caf.

The pilot briefings also called for caf, but if a request included both sweet pastries and meat rolls, it meant there would be a mission. So when the request came in this morning, he knew he had his opportunity to earn all that money.

He delivered the cart of refreshments to the pilots' main briefing amphitheater and then loitered out in the hall with a datapad and a second cart of caf, offering cups to anyone who asked for them. Soon enough, the pilots of *Mon Remonda*'s four starfighter squadrons began filing in.

He waved at the huge Rogue, the one almost too tall to fit in his cockpit with the canopy down—Tal'dira, the Twi'lek. "Lieutenant, can I have a moment?"

Tal'dira frowned at this odd request. He glanced at the other Rogues, as though to gauge whether they, too, found it out of keeping, but they swept past him into the briefing chamber. "Well," he said, "only a moment. The briefing is about to start. You're Kaley, aren't you?"

"Galey. And I have an important message for you. From someone who's finally realized she'd like to meet you." He beckoned Tal'dira and walked around the nearest corner.

The pilot followed, an intent expression on his face. "You don't mean—"

"Here's what she has to say. 'Wedge Antilles hops on one transparisteel leg.' "

Tal'dira rocked back on his heels, his expression shocked. He swayed on his feet and reached out to steady himself against the wall. "No."

"It's true. He really does."

The Twi'lek gripped his head as though to restrain some explosive force within it. "I *hate* that."

"Me, too. We all do."

Tal'dira stood upright again, with a new look in his eyes. "But I can put a stop to it."

"And you should. But wait until after the meeting. Then you can do it in an X-wing."

"You're right." The pilot slapped Galey on his shoulder, propelling him into the wall. "You're a good friend."

"As are you." Galey thought about giving Tal'dira a return blow, then decided against it. "May the Force be with you."

Tal'dira nodded briskly and turned back toward the briefing amphitheater.

Galey breathed out a sigh of relief and rubbed his shoulder where it still stung. He hoped the other Twi'lek wouldn't be quite so violent.

"FOR THE LAST FEW HOURS," Wedge said, "we've been in hyperspace en route to the Jussafet system."

A hologram starfield popped up to the left of the lectern where Wedge stood. It showed a cluster of stars near a fuzzy diamond-shaped nebula. One star blinked yellow in a decidedly mechanical fashion. Donos nodded; he remembered Jussafet from discussions of strategic moves into Warlord Zsinj's territory.

Wedge continued, "Jussafet is in the nebulous border territory between Imperial and Zsinj-controlled space. Jussafet Four is a habitable planet with some mining businesses, but the system's real wealth is in asteroid mining; they have an asteroid belt that is the remains of a large iron-core planet that broke up.

"Earlier today, Jussafet Four sent out a distress call to the Empire, talking about a full-scale invasion by Raptors, Zsinj's elite troops. A Duros ship approaching the system to do some under-the-table trading heard the transmission and relayed it to the New Republic. We're going in to stomp on the Raptors, and hopefully *Iron Fist,* as well as to do some good for the people of Jussafet."

Donos raised a hand. "What are the odds that Imperial forces will also come in to stage a rescue? It'd be nasty to fight a three-way."

Wedge nodded. "It would. Odds are low—the Empire's having enough trouble with us and Zsinj that it is likely to mount a more meticulous response, determining enemy strength, assembling a precise task force, that sort of thing. But it's possible. We'll be taking some steps to keep them from knowing our full force strength, too. *Mon Remonda* is going into the system with a couple of the fleet's frigates, but *Mon Karren* and the *Allegiance* will be waiting outside the system, ready to jump in if needed."

Corran Horn's hand was up next. "And what are the odds that this is another Zsinj trap?"

"Again, possible but not likely. The Duros monitoring of the battle in the asteroid belt and on Jussafet suggests that we're looking at a large force of Raptors, fully engaged, not just the whispers and rumors we're used to.

"We'll launch as soon as we drop into the system. Polearm's A-wings will take point and make the initial flyover on Jussafet Four. Rogue Squadron and Nova's B-wings will head into the asteroid belt to begin purging it of Zsinj forces. We have four flyers of Wraith Squadron active, and they'll escort shuttles of New Republic ground forces in to Jussafet Four."

Face Loran, leaning forward so as to keep his injured back from making contact with the chair, spoke up. His voice emerged as an uncanny impersonation of Tal'dira's. "This time, the Wraiths can do the baby-sitting. Now, and forever."

The pilots laughed. All, Donos noted, except Tal'dira, who kept his attention on the desktop before him and didn't react. Corran Horn gave Tal'dira a curious glance.

"That's it," Wedge said. "Your astromechs and nav computers have your navigational data. Good luck."

As they filed out of the amphitheater, Face and Dia caught up with Donos. "I wish I were flying with you," Face said.

"I'm glad you're not," Donos said. At Face's startled expression, he relented, smiling. "I so seldom get to be in charge of anything, the change is welcome. You just get injured anytime you like."

"Thanks," Face said. He stopped in the hall beside the caf cart and picked up a cup. "Thanks, Galey."

"No problem, sir."

As they continued down toward the starfighter hangars, Donos heard Galey say, "Excuse me, Flight Officer Tualin! A moment of your time?"

IT WAS HARD for Tal'dira to run down his preflight checklist. His thoughts were far away. How could Wedge Antilles, hero of the Rebellion, of the New Republic, fall so far as to hop on one transparisteel leg? Nothing short of the Emperor's magic could have wrought such a change in him. Rage grew within Tal'dira and he struggled, as only a true warrior could, to keep it in check.

"Rogues, announce readiness by number."

When his time came, Tal'dira said, "Rogue Five, four lit, three at full capacity, one at ninety-nine percent." His starboard lower engine was still not optimal. He'd have to insist that it be brought up to a reasonable level of performance.

After he killed Wedge Antilles, of course.

A HANGAR KLAXON warned the pilots that they were dropping out of hyperspace. The twisting, whirling morass of color outside the magnetic shield between the hangar and vacuum abruptly snapped into a simpler image: a starfield. One small planet hung, bright and round, near the upper right corner of the magcon field.

One by one, the Rogues shot through the field and formed up a kilometer from *Mon Remonda*. Tal'dira, leader of Two Flight, settled in beside his wingman, Gavin Darklighter. He felt his heart race as the moment crept toward him.

One bit of comm traffic caught his ear, a transmission from a fellow Twi'lek: "Polearm Two to Polearm Leader. I have a critical failure of my sublight engine. I'm down to fifty-four percent. Forty. Twenty-eight . . ."

"Two, this is Leader. Drop out of formation and head on in. Maybe next time . . ."

On Tal'dira's sensor screen, eleven members of Polearm Squadron leaped forward, drawing away from *Mon Remonda*, approaching distant Jussafet Four.

Tal'dira's astromech transmitted the unit's course to his navigation system and he absently reviewed numbers he would never use.

"Rogue Leader to group. On my count, ten, nine, eight . . ."

"WRAITH FOUR, you are out of position."

Tyria looked up, startled. She *was* out of position. She should be maintaining her distance from *Mon Remonda* and letting her fellow Wraiths—Donos, Lara, and Elassar—plus four shuttles, form up on her.

Then why had she heeled over and goosed her thrusters, heading toward the bow of *Mon Remonda*? Her hands had acted without her brain being engaged.

Ahead, she could see one lonely A-wing making a torturous, slow turn back toward *Mon Remonda,* an obvious case of engine failure.

Obvious . . . but false. Adrenaline jolted through her as she saw through the A-wing's moves, through the cockpit, through the skin and blood of its pilot to the mind beneath. "*Mon Remonda,*" she shouted, "bring your shields up. Polearm Two—"

"—IS FIRING ON YOU!"

Han Solo didn't hesitate. "All shields up full!"

The A-wing fired. The transparisteel viewport giving him and the bridge crew an unparalleled view of space darkened as it tried to cope with the A-wing's linked laser blasts. Then it shattered.

To Solo's eye, the shards of viewport floated into the bridge, then immediately reversed direction and fled to space . . . vanguard for the atmosphere of the bridge.

"FOUR."

Tal'dira reached up to flip the switch setting his S-foils to combat formation. They parted and his targeting computer came online.

"Three."

Tal'dira heeled over so his weapons aimed straight at the rear end of Wedge's X-wing. He began to swing his targeting brackets over toward the starfighter.

"Two . . ."

"Leader, break off!" Horn's voice.

Tal'dira, jolted by the interruption, fired before his shot was completely lined up. Wedge, impossibly, was already reacting to Horn's warning, breaking to starboard. But Tal'dira was rewarded by the sight of his lasers, cycling two by two, chewing through the port rear of Wedge's X-wing, blowing one fuzial thrust engine completely off, punching deep into the rear fuselage.

The comm system was suddenly loud with many voices, most of them distressed. Wedge's snubfighter continued banking to starboard and lost relative altitude, and Tycho was keeping pace with him as only the most experienced of wingmen could.

Tal'dira smiled. This would be a challenge. Good.

A BLAST OF air shoved Solo from behind—shoved him nearly out of his commander's chair and toward the hole in the forward viewport. He hung on to the chair but moved toward the hole anyway—the armature from which the chair was suspended swung inevitably in that direction. He could see, a few meters over, Captain Onoma in a similar predicament, being guided by his chair as though it were a mechanical throwing device toward the fatal exit from the bridge.

An alarm Klaxon sounded, loud even over the shrill whistle of air escaping the bridge. Solo saw the main door out of the chamber closing, an automatic safety measure.

When it closed, he'd be dead. The last of the bridge atmosphere would be out there in deep space, and he'd experience the joys of explosive decompression. So would every other crewman on the bridge.

He got one foot down to arrest the swing of his chair armature. Fortunately, artificial gravity was still working and he stopped his forward motion.

Then he drew his blaster and aimed for the control panel beside the main door. He fired, was rewarded with seeing the panel buckle inward under the blast—

The door stopped.

Now the bridge crew had a chance to make it to the door. But air was being vented from one of the ship's main corridors. They had to get through the door past that wind blast . . .

And the A-wing was still out there.

"AND YOU'RE IN a position to speak for the New Republic," Dr. Gast said.

Nawara Ven, Twi'lek executive officer for Rogue Squadron, nodded. "I have been so authorized by the Inner Council. And as soon as we can come to some arrangement, you can be free of all this." His gesture took in the tiny, plain stateroom that served as Gast's cell. Ven sat on the room's only chair, while Gast stretched out on the bed, leaning back against the wall.

"Well, you know what I want. A million credits, free of tax. Amnesty for all crimes, known and unknown, that I am alleged to have committed. And a new identity."

"No," Ven said. "We can offer amnesty for all crimes you offer all details on. If you hold something back, it remains live. And we can offer one hundred thousand credits. Enough for you to make a good start for yourself. But you're not going to be wealthy at the expense of the New Republic. Every credit we give you could mean the life of one of our people."

"Every detail I give you could mean the life of ten of your people," she said. "I'll buy into the full confession thing. But one million credits stands." Distantly, an alarm Klaxon began to sound. "What's this? More warfare against Zsinj? I wonder who's going to die today?"

Ven struggled to keep his voice under control. "We certainly don't employ torture or murder like the Empire," he said. "On the other hand, we could keep you in custody in some free-trade port while we assemble charges, and make no secret of the fact that we have you. How long would it take Zsinj to find you, do you suppose?"

Her expression became ugly. "For that, I hold back one detail you'll never know about, and some of your oh-so-precious people die. How about that, you subhuman nothing? Give me a *human* negotiator."

There was a sound beyond the door, an unmistakable one: two blasts in quick succession, two scrapes and thuds as bodies hit the floor.

Ven stood. He grabbed the side of Gast's bed and yanked, precipitating her to the floor. He shoved the bed over on her, then slid to stand beside the door.

"Hey!" she said. The bed rocked as she struggled to free herself.

The door slid open. A blaster gripped in a large human hand entered first. Ven grabbed the blaster, twisted it up.

He had a brief glimpse of the man he was wrestling with: big but not tall, fleshy, with red hair. Then burning liquid washed into his eye. He yelped, instinctively turned away from the pain.

A meaty fist slammed into his jaw, knocking him to the floor. He shook his head to clear it, belatedly realizing that it was hot caf in his face.

Above him, the attacker looked at the wriggling bed and fired into it—twice, three times, four. There was a female shriek in the middle of that.

Then the assassin turned to aim down at Ven.

Ven kicked out, shoving against the bed frame, and slid

out partway into the hall. The assassin's shot struck the flooring between his legs.

Ven found himself between the two door guards, both slumped, dead. He grabbed at the blaster pistol still in the hand of the one to his left. He brought it around, even as he saw the assassin aiming—

Ven didn't bother to aim. He fired, heard the distinctive crackle of blaster beam frying flesh as his shot took the assassin in one ankle. The big man yelped, fell, his blaster aiming in straight at the Twi'lek—

Ven fired again. This shot took the assassin right in the nose, snapping his head back, filling the chamber with even more burned-flesh odor. The big man fired, whether intentionally or as a dying spasm Ven didn't know, and his shot hit the doorjamb.

Ven rose. There was no more wiggling going on behind the bed. Knowing what he was likely to see, he pulled the bed from against the wall and looked at what lay beyond.

"POLEARM TWO," Tyria said, "power down and announce your surrender or I'll blow you out of space." She toggled her S-foil switch and felt a hum as the foils assumed strike position.

The A-wing heeled over and accelerated, moving behind the protective bulk of *Mon Remonda*, out of her sight.

TAL'DIRA SMILED AS he heard the pure tone of a good targeting lock on Wedge's X-wing, but the noise garbled as Tycho slid in between target and prey. Tal'dira dropped relative altitude, hoping for a quick shot under Tycho, but the captain mimicked his move, remaining an obstruction.

Now Tycho was an easy target, and so close—a proton torpedo would turn him into a billion fiery specks. But

Tal'dira shook his head at the notion. Tycho wasn't his enemy. Tycho wasn't the traitor. "Captain Celchu, get out of the way," he said. "I have a job to do."

He spared a glance for his sensor board. The other Rogues were staying in position—all but Rogue Nine, Corran Horn, who was moving out to a position some distance from the Rogue formation but not approaching.

Tycho's voice came back. "Rogue Five, power down all weapons systems and return to *Mon Remonda* immediately or we will be forced to regard you as an enemy. And destroy you."

"I'm not the enemy! Wedge Antilles is the enemy, that one-leg-hopping maniac! Celchu, clear my field of fire!"

Wedge, his X-wing moving sluggishly, continued his loop around to starboard. Tycho kept on him, keeping stubbornly between him and Tal'dira. The Twi'lek pilot gritted his teeth, sideslipped port, then starboard, but Tycho was always there, in the way.

SOLO PUSHED OFF from his chair armature and staggered toward the door. Captain Onoma, approaching from the other side of the bridge, reached him and grabbed him.

They made two steps, three, but then, as they neared the doorway, the wind increased—channeled tightly by the doorway, it was more ferocious the closer they got. Solo felt his forward motion stop; then his left leg slipped out from under him and he went on one knee. His ears popped as the air pressure continued to drop and his head felt as though it would burst.

So close, so close—he and Onoma could reach out almost to the doorframe. But the roaring air stopped them dead.

Dead.

Then light from the corridor was partially blocked off and a long, hairy arm reached from the other side of the door to grip Solo's. It was like a fur-covered vise clamping over his wrist. It hauled and suddenly Solo and Onoma were both through the doorway, staggering into the corridor, still battered but no longer endangered by the howling wind.

"Chewie!" Solo turned back to his rescuer. He grabbed the doorframe with one arm, Chewbacca's waist with the other, helping pin the Wookiee in place.

Chewbacca reached in again and hauled, dragging the bridge communications officer out. Then again, and again, yanking each bridge officer into the comparative safety of the corridor. There was an explosion from the bridge or from beyond it, and Chewie lurched backward, bleeding from the chest from what looked like shrapnel. The Wookiee shook off the sudden shock and looked back in. He bellowed, noises that would sound like an animal roar to most people but which Solo knew to mean "All out."

"No, there's one left," Solo said. He looked around. "Golorno, sensors."

"Dead," Onoma said. Even with the gravelly tones of Mon Calamari speech, Solo could make out the pain, the regret in his voice. "Out the viewport."

Solo grimaced. "Chewie, let's get this door closed." He heaved against the metal barrier. Chewie flexed one arm and slammed the door closed.

TYRIA'S SENSORS WEREN'T much use. This close to *Mon Remonda,* she couldn't even detect Polearm Two as an individual ship. He had to be hugging the hull pretty closely.

Perhaps if machinery couldn't help her, the Force could. She concentrated on Polearm Two, on his A-wing—

No, that was wrong. She leaned back, cleared her thoughts. Closed her eyes.

Mission, he had a mission. He was going to destroy the bridge or someone in it.

She opened her eyes and banked toward the bridge, amidships and topside . . .

As she cleared the horizon of the ship's curved hull, she saw the A-wing lining up for another shot at the bridge. Her targeting computer announced a clean lock on him.

"Don't," she said. But there was no time for a lengthy plea, for words that might get through to reach this madman. A few more degrees of turn, and he was in line, poised, a beautiful target—

She fired. Her proton torpedo hit and detonated before she registered that it was away. Polearm Two was suddenly nothing more than a bright flash and thousands of needles of superheated metal hitting *Mon Remonda*'s skin and heading into outer space.

"CAPTAIN, PLEASE," Tal'dira said. "It is not in my nature to beseech. I beg you get clear of my shot before I have to kill you, too."

But the voice that answered was Corran Horn's, not Tycho's. "Tal'dira, this isn't honorable. You shot him in the back."

Tal'dira checked his sensor board. Wedge's maneuver was leading him back and around toward Rogue Nine. In just a few moments, he would be forced to run a head-to-head against Horn. Tal'dira shrugged. He could take the Corellian pilot. He could take anyone.

Dishonorable. But that word burned at him. His first shot *had* been dishonorable. How could he have done that?

Because Wedge, that one-transparisteel-leg-hopping traitor, had to die.

But Tal'dira couldn't betray his honor to kill him. It was impossible.

Yet he *had.* And he knew, deep in the portions of his mind still functioning, that he would again. He'd throw away his honor to kill Wedge Antilles. And he'd never turn away from his quest to kill his former commander.

He heard a groan, knew it to be his own. That meant he would die without honor, shaming his family, shaming his world.

No. He shook off the thought, raised his head. *Honor above all.*

Wedge and Tycho were now heading straight for Corran Horn, Tal'dira tucked in neatly behind them. In another few moments, he'd be within good firing range of the Corellian.

He adjusted his shields, then switched to lasers and opened fire on Tycho.

Far ahead, Rogue Nine fired.

THERE WAS A BRILLIANT flash from behind Wedge. He glanced at his flickering sensor board.

Rogue Five was gone.

In other circumstances, he would have had words of praise for such accurate shooting. But no Rogue would accept praise for downing one of their own. Wedge felt sick. When he spoke, he was not surprised to find that his voice was raspy with his effort to keep his emotions in check. "Rogue Nine, are you fit to fly?"

There was a moment's delay. "Fit, sir."

"Rogue Two, take the group in. You're in command. I'm going to swap out X-wings and rejoin you."

"Yes, sir." Tycho didn't sound any less pained than Wedge. "Thanks, Two."

"You're welcome, Leader. Rogues, Novas, form up on me. We're going in." Tycho banked away and Corran moved up in formation with him.

8

THE MISSION, WHICH had begun in disaster, ended in disaster; but not for Solo's forces.

The A-wings of Polearm Squadron identified and strafed numerous sites of Raptor activity on the ground at Jussafet Four. Raptor shuttles were caught on the ground and shot to pieces, their occupants scattered, easier prey for the Jussafet ground forces. Soldiers deposited by shuttles, with air support provided by Wraith Squadron, overran and took the Raptor base camp near the Jussafet capital.

Rogue and Nova Squadrons, led initially by Captain Celchu, then by Wedge Antilles once the commander returned to the combat in Wes Janson's X-wing, cruised through the asteroid belt, wreaking havoc on the sparse units of TIE fighters and single corvette Zsinj's forces had deployed.

By monitoring the escape vectors of the smaller vessels chased off by Rogue Squadron, the crew of *Mon Remonda*, working from the vessel's auxiliary bridge, was able to determine the position of the assault fleet and give chase. The fleet consisted of two sturdy *Carrack*-class cruisers and a heavily modified cargo vessel . . . and as these three vessels detected the approach of the Mon Calamari cruiser, they turned spaceward and entered hyperspace.

No words of thanks came via comm from the Jussafet defenders—small wonder, since this was an Imperial world, its defenders doubtless looking on their liberators with as much suspicion as gratitude—but most of the starfighters picked up anonymous transmissions expressing thanks, sometimes wrapped in profanity directed against the New Republic.

Han Solo directed the soldiers on Jussafet Four to appropriate any Raptor vehicles and prisoners they could, leaving the rest for the planetary defenders.

WEDGE, BONE-WEARY—and not from the hours he'd spent in the cockpit—had the Rogues lined up for final approach to *Mon Remonda* when the word came. "Sensors show an Imperial Star Destroyer leaving hyperspace and entering the Jussafet system. It's still outside the system's mass shadow and can turn and run at any time. It's approaching slowly."

"Thanks, bridge. Rogues, form up on me. We'll cruise out that direction." Cruise was about right—the Rogues didn't have enough fuel left for another protracted trip and dogfight. The Rogues took up position and headed out at a pace that, for them, was quite leisurely.

A few minutes later, a new voice took the comm, Solo's. "Rogues, return to *Mon Remonda*. Star Destroyer *Agonizer* is communicating. They want to have a face-to-face with you, Rogue Leader."

Wedge raised an eyebrow. "Is *Agonizer* a Zsinj unit or Imperial?"

"According to our latest records on this ship, about a year old, she's Imperial."

"Interesting. I guess I'd better go over and see what they want."

"Negative, negative. You're too likely a prospect for assassination. Me, too. I've transmitted a recommendation that Captain Onoma make the visit. Wait a second." The delay was nearly a minute. "They didn't like that idea. Probably because he's Mon Calamari. They're willing to accept someone out of your squadrons."

Wedge ran a roster review in his mind. His Rogues were bone-tired, and he really needed to gauge their reaction to Tal'dira's death . . . and find out what had led up to it. "Ask Face Loran to volunteer. I think he'll satisfy their requirements."

"Done. Come on back in."

FACE HAD BEEN part of a mission that had landed aboard a Star Destroyer before—in his case, the Super Star Destroyer *Iron Fist*—but then he'd been in disguise, an apparent ally of the people he was visiting. This time he came as an enemy under temporary truce, and he could feel his heart rate increase as his X-wing rose into the hangar bay in the underside of the gigantic vessel. On repulsorlifts, he drifted laterally toward the Imperial officer waving the glow rods, and set down where the man directed, between two half squadrons of TIE fighters.

As he climbed down the ladder from his cockpit, an Imperial naval lieutenant bowed to him. "Captain Loran? The admiral is waiting."

"Good." Face returned the bow. Then he looked up at his R2 unit. "Vape, if anyone comes within three meters, activate self-destruct."

His astromech gave him a happy beep in the affirmative. With luck, none of these Imperials would actually risk such an approach to determine that, in fact, this X-wing had no self-destruct mechanism.

Two halls and two turbolifts later, the lieutenant led Face into a conference room. The oval table overflowed with food—cooked dishes, platters of fresh fruit, containers of wine, vases stuffed with fresh flowering plants. Struck by the ostentatiousness of it, Face laughed before he could check himself.

The room's sole occupant, a lean man, clean-shaven, of

graying middle age, smiled from his chair behind one of the flower arrangements. "It is a bit pretentious, isn't it?" He rose, revealing that he wore an admiral's uniform, and approached, his hand out. "Still, appearances must be maintained. Admiral Teren Rogriss."

"Garik Loran, Captain, New Republic Starfighter Command." Face shook his hand.

"And let me say I thought your holodramas and comedies were puerile, badly written things—though you rose above your material."

"Of course they were puerile. They were Imperial productions. But thank you."

The admiral barked a laugh. His amusement seemed genuine. He gestured for Face to sit. "Please, help yourself. Protocol demands I put it out, so we should eat it. But I won't keep you long. Time presses for me as I'm sure it does for you." Following Face's lead, he sat, and immediately helped himself to what looked like a plate of small boiled eggs drenched in some sort of syrup. "What I'm going to tell you is entirely unofficial. Make announcements about it, transmit queries to us along official lines, and we'll denounce it as typical Rebel lies. On the other hand, it does come down from the highest levels."

"Go ahead." Face tried one of the eggs. The fluid dressing was tart and not sweet at all; the yolk had been replaced by some sort of meat filling, though he had not seen a seam on the boiled surface of the egg. It had the rich taste of something that took a fair amount of preparation and cost a lot, so only the wealthy forced themselves to think they liked it.

"Our differences, Imperial and Rebel, are not going to go away. We'll be enemies until we die."

"Probably."

"But we both have a mutual enemy. It would profit us both to be rid of him. I am, in a sense, the counterpart of your General Solo."

"You lead a task force whose goal is to get rid of Zsinj."

Rogriss nodded. "Once we're done with him, we can go back to our very personal ideological differences, without having to invite anyone else to play."

Face snorted. "You're not like most of the Imperial officers I've talked to."

"True. What do you think?"

"I think it's a grand idea. But I can't speak, even unofficially, for the New Republic. Or even for this fleet. All I'm authorized to do is listen, and to report what I hear to my commanders."

The admiral smiled. From a pocket, he produced a datacard and slid it to Face. "Once we're out of system, you can reach me via HoloNet on the frequency and at the times this file indicates. If I receive a transmission from General Solo, directed personally to me, conveying any message whatsoever, then I will take it that you agree."

"And then what?"

"And then I transmit to you every piece of recorded data we have on Zsinj's campaigns. His strategic and tactical moves against worlds, what we understand of his overall strategy, what we know about his forces. And I'd expect a similar transmission from you. Each of us may know something about our mutual enemy that the other can exploit."

Face nodded. "An interesting notion. And if it became officially known, you'd be executed for collaboration with the enemy."

Rogriss nodded. He seemed so cheerful that Face might have been suggesting that his crew visit Coruscant for a bombardment raid. "As might your General Solo. But that's a worst-case possibility. Best-case is that Zsinj dies."

"True." Face pocketed the datacard. "One last question before I leave. Why are Baron Fel and the One Eighty-first working with Zsinj?"

The admiral's face lost most of its good cheer. "I can't

guess about Fel's motives. He defected to your side, then was gone for some years. Now he's defected from the Rebels to someone new. He's a compulsive traitor, I'd say. But I'll tell you this: He's not in charge of the One Eighty-first."

"How is that?"

"The real One Eighty-first is still serving the Empire with loyalty and skill, under Turr Phennir. Fel has assembled new pilots, called them the One Eighty-first, and slapped some red stripes on their starfighters to duplicate the fighter group's colors. Perhaps he thinks that he *is* the One Eighty-first, so wherever he goes, the group follows; that would be in keeping with the sort of colossal ego you see in fighter-group commanders. But it's not the truth."

"Interesting. Thank you for your candor." Face stood.

Rogriss nodded. He gestured at the tabletop. "Would you care to pack a lunch before you go?"

Face laughed.

IN THE HOURS of what would have been night on Coruscant—the timing by which *Mon Remonda*'s activities were scheduled—Solo and Wedge met in the general's office.

Solo looked as tired and dispirited as Wedge felt. And, Wedge noted, not for the first time, when Solo decided to drop his mask of roguish irresponsibility—as he had now—he could look angrier than any man Wedge had ever met. That's how it was now; while they'd been reviewing the attacks by the two Twi'leks, the general's face had set in lines that would strike fear in the heart of a subordinate or an enemy.

"Are you going to accept Rogriss's offer?" Wedge asked.

Solo's features softened. He nodded.

"Pending confirmation by Fleet Command?"

"No. I have very broad powers regarding the search for Zsinj. I can do this without anyone's say-so." Solo quirked a self-deprecating smile. "Until they decide that I've completely failed, I'm still a very important man.

"Which reminds me. Since I still seem to be important to Zsinj, I'm going to go forward with this plan by your pilots to mock up a *Millennium Falcon* and see if we can lure Zsinj to us with it."

"I'm glad to hear it. It has a chance."

Solo's smile faded. "Whatever this Twi'lek madness is, it's spreading," Solo said. "A little before the assassination attempts against the two of us, Councilor Mon Mothma was nearly killed by her bodyguard, a Gotal. She's badly injured. In the hours after that, there were two incidents of shooting sprees by Gotal soldiers, one in a barracks hall frequented mostly by humans, one in a holotheater. Dozens died. One of the killers was cut down by soldiers; the other turned his blaster on himself."

"Just as Tal'dira did," Wedge said.

"Huh? Corran Horn killed Tal'dira."

Wedge shook his head. "I saw this when I correlated all the sensory data from Tal'dira's attack. In the instant before Corran Horn fired, Tal'dira shifted all his shield power to rear shields. His bow was unprotected. In a sense, he committed suicide."

"That doesn't make any sense. I can see a fanatical assassin killing himself after his objective is achieved—but not before."

"I don't understand it either. Do you have anything on the cafeteria worker, Galey?"

Solo grimaced. "No known motivation . . . which means probably money. No sign of contact with insurgents or enemies. He's spent a lot of time since we left Coruscant on shuttle simulators. He might have been able to fly one of our *Lambda*-class shuttles out of here after he finished his job."

"But he's the key. The fact that he was sent to kill Gast means that he was working for Zsinj. The fact that he was seen speaking to both Tal'dira and Nuro Tualin means that he was involved with them, and therefore with the whole supposed Twi'lek conspiracy, which makes it a certainty that Zsinj is behind that."

Solo took a deep breath. "Unfortunately, our knowing that doesn't mean that everybody understands it. I have one more piece of news. Very, very unfortunate news."

He told Wedge.

IT WAS A FEW hours later, a few minutes after most of the pilots and civilian crewmen began their day shifts. In his own office, Wedge looked at the three good people he'd assembled and prepared to give them what might have been the grossest insult he could offer.

Nawara Ven gave him a close, evaluative look. It was obvious to Wedge that he knew something bad was up. It was harder for him to read Dia Passik's face. His chief mechanic, Koyi Komad, looked unsure.

"I have orders from the Provisional Council," Wedge said. "The effect on our immediate group is that I'm obliged to take you three temporarily off active duty."

Koyi registered shock. Dia's eyes narrowed. Nawara Ven nodded, as though this were what he expected. "It's because we're Twi'leks," he said.

"I'm afraid so."

Koyi's voice climbed a register in indignation. "I don't believe this."

"Believe it," Dia said. "It's fleetwide, isn't it, Commander?"

Wedge nodded.

"So much for the human promises of equality among the species," Koyi said. Her voice was bitter. "I don't have to stand by and be treated this way. You know how many jobs, civilian jobs for a *lot* of money, I've turned down? But no, I transferred back to the Rogues. I stayed with you after Zsinj blew down Noquivzor Base on top of us and killed almost everyone I worked with. I did this because the Rogues were the spearhead of this cause I wanted to support. A galaxy where species didn't matter. Now that's gone."

"It's not gone," Wedge said. "It's taken a body blow, but it's not dead."

Koyi gave him a smile, but there was neither amusement nor friendliness in it. "So I'm off duty. I have some reading to do. May I be excused, sir?"

Wedge nodded. "For what it's worth, Koyi, I'm sorry."

"I'm sure it's worth something, sir." On her way out, she said, "Ask me in a year and maybe I'll know what."

"I think I should go too, sir." Dia rose.

"How are you doing, Passik?"

"The Provisional Council has just announced to all the New Republic that *I'm not worthy*." Her red eyes flashed for a moment. Then she managed a smile. It wasn't, like Koyi's, a bitter smile. Wedge recognized it as mockery. "Fortunately, their opinion is worth nothing next to my squadmates'. I think I'll go keep company with them. I'd do that any day rather than slum with the Provisional Council." She saluted and left.

Nawara Ven said, "That was a lot of insolence for you not to dress her down."

"I feel almost the same way she does. I'm not sure when the last time was I felt this low. I just can't believe Tal'dira turning against us the way he did." A memory jogged at him. "Can you tell me something? Does the phrase 'one-leg-hopping maniac' have any special meaning in Twi'lek culture?"

Ven smiled. "You're asking me?" He gestured down to the lower portion of his right leg, the one that had been amputated in Ven's last mission as a Rogue Squadron pilot.

"I'm sorry. I forgot about that. But, yes, I'm asking. It's serious. It's what Tal'dira called me just before he died."

"Oh." Ven's eyes lost focus as he stared back into his memory. "I can't think of one."

"Odd. What would cause him—" Wedge's eyes opened wider. "Cause. Effect. What's the cause and what's the effect?"

"I'm not following you—"

"It didn't matter whether Admiral Ackbar died. Or Mon Mothma. Their assassins were successful."

"What? No, they weren't."

"Yes, they were. Koyi Komad was their first victim."

Ven's expression suggested that he was within seconds of calling in the medics to deal with his commander.

"Get the Wraiths together," Wedge said. "We're going to conduct one of their insane speculation and planning sessions. Pilots' lounge. And invite any Rogues who want to attend. As usual, with Zsinj, we have to dig one level farther down." Wedge was in the corridor before Ven had a chance to rise to his feet.

ALL THE WRAITHS were there, except Runt and Janson, whose injuries kept them in bacta-tank treatment for the time being, and so were Tycho, Hobbie, and Corran Horn of the Rogues. Donos decided that Tyria and Horn looked unusually glum, and couldn't blame them. At least Tyria had someone to offer her support; Kell stayed next to her. The others were keeping a little distance between themselves and Horn; whether it was out of respect for his feelings or because of their own unease at being in the presence of someone who had just killed one of his squadmates, Donos couldn't tell.

Wedge walked in, his bootheels clattering. "So we know about a sudden rise in terrorist activity by Twi'leks," he said without preamble. "We've determined to our own satisfaction that Zsinj is behind them."

Ven said, "Though we lack evidence to prove it conclusively."

"Not important for our discussion. Why is Zsinj doing this?"

"To hurt the New Republic," Kell said. "Losing Admiral Ackbar and Mon Mothma would be a serious blow."

Wedge took a seat and nodded. "Sure, it would. And they'd be replaced by people who probably aren't quite as good as they are at their tasks. If everyone on the Inner Council were murdered, we'd have an Inner Council that was just a little less adept at doing what it does. Not exactly a master stroke on Zsinj's part." He leaned forward, still oddly intent. "This morning at six hundred hours I was obliged to relieve every Twi'lek aboard *Mon Remonda* of active duty. And that, I think, is what Zsinj wanted."

"To be rid of our Twi'leks?" Kell asked.

Wedge shook his head, but it was Horn who spoke up. "Suddenly the Twi'leks are second-class citizens. Rumor has it that Gotals will be next because of the attempt on Mon Mothma's life and the follow-up shootings."

Lara said, "Twi'leks and Gotals don't make up much of a percentage of the New Republic armed forces. They're not even signatories to the New Republic; there are just a fair number of them in service. I mean, their loss is important, sure . . . but it's not going to cripple the fleet."

"It'll cripple the entire New Republic," Wedge said. "Right now, it's one species making up a fraction of one percent of the New Republic population. But we suddenly have a precedent that divides them from the New Republic. In their eyes, it casts humans as villains. To human eyes, the Twi'leks and Gotals are already starting to look like villains. What if, tomorrow, it's a species that has been with the Alliance since the start of the Rebellion? An important contributor to the New Republic cause?"

Donos saw the Wraiths and Rogues looking among themselves as the idea took root. He drew a breath. "Until this three-pronged attack on you, sir, and on General Solo and Doctor Gast, we had no real reason to believe that it was Zsinj's work."

"Correct," Wedge said. "It could have been an Imperial project, a criminal action, or an actual species-based conspiracy. But in trying to kill us under the same umbrella of this false conspiracy story, he's shown his hand."

"Which does us no good," Donos said. "We're not going to be able to convince the Provisional Council of this theory."

"Why not?" Wedge looked challenged, rather than angry, at the statement.

"Who's going to convince them of it? Ackbar? He trusted the Twi'lek who almost killed him. Mon Mothma? She's injured, not capable of leadership at the moment. Princess Leia? Off on some diplomatic mission. Han Solo? He'd have to leave the fleet, and abandoning his task is not the way to make the Provisional Council confident in him. You?" Donos repressed a wince at the words he'd have to say. "You, sir, also trusted the Twi'lek who almost killed you."

Wedge nodded. "Correct. But here's the answer to your question. To convince the Provisional Council, we're all going to become geniuses."

"I vote we start with Elassar," Lara said. "He has the farthest to go."

The Devaronian pilot winced. "No more. I surrender."

"What kind of geniuses?" asked Ven.

"Prophetic ones. The kind who can tell the Provisional Council just what's going to happen next. What's Zsinj's next step? If we can predict it, we can convince the powers that be that they're dealing with a methodical plan of Zsinj's . . . not a conspiracy of terror against humankind." He looked among them. "Otherwise, in six months, a year, the New Republic consists of humans on one side, nonhumans on the other, no possible trust or interdependence between them . . . and Zsinj can march in and take whatever he wants."

"I have a thought." That was Piggy. "A theory. About where I fit into Zsinj's plan."

"Go ahead."

"We know for a certainty that Zsinj has for some time been trying to create very intelligent examples of humanoids not known for their intelligence," Piggy said. "The question, especially as it relates to your other theory, is why?"

"Obviously," Tycho said, "to have intelligent agents who could infiltrate those species, and therefore not look out of place in locations where those species are found."

"Correct." Piggy nodded in the exaggerated way of Gamorreans. "But that's only part of the equation. What does a leader require in an agent in addition to intelligence? More important than intelligence?"

"Loyalty," Lara said. Her voice seemed a little sad. Donos gave her a close look. She saw his sudden interest, shook her head to suggest that her momentary disquiet was nothing.

"Correct," Piggy said. "Yet I am not loyal to Zsinj. I underwent no indoctrination from youth, nothing like the teaching the stormtroopers receive. Why not? Was I just a laboratory test specimen? Was I to be purged when tests on me were complete?"

Nawara Ven nodded. "Possibly so."

"Yes. But consider. Zsinj would not have embarked on a process like the creation of me and the other hyperintelligent humanoids without making some provision for loyalty. What if he found a way to instill it by force rather than through training?"

"Like brainwashing." Tycho's voice was flat, hard. Donos noticed that the captain now sat absolutely still. Small wonder: Tycho had at one time been suspected of being a brain-washed agent of Ysanne Isard, the former head of Imperial Intelligence. "You think the assassins were brainwashed by this technique."

"Yes," Piggy said. "But we know we're not facing brain-washing as we have experienced it before. The Twi'lek who attacked me and Admiral Ackbar might have been brain-washed, but he was missing only for a week—a possible, but very short—amount of time to do such a thing. From the time he joined Rogue Squadron, what was the longest time Tal'dira was out of sight of the other members? His longest leave?"

Tycho and Wedge conferred, and Tycho said, "About a day at a time. Various leaves on Coruscant."

"One day." Piggy nodded. "If we assume that Tal'dira was a victim and not a conspirator, then he was brainwashed in less than a day. Surely such a treatment must leave evi-dence on the body of the victim. Signs of probes. Blood chem-ical imbalances from drug treatments. Neurological disorders. Something."

"Unfortunately," Wedge said, "we don't have Tal'dira's body to examine. Or Flight Officer Tualin's. We might be able to put in a request to Admiral Ackbar to see if he can perform autopsies on his attacker and Mon Mothma's. And the two Gotal shooters."

"If only Doctor Gast had survived," Piggy said. "I feel no sense of loss at her passing; in fact, I am met with relief. But in retrospect, I wish we had the knowledge she possessed."

Wedge and Nawara Ven exchanged a glance. "We'll have to do without," Wedge said. "All right, let's get to work on these theories of ours . . . and see whether we can have suc-cessful careers as prophets as well as pilots."

IT DRIFTED OFF the bow of *Mon Remonda,* a saucerlike shape with two forward prongs signifying the bow and a small cockpit projecting from the starboard side to give the ship an off-balance look.

To Wedge's eye, it looked just like the *Millennium Falcon*, except that its top-hull dish antenna was much smaller. A shuttle occupied by Donos, Corran Horn, and the Wraiths' chief mechanic Cubber Daine, Corellians all, plus Emtrey, the Rogues' quartermaster, had escorted the battered-looking freighter from a scrapyard in the Corellian system, where such craft were most common . . . and cheapest to acquire.

"Ugliest ship I think I've ever seen," said Solo.

Captain Onoma, standing on the other side of Solo at the bridge's new forward viewport, wrinkled his forehead in a fair approximation of a human frown. "It looks like the *Falcon* to me."

"Nothing could look less like the *Falcon*," Solo said. "You could slap a paint job on a desert skiff and it'd look more like the *Falcon*." He sighed. "Still, with Chewie in charge of dressing her up, she might be able to fool Zsinj for a couple of minutes. What did our crew of Corellians pay for her?"

"They traded that hyperspace-enabled TIE interceptor Shalla Nelprin took off *Razor's Kiss*."

Solo looked at him, eyes wide. "That's crazy. Trade a valuable combat-ready starfighter for that hunk of junk?"

"No. They traded a valuable combat-ready starfighter for a chance to blow Zsinj up."

Solo's features settled into calmer lines, though he still looked tired, stressed. "Oh. Well, that makes sense. She'll never have the *Falcon*'s speed. Without a few years' head start, Chewie won't be able to make her insides work like the real thing."

"We don't want him to," Wedge said.

"How so?"

"Because if they count on this new ship being the *Falcon*, our modifications can trip them up. For example, the *Falcon* isn't packed with high explosives."

Solo shuddered. "There's a very good reason for that."

"Right. But since the *Falcon* isn't packed with explosives, you'd never send her into a crash dive into the side of a Super Star Destroyer. With this hunk of junk, you wouldn't feel any such compunctions."

"Except for not wanting to die."

"Well, that's what escape pods are for. You know what I mean."

"Yeah. Yeah." Solo returned his attention to the Corellian YT-1300 transport hanging off the bow. "All right. Secure Bay Gamma One to authorized personnel only and direct this flying trash receptacle there. Let's get to work."

IT DRIFTED OFF the bow of *Iron Fist,* a nightmare vessel. Her bulk was an irregular oval of wreckage more than three kilometers long held together by thousands of kilometers of cabling. Around the wreckage was a superstructure—a cluster of engines at one end, a wedge-shaped bow at the other, a gigantic spar of metal connecting them and acting as a frame for the envelope of wreckage to hang upon. The name, barely visible on the bow, was *Second Death.*

"Ugliest ship I think I've ever seen," said Zsinj. His face shone with admiration. "Melvar, you have done a magnificent job."

The general gave him a little bow. "There are a dozen explosive pockets within the body of the wreckage; they will send the components of *Razor's Kiss* out in all directions. There are more explosives in the engines and bridge, sufficient to remove most evidence that these extra components ever existed. It should be convincing. Unfortunately, she's slow. She can't be expected to keep up with *Iron Fist* or other elements of our fleet."

"Pity. Still, we'll do what we can. How does the crew escape?"

"Both bow and stern are equipped with a *Sentinel*-class landing craft. The crew has a chance not only to evacuate, but to fight their way out of pursuit." Melvar offered a little sigh. "The crew doesn't know that if a capital ship approaches within a kilometer before they've engaged the hyperdrive, they, too, will detonate. The crew will not be captured, will not be able to betray your secret to the Rebels."

"Excellent. Fine work, as usual. Give her a station in the fleet, outside of visual range of any of the other vessels. I am so pleased." Zsinj smiled. He hoped he'd never be forced to utilize the hideous amalgamation that had earned his approval and praise. Using it meant failure on his part—meant he'd been beaten and needed to hide to lick his wounds. But he liked to keep his options open. "Oh. What about the Nightcloak function?"

"Working . . . mostly. Would you like a demonstration?"

"Please."

Melvar held up his comlink. "*Second Death,* this is General Melvar. Activate and initiate Nightcloak."

"Yes, sir," came the tinny voice from the comlink. "Deploying satellites."

Tiny flares erupted from *Second Death,* four from the bow and four from the stern, deploying at precise angles so they suggested the corners of a wire-frame box surrounding the junkyard vessel. After a few moments of flight, the satellites ceased their acceleration; their burn trails vanished and they became all but invisible in the starfield.

"Nightcloak engaging," said the comlink.

And *Second Death* was suddenly gone.

Where she had been, where the space around her had been, was blackness. Not starfield—not even the stars were visible through it.

Zsinj offered a little exhalation of happiness. "Sensors, give me a reading on *Second Death.*"

The sensor officer in the crew pit below examined his screen. He took on a stricken look as he raised his head to face the warlord. "Nothing, sir. We don't even get a return on the active sensors. It's a sensor anomaly."

"Fine, fine."

Out in space, stars briefly flickered through the darkness, then shone brilliantly again, and *Second Death* once more floated before them.

Melvar frowned. "*Second Death*, I didn't order an end to the test."

"Sorry, sir. System failure. It's still not entirely reliable."

"Well, bring in the satellites and get back to work. Until it's one hundred percent, it's not adequate. Until it's one hundred percent, we're not happy with you. Melvar out." The general pocketed the comlink and turned to his warlord. "I'm sorry, sir."

"Don't be." Zsinj waved his apology away. "It's a fine demonstration. A wonderful adaptation of what we're accomplishing at Rancor Base. They'll have it done in time. Or else." He smiled.

In *Mon Remonda*'s pilots' lounge, in stuffed chairs dragged against the viewports to suggest thrones, sat Wes Janson and Runt Ekwesh.

Standing before them, Face said, "For intercepting great quantities of damage so the rest of us didn't have to, your crowns, o mighty ones." He took circlets made of flimsy material and placed one on each pilot's head. "For enduring medical treatments without whining, for surviving days of bacta bath without crying, for emerging from your treatment without asking for extra cake and sweetening, your royal scepters." He placed a wooden dowel, its end decorated with tassels and ribbons, into the hand of each pilot. "And now, receive the accolades of your subjects."

He stood aside, and the gathered Wraiths and Rogues hurled confetti upon them, a rain of color and rubbish.

Janson blinked against the atmospheric assault and turned to Runt. "This is the last time, positively the last time, that I suggest to Face that the squad doesn't always show enough appreciation."

Runt nodded. "We agree. Do all kings have to suffer this?"

"Well, any king with Face Loran as his majordomo."

"And now," Face said, "the two kings fight each other to the death, and we space the loser."

"Whoa, there." Janson stood and shook confetti from his hair. "Try again."

"We space the winner?"

"One more."

"We buy you a drink."

"That's more like it."

As the pilots drifted back to their seats, Shalla dropped gracefully in a chair beside Piggy's. "Tell me something," she said.

"Yes?"

"The other day, you said that you were relieved when Doctor Gast died. Why relieved?"

Piggy took a few moments to answer. Shalla wondered whether he was considering his response, or debating whether to tell her to go to hell. Finally he said, "It takes pressure off me. Pressure of decisions."

"I don't understand."

"As far as I know, I am the only one of my kind. I am not fit to be among normal Gamorreans; I make them nervous and I am dismayed by their presence. Their violence, their simplicity. So I will never find a mate, a Gamorrean female, to my liking. I had sometimes wondered if Gast had created one . . . or if she might do so, if I compelled her. Even so, such a relationship would endure in frustration and sadness. If I understand it correctly, the changes made to me are not genetic; I could not pass them on to offspring. So I could not have children with my mental and emotional characteristics." He raised his hand, studying the Churban brandy in the glass he held. "In that sense, I am alone . . . and *should* be alone. Doctor Gast's continued existence led me to hopes I should not have entertained. Now that she is dead, I can be more responsible."

"I'm sorry." On impulse, she reached out and took his other hand. "But in one sense, you're wrong."

He sipped at the brandy before replying. "How so?"

"You're not just flesh and bone. You don't just pass along your genes. If you had children, you'd be giving them your ideas, the example of your courage and commitment, all the things that come from the way you relate to the culture you've chosen. And those things you can pass along to others who aren't your children. Intellectually, emotionally, your parents and children aren't related to you by blood at all. I know that may be small consolation."

He downed the rest of the brandy, and after a moment his lips curled up in a near-human smile. "Well, it is *some* consolation."

"Would you like to dance?"

"Would you like to have your toes smashed flat?"

"I have fast feet."

"True. Well, the risk is all yours." He heaved himself up, then helped her to her feet.

Other dancers were already in motion on the portion of the lounge the pilots had cleared of furniture. Face and Dia had center stage, moving to a classical theme of ancient Coruscant, and Donos and Lara were now moving to join them.

"They're not really together," Dia said.

Face glanced over at Donos and Lara. "How do you figure?"

"She's tense. Keeping a little separation between them. Her expression keeps softening, she keeps smiling, as if she's really enjoying herself. Then she tenses and withdraws. It's a little cycle she keeps running through."

"Oh, you're good at this game. But you missed when she gave him the opportunity for a kiss. A deliberate invitation."

"No, she didn't."

"She did." He gave her a superior little smile.

"When?"

"A moment ago. Did you see her lower her eyes, then raise them and make that little twirling motion with her finger?"

"Yes. I assumed she was describing something. She was talking."

"She *was* describing something. That's what makes it so subtle, the way she blended the cue in, the way you're supposed to. It's—" Then Face stiffened, nearly losing the rhythm of the dance, and looked back at the other couple.

"It's what?"

"Coruscant charm signing."

"I don't know what that is."

"It's something like the language of flowers. You know how on some worlds the precise flower you give someone, the number, the arrangement, all has specific meaning."

Dia nodded. "It's a human custom. A new way to miscommunicate so you can find reason to kill one another."

"That's an interesting interpretation . . . anyway, charm signing is sort of like that. It's confined to the social class of Imperial officer trainees from wealthy families and their circles. It came out of Coruscant long before the rise of the Empire, but it's mostly confined to the Empire these days; most of the former Imperial officers serving with the New Republic weren't of that social order. Anyway, she gave him the correct sign for 'I'd accept a kiss.' He just didn't know what it meant."

"Is that a reason for you to be so startled?"

"Well, yes. Lara keeps saying 'Coruscant' to me, without meaning to. When she's distracted, when she's upset . . . not when she's in control. Sometimes she'll walk like a native throneworlder—you know the sort of hunched-in, 'don't touch me' body language?"

She nodded.

Face thought back. "And then, things she knew about Coruscant commerce. Pretty elaborate for someone who'd been employed there only for a few weeks. And that incident at the Galactic Museum. The old man who thought she was— what was the name he called her?"

"Edallia Monotheer."

Face looked at her with real surprise. "How did you remember that?"

"A trick of the trade. When you're a slave dancer, you remember the name of everyone you are introduced to by your owner. If you fail, you're beaten . . . or worse."

"I'm sorry." He pulled her to him, an embrace of apology. "I always seem to do something to remind you of those times."

"It's not your fault." Her voice was a whisper. "I can't seem to give up on it. Sometimes I think I say things like that to remind other people of what I used to be—when *I'm* the only one who needs to remember." She sighed, as if releasing some sorrow into the air. "What are you going to do about Lara? Ask her how she knows this charm signing?"

He shook his head, brushing his cheek against hers. "I'm going to put in a request for information. To New Republic Intelligence."

"But later," she said.

"Later."

A COUPLE OF hundred meters away, Wedge trotted up the access ramp to the YT-1300 freighter hidden away in one of *Mon Remonda*'s hangar bays. Crashing and clanking noises drifted down from the freighter's upper hull, accompanied by the deep rumbling of Chewbacca's complaints. But no human words accompanied the rumbling.

He found Han Solo in the vessel's cockpit. He dropped into the copilot's seat beside the general.

"I thought you'd be at your pilots' welcome-back party," Solo said. He didn't turn his attention from the forward viewport. Across the floor of the hangar, cluttered with tools and repair carts, was the rectangle of lights outlining the hangar's magnetic containment field. Beyond that, dim because of the hangar's light, were stars.

"I stopped in," Wedge said. "I didn't stay too long. It tends to make the children nervous."

Solo managed a faint smile. "I know what you mean. I used to be one of the guys. Now I walk into a room and all conversation stops. I didn't imagine, when I accepted this job, that I'd become some other thing. An outsider."

"Sometimes that's what an officer is. Someone who's 'one of the guys' can't maintain discipline."

"I suppose."

A furious hail of metallic banging made conversation impossible for a moment. It was followed by an unusually lengthy and articulate stretch of grumbling from Chewbacca.

Solo said, "He hates this wreck almost as much as I do."

"Why do you hate it more?"

"Because, despite everything I said, it's just enough like the *Falcon* to make me homesick."

"For the *Falcon*? Or for Leia?"

Solo rubbed his face, easing away some of the lines of tiredness. "Yeah."

"I never really understood why you left the *Falcon* on *Rebel Dream* when she went on her mission. You could have stored her on *Mon Remonda*."

"It's just . . . I'm not sure." Solo stared off into the distance of space. "The *Falcon* is the thing I value most. Not the person I value most, but the thing. I think I left her with Leia so Leia would know."

"That you trusted her with what you valued most."

"Something like that. And I wanted her to remember me."

"As if she'd forget."

"Sometimes I think she should." Solo was silent a long moment, and when he spoke again, his voice was quieter. "I don't deserve her. And someday she'll realize that. When she's away from me, I think, 'Maybe today's the day. Maybe today she'll figure it out and get on with her life.' "

Wedge shook his head. "That's ridiculous."

"No, it's not. She's the one with the goal, the plan for her life. She's a driving force in the New Republic. Without her, I don't have a place. I'm just a drifter with an irresistible dose of roguish charm. And someday she'll get tired of the charm and there won't be anything else for me to offer her."

"You know," Wedge said, "I can't do it myself, because you're my superior officer. But I could call Chewie down here, and tell him what you've just said, and then he'd beat you nearly to death with a hydrospanner. Maybe then you'd figure out how wrong you are."

Solo managed a smile. "I think maybe that's why I volunteered for this Zsinj assignment. I thought it was because of how I felt when I heard about his bombardments. His assaults on defenseless worlds. I could just see myself as a child on the streets, looking up to see the turbolaser blasts coming down to destroy the little bit of world I could call my own. But, really, it might have been just to show Leia, 'Here I am, see, I can function in your world.' But after months of it, I just get tireder and crazier. I find myself wishing I could leave Zsinj be, and Leia could come home right now, with her mission unfinished, so things could go back to the way they were. And if she knew that, she'd be ashamed of me."

"It's a natural human emotion. And I have a three-stage plan to let you get back to the way things used to be."

That caught Solo's attention; he looked at Wedge for the first time since he'd boarded the freighter. "How?"

"Stage One." Wedge opened a comm channel on the co-pilot's control board. "YT-1300 to bridge. This is Commander Antilles. Please cut all lights in Bay Gamma One."

A few moments later, the overhead lights darkened. Chewbacca made a noise of complaint.

Wedge said, "Including the magcon shield indicator, please, bridge."

The rectangle of light around the magcon field faded. Now they sat in near-perfect darkness, illuminated only by the stars outside the field. They hung there, perfect, not blinking because there was insufficient atmosphere to make them twinkle, a perfect space vista.

Solo fell silent, just staring at the view for a long moment. "That's nice," he said. "I think you're right. I could use more of that. What's Stage Two?"

"Well, you're not the only member of the crew who could benefit from some blissful irresponsibility right now. So I'm going to stage an insurrection and seize control of *Mon Remonda*."

Solo gave a curt laugh. "Wedge Antilles, mutineer. That I have to see."

"Bring your Wookiee and I'll show you."

DONOS AND LARA walked into the officers' cafeteria and stopped short. It didn't look the way it was supposed to.

Tables, normally arrayed in neat rows, had been dragged out of line into zigzags, into four-table rectangles. Though the chamber was sparsely occupied, even that was different; normally the diners would be scattered across the chamber, but now they were concentrated at three or four tables.

Donos and Lara approached the closest table. The one

where their commander sat with General Solo and Chewbacca. Sabacc cards were laid out on the table before them.

"Excuse me, sir," Donos said, "I hate to interrupt—"

Wedge looked up. "What did you call me?"

"Uh, sir."

"Who do you think I am?"

Donos glanced at Lara, but she seemed as puzzled as he. "Commander Wedge Antilles, New Republic Starfighter—"

Wedge shook his head. "No, no, no. I just look like him. If I were Antilles, wouldn't I be wearing appropriate rank insignia?"

It was true; he wore none. For that matter, neither did General Solo.

"In fact," Wedge said, "what's that *you're* wearing? Lieutenant's insignia?"

"Uh, yes—"

"Off," Wedge said.

"Off," Solo repeated.

"Off off off off," Wedge said.

Donos pulled the rank insignia from his jacket. Lara followed suit with hers.

Wedge visibly calmed. "That's better," he said. "Wait. Where's your astromech?"

Donos's mouth worked for a moment as he considered responses. "I don't think I have an answer that will please you. Sir. Or Not-Sir. Whoever you are."

"You certainly don't. The astromechs are the backbone of Starfighter Command. Hardest-working beings in the galaxy. They need some rest and recreation, too. Don't you agree?"

"I, uh, I do."

"Good. Get out. Don't come back without your astromechs." Wedge gathered up the sabacc cards. "New hand. Who's in?"

———

WHEN FACE WANDERED IN, his R2 unit Vape wheeling along behind him, the cafeteria was more than half-full. It was also loud; card games and conversations dominated most of the tables. Some of the kitchen staff appeared to be on duty, bringing out drinks and various sorts of snacks, but they cheerfully exchanged sharp words with the officers present in a way they'd never do under ordinary circumstances. Officers sat with enlisted men and women, and, though uniforms suggested which was which and the services being represented, there were no rank insignia to be seen.

Chewbacca waved him over. Face and Vape moved up to his table.

Over his hand of cards, Wedge gave him a cool appraisal. "It's the one who looks like Captain Loran. But he has his astromech and no rank. He'll pass."

"Thank you, uh, one who looks like Commander Antilles."

"He catches on quickly," Wedge said. "One second. Vape, cold one."

A trapezoid-shaped plate at the top of Vape's ball head slid open. There was a *chuff* of compressed air, and a condensation-dewed bottle leaped up into the air. Wedge caught it with his free hand and set it down on the table before him. "Thanks, Vape. Thanks, one-who-looks-like-Face. That'll be all." He turned back to his game.

Face said, "You weren't supposed to know about that. And it certainly shouldn't have worked for you."

"I look just like the group leader. That gives me special privileges."

"Besides, it was my last one."

"Well, come back when you're fully stocked."

The others at the table—men and women who looked like General Solo, Chewbacca, Captain Todra Mayn of Polearm

Squadron, Gavin Darklighter and Asyr Sei'lar of Rogue Squadron, laughed.

Face turned away. "Run along and play," he told Vape. "This is going to be an interesting evening."

WEDGE'S MUTINY OF anonymity spread through the ship with a sort of quiet persistence. No officers on duty abandoned their tasks to join it, but crewmen coming off duty gravitated to the officers' cafeterias and, when the mutiny became too populous, into adjoining noncommissioned crew cafeterias, briefing halls, and auditoriums as well.

And nowhere in the mutineers' sections of *Mon Remonda* were name tags or rank designations to be found. Donos, walking the perimeter of the mutineers' sections with Lara in a state of baffled good humor, saw Rogue mechanic Koyi Komad win a week's wages from Captain Onoma in a card game as bloodthirsty as any TIE fighter vs. X-wing engagement. He saw Chewbacca simultaneously arm wrestle a naval lieutenant and a civilian hand-to-hand combat trainer so vigorously that both humans were thrown to the floor; they arose laughing and massaging wrenched arms.

Astromechs huddled in corners, exchanging chirps and trills that few organisms could interpret but that apparently kept them highly amused. Donos and Lara had to stop short of a portion of floor bounded by lines of observers; a group of R2 and R5 units sped through a twisting, winding course marked by colored tape on the floor. Curran Horn's Whistler was in the lead, Wedge's Gate was in second place, and both units were tweetling in the excitement of the moment.

Whistler and Gate maintained their one-two standings across the finish line and a crowd of bettors erupted in cheers and catcalls. Donos heard Horn's voice rise above the crowd noise: "I told you, I told you. Next time, make it an obstacle course with security measures. Whistler will still smoke them all."

"If I weren't sure I was only half-crazy," Donos said, "I'd be certain I was hallucinating."

"Your logic is faulty," Lara said. "If you were zero percent crazy, you'd be certain you weren't hallucinating. If you were one hundred percent crazy, you'd be equally certain this was real. Only at your current state of fifty percent insane do you doubt what you see."

"No fair. If I take you back to the pilots' lounge and dance with you again, will you stop picking at my flaws in logic?"

"Sure," she said. "That was my motive in the first place."

THE MUTINY ENDURED from early evening to late evening of the next calendar date, with a pair of sabacc games the last to break up, and galley workers grumbling only halfheartedly as they swept up the trash left behind by a day of blissful, if intermittent, irresponsibility.

Solo and Wedge were among those who abandoned the last surviving card game. Solo rubbed tired eyes and said, "Not bad, man-who-looks-like-Wedge. What's Stage Three?"

Wedge gave him a smile he might have learned from a toothy Bothan. "In Stage Three, we track down Zsinj and blow him up."

"Good plan. I like it."

9

THE NEXT MORNING, once hangovers were shaken off and infusions of caf had taken hold, the crew of *Mon Remonda* moved more briskly, with weeks of frustration and bone weariness at least partially shaken loose.

At a briefing of the Rogues and Wraiths late in the day, Wedge said, "For those of you who were curious, tomorrow's mission does not seem to have been endangered by the mass amnesia that seems to have struck my pilots—no one seems to be able to recall what he was up to yesterday." That drew some chuckles. "Assuming our brains are working correctly again, we can probably get through a preliminary operational briefing now."

He tapped keys on the lectern keyboard and a holoprojection sprang into existence beside him. It showed a solar system—medium-sized yellow sun and a dozen planets around it. Their orbits were indicated by glowing dotted lines. "This is the Kidriff system. It's along what we think of as the Imperial/Zsinj border, as far coreward as Zsinj's influence extends. Its occupied world, Kidriff Five, is a very wealthy one, a heavy trade depot that develops and exports metal alloys—several improvements in Sienar TIE fighter hulls in recent years came about because of Kidriff developments.

"Kidriff Five's government patterned the world's building and expansion plans very heavily on Coruscant, as a way of becoming more attractive to the Empire and the Imperial court." Wedge activated another image, and the holoprojector displayed a city vista—a seemingly endless sea of skyscrapers that would not look out of place if dropped whole onto Coruscant. The sky, however, was not as hazy or as thick with storm clouds as Coruscant's typically was. "It wouldn't have been a bad site for Ysanne Isard to set up her government seat in exile—except, by the time the Rogues threw Isard off Coruscant, Kidriff had already fallen to Zsinj.

"We've recently received a lot of data on Kidriff and other Zsinj-occupied worlds in Imperial sectors. Analysis showed that the data had been scrubbed of certain types of information useful to the New Republic. But the scrubbing seems to have been hasty, and did not entirely eliminate the fact that there had been activity by a pro–New Republic faction in the months before Zsinj took over." Wedge called up another image, this time of a region seemingly divided equally between stretches of skyscrapers and stretches of heavy rust-colored foliage. "Kidriff Five's Tobaskin Sector. Seat of their rebel activity, which may or may not still exist. That's our target."

Janson spoke up. "And what do we do there, chief?"

"Very little, actually." Wedge brought up the image of a Corellian YT-1300 freighter. "This is not the *Millennium Falcon*. It's our simulacrum, which Chewbacca and a few unlucky mechanics have been transforming into a likeness of the *Falcon*. They painted false rust on good hull and put good paint on rusty hull so the blotches match up, and have made some other modifications. We've dubbed it the *Millennium Falsehood*. We're given to understand that it's approximately spaceworthy."

From the back of the briefing hall, Chewbacca uttered a sustained grumble that left the pilots no doubt that the Wookiee didn't think much of the freighter.

Wedge continued, "Chewbacca and I will pilot the *Falsehood* to Tobaskin Sector and land in one of those forest tracts.

We'll let off a couple of intelligence operatives who are going to try to make contact with any surviving pro–New Republic factions there. But our main job is to wait there until we're seen, then take off for space."

"Which accomplishes what?" Janson asked. "Actually, I know the answer. But I thought you ought to have at least one shill in the audience."

"Good to see you're developing a skill you can use in civilian life," Wedge said. "This allows the apparent *Millennium Falcon* to be seen well within Zsinj's territory on a world where Zsinj knows there has been pro-Rebel activity. It's one piece of data that will pique his interest. We're going to do this again and again. At a certain point, when the *Falsehood* has developed a predictable pattern of mission activity, Zsinj will, we hope, show up to destroy her."

Lara raised a hand.

"Notsil."

"Um, I don't know whether this has entered your mission planning, sir, but if you go to an Imperial world, they'll probably want to kill you. And if you do land and let yourself be noticed later, they'll probably want to kill you then." She gave him a look as though she were an ingenue full of pride in her sudden tactical realization. Pilots around the amphitheater laughed.

"This had occurred to us. Data on the Kidriff system suggests that their security is very lax in order to promote fast, efficient trade—they're far more interested in making sure cargo gets taxed than in protecting government and military installations, which tend to be buried very deep and hard to hit. So our belief is that we can just fly the *Falsehood* in. We'll kill our transponder stream once we're low enough, so they won't know where we landed. They'll assume it's a smuggler's ploy and look for us. We'll be going in with Captain Celchu's X-wing coupled to our hull, and he'll detach to act as our escort on the trip back out. But before we go in, the

Wraiths who are assigned TIE interceptors will go in and make a preliminary landfall. If their security queries are more difficult than we suspect, they can signal us and wing out of there. Otherwise, they'll be on hand to join Tycho for escort duty on the flight out. The rest of the Rogues and Wraiths will be orbiting the planet's primary moon to offer additional support when they chase us off-world."

Wedge looked among the seated pilots. "We'll be taking out targets of opportunity, mostly enemy starfighters, on the way out. Our mission is to disengage with as little loss as possible. Does anyone see any specific flaw in this operation?"

Runt sneezed. He looked around, embarrassed. "Sorry. No flaws. Just bacta tickle in our sinus cavities."

"Which brings up another point," Wedge said. "The medical reports of the Wraiths who sustained burns look good. I don't see a sign that any Wraith has not recovered sufficiently to be part of this operation. But if any of you does still feel that he's not up to the mission, let me know privately. Believe me, no one will hold it against you."

There was silence.

"Any more questions? No? Tomorrow morning we'll get the final flight data, drop out of hyperspace outside the Kidriff system, and execute this thing. Until then, get some rest. Dismissed."

As THEY FILED out of the briefing chamber, Elassar said, "I don't know. I have a bad feeling about this one, a bad feeling."

"Why?" Face asked. "When we were going into the briefing, you were as happy as a bantha on a mountain of blumfruit."

"Runt sneezed."

Face looked the younger pilot. "Why, yes he did. I forgot about that. Doomed the whole lot of us, did he?"

"No, this is serious. He sneezed right when the commander

got to the point where the commander asked about flaws in the plan. That means there *is* such a flaw, and we didn't notice it, and Runt will be in trouble then."

"No, no, no." Face shook his head. "That's what it would have meant had it been an accidental sneeze. But it wasn't. It was a deliberate sneeze."

Elassar looked at him, his expression puzzled. "Why would he sneeze deliberately?"

Lara said, "He was clearing his chamber."

"What chamber?"

Face leaned in, his expression conspiratorial. "We're working on a secret weapon for desperate situations on our commando raids. Runt is strengthening his lungs, his sinus cavities."

Lara said, "Before each mission in which we go into the field, we load Runt's nose with plasteel ball bearings."

"Then," Face said, "if we're captured and end up in the hands of just a couple of guards, Runt can take in a deep, deep breath and sneeze those ball bearings out at them."

Lara nodded, her own expression earnest. "In secret tests, we've clocked the ball bearings erupting from his nose at just over five hundred klicks per hour. Definitely subsonic, but still fast enough to penetrate flesh and light stormtrooper armor."

Elassar looked back and forth between them. "Hey, wait a minute. That would never work." The two conspirators dissolved into laughter, and he continued, his voice petulant, "I was being serious. Can't you be serious? Someone's going to be in trouble."

"You just summon us up some luck," Face said. "We're relying on you."

ROSTAT MANR was good at his job. As a Sullustan, he was supposed to be adept at piloting, at navigating, but he knew that he and his fellow Sullustan ship handlers had gotten their reputation far more through hard work than through natural inclination.

Rostat had been rewarded for his hard work, too. For four years he'd flown Y-wings for the Rebel Alliance—now known as the New Republic. Less than a year ago, sick of war, certain that he'd done his duty for the cause he believed in, he accepted a position flying tugs for a civilian firm: Event Vistas, a cruise-vessel line. Only a few months ago, he'd been promoted to chief pilot aboard *Nebula Queen,* one of the line's newest and most beautiful cruise vessels.

But now, he was in danger of losing all he had gained. The thought, as he stared out the viewport at the growing circle of color that was the planet Coruscant, made him sad.

He couldn't tell anyone. They'd laugh at him. Then they'd demote him . . . at best.

For no one wanted to employ a pilot with Ewoks in his nose.

He could feel them dancing, hear the faint, tinny sounds of their music and singing as they made merry in his nostrils. All the digging he'd done had failed to dislodge them. He couldn't think about anything but the Ewoks, and what it would take to rid himself of them.

All he had to do was crash *Nebula Queen* down upon Coruscant's surface. Then everything would be all right. He smiled. Soon, soon.

As the cruise ship reached the point it should have maneuvered into high Coruscant orbit, Rostat kept her headed into the atmosphere. A carefully calculated approach, the precise speed and angle needed for her to breach the planetary atmosphere without igniting. He really needed for enough of the ship to be left to hit the planet's surface, after all.

"Rostat?" That was his captain, a human female originally from Tatooine. Other humans described her as old and leathery, but Rostat didn't have their perspective on human features. "What are you doing?"

Rostat looked at her, trying to mask his alarm. "You know, don't you?"

"I know you're out of your approach plane."

"No. I mean, about my nose."

She gave him a look that suggested she *didn't* know. But she had to be shamming. She had to be in on it. Perhaps she'd even been the one who put the Ewoks up his nose.

Seized with a sudden fear of what she was, what she might do to him next, he drew his duty blaster and fired on her. It was point-blank range; he would have had to go to some effort to miss. His shot took her in the side and she fell over.

But it wasn't a blaster shot. He looked curiously at his issue sidearm. It was set on kill, but a stun-level beam had emerged. Curiously, he flipped the switch between blast and stun, but no sound emerged. Perhaps the mechanism was broken.

No matter. She was unconscious, and she would stay that way long enough for the ship to crash. And relief would be his.

But the *Nebula Queen*'s control board now showed her altitude gaining, not dropping. He stared curiously at the numbers, then took the pilot's controls again.

They didn't respond. The cruise liner began climbing back up into her proper orbit. He ran a quick diagnostic. It indicated that the auxiliary bridge currently had control.

He brought up the ship's intercom and called the auxiliary bridge. When the picture swam into focus, it showed that bridge's control seat. In the command chair was another Sullustan, a very junior officer Rostat knew. "Nurm," he said. "What are you doing?"

Nurm looked uncomfortable and glanced off-screen. "I've seized control of the ship," he said.

"Return control to the main bridge," Rostat said. His nose was really itching. The Ewoks had to be mounting a major celebration in there.

"No," Nurm said.

"Give me control right now," Rostat said.

"Make me," Nurm said.

"However you want it. Your career is at an end." Rostat switched off.

He waited for a moment, settling his temper, and then made a sudden motion, driving his finger into his nose as fast and deep as he could.

No good. The Ewoks got away, leaping up above his probing finger, as they always did. He sighed, took up his blaster, and headed aft.

Moments later, he charged into the auxiliary bridge with his blaster at the ready.

There was no one in the control chair. But there was motion to his right. He spun—

Too late. Nurm fired first, his stun blast washing across Rostat's chest. Rostat felt his body go numb and watched with a detached sort of interest as the floor angled up and knocked at his head.

Then he knew only blackness.

NURM LOOKED ANXIOUSLY at the fellow officer he'd just shot. "Will he be all right?"

The man to whom he spoke, a human in the uniform of a colonel, rose from behind the communications console. He moved over to Rostat's body and prodded it with his toe. "He should be. If we can figure out what's wrong with him."

"I couldn't believe it. You showed it to me, and I still can't believe it. He wanted to crash us."

"I don't think he did. There's something very wrong going

on in his head, though. But you've saved him from scandal, or death, or both."

"Why did you want me to shoot him? I've barely qualified with blaster pistols! I'm a civilian!"

The officer gave him an enigmatic smile. "It's important. Believe it or not, the fact that you shot him instead of me may save additional lives. Just remember the story as I've given it to you."

He brought out his comlink to summon members of ship's security to take Rostat into custody, then transmitted a few words, a mission-accomplished code, to his commander.

IN AN ORBITAL station in high orbit above the far side of Coruscant, General Airen Cracken, head of New Republic Intelligence, received the officer's signal. He responded with a few words of congratulation and signed off. He'd get the full report and offer more appropriate words of praise later.

He returned to the ancient, scarred desk that served him as a reminder of his many campaigns and years of service, and felt the first stirrings of relief. Suddenly, a picture once made up of shadows and inexplicable shapes was beginning to assume a form he could understand.

On his personal terminal, he called up a communications file, a full holo, and advanced it to a mark he'd placed earlier.

Wedge Antilles's face and upper body appeared at one-third scale just above Cracken's desk. The pilot seemed to be seated behind a desk of his own, and there was nothing but white bulkhead wall behind him.

"Now that the Warlord has persuaded the New Republic to institute measures that can be used as precedents when dealing with future incidents, his next step must inevitably be to make a breach between the New Republic and one of the member species that has contributed significantly to our success.

"Logic suggests that the Mon Calamari would be the best choice, since without their engineering expertise and their heavy cruisers we would have had a much harder time of this war than we've had. But we suspect that this brainwashing treatment may be confined for now to mammalian and near-mammalian species—it would be much, much harder to devise a treatment that was equally functional across the wide range of all sapient species types. So our prediction is that it won't be Mon Calamari or Verpines at this time.

"Our best guess is that the next attack will come from Sullustans or Bothans. And we have some ideas about that." Wedge typed something into the datapad before him; Cracken supposed that he was consulting notes.

"Gotals are known as expert hunters. And for the last several years, Twi'leks, who have traditionally been thought of by Imperial humans as traders, and not particularly bold beings in general, have been trying to impress on human cultures the importance of their warrior tradition. We think it's significant that the Twi'lek and Gotal disasters have involved single warriors wreaking havoc. In our opinion, the assaults to come will correspond in some way to popular stereotypes and misconceptions about the species whose members initiate them. If the next attack is Bothan, it will involve computer slicing—such as, perhaps, falsified data transmissions that cause disasters. If the next attack is Sullustan, it's likely to involve a piloting or navigating mishap costing hundreds or thousands of lives. Either way, if it is remotely possible, it's important that the agents of these attacks be taken alive. Our hope is that they are under compulsion to do what they're doing, and that the brainwashing technique leaves some consistent physiological evidence that New Republic medics can detect."

Antilles shut his datapad. His gaze, unsettlingly enough, seemed to seek out Cracken's. "That's the best we have to offer, General. But if our predictions come anywhere close to the reality of the next set of mystery terrorist activities, you can rely on it being an attempt by Zsinj to create more chaos within the New Republic, and you can head off the damage his effort might otherwise cause.

"Thank you for your time, General. Antilles out." The hologram of Wedge faded.

Cracken sat motionless for long moments. The first time he'd heard this transmission, he'd shaken his head and wished, once again, that flyboys would just keep their attention on their cockpits and out of Intelligence affairs. The second time, after Cracken had reviewed the evidence on the Twi'lek and Gotal assaults, it had made a frightening kind of sense . . . and Cracken had begun devoting resources to an investigation based on the possibility that the Antilles theory was correct.

Now, Cracken wished that one flyboy, Wedge Antilles, would pay less attention to his cockpit and devote some more of his thinking to Intelligence affairs.

Perhaps he could be lured out of Starfighter Command and over to Intelligence.

Cracken made an exasperated noise and shut down his terminal. No, not in this lifetime.

He turned his attention to the ongoing search for evidence of an upcoming Bothan code-slicing effort that would end in disaster.

FACE LORAN WOKE to the sound of passerby conversation out in the corridor. He stretched, enjoying the luxury that was to be his—a few minutes of lazy rest before his alarm went off.

Then he glanced at the chrono beside his bed. The time was half an hour after his alarm should have awakened him. He hadn't set it.

He swore and threw his sheets off. He had just enough time to clean up and dress before mission briefing, if he hurried.

A portion of his terminal's screen blinked at him—sign of new mail, not yet reviewed. He typed in a command to transfer it all to Vape, his astromech—he'd read it when nothing else was going on during the Kidriff mission.

THE LAUNCH BAY assigned to the Rogues and Wraiths hummed—not just with activity, but with the bone-cutting whine of X-wing repulsorlift engines being tested as pilots went through their prelaunch checklists. And it was cold, the launch door opened to space, only the magnetic-containment field keeping the atmosphere safely within . . . and magcon fields did an inadequate job of retaining heat.

Wedge watched the activity, looking for undue stress or worry on the part of his pilots.

Gavin Darklighter. The young Rogue would be flying without a wingmate. He'd been sobered by Tal'dira's death, and still looked unusually serious, but showed no sign of distraction.

Corran Horn. It had been only days since he'd killed a squadmate, and the speculation that Tal'dira had been brainwashed, not a traitor, and therefore theoretically possible to save, had to be eating at him. He showed no sign of it, his real emotions safely hidden behind the mask of professional civility that CorSec and other police personnel wore when dealing with strangers.

Tyria Sarkin. She'd also been forced to kill a fellow pilot. She made no secret of her distress, and even now, as she donned her helmet and climbed into her X-wing cockpit, there was a sad look to her eyes. But, unlike Horn, she hadn't had to kill a squadmate, a friend. And she hadn't been as isolated as Horn; Kell had been there for her. Kell had even persuaded her to talk to Wes Janson, the man who had been obliged, many years before, to kill Kell's own father under not dissimilar circumstances. Janson had said it had helped her. Though Tyria wore her emotions very close to the surface, Wedge felt he had little to worry about with her.

Dia Passik. She would not be flying today; the decision handed down by the Provisional Council made it impossible for her to come along. But it didn't prevent her from participating in other ways; she was present, out of uniform, moving from starfighter to starfighter, offering a recommendation here, a wish for good luck there. And, when she thought no one was looking, a kiss for Face.

Elassar Targon. The Devaronian pilot was busily sticking figurines made of hard-baked bread on various portions of Runt's X-wing's hull while the Thakwaash pilot ineffectually tried to shoo him away. More charms. Wedge sighed.

"You can't just stay here and avoid it," Janson said.

Wedge looked at the Wraiths' XO. "Come again?"

"You can't just hang around here, Commander. You have to get to the *Falsehood* and face your mistake."

"What mistake is that?"

Janson grinned. "Well, of course, you're taking Han Solo's place in piloting the *Falsehood* because he really can't keep on relinquishing command of the fleet for joyrides."

"Correct. No mistake I can see so far. I have more experience with Corellian freighters than anyone on *Mon Remonda,* excepting Han Solo."

"And you asked him if Chewbacca would be interested in coming along as copilot and mechanic. He has all that experience keeping disintegrating junk together as it flies."

"Correct so far."

"And the general said, sure, Chewie would be happy to come along."

"You're three for three."

"Wedge, you don't speak Wookiee."

"I—oh, Sithspit." Wedge felt some color rising into his face. Janson was right: In all the mission planning they'd done, he'd failed to remember that he wouldn't be able to understand anything his copilot said, though Chewbacca could certainly understand Basic.

Janson just stood there, his expression merry.

Wedge sighed. "Check with Squeaky and Emtrey. I can't issue orders for them to go, but if either is willing to volunteer, I'd appreciate it. Preferably Squeaky." Though 3PO units normally had protocol skills as part of their programming, including diplomacy and instantaneous translation of a staggering number of languages, Emtrey's programming was optimized for military functions; Squeaky's was better suited to this mission.

"Will do."

"You haven't mentioned this to the pilots?"

"Well, yes, I sort of blurted it out when it occurred to me."

"And what did they say?"

"They put down bets on what you'd do. So then I had to go to all the other pilots so they could get their own bets down."

"Who won?"

"Tyria Sarkin. She said you'd say 'Sithspit.' "

"You know, you've finally earned my gravest revenge."

"You don't ever take revenge. That's beneath Wedge Antilles, Hero of the New Republic."

Wedge gave him a smile, one full of teeth, and Janson's own grin faltered. Wedge said, "Dismissed."

KELL TOOK POINT, Elassar tucked in behind and beside him as wingman, and led his TIE interceptor unit in toward Kidriff Five. The other wingpair, Janson and Shalla, stayed off to their starboard at the distance prescribed by Imperial regulations.

The world called Kidriff Five gradually grew in their viewports. The planet, at least the hemisphere they could see, seemed to be dominated by three colors: blue for seas and rusty red for vegetation, and a lesser amount of gray-white where the planet's greatest cities lay.

Comm traffic also increased as they neared the planet. First was an automated signal directing them into one of the preapproved approach vectors. As soon as that signal arrived, Kell transmitted a tight-beam signal back to the *Falsehood* indicating where they could expect first comm contact.

As they entered the approach vector, they could see, far ahead of them, tiny lights—at the distances shown on their sensors, these had to be massive cargo vessels approaching the planet.

When they were close enough to the planet that Kell could see nothing but its surface unless he leaned much closer to his viewport, they received the first live transmission. "Incoming flight, four Sienar Fleet Systems interceptors, this is Kidriff Primary Control. Please identify yourself and your mission."

Kell activated his comm unit. "This is Drake Squadron, One Flight, out of the *Night Terror,* Captain Maristo commanding. We're here for rec-re-a-tion." The emphasis he put on the final word suggested a pilot who'd been away from any sort of entertainment for too long. "Inbound to Tobaskin to see how much rec-re-a-tion a cargo bay full of credits will buy."

"Acknowledged, Drakes. Transmitting your revised approach vector. Will your ship be arriving later?"

"Negative, we're here solo." And that lie conveyed a second lie to the traffic controllers on Kidriff Five: that Drake Squadron consisted of hyperdrive-equipped TIEs. This suggested, in turn, that its pilots were very important people. It wasn't uncommon for high-ranking officers to take their personal TIEs, with a lower-ranking officer as theoretical commander to act as a shield of anonymity for them, on a junket like this.

"Understood. Leave your transponders on at all times, by planetary ordinance. Enjoy yourselves, and welcome to Kidriff Five."

Kell compressed the exchange and transmitted it, and the point in space where he'd received the opening words of the greeting, back to the *Falsehood*.

"I DO RECEIVE combat pay, don't I?" The speaker was Squeaky, situated behind Wedge's seat on the *Millennium Falsehood*.

"If we're fired upon, yes," Wedge said. "Otherwise, you just get hazardous-duty pay."

Chewbacca grumbled something. Squeaky said, "Shut up, you."

Wedge grinned. He'd never met a 3PO unit as verbally abusive as Squeaky. Most of them, because of standard programming and because they knew themselves to be defenseless, attempted to ingratiate themselves with everyone they met—usually with so much talk they ended up aggravating those they wished to befriend. But Squeaky was a manumitted droid, owned by no one, and had a few quirks. "What did he say?"

"I don't have to translate comments like that."

"Translate everything. I'll decide what's important and what's not."

"He said he could guarantee I receive combat pay by pulling off my legs and hitting me with them."

"Well, that was very generous of him. You should have said 'Thank you, maybe later.'"

"Sir, I think you lack an understanding of this Wookiee's violence-laden humor."

———

AS SOON AS they dropped to within twenty kilometers of the planetary surface over Tobaskin Sector, which was already under nightfall, Kell and his fellow Drakes began receiving transmissions from sector businesses—some data, some sight and sound, all extolling the virtues of various entertainment spots in the region. One transmission was the city government's visitor's package, including maps of the region with hundreds of clubs, bars, hostels, and other businesses highlighted.

As if unsure as to which of the city's many offerings to choose, Kell led his group out over one of the sector's deeper forest tracts. As his pilots exchanged banal comm traffic about which sites would offer the most recreation, Kell scanned the forest floor for life. And when he'd chosen a spot that included a clearing large enough for the *Falsehood* but was so deep within heavy forest that it seemed humans did not frequent it, he transmitted that data back as well.

They found a personal-vehicle landing zone near a district full of brilliantly lit entertainment businesses. They came to rest there and emerged from the top hatches of their interceptors.

Kell pulled his helmet free, dropped it onto his pilot's couch, and began removing other pieces of piloting paraphernalia he wouldn't be needing. "Drake Two, Drake Four, keep all your gear on. You'll be staying with the interceptors."

Shalla nodded. She slid down to the ground in full gear and stood at attention before her starfighter, a guard on duty.

"Aw, no." Elassar sounded heartbroken. He clutched his chest as though someone had shot him. "Why me? I'm the youngest, I'm in the greatest need of fun."

Dressed only in his black jumpsuit, Kell slid down to his wing pylon, then dropped to the ground. He clambered up Elassar's interceptor and leaned in close to the younger pilot. "Let me ask you something, Elassar."

"Fire away, sir."

"You go into one of these wonderfully diverting bars."

"Yes."

"You put down your credits."

"Sounds good so far, sir."

"You take off your helmet."

"Well, I'd certainly want to at some point. Even if I were only getting a drink."

"What do the other patrons see?"

"Well, they see the galaxy's best-looking—oh."

"Devaronian pilot."

"Right, sir, I get it."

"How many Devaronian TIE interceptor pilots do you suppose there are in the Empire?"

"I understand, sir, I really do."

Kell shook his head and dropped to the ground.

WEDGE SET THE *MILLENNIUM FALSEHOOD* down so gently that not even he was fully aware of the transition between repulsorlift support and the settling of the hydraulic landing skids.

Chewbacca rumbled something.

Squeaky said, "Well, of course that was a good landing. He can't afford to set this flying trash heap down any harder. Pieces would fall off."

Chewie's grumbling became louder, more eloquent.

"What do you mean, this is a good ship? Just this morning you were calling her names that would peel new paint off a hull. You're disagreeing with me just to be disagreeable."

"Captain's leaving the bridge," Wedge announced. "Chewbacca, the controls are yours."

He trotted back to the top of the loading ramp and found his passengers gearing up, ready to leave. One man and one woman, both with dark hair and unmemorable, average features, dressed in black pants and tunics decorated with dazzling bright zigzag stripes—this season's very definition of tourist in certain portions of the Empire.

They'd never told Wedge their names. He thought of the man as Bland One, the woman as Bland Two.

Bland One turned to him, extended a hand. "Thanks for a smooth flight. Much better than some insertions we've been through." Bland Two nodded; Wedge couldn't remember her saying a word.

Wedge shook his hand, then activated the ramp control. The access ramp whined but did not budge.

"I have one pilot," Wedge said, "who'd be certain that you jinxed it with the compliment." He stomped down on the nearest portion of ramp. The mechanism's whine increased in volume, then the ramp lowered. "Good luck."

Then they were gone, and the ramp closed again with less complaint.

By the time Wedge returned to the bridge, Tycho had decoupled from the top hull and his X-wing was settling to the ground just ahead of the *Falsehood*'s cockpit. Then the X-wing appeared to vanish as its lights faded. Suddenly they were in darkness, the trees all around them acting as an impenetrable wall between them and the city lights. Their only illumination was the two spots of gold light marking Squeaky's eyes.

"Well," said Squeaky, "what shall we do now? I know many mnemonic games. Compare Storerooms is a good one."

Chewbacca rumbled something.

"No, I don't know Droid-Crushers."

Rumble.

"What do you mean, you'd be happy to demonstrate? Oh, ha, ha."

Wedge sighed. For such a short flight in, this was going to be a long mission.

———

IT WAS LONG after the Rogues and Wraiths settled into their parking orbit around Kidriff's moon that Face remembered his unread mail.

"Vape, put that new storage through to my comm screen. In order of reception, please."

First was a letter, text only, from his sister, now at school on Pantolomin. It was chatty, full of details of everyday life, much as Face remembered it. A bright bit of home to distract him from the bleak lunar scape that was his sole viewing pleasure right now.

The second, and last, item was from New Republic Intelligence. He had to wade through screen after screen of standard admonishment that he was not to distribute this material, upon pain of trial and incarceration, before he got to the meat of the message and remembered what it was all about: his recent query concerning Lara Notsil and Edallia Monotheer, the name she'd been called by the old man on Coruscant.

The enclosed material was all classified secret; nothing had a higher secrecy rating. He hoped the answers he was looking for weren't hiding behind a more stringent level of classification, a level he couldn't access.

The file on Lara Notsil contained little information he didn't already know. Much of it she'd told him and the other Wraiths at one time or another. Born on a farm in Aldivy. Decent grades in school. No indication of special aptitudes other than agriculture. Then, the data derived from her own accounts and a little independent verification: how her community refused to offer aid to the enemy by turning over stockpiles of grain and meats to a former Imperial admiral by the name of Trigit, how Trigit's ship *Implacable* had bombarded the town out of existence. How follow-up troops had found a survivor, Lara Notsil, and taken her up to the ship. How Trigit, taken with the girl, had kept her half-comatose on a steady diet of drugs and made her his unwilling mistress.

Until Wraith Squadron and allied troops had destroyed *Implacable*. Until Lara had escaped in Trigit's personal evacuation pod.

A rather sparse account. But colonists like the Aldivians, given to raising their crops and children, didn't devote a lot of time to more extensive personal records. On some colonies, they didn't even carry identification.

Then the file on Edallia Monotheer. For all that she was born on Coruscant, a planet notable for the extent and quality of its citizen records, her account was scarcely longer than Notsil's. It had been reconstructed from interviews; all primary sources about her appeared to have been destroyed.

Born about fifty years ago. Trained to be an actress. She'd caught the eye of Armand Isard, father of Ysanne Isard; he was the head of Intelligence throughout most of the reign of Emperor Palpatine. Monotheer had trained as an Intelligence agent and had executed many successful missions for her superiors.

Then, according to this account, she had been arrested and convicted of treason, along with her husband. Both were executed for funneling information about Imperial Intelligence to anti-Imperial factions on Chandrila. An opinion annotated by some anonymous New Republic Intelligence analyst suggested that this was a standard technique to cause the death of a subordinate who had committed some less significant offense, and that Monotheer had had nothing to do with the Rebel Alliance.

Husband. Face found the link to data on Monotheer's immediate family and brought it up.

There was not much of interest there on her husband. He had a history similar to hers. There were rumors that the two of them had had a child, but there was no data on file about this.

But far more interesting than the husband's history was his name.

Dalls Petothel.

Face felt his stomach sink.

"DAWN," SAID SQUEAKY.

The one word, emerging out of blackness, jolted Wedge out of his light doze. He looked around but could still see no illumination other than the droid's eyes. He rubbed his eyes and swung his booted feet down off the command console. "It doesn't much look like dawn."

"If you look straight up, you can see the sky brightening. All these trees and the buildings beyond keep the early-morning light from reaching us," Squeaky said.

Chewbacca stretched, making loud tendon-popping noises, and rumbled something.

"Well, yes, since we don't have any light in our eyes, I could have let you sleep a few more minutes," Squeaky said. "But I was under the impression that the commander here wanted to know when dawn was. Because as soon as it's day, the more likely it is we get seen. Or hadn't that thought penetrated the mass of fur shielding your brain from outside stimulus?"

Grumble.

"Well, yes, technically, it is light rather than chronological markers for daytime that make it more likely we'll be seen, but my point still holds—"

"Quiet," Wedge said. "We may have something."

On his sensor screen, a small blip had just crossed, in a straight line, a portion of this belt of forest about a kilometer to their south. It had looped around and was now crossing the same forest a hundred meters or so north of its last passage. As they watched, it completed this crossing and looped back again.

"A search grid?" Squeaky suggested.

"Yes. But it's the only vehicle doing that in the area. So

there's not a concerted search going on." Wedge read the text register on his sensor board. The vehicle was tentatively identified as a sort of high-altitude floater routinely used by police forces on Imperial worlds. "Probably just a routine flyover of his territory. He should be here in about fifteen minutes." He dialed down the broadcast power of his comm unit and activated it. "Two?"

"I see it, Leader."

"Just checking. Begin your preflight preparations. Out." He brought the comm system up to full power and selected an encryption code, then transmitted one phrase: "In the green."

A moment later, he received an answer, encrypted the same way. "Two lit." Kell's voice.

"Drake Squadron is getting ready," Wedge said. "Now we wait for the locals to flush us."

10

I N THE GRAYING hour of dawn, the police floater heeled over
so far that Wedge was certain that its pilot would tumble
out of his seat if not for strap restraints and the vehicle's bubble top. The pilot looked down at the *Millennium Falsehood*,
reached for his control board as if to activate his comm system, then spotted Tycho's X-wing.

Even with the distance between them, Wedge could read
the shock on the pilot's face. "Let's go," he said.

Rogue Two's nose elevated until the X-wing was pointed
almost straight up, and then Tycho kicked in his main thrusters, shooting the snubfighter into the air straight past the police floater. He missed the smaller vehicle by less than two
meters. The police pilot unnecessarily slid sideways to get
clear of the X-wing's passage.

Wedge duplicated Tycho's maneuver, putting the *Falsehood* into a steep climb. Above, he could see the glow of Tycho's engines. "Chewie, the comm system is yours," he said.

Chewbacca activated the comm unit. He grumbled and
roared into it across an open channel. By agreement with
Wedge, these would be insults and curses in the Wookiee's
language.

The *Falsehood* reached the altitude of the top of this sector's highest buildings. Wedge leveled off, still traveling in
Tycho's wake, a sharp maneuver that brought a startled ex-
clamation from Squeaky . . . followed by a clatter of metal on
metal.

"Forget to strap in?" Wedge asked.

"I never forget anything, sir," the 3PO unit said, his tone a bit miffed. "I merely failed to add 'strapping in' to my list of things to do. Could you hold her level for a moment?"

"No." Wedge sideslipped to go around an aggressively tall skyscraper. There was another clash and scrape of metal from behind. Tycho rejoined Wedge from the other side of the skyscraper, his X-wing dancing around the Corellian freighter with the nimbleness only a starfighter could manage.

Chewbacca grumbled something and indicated the sensor board. Wedge spared it a glance. It showed a lot of air traffic, most of it moving in what appeared to be patterns unrelated to the *Falsehood*'s flight. One group of signals, their number indeterminate because of their proximity to one another, followed in their wake at a distance of more than two kilometers; they faded in and out of the picture as they dipped down below the level of ground clutter and emerged at intervals. "That's Kell and the Drakes," Wedge said. "We still need to be sure we've been spotted by the world authority—"

A strong signal, a blur representing six or more starfighters, appeared to the north, closing fast.

"There we go," Wedge said. "Let's bounce out."

Tycho said, "Consider it bounced." His X-wing vectored straight for space.

"Oh, no," Squeaky said.

Wedge hauled back on the controls and the *Falsehood* followed.

KELL SAW TYCHO and the *Falsehood*'s sudden flight for space, and the signals from the distant pursuers just as abruptly showed altitude gains. He put his interceptor in an upward course—a near-intercept course aimed at a point not far behind the pursuers of the *Falsehood*.

As they climbed, he got a clearer look at the group behind

the *Falsehood*. It was a full squadron, identified by the sensors as TIE fighters. They'd be on the top of Wedge and Tycho pretty soon, certainly before the *Falsehood* left the atmosphere.

"Drake Squadron, this is Kidriff Primary Control. Please disengage pursuit of official government forces. This is an internal matter."

"Kay Pee See, this is Drake One. We've been hoping to evaluate your pilots. Rumor rates them pretty high. Shall I go back and tell the admiral that you wouldn't let us?"

"That's affirmative, Drake One. Break off pursuit now or we'll have to view your action as a hostile one. We'll apologize very sweetly to the admiral and your survivors."

Kell cursed. Not every aspect of Kidriff security was sloppy. He put all discretionary power to thrust and gained even faster on the *Falsehood*'s pursuers.

JUST AS THE AIR thinned to the point that the stars shone with brilliant, unblinking clarity, the first laser blast sizzled past the Corellian freighter's port side. "A long-distance shot," Wedge said.

Tycho's voice came back, "Easy to hit a flying bathtub like the one you're driving even with a long-distance shot. Permission to engage?"

"Not yet. Wait until it gets complicated." Wedge spared a moment to look at his sensors. The squadron of TIEs was only a kilometer back. Kell's Drakes were only half a klick behind them and closing fast. And a new signal was on the board—a second full squad of TIEs from the ground base. It was going to get complicated soon.

Moments later, a shot hit the rear shields. On the sensors, Wedge saw two wingpairs of TIE fighters peel off and curve around toward Kell's group. "That's it," Wedge said. "Rogue Two, you are free to engage. Chewie, you have the controls." He unbelted and moved aft.

"Sir?" said Squeaky. "You're not leaving this disagreeable ball of hair in charge of a whole ship? Sir?"

Wedge clambered into the upper gunport turret and powered up. His targeting grid immediately lit up with glows, most of them red—enemies. Two were out ahead of the others, firing as they came, probably aiming to overtake the freighter, turn, and fire from ahead, forcing Chewbacca to adjust the ship's shields on a constant basis.

The first of the lead TIE fighters shot past, firing; a laser hit rocked the ship. Wedge let that one go, but timed its passage, then sent his gun turret swinging in its wake even before the second TIE reached him. That TIE flashed through his crosshairs and he fired.

The TIE erupted in a ball of expanding gases. And abruptly Rogue Two was darting out from beneath the freighter, tucking into the lead TIE fighter's wake, firing quad-linked lasers. The TIE pilot, having lost sight of the X-wing on his sensor board, having assumed he was too far laterally for the *Falsehood*'s guns to track him, wasn't maneuvering. Tycho's lasers chewed through his port solar wing and he tumbled—an uncontrolled roll that, if he were not rescued soon, might never end.

Two down. Twenty-two to go. Wedge reset and waited.

"KEEP IT SLOW," Kell said, "and keep it sluggish until we break. Remember, we're supposed to be hyperspace-equipped, less maneuverable—they'll already have been told what they're facing." He sent his TIE interceptor into a comparatively gentle westward curve, drawing two of the fighters above into his wake, and was pleased to see Elassar mimicking his move. Janson and Shalla curved off eastward equally lazily.

His sensor system shrilled, indicating an enemy laser lock, and he shouted "Now!" and cut hard to starboard. A green laser blast illuminated space where he'd been just a moment before, and two TIE fighters followed the blast, caught off guard. They began their turn, but Kell continued his ferocious maneuver, feeling his chest compress as the interceptor's inertial compensator failed to keep up entirely with the g-forces he was generating.

His targets swung into view from the right side of his viewport. They, too, were now curving to starboard, but he'd caught them off guard, and had the advantage of a few seconds of controlled maneuvering. The leftmost of them jittered in his targeting brackets. He let it go—that was the easier target, and that was for his wingman. The second TIE now crossed into his targeting bracket and jittered, sign of a laser lock.

He fired. His green lasers bit into the TIE's fuselage where it glowed brightest.

Suddenly the TIE's engines glowed much brighter. Smoke and sparks emerged. The fighter banked to port and down, toward the planet's surface. As more and more sparks emerged, it looked like nothing so much as an artificial comet heading for its final resting place.

The second TIE was still intact. It continued looping around to starboard, cutting its maneuver more tightly than Kell could, and was now well out of his targeting brackets.

Then a barrage of lasers struck the fighter from Kell's left. The shots tore through its left solar wing array, turning the wing into a mess of shrapnel, then marching across to the fuselage. The fighter detonated, hurling speeder bike-sized pieces of itself in Kell's path. He juked around the closest of them and reswallowed his stomach.

Who'd fired that shot? He checked his sensors. "Drake Two? Where were you?"

"Sorry, Drake One." Elassar's voice was sheepish. "When you broke to starboard, I made a mistake and broke to port. I had to loop around to rejoin you."

Kell shuddered. His wingman had been gone for those long seconds, and his rear had been unprotected. He'd talk to Elassar about it later. "Nice shooting, Drake Two. Let's rejoin General Solo," he added for the benefit of the planetary listeners who would someday soon crack this set of broadcast encryptions.

"Yes, sir." Sensors showed Drake Two coming up in his wake, and Drake Three and Drake Four returning to the primary course with their targets now off the screen. But the second group of TIEs was much closer.

That trick, pretending to be heavily laden with hyperdrives, wouldn't work a second time, Kell knew. But it had helped even the odds. That was good enough for now.

ANOTHER TIE HAD fallen victim to Wedge's guns by the time the leader of the first TIE squadron got smart. The five remaining TIEs drifted out of the engagement zone and dropped back toward the intact squadron that was rapidly catching up.

Wedge deployed the Drakes behind him in two pairs and kept Tycho between them, giving him a five-pointed shield of fighters to his aft. They were well clear of the atmosphere now, outbound toward the planet's primary moon, but the remaining squad and a half of TIEs was gaining rapidly. "Chewie? How are we doing?"

He received a long set of rumbling commentary in reply.

"Squeaky?"

"He says, in his almost preverbal fashion, that the shields are holding, but the relays that permit adjustment of the shields are, as he puts it, 'twitchy.' He thinks some of them may fail if he continues shunting power between them."

"Wonderful. All right, Chewbacca, put them in their default settings. We go with fixed shields for now."

Another long-range shot struck the *Falsehood*, rocking the

freighter. Wedge heard mechanical crashes as something was jarred loose from a corridor housing. "Break and fire at will," he said, and saw his escort move out and prepare to engage the enemy again.

Then there was a sensor signal from ahead of the *Falsehood*—a big, complicated signal. And red lasers flashed from ahead, all around the freighter, into the ranks of the pursuing TIE fighters.

Chewbacca rumbled something.

"He knows that, you walking dirt trap. It's the Rogues and the Wraiths."

ON LARA'S SENSOR SCREEN, the cloud of TIE fighters suddenly became bigger, more diffuse, then resolved itself into seven wing-pairs and one trio of starfighters.

"Group, this is Rogue Nine." She could almost recognize Corran Horn's vocal characteristics in the comm-distorted words. "Remember not to fire on the interceptors. They're Wraiths, and they might cry. S-foils to attack position. Break by pairs and fire at will."

Face immediately rose relative to the plane of their flight, heading up and away from the centerline of the conflict to come. He also decelerated, dropping behind the rest of the group. Confused, Lara stayed tucked in behind his starboard. "Wraith One? Two. What's our tactic?"

Face was a moment in replying. "You'll see," he said.

The other Rogues and Wraiths fired, a column of red lasers that passed harmlessly around the *Falsehood* and her escort but with less delicacy through the oncoming TIEs. Lara saw one fighter ignite and blow apart.

But Face held his fire and so did she.

A moment later, she thought she understood. The screens of TIEs and X-wings crossed, with pairs of starfighters maneuvering wildly to get behind one another. A pair of X-wings shot out of the flurry of activity with a pair of TIEs in close pursuit. Face angled toward them and accelerated, diving opportunistically toward them, and opened fire. His shots caused the TIE fighter to spook and pull away from its prey, but Lara's laser fire was more accurate—her concentrated fire punched through the TIE fighter's top hatch. There was no explosion, but the thin atmosphere in the fighter vented and the starfighter went into straight-line flight, out and away from the engagement zone.

"Nice shooting, Wraith Two. Thanks." The comm unit identified the speaker as Ran Kether.

"Happy to oblige, Rogue Seven."

Surely Face would now dive into the main body of the fight. But he didn't. He circled around the periphery of the battle. Frowning, Lara followed. She knew her duty, even when she didn't understand it.

TYRIA WAS IN the flow of the moment. Even when she wasn't looking at her sensor board, she had a grasp, a comprehension she'd never really enjoyed before, of where the fighters around her were in relation to her and to one another. She knew what they intended. A moment before they maneuvered, she knew which way they would turn.

Three pairs of starfighters—Corran Horn and Ooryl Qyrgg in the lead, two Kidriff TIE fighters behind them, gaining to optimal distance for a shot, and behind them, Donos and Tyria, unable to gain on the lead Rogues.

Ooryl fell a little behind and Horn swung ahead and slightly below him. The maneuver gave Horn a split second of advantage, since his pursuers couldn't see the first signs of his next action. Suddenly he was behind Ooryl, losing ground to the TIEs so quickly that they overshot him. One TIE fighter, its pilot obviously experienced, banked to port. The other hung there in place for a moment, and Horn took his shot, a quad-linked laser barrage. Tyria couldn't tell where it hit the TIE; the enemy starfighter blew so suddenly that she wasn't able to register the impact.

Both Horn and Ooryl banked in the wake of the escaping TIE.

"How'd they do that?" Tyria asked, surprised. She hadn't felt the trick maneuver coming, hadn't predicted it. "That was too fast for them to have said anything."

"Experience," Donos said. "Less chatter, Wraith Four."

"Sorry."

"I'M HIT!" The voice was young, a little panicky. "Losing shield power. Smoke in my cockpit. Lasers indicate malfunction."

Lara checked her board. The transmission was from Rogue Eight, "Target" Nu, the Rodian. He was separated from his wingmate and had a pair of TIEs on his tail.

"I'm coming." That was his wingmate, Kether. "I'm—I'm hung up here."

"Rogue Eight, this is Wraith One." Face's voice. "Come to one-nine-four. I'll head in straight toward you and head-to-head your pursuit. You pair up with Wraith Two out here and stay clear of the engagement."

"Thanks, Wraith One." The blip that was Rogue Eight vectored toward her and Face. Face headed straight toward it, leaving Lara hanging out in the void.

She didn't object. She didn't ask for orders. She knew what was required of her.

But she wondered, and her confusion gradually turned to cold worry in her stomach.

SEVEN FIGHTERS OF the combined TIE pursuit force, including the one Face vaped on his head-to-head run into the center of the engagement zone, were destroyed before the pursuing squad leader ordered an evacuation. Donos decided that the man had to have been assuming the TIE fighter's greater speed and maneuverability would give him all the advantage he needed against a numerically superior mixed force. But against the Rogues and Wraiths, he was wrong.

The surviving TIEs fled planetward, doubtless to form up with yet another flight group and come once again after the Rogues and Wraiths. But this time they wouldn't catch up.

Donos responded to Wedge's order that the group form up on the *Millennium Falsehood*. But on his sensor board, Wraith One and Wraith Two maintained their distance, paralleling the main group's course a dozen kilometers out.

LARA COULD STILL hear a little high-pitched alarm in Rogue Eight's voice, but that situation seemed to be under control. "I'm getting regular power fluxes but no serious drops. I've had to shut down one starboard engine but I can limp in on three."

"Group, this is Leader. As soon as we have a little bit of moon horizon between us and the planet, the Drakes are going to separate and head on out to Rendezvous Point Beta. The rest of us will vector back into space the planetary sensors can scan, and will then make the jump to Rendezvous Point Alpha. Rogue Two, I want you to delay your jump thirty seconds to make sure all our damaged snubfighters make the transition to hyperspace."

"Leader, Two. Understood."

"Wraith One, Wraith Two, rejoin the group and prepare for jump."

Face's voice was next. "Leader, this is Wraith One. We need to jump from here and follow you in."

"Explain that, Wraith One."

"On a private channel, if you please, Leader."

The worry in Lara's stomach turned into fear. There were only so many reasons Face would refuse to let them return to the group. Most of them involved one or the other of them being a danger to the group, such as if one of their X-wings were threatening to blow up.

Face was protecting the group, or someone in the group. And Lara was certain she knew who. He was protecting Wedge. From her.

Face's voice was off the comm waves for a couple of minutes. Then he returned. "Wraith Two, have you double-checked your nav course?"

"No," she said. "You know, don't you, Face?" Her voice emerged as a choked whisper and she wondered if the comm unit would even pick it up.

"I know that you're Gara Petothel," he said. His voice was quieter, more gentle than she expected it to be.

She felt a snapping sensation in her chest, as though her breastbone had broken. And then there was the sensation of loss—of the sudden departure from her life of everything she considered important.

But it didn't feel quite the way she expected it to. Pain there was, certainly, but she also felt a sudden relief, an absence of the weight she'd been carrying around since first she decided she no longer wanted to serve Zsinj, since she decided that her alliance with the Wraiths was fact, not fiction.

Like an animal in a hunter's steel-jaw trap, she'd finally lost that part of her the trap held. The pain was indescribable. But there was freedom as well. And she knew that she didn't need to cry anymore.

"I never betrayed you," Lara said. She was surprised at how calm her voice sounded.

"I'm glad."

"I tried so hard just to be Lara. But they wouldn't let me. The whole universe wouldn't let me."

"Lara, I'm sorry," Face said. "I have to place you under

arrest pending investigation of this whole mess. Power your weapons systems down. Set your S-foils to cruise position. Don't attempt any sudden maneuvers."

"Understood, sir. I'm complying with your orders."

FACE FELT SICK to his stomach. He had wished, futilely, that he'd been wrong. But Lara had confirmed it.

A sudden fear struck him. He had been on a private communications channel with Lara, had switched to squadron channel to handle the Target Nu situation and then to respond to Wedge's order that he move back to the formation, had switched to a private channel for his quick talk with Wedge—and then had gone back to his private channel with Lara. Hadn't he?

He looked at his comm board. He was now set to squad frequency. He'd spoken last to Lara on an open channel.

His stomach suddenly got worse.

DONOS HEARD THE WORDS but didn't understand them. "I know that you're Gara Petothel." He knew that the name Gara Petothel meant something to him but he still couldn't force his mind around the meaning of those words.

Ah, that was it. Naval officer Chyan Mezzine, a communications and intelligence specialist, had betrayed the New Republic by sending critical information to Admiral Apwar Trigit, a minion of Zsinj. Some of that information was what Trigit used to annihilate Talon Squadron—the X-wing unit commanded by Donos. Only he had survived. Then, later, the New Republic had put out a bulletin on her, indicating that her real name was Gara Petothel, that she was actually a deep-cover agent for Imperial Intelligence. Later, she had been declared dead, another victim of the destruction of Trigit's Star Destroyer, *Implacable*.

But Lara Notsil *was* Gara Petothel.

Lara Notsil had destroyed his command. Had killed eleven pilots he had bound together.

Suddenly he was back there, in the smoky skies above the volcanoes of Gravan Seven, as ally after ally was ripped from the sky by Trigit's pilots and their ambush. Again he felt the pain of their deaths. It was a selfish pain, part loss, part realization that he had failed them, part understanding that his life had changed in a way he could never set right.

The howl that escaped him was no animal noise. It was the wail of a man who'd just lost everything dear to him . . . and who suddenly had the destroyer of his happiness in his sights.

IN SPITE OF comm distortion, the howl made Face's skin crawl. He knew who it had to be, and a glance at his sensor board showed Wraith Three turning away from his course to the rendezvous point on an intercept course with Face and Lara.

Wedge's voice did not sound amused. "Wraith Three, this is Leader. Return to your original heading."

Donos did not deviate from his new course.

Face said, "Wraith Two, come to three-three-two and accelerate to full speed." He himself did as he'd ordered, turning away from Donos and running before him. Lara stayed with him.

IT'S HAPPENING AGAIN.

The words were a wail of anguish inside Tyria's mind.

Once again a fellow pilot was making an assault on a friendly target.

She turned in Donos's wake and returned her S-foils to attack position.

Once again she had to put a fellow pilot in her weapon sights.

But this time her target was not just an ally but a friend. A squadmate. "Myn," she said, "please don't do this."

WRAITH THREE CAME on inexorably but could not gain on Face's and Lara's X-wings. But he could fire a proton torpedo, which would cross the distance between them in seconds and could achieve a lock on Lara.

Face neatly sideslipped his X-wing behind Lara's. "Wraith Three, hold your fire. If you fire, I'm your primary target."

"Wraith Three, power down or I'll be forced to fire." The words were being choked out, the voice identifiable as Tyria's.

"Wraith Four, this is Wraith One. Do not fire, whatever happens. This is not the same as the Jussafet situation. Acknowledge."

"Acknowledged, sir."

Lara, her voice raspy with pain, said, "Maybe you ought to let him shoot me, sir. Get out of the way."

"Shut up, Two."

Face's sensor board howled, a new noise—the distinctive wail signifying a proton-torpedo launch. Donos had fired.

"Wraith Three, detonate your torp *now*." Face made no effort to keep alarm out of his voice; that would have required concentration. He maintained his position immediately behind Lara's X-wing and put all available power to his rear shields. He kept his free hand on his ejection lever. "Three, blow the torp, I'm your target." From the moment of launch he had only a few seconds before the torpedo hit, and most of that time was already gone. "Detonate, dammit!"

The universe behind Face filled with bright blue fire. His stern shuddered as though he'd been rammed and his cockpit was suddenly filled with smoke, the howl of damage alert sirens, Vape's mechanical shrieks of dismay, and the rumble and tremble of failing vehicle systems.

But he was still alive. Either the proton torpedo had detonated at the very outer edges of his rear shields, or Donos had detonated it prematurely—barely prematurely.

Bitter anger swelled within him. "Congratulations, Three," he said. "I may be your newest kill."

DONOS JERKED UPRIGHT in his cockpit, confusion clearing from his mind like smoke sucked into hard vacuum. On his sensor screen, Wraith One was maneuvering erratically as Two continued on the straight-line course she'd been assigned. "Face—One. I'm sorry—" He tried to regain control of his voice, his thoughts. "Hold tight. I'm coming in for a flyover. I'll check external damage."

His astromech, Clink, shrieked at him and the shrill tone of an enemy targeting lock assailed his ears. That, and Tycho's voice, hard and cold as Donos had ever heard it. "Abort that maneuver, Wraith Three."

"But Captain, I'm closest, I have to see—"

"Deviate from your current course and I will blow you out of space." There was no questioning the deadly seriousness of Tycho's tone. "Wraith Four, do a flyby on Wraith One and report signs of damage. Wraith One, do you copy?"

Face's voice was nearly as cold as Tycho's, but his words were harder to understand, drowned by the cockpit alarms from his damaged snubfighter. "I read, Rogue Two. My fighter's holding together for the moment."

"Good. Wraith Two, swing back around and form up with the group."

There was a perceptible delay. Then Lara's voice came back, strained, but not racked with pain as it had been moments ago. "I don't think so, Rogue Two."

"That's an order, Wraith Two, a direct order."

"I've already surrendered once," she said, "and have subsequently been fired on by an officer of this group. I no longer have any faith that I'll survive long enough to meet a court-martial."

"Wraith Two, this is Rogue Leader. You know you'll make it now. The situation is under control."

It was true; Donos was maintaining straight-line flight under Tycho's guns. He wasn't sure he was capable of doing anything but following orders. It wasn't fear of death at Tycho's hands that kept him in line—it was shock at what he was certain he'd just done.

"What I know is that you don't believe me," Lara said. "You don't believe that I'm a loyal Wraith. You don't believe that I've never done anything to compromise this unit."

Wedge abandoned the formality of call numbers. "Lara, if what you're saying is the truth, the court will bear you out. I can confidently state that Nawara Ven will take your case. He's the best."

"But that's it for me with the Wraiths. I'll never be able to fly with you again. I'll never be able to help you. To get you out of a jam. I can never undo what I've done. Never."

"You're probably right, Lara. That's the way it is. Now come around."

When her voice returned, it was not Wedge she addressed. "Wraith One? Can you hear me?"

Face's voice was still strong, and this time was not accompanied by alarms—he'd obviously taken steps to quiet the sirens in his cockpit. "I read you, Two."

"I want you to understand something. I don't care if you understand it now. I want you to understand it later. I have never betrayed the Wraiths. I will never, ever betray the Wraiths. Do you read me?"

"I . . . hear what you say."

A moment later, she said, "Myn?"

Donos jolted. He opened his mouth to answer, but he

didn't know whom he'd be talking to. Lara, the woman he'd wanted to come to love, or Gara, the woman he'd sworn—and now attempted—to kill.

"Myn?"

He sat there, paralyzed by indecision, and did not answer.

Lara's X-wing leaped out of sight and off the sensors as it made the jump into hyperspace.

IN THE ROGUE and Wraith squadrons' landing bay, Donos climbed down out of his cockpit. His back was so straight it hurt. He needed that pain. He needed the constant reminder that he had to get himself back under control.

He'd lost control. He'd lost Lara. He'd lost everything.

Wedge waited for him at the foot of the ladder. Donos turned to face him and took a step back without intending to. Wedge's body was as still as if carved from ice, but there was nothing cold about his eyes. They were full of anger, more intense anger than Donos had ever seen in them.

"One reason," Wedge said. "I'd like to hear *one reason* why I shouldn't ship you off to Coruscant and put you up on charges of gross insubordination."

Donos stood at attention, every muscle he was aware of locked into place. He kept his gaze fixed above Wedge's head and took a deep breath as he got his thoughts in order. "Logically speaking, I should not be tried for insubordination, sir, because insubordination is generally a deliberate act. I do not believe I was in my right mind when I fired upon Flight Officer Notsil. I can't even remember doing that." He couldn't bring himself to refer to her as Gara Petothel, even in his own mind. His hard-won control might slip again.

"Temporary insanity?" The tone of Wedge's voice suggested the frown Donos could see only in his peripheral vision. "That sounds like a dodge to me, Lieutenant."

"I'm not sure it's temporary, Commander." Donos couldn't

keep the dejection out of his own voice. "You and Face, Captain Loran I mean, are aware of my . . . earlier difficulty."

"Difficulty" was something of an understatement. Weeks after the destruction of Talon Squadron, when Donos's R2 unit, Shiner, the only other survivor of the Gravan mission, had been destroyed, Donos had lapsed into a near-catatonic state. Only the intervention of Kell, Tyria, and Falynn Sandskimmer—herself now dead for many weeks—had brought him out of that withdrawal. "I submit," Donos continued, "that I was not in my right mind when I fired on her, and I no longer have any confidence that I'm in my right mind at other times. With respect, sir, I tender the resignation of my commission and of my place in Wraith Squadron."

Wedge didn't answer immediately. Donos could see the top of his head as the commander looked right and left, communicating with the other senior officers by what might have been a combination of shared experience and telepathy.

"I'll consider your request," Wedge said, "while you consider a question I may oblige you to answer at some later time. If we encounter Lara Notsil in the future, in a combat situation, which of the Wraiths would you prefer to vape her in your place?"

The question was like a blade of ice thrust straight into Donos's gut. He opened his mouth to respond, but Wedge said, "Quiet. I don't require your answer yet. Dismissed."

Donos turned away, past the eyes of the Rogues and his fellow Wraiths.

He saw anger in some of them, confusion in others. A sort of sick pain in Tyria's. What he'd almost made her do—kill a second fellow pilot.

She'd never forgive him.

It didn't matter much. He'd never forgive himself.

Behind him, he heard Wedge directing his anger against another target. "Captain Loran. You and I need to talk. My office. Right now."

———

LARA'S FIRST JUMP had just taken her clear of the Kidriff system. Her second, initiated after she'd had a chance to consult her astromech Tonin's memory, would take a while to complete. It would bring her back to the Halmad system, where she and the other Wraiths had once pretended to be a band of pirates called the Hawk-bats.

In abandoned Hawk-bat Station, she'd be able to refuel, to initiate a new communication, to make some modifications to Tonin.

But for now, she was left with her thoughts.

Her one thought.

Lara Notsil is dead.

Lara had been a temporary identity. Something to keep her out of the hands of the New Republic while she figured out a way to persuade the warlord Zsinj to employ her. Then it had been a convenience, a means to infiltrate the Wraiths in order to improve her worth in Zsinj's eyes. Then, when she'd come to realize the depths to which her early teaching had programmed her to accept Imperial ideas of rule as infallible, when she'd realized that she could never serve Zsinj or the Empire again, Lara Notsil had become a gradually eroding shield between her and the day the Wraiths would turn against her.

That day had come. Lara Notsil was no more.

Who was she, then? Not Gara Petothel. That was the name she'd been born under, but Gara had been such an unhappy creature, a servant of Imperial Intelligence, a young woman with no goals of her own. With no future.

No one, no family member or friend, who'd known her under that name still lived. So Gara Petothel was dead, too.

But Kirney Slane—an identity she'd worn for a few weeks when she learned many of the techniques of the intelligence agent. Kirney was nothing but a young woman wandering through the wealthy-officer stratum of Imperial culture on Coruscant. She'd attended dances, flirted with officer candidates, shopped.

She had been worthless. But she had been happy.

Lara wondered if she could take that long-abandoned identity and give her some worth. And even, perhaps, retain some of her naive cheer, her certainty that life was worth living.

Gara Petothel is dead. Lara Notsil is dead. I will answer to those names. But they are no longer mine.

I am Kirney Slane.

I have no life yet.

I will make one, or die in the attempt.

She thought about Donos. He, too, had attempted to kill Gara, with at least as much reason as she had.

He'd been right. They were more alike than she had realized.

"YOU DON'T THINK," Wedge said, "it could have waited until we returned to *Mon Remonda.*"

"No, sir," Face said.

"She had plenty of opportunities to vape me or any of the rest of us prior to today. That ranks her pretty low as a threat."

"With all due respect, sir, I thought about that. If we think that way, we have to presume that Lara was not working for Zsinj or the Empire. Because if she was an agent, she could have been following her employer's plan or schedule. I mean, Galey the cook also had plenty of opportunities to stick a vibroblade in you or the general. So, if we follow your logic, the fact that he didn't attack someone between the day *Mon Remonda* returned to space and the day he killed Doctor

Gast means he was trustworthy all those days." He offered Wedge an expression of regret. "Sir, I did what I thought was right for the unit."

"What does your gut tell you?"

Face looked away for a long moment, then returned his attention to Wedge. "My gut says she was telling the truth. That she was a loyal Wraith."

"But you didn't believe your gut instinct."

"Yes, sir, I did. But I didn't rely on it. If I had, and I'd been wrong, whatever she did would have been my fault."

Wedge nodded. "All right. Face, off the record, I think you fouled up, and this situation could have been resolved in a less catastrophic fashion if you hadn't."

Face nodded, his expression glum.

"But there's nothing wrong with your logic. It wasn't entirely a bad call. Just one made on incomplete data. I need you to understand that an officer who can't rely on his own gut instinct is an officer who shouldn't be commanding others."

Face considered that. "I imagine you're right, sir."

"So work on it. Now get back to your unit and see if you can patch them up emotionally."

Face had been gone only a moment when someone knocked.

Wedge shook his head. This was not going to be a good afternoon. "Come in."

Donos entered his office and stood at attention.

Wedge let him remain that way. It had been a very few months ago that Donos had entered one of his offices for the very first time, remaining stiffly at attention just like this. Now, as then, the pilot's features were expressionless; his gaze was carefully fixed on the wall over Wedge's head.

"Yes?" Wedge said.

"After due reflection, I have concluded that my earlier intention was the correct one. I have come to formally resign my commission. It's my only possible course of action."

Wedge waited, but Donos didn't elaborate. "Why?"

"I have performed acts that are an embarrassment to this unit and that will inevitably result in the end of my flying career. I feel that it is best to end it myself, without further inconvenience to you or to the unit."

Wedge regarded him steadily. Yes, this was just like the first time, with Donos's true thoughts hidden behind the mask of his face, kept rigidly at bay by his personal discipline. And his words had been so precise. "I'm sorry," Wedge said, "I didn't catch all of your last statement. 'To end it myself—'"

"Without further inconvenience to you or to the unit. Sir."

Wedge sighed. He rose, unfastened his right boot, drew it off, and stood it upright on his desktop. "You, too, Donos. Your right boot. Put it there."

Confusion struggled with the imperturbability on Donos's face. "Sir, I don't understand."

"Do it."

When Donos complied, setting his boot beside Wedge's, the commander sat, putting his feet up on the desk. "Lieutenant, sit down. Put your feet up. That's an order."

They sat, two officers each with one boot off, their feet up on the desk, for long moments of silence. Finally Donos said, "Sir, I don't think you're taking my request seriously."

"You'd be surprised at how seriously I'm taking it. Now, start that little speech again, Lieutenant. Come on, you know it. It goes, 'I have performed acts that are an embarrassment to this unit . . .'"

"You're mocking me."

"No, I'm testing a theory. I think that in this ridiculous pose, you won't be able to convincingly recite the speech you have so laboriously written for yourself.

"Let me guess," Wedge continued, and began counting off

items on his fingers. "In your resignation speech, you take full responsibility for your actions. You throw yourself into the path of the oncoming investigation so that the unit will not suffer. You apologize eloquently. And with your words, you anaesthetize yourself so you don't have to feel anything when your fellow pilots look at you or when your superior officers tell you what they think of you."

Donos's face flushed. He rose. "I didn't come here for you to make fun of me—"

"Sit!" Wedge made a bellow of the word, and Donos flinched. "And get your feet back on top of the desk. Right now."

Donos complied. His face did not fade to a normal color.

"That's better. Now, let's have it without the speech. In not just your own words but your real voice. Start."

Donos looked as though he were silently practicing swear words. Then he said, "I'm here to resign my commission in Starfighter Command."

"Because you want to, or because you feel you ought to?"

"Because it's better to punch out before the oncoming missile hits you."

"Well, that's an ironic turn of phrase, in light of today's events. Who is the incoming missile?"

"Whatever board investigates the events at Kidriff Five. And, if I may say so, sir, you."

"I'm going to drum you out of Starfighter Command?"

"Yes, sir. You'll have to."

"I do not invite you to speak for me, Lieutenant. But let's assume that I don't have to do this, that the investigating board will do it. Why will they do it?"

"Because I deliberately shot at a fellow pilot, or a surrendering enemy, or whatever she was—" Donos's voice was suddenly hoarse "—in the face of a superior's orders not to do so."

"When we landed, you said that you didn't remember

having fired. You didn't remember anything about the critical seconds in which you turned toward your target and shot off a proton torpedo. Do you remember those events now?"

"No, sir."

"So how do you know you fired deliberately?"

Donos frowned. "I—I—Can I put my feet down? I feel silly."

"You may not. You're supposed to feel silly. It makes it much harder to baffle me with elegantly designed speeches. What you *may* do is take your time in answering."

Donos did. He took several long breaths and his face returned to a normal color. Finally, he said, "My assumption that I fired deliberately comes because such an act is completely in keeping with my mental state whenever I thought about what I'd do if I ever had the betrayer of Talon Squadron under my guns."

"Very good. That's a real answer. Now, tell me, based on your *memories,* not what's consistent with your feelings prior to this event: Did you deliberately fire on Lara Notsil?"

"I don't know."

"Did you deliberately disobey the orders of a superior officer?"

"I don't know."

"Very well. I'm going to put the incident down as 'accidental discharge of a weapons system' for the time being. That's the way it goes in the record until an investigation determines otherwise."

"And when the investigation determines otherwise, I go through a court-martial."

"Possibly. But they might not determine otherwise. We may never know. And if they're obliged to accept the 'accidental discharge' theory because nothing else can be determined, your career will probably survive it. There will come a time, in the far future, when a peacetime Starfighter Command has too many pilots, and a blemish much less significant than this one will torpedo a career . . . but that'll be a long time in coming." Wedge gave Donos a frank and evaluative stare, one he knew to be intimidating. "Donos, do you know what I think happened?"

"No, sir."

"I think that when you realized that Notsil had been partially or completely responsible for the deaths of your fellow Talon Squadron pilots, you lost all control and tried to kill her, in spite of danger to your fellow pilots and in spite of orders from a superior officer."

Donos's face registered shock. "That's what I've been trying to tell you. That's what I've been trying to accept responsibility for."

Wedge shook his head. "You haven't been trying to accept responsibility. You've been trying to avoid it. Responsibility involves owning up to what you've done wrong and trying to make up for it."

"I . . . don't understand. Once again, I have no idea what you're saying."

"Why did you lose control? More specifically, why were no members of your squadron aware that you might lose control?"

"Obviously, there's something still wrong in my head."

"And obviously, you've discussed this problem with the medics."

"No, sir."

"You've discussed it with your wingmate."

"No, sir."

"Whom have you discussed it with in order to improve the situation?"

Donos looked away, struggling to keep distress off his face. "No one, sir."

"Donos, *that's* the responsibility you've dodged. Now, either you're fit to fly or you're not. How do we find out?"

"I guess I talk to the medics."

"Talk to one of your squadmates first. One or more of them. Venting whatever pressure is in you is easier to survive if it's done in atmosphere rather than in vacuum. And then talk to the medics."

Donos didn't meet his gaze, but nodded.

"You're off the active flying roster until someone can tell me whether you're fit to fly. And you're not the person to tell me."

Finally Donos looked at him and nodded again. "Understood, sir."

"You did one thing right today, Donos. You probably don't even know it. Your flight recorder and your astromech both indicate that you detonated your torpedo before it hit Captain Loran."

"I don't remember that, either."

"But it's the one reason that stands between you and my instant acceptance of your resignation. Dismissed."

Donos took his feet from the desk. "Before I go, may I ask something?"

"Go ahead."

"In the bay, you asked me something. You asked if we met Lara again, which Wraith I'd want to kill her instead of me. I still don't understand why you asked. What the question even means."

"Well, answer the question. Then I'll explain why I asked."

"I'm not sure I *can*. I don't want to kill her, not anymore. I don't want her to be dead. I'm not even sure I want her punished. She was an enemy when she gave Admiral Trigit the data on my squadron, then she became something that wasn't an enemy." His shrug suggested helplessness. "I don't know *what* I want."

"That's what I thought. One reason I asked was to gauge your reaction to the thought of somebody killing Lara. You didn't like that idea. And I also asked so you'd think about this: If we run up against her in an adversarial situation, and—in the faint likelihood that you'll be piloting by that time—you lose control again and assault her, you may provoke her into fighting back. Correct?"

"Yes, sir."

"If your squadmates see you having trouble with an enemy, they may come in to help you. Correct?"

"Yes, sir."

"Which puts them in the position of possibly having to kill her. Which also puts her in the position of possibly having to kill one of them. The other half of that question was, which of your squadmates are you willing to sacrifice?"

"None, sir."

"Then get your head fixed. Or I *will* accept your resignation."

Donos rose and saluted. The expression on his face was a glum one. But, Wedge reflected, at least it was an expression.

When Donos and his boot were gone, Wedge let out a sigh and tried to relax. He'd had too many years of command not to have some experience at taking the attention and thoughts of a pilot and redirecting them, but it was still an effort, one that filled his gut with acid.

Donos was on the edge. Wedge recognized that. One step the wrong way and he'd be lost as a pilot, too erratic and undisciplined to be trustworthy.

But he hadn't quite taken that step, and if Wedge could keep him from taking it, he'd save the New Republic the staggering number of credits that had been spent on Donos's pilot training. He might even save a man whose warlike skills and impulses would not translate well to civilian life.

There was another rap at the door.

"Come."

Wes Janson strolled in, datapad in hand, and stopped short. He stared at Wedge's bootless foot. He said, "Should I ask?"

"Not unless you'd like me to decide on a new place for my boot to go."

11

S HE WAS DRIFTING, in pain, and knew she did not want to awaken. But something would not let her sleep. Not just the pain in her back. She opened her eyes.

Pink, she was floating in a sea of pink. No, nothing so poetic—she was suspended within a bacta tank, and the pain she felt suggested she was going to be here for some time to come. But a female technician with a perky smile was outside, gesturing for her to rise to the top, so she gave a few feeble kicks and floated up through the cloying liquid.

When she broke the surface, a hand, a male hand, reached down to help disengage the breather unit from her face. When her vision cleared, she recognized the individual leaning across the top of the bacta tank, reaching in to assist her: it was that Twi'lek lawyer, Nawara Ven.

"Doctor Gast," he said, "I have an offer for you. One half a million credits. Amnesty for all crimes to which you provide confession and full details. And a new identity—quite easy to manage, as you are already officially dead; only a couple of medics and three officers know you're still alive. But this offer is only valid if you can tell us, among other things, the biological signs and markers that indicate when someone has been subjected to Zsinj's brainwashing techniques."

Gast let a slow smile spread across her features. "My, you *have* been doing your research."

"WE'LL KEEP TODAY's meeting short," Wedge said. He looked out over his audience of pilots, trying to gauge their mood.

They were quiet. Few wisecracks. Little banter. They were even refraining from badgering Elassar Targon. A bad sign; morale was low.

"A recent attempt by a Sullustan pilot to crash a luxury liner onto Coruscant was thwarted by a fellow Sullustan officer. An attempt, also on Coruscant, by a Bothan civil services employee to cause an explosion at a power center was thwarted by his supervisor. Though, officially, both incidents were prevented by fellow workers, unofficially, they were prevented by New Republic Intelligence—who were following the blueprint we sent them for Zsinj's operations. General Cracken sends his personal congratulations to the members of Wraith Squadron and Rogue Squadron who participated in our prediction sessions. Yes, Face?"

"Does this mean that the order keeping the Twi'lek crewmen off active duty is rescinded?"

"No. Officially, it's not." He nodded toward Dia Passik. "Unofficially, it is, pending an upcoming vote by the Provisional Council. Dia, you're back on duty."

"That's not good enough," Face said.

"I know," Wedge said. "Zsinj has still wounded the New Republic. We're going to have to bear up under it until the wounds close, and be happy that we prevented similar measures from being handed down against Sullustans and Bothans. But, Dia, it's up to you. Do you want to fly?"

"I'll fly," she said. "I want my shot at Zsinj."

"Good, because we have a heavy schedule ahead of us." Wedge activated the holoprojector. The image of a broad belt of stars appeared beside him, with numerous points of light blinking within it. "We're going to be bouncing in and out of Zsinj-controlled space, hitting his territories in some places, showing up in our ersatz *Millennium Falcon* in others. We'll also be moving through the borders between New Republic territory and Zsinj's, performing some routine assaults. Horn?"

The Rogue pilot lowered his hand. "Sir, Lara Notsil isn't just gone, she has to have defected. She really has nowhere to go but the Empire or Zsinj, and that's a fifty percent chance that the *Falsehood* scheme has been compromised."

"That's a very good point. It all boils down to the question of whether or not we believe her last transmissions. That she still considers herself a loyal Wraith. That she never betrayed us. Do you believe her?"

"No," Horn said. "She may have believed what she was saying. But after talking to some of the Wraiths about her behavior, reviewing her conduct before Kidriff Five, I tend to think she's a situational conformist with a few bolts loose in her skull. If she ends up in Zsinj's hands, she'll probably end up being a loyal officer of Zsinj's."

"That's a reasonable interpretation," Wedge said. "Don't think I haven't considered it. But I don't believe it. I think that the *Falsehood* plan will remain secure, just as the Hawk-bats plan did. However, since I'll be staking my life on this conclusion, and those of my pilots, I'll accept, without prejudice, any request for transfer any of you has to offer me. Make them through routine channels after this briefing.

"More good news. We are now in the possession of information about the blood markers that indicate Zsinj brainwashing in a variety of humanoid species. All members of this task force, from General Solo to the most junior civilian crewmen, will be tested, and anyone returning from a shore leave or unmonitored departure from the fleet will be retested. We will not face the tragedy of Tal'dira and Nuro Tualin a second time." He saw some expressions brighten.

"All right. Among our new weapons is a lot of data about the way Zsinj moves into a system currently in enemy hands and acquires control of businesses there." That had been another benefit of the first interview with Dr. Gast; her uncle

had helped him acquire his majority share in Binring Biomedical on Saffalore, and had told her of the precise techniques he had used. "On Zsinj-held worlds, we'll be making
strikes against the businesses that have to be providing him
with the greatest amounts of money or necessary matériel,
and we'll be escorting more appearances by the *Millennium
Falsehood*—both to lure him into an attack on General Solo
and, we hope, to make him paranoid about treason on worlds
he holds."

There was more to it than that, details Wedge couldn't
give his pilots. There were no Imperial-held worlds on the
task force's hit list, because General Solo was forwarding to
Admiral Teren Rogriss that same information about Zsinj's
business dealings. New Republic Intelligence would be ferret-
ing out Zsinj-held businesses in New Republic territories,
hoping to use some to lure Zsinj into a trap, cutting off Zsinj's
precious pipelines of money and matériel from others . . . and
Imperial Intelligence would be doing exactly the same thing
in Imperial-controlled territories.

General Solo and Admiral Rogriss, senior officers of two
enemy governments making agreements that would be easy
to interpret as treasonous . . . Wedge had to shake his head
over that. It took a menace like Zsinj to make temporary allies of two men who would otherwise be bitter opponents.

"So. Mission One." He shifted the holoprojector image to
a single solar system, that of a red gas giant. "This is the Bels-
muth system in Zsinj-controlled space. On the second planet
in the system is what used to be one of the Empire's finest
technical universities. Now it's an academy for Zsinj's pilots
and officers. Two days from now, it's going to be a series of
craters. Rogue Squadron will escort Nova Squadron in from
north of the facility . . ."

———

"LIEUTENANT PETOTHEL. Delighted to meet you."

At the foot of the ladder to her X-wing cockpit, Lara shucked her helmet and turned to face the speaker. The man advancing toward Lara was tall and lean, with the cruelest features she'd ever seen on a human being. The nails on the hand he offered gleamed like mirrors. She suspected that they were as sharp as a vibroblade.

She put on a broad smile that masked the sudden churning in her stomach. "I recognize your voice. General Melvar?" She took his hand.

"Correct. Welcome to *Iron Fist*. And thank you for dressing for the occasion."

Lara smiled. She'd left her New Republic flight suit at Hawk-bat Base and was now dressed in a TIE fighter's black jumpsuit, though it was adorned with the standard X-wing flight gear. "I can't tell you how happy I am to be here at last."

Melvar's gesture took in her X-wing and her astromech, which was now being extracted from its berth by a hangar electromagnet. "Are you making a presentation to us of this vehicle?"

"No." She laughed. "This Rebel starfighter and its astromech are all the property I have in the galaxy. If the warlord doesn't choose to employ me, I'll need them to continue on. To find someplace to call home."

"Oh, I think the least you can count on is a medium-term civilian contract. You're far more likely to receive an officer's posting on *Iron Fist*. But let's find out." Melvar led Lara out of the hangar, which otherwise was occupied by Imperial-style vehicles and personnel. From the number of TIE interceptors and *Lambda*-class shuttles, she suspected that this was the senior officers' hangar.

She was sure of it a minute later—its proximity to Zsinj's personal office made it a certainty. She was led into the presence of the warlord like an honored guest. Zsinj actually rose as she entered the office, giving her a little formal bow. "Gara Petothel. So happy to meet you at last."

"You're the warlord," she said, keeping her voice pert. "I won't try to compete with you in degrees of happiness."

Zsinj's smile broadened. "Very good. She gives me my due, yet steals it back by making her presence the one that induces more happiness. Did you see that, General?"

"I saw." The general hovered, standing a meter behind Lara's chair, to the left. She forced herself to stay relaxed. She couldn't let him know how tense his presence made her.

"Lieutenant Petothel—may I call you Gara, at least until we have questions of your employment settled?"

"Please do."

"Gara, we must know." The general's mobile features took on an expression of sympathy, of worry. "We dispatched a team to make arrangements for your employ, and possibly your extraction, to Aldivy. We received word from their contacts several days later that our agents had been found—or, rather, their bodies, badly decomposed. What happened?"

Lara offered a little sigh of vexation. "I traveled to Aldivy in the company of an officer of Wraith Squadron. I'd intended to make an offering of him and his X-wing to the contact team. He was the final member of Talon Squadron, which I helped Admiral Trigit destroy. I thought he was one lingering detail I ought to deal with. But what I didn't know until later is that the idiot had fallen in love with me. He was supposed to stay with the X-wings; instead, he followed me. Well, in my opening negotiations with your captain, my brother— that is, the real Lara Notsil's brother—got testy, drew a blaster, just a show of intimidation . . . and Lieutenant Donos fired upon him, killing him. Then he finished up by killing your captain. I had to cover up my tracks after that, not attempt any further communications with you for a while, as I was under some scrutiny during the review."

Zsinj nodded. "But, obviously, you came away clean."

"Oh, yes. For a while. Unfortunately, on Coruscant, one of the Wraiths stumbled across some information on my mother, who'd been with Imperial Intelligence. He noticed a resemblance, did some research . . . and then confronted me during a mission. With my cover blown, with it now impossible for me to uncover any more information to offer you, I fled."

"How did you manage to contact us?"

Though Zsinj's expression was open, innocent, Lara knew he had to be aware of every fact of the story. Still, she was playing his game by his rules. "When my so-called brother contacted me initially, he mentioned a company that might want to employ me—that is, Lara, his real sister. After I was forced to flee *Mon Remonda*, I decided to look into that firm, in case it was a front for your operations. And it was, one you'd set up only a couple of weeks prior to the first contact I received."

"Well, excellent." Zsinj reviewed a screen full of data on his terminal, data Lara could not see. "I am, unfortunately, too pressed for time to give you all the attention I should like, so let's jump straight into the dogfight, shall we? I can offer you a commission at the rank of naval lieutenant. You'd be an analyst aboard *Iron Fist*. While you go through your first few weeks of orientation, we'd like to pry from you every bit of knowledge you can give us on *Mon Remonda*, General Solo, Commander Antilles, and Antilles's squadrons. Does that suit you?"

Lara made her voice a purr. "It suits me very well. May I keep my X-wing and R2?"

Zsinj's face registered mild surprise. "Why would you want to? We can give you something far better."

"Well, they're souvenirs. Of my victory over a rather vehement idiot named Atton Repness. They used to belong to him."

Zsinj exchanged a blank look with Melvar, then shrugged. "Of course. We have a deal, then? Excellent. Welcome to *Iron Fist*, Lieutenant Petothel."

Lara shot to her feet, schooling her features to absolute blankness, and saluted.

Zsinj looked startled for a moment, then chuckled. "I admire the way you switch gears, Lieutenant. You're off duty until we come up with an itinerary for you. One of those pasty-faced ensigns out there will take you to your new quarters and act as your guide for your first few days. Wander as you will. And welcome." At last, he returned her salute.

"Thank you, sir." With military precision, she spun on her heel and exited the office.

THE "PASTY-FACED ENSIGN" awaiting her outside was anything but. Tall, dark-haired, and solemn, he had the hard look of a front-line soldier who'd received a field promotion. He identified himself as Ensign Gatterweld and led her first back to the hangar where her X-wing waited—so that she might pick up her R2 unit, Tonin—and then to her quarters. He spoke little.

It was a long walk, and the finality of what she'd done finally hit Lara.

She was surrounded by countless tons of machinery whose sole purpose was to rain death down on people she had ultimately chosen to protect.

Except for one R2 unit, she was alone, a secret enemy of those who now employed her, a public enemy of those to whom she desperately wanted to return.

She saw a trapezoidal little utility droid zipping along the hall, steering like a frightened animal out of the path of officers walking along the corridor, and imagined herself the human equivalent of such a machine—so small and inconsequential that she posed no threat, that she could not determine even the smallest detail of her own fate.

Then, five steps later, she realized how she was going to destroy *Iron Fist*.

"What do you think?" Zsinj asked.

Melvar let his features go slack. All the menace and cruelty in them vanished. "Certainly, some of what she was saying was the truth. I just have difficulty trusting Intelligence types."

"Such as yourself."

"I was never with Imperial Intelligence. I just saw them as a likely enemy and schooled myself in their skills and tactics." Melvar shrugged. "I've received early word from the technicians examining her astromech. It's a new-model R2, very much state-of-the-art, and has received a recent memory scrub. It remembers the jump from Aldivy to our rendezvous point, but nothing else. It had a restraining bolt on it when she arrived."

Zsinj smiled. "Very appropriate. Innocuously appropriate. Keep a close eye on her. Extract every possible bit of information out of her. If she remains loyal, reward her. If she proves to be disloyal—"

"I can guess the rest."

"Why me?" Janson asked.

He lay on his bunk, hands behind his head, looking dubiously at his visitor.

"I can't go to a friend," said Donos. He sat in Janson's chair, leaning back on its rear legs so his shoulders rested on the wall. "I don't have any."

"Not since you shot at the last one."

Donos managed a mirthless smile. "I can't go to a subordinate officer. I'd just feel uncomfortable. Or to a superior."

"Which leaves the rest of us lucky lieutenants."

"Pretty much."

"So talk. I'm game. It's been years since I ruined the life of a fellow lieutenant. Well, weeks, anyway."

"I'm not sure where to begin. I don't know whether I'm crazy or not. I just know that before Talon Squadron was destroyed, I was a different man. Self-control, self-composure were easy. Afterward, I had to work so hard to manage everything. If I didn't . . ."

"If you didn't, what?"

"I don't know. I never found out. I was so good at managing everything. Except for that collapse. And the other day, with Lara."

"How many times did Lara slap you?"

"*Slap* me? Never."

"Why not?"

"I never gave her reason to."

"Right. Since you became a pilot, how many times have you been picked up by military police for being drunk and belligerent?"

"Never."

"But you drink."

"In moderation."

Janson sighed. "You see, I was operating under the assumption that you'd actually died with Talon Squadron but had failed to notice. But I was wrong! You've been dead since you joined Starfighter Command. Maybe longer, maybe since you were with the Corellian armed forces."

Donos frowned. "I'd appreciate it if you'd explain that."

With a single, fluid move, Janson sat upright, spun ninety degrees to his right, and set his heels on the floor. "Sure," he said. "It's simple. You're dead. I'm not. Let me demonstrate."

He stood up on his bed, then began bouncing up and down. "Did you ever do this as a kid?"

"Of course."

"Did you ever do it as a grown-up?"

"Of course not."

"You say 'of course' a lot, and it's always wrong. Tell me, Myn. How do I look?"

"Well, stupid."

"Exactly!" With an exuberant bound, Janson leaped off his cot, smacked his head on the ceiling, and swore as he landed on the floor again. He rubbed his head and glared at the treacherous ceiling. "When was the last time you looked stupid?"

"I don't know."

Janson leaned in close to him. "Try to understand this. I'll say it slowly. I want you to remember it for the rest of your life.

"You can't look dignified when you're having fun."

"Assuming that's true—so what?"

"If you're not having fun, you're not enjoying your life. If you're not enjoying your life—why even bother being alive?" Janson gave an eloquent shrug. "Myn, I'm living on borrowed time. I've nearly been killed more times than, than, well, more times than you've been slapped, certainly. If I wait until some imaginary distant point in my life to start enjoying it, I'll be dead before I get there. But if I get killed tomorrow, at least I can be pretty sure that I enjoyed myself more than whoever's killing me. You understand?"

"Not really."

Suddenly deflated, Janson sat on his bed again. "Let's try it a different way. You want to be in control so you don't foul up some horrible way. But you're so in control that you're basically a walking dead man. Since you're dead, you had nothing to offer Lara. You have nothing to offer Wedge—he's got *plenty* of dead pilots, doesn't need another one. Most of them are smart enough to stay where we plant them, though."

"So what do you recommend?"

"Get drunk. Get slapped. Do something you always wanted to do as a child, especially if it's something that would humiliate you today. If you're going to get kicked out of Starfighter Command, make it for something you can be proud of." Something beeped in one of Janson's pockets. He pulled it out, a comlink, and held it up to his ear to listen. He brightened. "Automatic signal. The Rogues and the *Millennium Falsehood* are back. No losses. Sorry, I have to run, have to figure out what to razz Wedge about." He darted for the door and was gone.

Donos shook his head. "I'm asking career advice from a nine-year-old."

THE DOOR TO the *Falsehood*'s hangar slid open before Janson reached it. Out came a repulsorlift cargo sled, pushed by a single *Mon Remonda* technician. On the sled was a crate, two meters long by one wide and high. The crate rocked on the sled and odd noises, like a faint and garbled voice, emerged from it.

Wedge walked out behind the technician and stopped short when he saw Janson. He made a noise of exasperation and slapped the gloves he carried into his open palm. "You weren't supposed to see that."

"See what?" Janson stared after the departing technician and cargo. "What was that?"

"That was Lieutenant Kettch."

Janson gave Wedge a close look. Wedge certainly didn't look crazy. "Um, please correct me if I'm wrong, but Lieutenant Kettch is fictitious. An Ewok pilot who doesn't exist. I should know. I made him up."

"He's not fictitious anymore."

"Now he's real?"

Wedge stepped out so the hangar door could close behind him. "On planetside, while we were waiting for the *Falsehood* to be spotted, Tycho found a store where they sold exotic animals to wealthy Zsinj supporters who enjoy that sort of thing. One of the 'animals' was a full-grown Ewok male named Chulku. When we were preparing to blast off and do our usual number on the pursuit, Tycho staged a jailbreak and we brought Chulku along. While we were flying back, I had an idea—if Zsinj ever does need to see the Hawk-bats, we could have an actual Lieutenant Kettch for him." He nodded after the sled. "Chulku is pretty bright, and we think we can teach him which TIE interceptor controls to touch and which not to—I doubt we can teach him to fly without years of education, but we can make him look authentic in a cockpit."

"That's crazy."

"Now we just need to build him those prosthetic hand-and-leg attachments Kettch is supposed to have so he can manipulate a starfighter's controls."

"Still crazy."

Wedge smiled. "And since you had the bad luck to witness his arrival, you get to be part of the crew who takes him food. Welcome to the conspiracy, Wes."

Janson shook his head. "Now I'm crazy."

THE TIE INTERCEPTOR hurtling toward Lara in a head-to-head run juked and jinked in what seemed like a random pattern, but the maneuvers did not seem to throw the pilot off. His linked laser fire angled in ever more accurately toward Lara's interceptor.

She, too, threw her starfighter back and forth, up and down, in an effort to keep the enemy laser fire from hitting her. She was successful—the two fighters passed with no damage to her craft. But she hadn't gotten off a single accurate shot at her enemy.

The second she flashed passed the enemy TIE, she hauled back on the flight stick, gaining relative altitude with such a sharp maneuver that she felt the g-forces pull her down into her pilot's couch despite the ship's inertial compensator. A moment later she was upside down and headed back the way she had come—

Straight into the path of her opponent.

The enemy pilot fired a split second before she could bring her lasers in line. Her TIE shuddered under the impact and slewed to port.

But it held together. There was no shriek of hull breach, no warning of imminent detonation. She'd been grazed.

"I'm hit!" she said. "I'm done for." She jerked her control yoke to send her spinning in the direction she was already headed.

She counted to two, then snapped her interceptor back around to face her opponent. The enemy TIE jittered in her targeting computer—

But he was much closer than she would have guessed, a mere quarter kilometer away, and was already lined up for a shot. Before she could hit her laser trigger, the sensor system shrieked a recognition of her enemy's targeting lock—

Then her viewport went dead.

The artificial gravity, which simulated zero gravity and high-angle maneuvers, turned off and she dropped at full weight into her pilot's couch. She sighed.

A voice crackled over her comm unit. It was deep, with a trace of the Corellian accent that occasionally crept into the speech of Han Solo and Wedge Antilles. "That was very good flying. And the last trick, pretending to be out of control, almost fooled me. I commend you."

"Who am I talking to?"

"My name is Fel. Baron Soontir Fel."

Lara's insides went cold. When she was a crewman aboard *Implacable,* she'd never even been aware of the presence of Fel and the 181st there, so secret had their mission been. Now, at last, she'd be able to meet the most dangerous pilot who served her enemies.

With her fear, there was a rush of elation. With Wraith Squadron, Lara had flown in simulators against Wedge Antilles, the best the New Republic had to offer. Now she had flown against Baron Fel. She'd competed against the very best pilots two governments had to offer.

Too bad she lost most of the time.

"A pleasure to meet you," she said. "I'm sorry I didn't offer you more competition."

"Don't be," he said. "You're very good. More work, and you might train up to the standards of the One Eighty-first. Shall I keep you in my records as a candidate for the group?"

"I'd be honored. Can I buy the victor a drink?"

"Unfortunately, I have more simulations to fly—and it appears that you don't. Some other time, though."

The hatch behind Lara opened and Ensign Gatterweld thrust his face in. "Need any help?"

"No, thank you." She was getting sick of the ubiquitous Gatterweld. Except when she was in her quarters, in the tiny office where she wrote her commentary on her time with Wraith Squadron, and in simulators, Gatterweld was there. Her shadow.

She unclipped the netting that, in a real TIE interceptor, would have kept her bound in place on the pilot's couch, and threw it to one side, then hauled herself backward and out of the open hatch at the rear of the ball-shaped simulator. Outside, the air was cooler and the omnipresent hum of *Iron Fist's* engines was in her ears again.

Gatterweld handed her the pack in which she carried her datapad and other equipment. He looked at the control board where her standings were displayed. "You did pretty well."

"Do you fly?"

"I can pilot shuttles now. I don't have the reflexes for starfighters. Hand to hand is my game. Where to now? The cafeteria?"

Lara checked her chrono. "No, it's late. I think I'll just turn in."

As they walked past the banks of control stations set up to monitor the simulators, she saw what she needed—a device she would kill for. A set of monitor goggles and attached microphone. They lay unguarded on one of the control stations, their owner away, perhaps on break.

As she and Gatterweld passed the station, she contrived to get her left foot tangled in his legs. He tripped forward, swearing, while she stumbled and fell sideways—snatching up the set of goggles and tucking them into her pack as she hit the floor.

He scrambled to his feet. "I'm sorry. Are you hurt?"

She took the hand he offered and let him half haul her to her feet. She winced as she put her weight on her left leg. "A bruise, maybe. Not your fault. I think I had a cramp from all the time in the simulator."

"Can you walk? I can summon a stretcher—"

"No, I'd better walk it off. Thank you."

SHE MAINTAINED THE PRETENSE of her limp all the way to the door to her quarters, and inside as well—though she hadn't spotted the holocam, she knew there had to be one. Or two, or three. She wasn't trusted, and with Zsinj in charge, that meant there were holocams on her in her quarters.

She set her pack down inside the closet and took a look around. She'd been given sizable quarters, appropriate to a naval lieutenant on track to promotion. She actually had a decent-sized bedroom with a full terminal and a closet, a small office, and a separate refresher chamber. Much better accommodations than she'd enjoyed on *Mon Remonda*.

Tonin, her R2, sat in the middle of the bedroom. He came alive when she entered, offering up whistles and clicks that she interpreted as a polite interrogative. He was almost a stranger to her now, had been so since she'd wiped his memory on Aldivy.

But that would change soon.

"I'm fine, Tonin. Just tired."

Once in bed, she deliberately changed position every two or three minutes, tossing and turning, a show of insomnia for whoever was monitoring her holocams. She did this for an hour. Then she sat up and ran a hand through her catastrophically tousled hair.

Tonin beeped another question.

"Sorry, but I'm going to need the patch of metal where you're resting. Scoot into the closet, would you?"

With a series of musical tones suggesting that he was hurt by her suggestion, Tonin rolled into the closet. He turned his head around so his main holocam eye could still observe her.

Lara rose and pulled the mattress from her bed onto the floor, then redistributed pillows and sheets on it. She made sure that one of the sheets reached as far as Tonin's wheels.

She reached into the bag in her closet and hunted around for something within it with her left hand. With her right, she extracted the monitoring goggles and scooted them under the edge of the sheet on the floor, then plugged the goggles' cord into a jack in Tonin's side, hoping—nearly certain—that her body shielded the action from the viewpoint of most of the places holocams might be situated in her room.

Finally she grasped the object that she'd pretended not to be able to find. She stood and stared at it, turning so the holocams could get a good look at it. A bottle of tuber liquor from Aldivy, nasty stuff the locals there adored.

She stared at it for long moments, as if contemplating its medicinal qualities, then shook her head and placed it on the top shelf of her closet. A moment later, she slipped under the sheets over her mattress, rolled around a moment to find the most comfortable spot, pulled the sheets up over her head, and lay still.

THE VERY JUNIOR intelligence officer watching this display began typing, ever so tentatively, into his terminal. *24:00 hours,* he typed. *Subject situated herself on mattress on floor. Entered sleep state almost immediately. First considered alcohol as soporific, but decided against. Cause of sleeplessness unknown. Bed too soft? Guilt?*

"Don't forget simple stress."

The voice sounded right in his ear and he jumped two handspans. He'd thought he was alone in the room. He looked up into the face of General Melvar. "Uhh, thank you, sir. We'd call that occupational anxiety or excitement from lifestyle transition."

"Do you get paid more for using more words?"

"No, sir, but the medics like them."

Melvar snorted. "Well, add it any way you want to."

"Yes, sir."

Melvar spared one last look at the overhead view of Lara's still bed, then left as quietly as he'd arrived.

WITH MOVEMENTS ALMOST imperceptibly slow, Lara drew the monitoring goggles onto her head and turned them on. The goggles, drawing power from the link with Tonin, activated with a faint hum.

She whispered, "Tonin. Aldivian colloquialism. Definition: Little Atton."

Then she waited.

If she was right, if she'd done her work correctly, the passwords she'd just spoken would be causing events to transpire deep within her R2 unit. The extra hardware she had buried within his power unit would be activating. The memory backup it contained would be pouring out across the droid's circuitry, appending itself to and overwhelming Tonin's current programming.

And in a few moments, once again, she would have a—

A single word, READY, appeared before her eyes. It looked as though it were sculpted out of metal and floating in darkness a meter from her, but she knew that it was merely being projected onto the goggles she wore.

"Don't communicate audibly," she whispered, though Tonin's transmission of his first query as text suggested that he understood the need for secrecy. The fact that all data being transmitted between them was going across a direct wire connection made it very unlikely that her observers would be able to detect their communication. "Before we do anything, I want to apologize."

FOR WHAT?

"For being selfish," she whispered. "I shouldn't have brought you. I've put you in danger. I may get myself killed here, and if I do, the same will probably happen to you."

I'M GLAD I'M HERE.

"Me, too. You're my only friend, Tonin." She closed her eyes for a moment, all too aware of how pathetic that sounded. Then she forced them open. "I also have to apologize for what I've done to you. I wiped your main memory on Aldivy. Anytime anyone but me puts a restraining bolt on you or opens you up, your memory will wipe. Anytime I say the right words, your backup memory will reload. So you may experience some memory gaps. I'm sorry. It's the only way to keep you safe."

I UNDERSTAND, LARA.

"I had an idea as to how we can destroy *Iron Fist*. You'll

have to do most of the work. But if we succeed, you may become the most famous R2 unit ever. Well, maybe second, after Artoo-Detoo."

THAT WOULD BE NICE. WOULD THE WRAITHS LIKE YOU AGAIN?

"No. They'll never like me again. So I have to do this for myself. I have to do this because it's right. I have to do this because I have nothing else to do."

WHAT DO I DO?

"Well, Zsinj, except when he's paying for really good employees and mercenaries, is notoriously cheap. Which means he probably won't have my quarters monitored when I'm not in them. If I stay away from my quarters all day long, that gives you plenty of time to work. I'll tell you what you need to do. But first . . . when we're alone like this . . . could you call me Kirney?"

YES, KIRNEY.

12

HALF AN HOUR after Lara's departure from her quarters the next morning, Tonin became active. He rolled out of the closet to the door, deployed and extended his fine-work grasper arm, and got to work on the door controls. Within minutes, he had rewired the controls and mechanism so he could open the door and close it fractionally as well as fully.

He opened the door a bare three centimeters and extended his video sensor through it nearly at floor level, giving him a 360-degree view of the corridor. A passerby was not likely to notice the slight gap in the doorway or the protrusion from it. He waited.

It was nearly an hour before his first opportunity arose. Certainly, in that time, many of the trapezoidal MSE-6 utility droids passed his doorway, but always under the eye of a passerby. This time, one little droid, rodentlike in its scurrying motion and nervousness, was alone, unobserved.

Tonin signaled it, a chirp that constituted a come-here order. The droid stopped its forward progress, turned toward the doorway, ran the request through its very simple processor, and determined that accepting this new order was not likely to delay accomplishment of its standing orders significantly. It approached the door.

Tonin snapped his heavy grasper arm out through the gap and snared the little droid. It gave a squeal of alarm and spun its wheels into reverse, but he hauled it up off its wheels. Tonin opened the door wide enough to accommodate his prey, then dragged the little droid through and closed the door.

Then he got to work.

He laid the utility droid on its back. Its wheels spun in helpless panic. With his fine-work arm, he popped open the access hatch on the droid's underside and extended his scomplink into the opening.

As new programming flooded its tiny brain, the utility droid quieted.

BY DAY'S END, Tonin was in command of three of the utility droids, and one had managed to bring him some of the components—magnetic track strips to replace wheels—he needed to begin their modifications.

WEDGE'S FOUR SQUADRONS—Rogue, Wraith, Polearm, and Nova—executed mission after mission, one after another, sometimes two in a single day. Most missions involved only one squadron. In others, one squadron would escort and protect the B-wings of Nova, or Wraith Squadron would be inserted at ground level and then ground-guide the precise bombing runs of one or two of the other starfighter units. Some missions involved nothing more than carefully inserting the *Falsehood,* then very publicly escorting the ship, usually with Wedge and Chewbacca at the controls, out into space and safety.

By the end of one week, the fighter pilots of *Mon Remonda* began to lose track of what day of the calendar it was, and had little time left to them for anything but mission briefings, the missions themselves, and sleep.

By the end of one week, between Wedge's missions and those an Imperial admiral was executing in another part of the galaxy, the Warlord Zsinj had lost more millions of credits than any New Republic fighter pilot could ever hope to accumulate.

MELVAR ENTERED THE WARLORD'S office as silently as ever. Zsinj, turned to stare into his terminal, didn't react. Melvar took the chair before his desk, no longer bothering to keep his movement quiet, and still there was no reaction. Finally, Melvar coughed.

"They're killing me." Zsinj shook his head sorrowfully as he stared at the data on the terminal screen beside his desk. "They want me dead, Melvar."

"Of course they do," the general said. "You're their greatest enemy. It is to your considerable credit that they want you dead."

"Look at this. My businesses are being seized up and down Imperial space—*and* Rebel space. The *Counterpunch* puts in at Vispil and is blown out of space by planetary authorities who refused to stay bribed. A half dozen of my best earners bombed out of existence on worlds within my own borders. Eight percent of my income eliminated in a week. And everywhere, the *Millennium Falcon* flitting around, fomenting more rebellion." He sighed. "And my Funeral Project crews around Coruscant? Suddenly, completely ineffectual. A half dozen acts of terrorism or sedition closed down almost before they're enacted. The rifts between humans and nonhumans in the Rebel government are healing. All my work, years of work, coming undone."

"Mere setbacks, sir."

"No. Can't you feel it? The hordes of my enemies are drawing closer, their claws outstretched, reaching for me." Zsinj heaved a sigh. "I think, I really think, they are poised to undo me. I think Doctor Gast talked before she died. I think the Rebels and Imperials are cooperating."

"Impossible."

"Not impossible. You yourself said I was their greatest enemy. What else could give them the incentive to cooperate?"

Melvar was silent for long moments. In all the years he'd worked with the warlord, this was not the saddest he'd seen him, but it was the most resigned, the most fatalistic. It was a startling change. The warlord had always been an unstoppable force of optimism and will. Now, despite the fact that his girth had not diminished, he seemed somehow reduced.

"Do you think they'll win?" Melvar asked.

Zsinj took a deep breath, then nodded. "I think, in a sense, they already have. They've stopped my processes. They've set their own in motion. Theirs are replacing mine, and I can't seem to do anything about it."

"So what will it take to pull a victory out of this? Tell me the minimum you need. We'll achieve that, and more."

Zsinj switched off his terminal screen and thought. He swung ponderously around to face Melvar and began counting off on his fingers. "One. We retain *Iron Fist*."

"Count on it."

"Two. We retain enough businesses to start again."

"That will be harder. As much as we've done to keep your businesses isolated from one another, some leakage of information has obviously occurred. The more they capture, the more they seem to be able to capture. But, statistically, they can't find everything. We'll have a solid core left."

"Three. We have time to rebuild, repair, recover."

"For that, we'll definitely have to use the *Second Death* for her intended purpose. But we can do that."

"Four. We come up with our next plan for the elimination of the New Republic."

"I think that means Rancor Base and the Force-witches. We have to learn what they do and how they do it. Another path we can take, weapons the Rebels and the Empire can't cope with."

"And Five. Which actually takes place before Three. We

kill General Han Solo and as many of his friends and aides as is humanly possible."

"That," Melvar said, "will be the most enjoyable part of the operation."

ZSINJ SHOWED UP at Lara's new work station in the bridge pit, as apparently cheerful as usual. "Lieutenant Petothel. How are you settling in?"

"Very well," she said. "I can't describe how good it is to be doing this kind of work again."

"Good, good. But the first few days you looked, if I may be indelicate, a little tired. Rings under the eyes. A general malaise."

She nodded. "It took me a while to get used to ship's routine. I had to make some adjustments to my sleeping patterns." Not surprising, as it had proved difficult to get any sleep when she was talking and programming with Tonin all night long. "But I'm over it."

"Have you had a chance to look over the data package I transmitted to you this morning?"

"Yes."

"Your conclusions?"

Lara became aware that the operatives at the consoles on either side of her, though they were continuing to do their work, were listening intently to this exchange. She smiled. Intelligence operatives were the same everywhere. "Well, first, whoever compiled that data did an inadequate job of making the events anonymous. I recognize the first mission as the *Millennium Falcon* escort to Kidriff Five. I was there, after all. Which means that Prime Target is the *Falcon,* and Secondary Target is, roughly, Commander Antilles's entire command of Rebel starfighters."

Zsinj nodded, his expression glum. "So much for secrecy. What do you conclude from their behavior?"

"General Solo is trying to separate you from the income that sustains your fleet, and is personally rabble-rousing while he's at it."

"Why?"

Lara gave him a smile that suggested contempt for their subject matter. It was easy; she only had to let her contempt for Zsinj rise to the surface. "He thinks he's an important man. That his presence is the only thing that can inspire Rebel sympathies in the population. Based on what I've personally observed of the man, I'd say he's desperate. He hasn't had any real success in his mission against you. If he fails, he gets replaced; if he gets replaced, he loses all his status."

"I never had the impression that he cares about status."

"He doesn't." She almost hesitated on the enormity of the lie she'd concocted, the one that Zsinj, in all his ego, must inevitably accept. "But the woman he loves does."

"Ahhh."

"He knows that as a dirt-poor smuggler, he can't keep a princess's affection. But as a Rebel general, he can."

"But only if he's successful."

"Correct."

"Interesting interpretation."

"There's more." Lara pressed on, hoping Zsinj would not detect the queasiness she was feeling.

She had an idea, based on the pattern the *Millennium Falsehood* was demonstrating, as to which world or worlds the ersatz Han Solo would visit next. But was this a conclusion that Zsinj and his intelligence people were supposed to have drawn, or had she come to a conclusion based on her superior knowledge of the Wraiths, a conclusion that would endanger her former squadmates? She didn't know, and the uncertainty ate at her. She had to trust her instincts, though, and her instincts said that the *Falsehood*'s mission profiles came about from meticulous planning that Zsinj was eventually supposed to interpret.

"They're progressing from world to world in your territories based on a number of factors. The degree to which a world is known outside the borders you control. Estimated planetary production that can be applied to your fleet funding. Proximity to New Republic space so they can make quick escapes. Comparative morale value of hitting specific targets. Suspected presence of pro-Rebel factions."

"I know that. Unfortunately, considering how many worlds I control, that still doesn't give us a pattern."

"Yes, it does. There's one more factor. Former trade relations, direct or indirect, with the planet Alderaan."

Zsinj rocked back on his heels. "That *would* make sense."

"Yes, sir. On such worlds, there's a higher likelihood that there will be people who sympathize with Princess Leia and the other Alderaanians who were off-world when the first Death Star destroyed that planet. Also, in my opinion, they're more likely to be planets that Princess Leia will have heard of, thereby increasing her recognition of Solo's deeds when he tells her of them."

"Very good, very good." Zsinj's eyes lost focus as he considered Lara's words. "What does that suggest Solo's next target will be?"

"I give a very high probability to Comkin Five, and just slightly less high a likelihood to the Vahaba Asteroid Belt." Comkin was a Zsinj-controlled world known for its candies and medicines—two industries inextricably tied together on that world—and Vahaba was known not only for its asteroid-mining operations but for the skill of its metal fabricators. She knew a little about Vahaba; it was in a well-populated cluster of stars, not far from Halmad, where the Wraiths had acted as pirates not long ago.

"Well. Interesting speculation. Thank you, Lieutenant."

Still distracted, Zsinj turned to depart the bridge, not even seeing Lara's salute.

GENERAL MELVAR CAUGHT up with Zsinj in the corridor just outside the bridge. "Well?"

"There's a proper query to give a superior officer. It's not 'Well?' Something more like, 'Sir, a moment of your time, I wished to inquire about your recent interview with the subject under observation.' "

Melvar said, "I can phrase all such requests so as to waste a maximum amount of your time, of course."

Zsinj smiled. "Never mind." He told him of Lara's speculations, then said, "What I don't know is whether she came to this conclusion honestly, or whether she was privy to some of their mission profile before she left *Mon Remonda* and is now presenting it as a sudden realization on her part."

"Either way, the information is valuable . . . so long as she's not leading us into a trap."

"We'll find out. Dispatch half the ready fleet to lie in wait at Vahaba, and we'll take the other half personally to Comkin."

DONOS LAY WAITING on the craft he had fabricated from rubbish.

Portions of the thing had begun their existence as the gravitational unit in a TIE fighter simulator. When coordinated with the simulator's computer, they would exert artificial gravity around the pilot, drawing him left, right, down, up, all in artful mimicry of the sort of g-forces the pilot would experience in sharp turns and other maneuvers.

But the simulator had grown old, had become too unreliable even for recreational use, and it had been dragged to a corridor outside a refuse chamber. There Donos, doing a tour of the unfrequented portions of *Mon Remonda,* a habit that had recently become part of his regular routine, had found it.

He'd liberated still-functioning portions of the gravitational unit. He'd installed computer gear to ensure that the unit would exert appropriate force downward even when the unit was tilting, would detect obstacles, would exert repulsorlift power against obstacles. To this he had added a padded layer that was part of the simulator's pilot's couch and a battery to supply power.

Now, in one of the ship's lonely cargo areas, he lay on his stomach atop the junk he had assembled. It hovered a half meter above the floor, humming, motionless.

Of course it was motionless. It had no engine, no motivation.

Except for him. And to set it into motion, to make it do what it was designed to do, would be to look stupid.

His legs extended off the back of his jury-rigged vehicle. He brought them down to gain purchase with the floor and kicked off, setting his craft into motion. He kicked again and again, building up speed as he floated between shelves of stored materials toward a distant bulkhead. Halfway down, he kicked once more, sideways, setting his craft into a spin, and drew himself into a ball atop it.

His floating sled spun haphazardly, coming within half a meter of a shelving unit before the sled's repulsor unit reacted to the proximity of the thing and bounced him back the other way. Like a ball, he careened from shelf to shelf across the open space in between, coming within handspans of impact but never quite hitting, while he floated toward the bulkhead wall.

Eventually, forward momentum almost spent, he floated to within a half meter of the bulkhead and came to a stop.

"Well, that looked good."

Donos rolled onto his side to get a look at the speaker. Wes Janson stood a few meters away. He must have approached up the walkway that ran along the bulkhead wall.

"I'm amazed it held together," Donos said. "I expected to have the whole thing fail halfway through and toss me into a stack of crates."

"Is it fun?"

Donos nodded. "Pretty much."

"You don't look too amused."

"I imagine I did a moment ago." Donos rose to his feet, gripped his craft by its one handle, and depressed what had once been a pilot's yoke trigger. The craft dropped as it depowered; he hauled it upright. "But even fun isn't much fun. I keep wishing Lara were here."

Janson nodded, sympathy plain on his features. "Yeah. But you're about to get more people here than you probably want. We're doing some inventory here in a few minutes. You probably ought to try the main corridor down in Engineering. It's long enough, and I'm sure the engineers would be interested in seeing your kludge."

"Probably." Donos checked his chrono. "A little later, though. I have somewhere to be."

THE MOMENT DONOS was out of sight, Wedge slipped out from a second-level shelf full of foodstuff packages. "Well, that was interesting."

"Wedge! Why don't you scare the other half of my life out of me? How long were you waiting there?"

"About fifteen minutes. During most of which, Donos just sat there, waiting to decide whether or not to play his game."

"Well, he did. A good sign."

"I hope so." Wedge reached behind the first row of stacked food crates and dragged another one up front. This one, like the others, was labeled BANTHA STEAK, DEHYDRATED,

250 GRAMS RESTORED, INDIVIDUALLY PACKAGED. But the top was ajar and the smell wafting from the crate, something like fruit and leaf compost, was not reminiscent of bantha meat. Wedge reached into the crate's top and drew out a bowl full of brownish lumps Janson couldn't identify. "Now, you've fed Kettch before, correct?"

"No. You and whatever crew you've been using haven't brought me in before now."

"That's right." Wedge led Janson toward the forward doors out of the cargo area. "There are still some security concerns, since Kettch was supposed to be a Hawk-bat, not a New Republic pilot. So we're limiting the personnel who see him. He gets one bowlful like this, three times a day. We have him set up near an officers' mess that General Solo isn't using, since he doesn't entertain. So you'll get water for Kettch from the mess."

"Right."

They passed through a small door into a secondary cargo area, this one much smaller than the one they'd left, its shelves full of crates labeled BULK CLOTH. From the rear, they approached a larger crate, one two meters by two meters by one and a half tall, which had been laid out in the aisle between rows of shelves.

"And now," Wedge said, as they got to the front of the crate, "you meet—uh-oh."

A door that had obviously been retrofitted onto the front of the crate lay on the floor, off its hinges. There was nothing within the crate but what looked like a bed of grass and cloth scraps.

"He's loose?" Janson said.

"He's loose." Wedge looked around. "But for how long? We've got to find him, keep to a minimum the number of crewmen who see him—"

There was a soft *patter-patter* of movement from the far end of the chamber, the bow end.

"We're in luck," Wedge said. "He's still in here." He extended the bowl of food. "Here, take some. Maybe we can lure him back."

Janson grimaced as he grabbed up a handful of the smelly Ewok food.

They headed forward, only to hear the forward door out of the chamber hiss open, followed by the *patter-patter* of bare feet and the door hissing closed again. Wedge headed forward at a dead run, Janson at his heels.

The door opened for them, revealing dimness beyond, then Wedge was skidding to a halt and Janson ran into him. They toppled over together, crashing into containers of some sort, and fluid, liters of it, splashed over them.

A sharp, poisonously clean smell forced its way into Janson's nose. "Sithspit, what's that?"

"Cleansing fluid of some sort. We must have hit a janitor droid's stash." Wedge sat up. Janson could see him wrinkling his nose even in the dim light. Somewhere else in the room, a door hissed open and closed again.

"Oh, this is no good," Wedge said. "He's running now because we're chasing him, and he's going to be able to smell us from kilometers away."

"So let's call in Kell and Tyria. They can hunt him down while we clean up."

"They're not part of our Kettch conspiracy." Wedge rose and moved away from the puddle. "Strip."

"What?"

"Get those clothes off. We'll rub some of the Ewok food over the parts of our skin that have the cleansing fluid on them. That should make it possible for us to get close to him." Wedge suited action to words, unzipping his jumpsuit.

"Oh, sure. Would you stand still if you were being approached by two naked men with Ewok food smeared all over them?"

"No, but I'm not an Ewok. Just do it." Wedge nodded

right and left. "Looks like there are two doors out of here. I don't know which one he took, but they'll both go into General Solo's mess. You take that one, I'll take this one."

"Wedge, this is the last time I'm feeding Kettch."

"Me, too."

THE DOOR OPENED for Janson and he crept through into the dimly lit room beyond.

Not three meters ahead stood an Ewok, wearing the traditional bonnet-style headgear of the species, his back to Janson.

Janson took a careful, silent step forward. The Ewok didn't react. One more step and he was in range—Janson lunged, grabbing the Ewok with his left hand, the one uncontaminated by Ewok food. "Got you!"

The Ewok didn't struggle. Nor did it weigh much. Janson looked at it. It wasn't a live Ewok; it was the stuffed toy the Wraiths had brought with them from Hawk-bat Base, the one they called Kettch.

Then Janson realized that the room was full of people—all the other members of Wraith Squadron. In the dimness, they stood like statues, in poses suggesting they'd been in the middle of a social gathering, in conversational groups of twos and threes, and then had been flash-frozen.

No, not frozen, exactly. They still breathed. Some swayed a little where they stood.

And none of them looked at Janson.

Janson stood still for a long moment, waiting for some reaction from them, or for some realization to set in and inform him why they'd be standing stock-still in a dimly lit room. None came.

So he held the stuffed Ewok toy before him and backed to the door through which he'd entered.

His bare skin touched metal and he flinched. The door had closed and wasn't opening for him.

He scraped the Ewok food off his hand against the door-jamb. Slowly, silently, his sense of unreality mounting, he walked sideways toward the other door into this chamber. To get there, he'd have to pass close to Piggy, Shalla, and Elassar, who were grouped close to the wall. As he neared them, he paused and reached out to touch Piggy, the Wraith nearest him.

His fingers encountered real flight suit and solid flesh beneath. He jerked his hand back. Neither Piggy nor any of the others reacted.

It was a dream, it had to be. And by the rules of dreams, doubtless there was to be some bad result if he failed to escape before the Wraiths awoke. In case he could short-circuit the process, he pinched himself, hoping to awaken prematurely, but he had no such luck. The scene remained before him.

Moving with less caution, he made it to the other door and backed into it . . . and his bare rear once again contacted metal as the door failed to open.

Well, then. There was one more door out of this chamber, which should open up into a corridor—a corridor that he could, with luck, duck down unobserved and perhaps reach the pilots' ready room, where he had another uniform in his locker. He continued sideways along the wall, around the corner . . .

He reached the doorway and turned into it. The door whooshed open. And beyond was Wedge, fully uniformed, bellowing, "Attention!"

The room lights blazed into normal brightness and Janson heard the Wraiths behind him snapping to attention. He felt his cheeks burn as he realized they had to be facing his bare backside.

Wedge looked at Janson, then at the Ewok toy he held protectively before him. "Lieutenant, you're out of uniform. And you know, wearing an Ewok as a swimsuit is a felony on some worlds."

Janson nodded. He could not keep a rueful grin from forming on his lips. "I have been so set up," he said.

"Good analysis," Wedge said. "You're showing real leadership potential, among other things. Lieutenant Nelprin?"

Shalla approached, standing beside Janson so he could see her without turning. In her hands was a folded mass of orange cloth. She unfolded and displayed it before him. It was a cloak, in New Republic flight-suit orange, with the words "Yub, yub, Lieutenant" stenciled on the back in black. She swept it across his shoulders and fastened it around his neck. Then she leaned in close and whispered, "Nice rear, Lieutenant."

Janson felt his cheeks burning hotter. "Thank you for noticing, Lieutenant." He handed her the Ewok doll and draped the cloak in a more concealing fashion about himself. "I take it this is revenge for that bet about your not speaking Wookiee?"

Wedge stepped into the room and the door shut behind him. "Well, for that, and for your antics with Lieutenant Kettch here and at Hawk-bat Base."

Janson couldn't keep the surprise from his face. "You knew about that?"

"Well, not at first, of course. Not for sure." Wedge threw an arm over Janson's shoulders and turned him, leading him back into the room, into the midst of the grinning Wraiths. "But you didn't do much of a job of concealing your tracks. The doll showed up immediately after your return from Coruscant, which meant that it was probably you or someone else involved with that trip. Then, after it was obvious that the doll was wandering pretty much at will, I had a transmitter sewn into it."

Janson winced. "You tracked its movements. And knew it was me. And waited all this time for payback."

"So, do you still think revenge is beneath Wedge Antilles, Hero of the New Republic?"

"I'm not sure anything is beneath you anymore. Who was playing Kettch? Or Chulku, or whatever his name was supposed to be?"

Wedge grinned. "The first time, we had Squeaky in the box you saw. He speaks Ewok, of course."

"Of course." Janson sighed.

Dia said, "I was the footsteps you were following a few minutes ago. And I was the one who splashed you with the bucket full of cleansers. Had to make sure you got plenty on you. We couldn't rely on you to fall correctly onto the buckets we'd placed."

Wedge accepted a small glass of amber-colored liquid from Kell, passed it to Janson. "A reward. You're taking it very well, Wes. Just remember that, when it comes to pranks, you have the necessary enthusiasm, you have the inventiveness, you have the experience . . . I have the resources."

"Granted." Janson sipped at the glass, made an appreciative face. It was Whyren's Reserve, a Corellian brandy with a rich, smoky flavor. "But it's over now. No ongoing punishment for me. Right?"

Wedge's expression became serious. "Well, not after the holorecording of tonight's events has been circulated."

"Tell me you're kidding."

"What, and deny the universe the chance to see a rear end that the Wraiths have proclaimed so hologenic?"

Janson didn't even try to keep the dismay off his face. "*Please* tell me you're kidding."

"I'll decide tomorrow. Tonight we celebrate."

Donos leaned in. "And remember what a very wise man once told me. 'You can't look dignified when you're having fun.'"

"If I knew who that wise man was," Janson said, "I'd shoot him."

———

THE NEXT MORNING, the last pilot to enter the briefing amphitheater was Donos. He remained standing until Wedge noticed him. "Permission to sit in, sir?"

"Why? You're still off the active list."

"I'd like to volunteer for this mission."

Wedge looked momentarily baffled. "Did I misstate myself? You can't fly."

"I'm not volunteering as a pilot, sir. Nothing in my current reevaluation indicates that I'm unfit to handle a ship's guns. I'd like to volunteer as a crewman on the *Millennium Falsehood*. I'm a Corellian, I know the equipment, and I'm a good shot." That was understating it somewhat; though his greatest talent was with a sniper's rifle, Donos was marksman-rated with most sorts of blaster and laser weapons.

"Good point," Wedge said. "Yes, you can attend the briefing; I'll decide on your request later." He stood behind the lectern and turned to the assembled pilots.

"Today is a standard 'let them see the *Falsehood* then run' exercise. Our target is the Comkin system. Comkin's security measures are more extensive than some we've recently encountered, so we can't count on smuggling in our TIE interceptor escort. However, Chewbacca has temporarily attached plating to the surface of the *Falsehood* that gives it a sensor echo much more like that of a YT-2400 freighter, and that plating will contain a bit of a surprise for Comkin's defenders. We have transponder data corresponding to that of a real YT-2400 mercenary trader, so we should be able to make it to the planet's surface; however, if we're identified on entry, we just evacuate and achieve our primary objective, another appearance by the *Millennium Falcon*.

"Another modification we've made to the *Falsehood* will allow for quicker response time by the support squadron when it's supposed to come in for rescue: we've installed a miniature holocomm unit worth more than the rest of the ship put together. Yes, Face?"

"Sir, is it a bad time to point out that a good shot of brandy is worth more than the rest of the ship put together?"

"Yes. Wraith Squadron will be our primary escort . . ."

MELVAR APPEARED SILENTLY beside Lara's station. His mild words contrasted with the cruelty of his features. "Baron Fel would like to see you fly."

"Really." Lara made a face suggesting that she was surprised and pleased. "You mean, for real, not in a simulator."

"For real. Broadaxe Squadron will be supplementing the One Eighty-first, and they're a pilot light. Would you care to suit up and fly with them?"

"I'd be delighted."

"Report to their ready room at thirteen hundred." Melvar gave her a mirthless smile. "Don't do too well. We'd hate to lose you as an analyst."

"I'll keep it in mind. Thank you, sir."

When he was gone, she stared at her screen, seeing none of the data on it, and tried not to shake. She prayed that she'd been wrong in her initial assessment, that the next *Mon Remonda* strike would be on any system other than Comkin Five.

For if she'd been right, she might end up facing her former squadmates in mortal combat.

COMKIN FIVE WAS a green-blue world circling a yellow star. As the *Falsehood* neared the planet's surface, blotches of color resolved themselves into blue sea, deep green tropics, and bands of cloud cover, with only the smallest patches of arctic ice.

"Pretty," Donos said. "What do we blow up first?"

Wedge, ahead of him in the pilot's chair, turned to glance

at him. "Write that down," he said. "That ought to be the Wraith Squadron slogan."

"Good point. Squeaky, record that."

"If I must."

Wedge's attention was diverted by data on his sensor board. "We've just been tapped by planetary sensors. Now we find out if our camouflage fooled them."

"I don't see how it can," Squeaky said, his voice even more petulant than usual. "On close examination, the extension off our starboard side just does not look genuine. And Chewbacca has failed to minimize the *Falsehood*'s forward mandibles, which are, if I'm not mistaken, characteristic of the YT-1300s but not the YT-2400s. We are, I think, probably dead."

Donos frowned at the two-tone 3PO unit seated beside him. Squeaky looked absurd in his ill-fitting clothing, a New Republic general's uniform. "Then why did you volunteer for this mission?"

"Habit?"

"No."

"Because I thought my absence would doom the mission?"

"Although Emtrey could have substituted for you."

Chewbacca grumbled something.

"Certainly not," Squeaky said, his tone turning indignant. "This is not fun, and I wouldn't miss you."

Chewbacca grumbled again.

"No, you don't keep having to remind me to belt in. I am firmly belted in. My belt is fixed with more finesse than that of any belt in this cockpit."

Donos shook his head. Maybe he ought to set up at one of the gunport turrets now.

LARA SAT IN her cockpit, drenched in sweat and feeling miserable.

It wasn't because the cockpit was more uncomfortable than usual, or because of the protracted amount of time she'd been in it.

She'd met the Broadaxe Squadron pilots and had been assigned a TIE interceptor and a wingman, the squadron commander. She'd gone through the routine power-up checklist and transferred, with the rest of the Broadaxes and the 181st, to another ship—a Dreadnaught, older than the Empire, named *Reprisal*. She remembered it from the Levian mission. Broadaxe Squadron occupied the Dreadnaught's fighter bay, while the 181st was divided among officers' bays and cargo bays. Lara shook her head over that; she'd have thought that the more prestigious unit would choose the more convenient bay.

She'd been among the last TIEs to land, and was positioned to be among the first to launch, her viewport a mere meter from the bay's magcon shield. Her temporary commander had laughed at her zeal, but there was another reason she wanted this position: no one was likely to walk in front of her TIE and see what she was doing inside it. Since she'd settled in, she'd been hard at work.

She had started by coupling her personal comlink to a datapad she'd stolen from another *Iron Fist* crewman while they were in the officers' mess. She didn't steal equipment on the bridge; it might be too easy to track back to her.

She recorded a lengthy message, one that turned her thoughts gloomy. Then she pulled up a panel beneath her feet, one that gave technicians access to the vehicle's laser power generators. She powered down all vehicle systems except the comm unit and exterior lights, which would allow her to pretend that the system was still fully powered—assuming no one ran a sensor scan on her, or that no one called, in the next few minutes, for immediate takeoff.

Leading from the power generators were power regulators, which could keep a fatal spike of power from frying vehicle systems in case the generators were hit or malfunctioned in combat. She opened one of the regulators, the one protecting the port-side laser cannons, and spliced in a set of cables. These she attached to the datapad's computer coupler port.

She activated the datapad and packed it into the cavity with the laser power generators, taping it securely into place. She left one wire, terminating in a simple thumb switch, trailing into the cockpit; she closed the access hatch over it, then taped the thumb switch to her pilot's yoke.

Finally, she recommenced power-up, hoping that her modification wouldn't cause any of the vehicle systems to fail, that her modification wouldn't activate any sensor she didn't know about.

If this worked, she was one step closer to *Iron Fist*'s destruction. If it failed, but she was otherwise very lucky, maybe her activities wouldn't be noticed. Maybe.

After a mere ten minutes of frantic activity, she began to get her breathing back under control.

The stars beyond the magcon field suddenly twisted and blurred as *Reprisal* entered hyperspace.

"This will be a short jump," her commanding officer said. "Prepare to launch on arrival."

THE *FALSEHOOD* WAITED in low planetary orbit, its crew watching the green, lush world slowly turn beneath them.

"It's been too long," Donos said. "They're on to us."

"Probably," Wedge said. He didn't look at all uneasy.

Squeaky said, "I see other vessels awaiting final clearance to descend."

"Either they're not on to us," Wedge said, "in which case our waiting here is standard procedure, or they're on to us, and they're having other vessels wait nearby so we won't get suspicious."

"Oh," Squeaky said. "But we're suspicious anyway."

"They failed," Wedge said.

"Will it matter if they destroy us anyway?"

"Not really." The console beeped at Wedge, and he leaned over to look at the comm unit's text screen. "We have final approval for descent to our primary target zone."

Chewbacca shook his head, making a nearly subsonic noise of dissent. He gestured at the sensor board.

There, approaching from planetary east in a similar orbit, was a large, indistinct signal.

"Looks like starfighters," Wedge said. "At least a full squad. All right, we go." He unbelted. "Donos, take the belly gunport turret, I'll take the top. Chewbacca, the controls are yours. Squeaky, you have the comm unit. Call in the Wraiths now, then bring in *Mon Remonda* on the holocomm unit, then stand by in your new mode."

"I'll be so pleased to make my debut."

"Only if they address you, now."

"Yes, sir."

Donos followed Wedge back to the turret access tubes and descended to his turret. He powered it up, swung his weapons back and forth a few times to gauge their speed and responsiveness. Meanwhile, he felt the *Falsehood* maneuvering as it pointed spaceward and accelerated away from Comkin Five.

Squeaky's voice came over the ship's internal comlink. "Chewbacca says estimated two minutes until the TIEs are in range. At least five until we're far enough away from the planet's mass shadow to enter hyperspace. Wraiths report that they will intercept us in three and a half minutes."

Wedge's voice was next. "So they have a minute and a half to batter us before we have reinforcements. We should be able to handle that."

Squeaky said, "Chewbacca says . . . oh, my. Oh, dear, dear dear."

Wedge said, "Report, Squeaky."

"Are you sure you want to know? It's not good."

"Do you want to walk home? Report."

"Chewbacca reports a capital ship dropping out of hyperspace along our escape vector. It's closer than the Wraiths, and it's deploying TIE fighters. Excuse me, TIE interceptors. Two squadrons. They are deploying in what he calls umbrella formation and approaching."

Wedge said, "And our pursuit?"

"They're, ah, they seem to be hanging back. Pacing us, no longer gaining."

"Driving us to the hunters. Thank you, Squeaky." There was a long moment of silence. "Chewbacca, make your course straight for the capital ship. When you're just outside the range of their tractors, deploy Package One and vector away. Then allow Package Two to deploy at its discretion."

A grumble sounded over the comm unit.

"He doesn't seem happy with your order, sir, but he's complying. Ah, ah, the capital ship is identified. A Rendili Star-Drive *Dreadnaught*-class heavy cruiser. Oh, it's the *Reprisal*! How nice to see it still functional. The *Reprisal* visited Kessel one time."

"Save your reminiscences for later. And put your mask on."

"Yes, sir." The droid's voice sounded resigned.

13

LARA PUT EVERYTHING into acceleration, hurtling toward the *Falsehood* as fast as she could travel. She shouldn't have been able to outstrip the other TIE interceptors of the combined units, but most of them dropped slowly back. In a matter of moments, she was at the fore with three other TIEs—her wingman and two interceptors of the 181st.

One of them communicated. "Anxious for battle, Lieutenant?" It was Baron Fel's voice.

"Anxious to show you what I'm made of," she said.

"Never let it be said that I'm not gallant," Fel said. "The first strafing run is yours."

She managed to project gratitude and excitement into her voice. "*Thank* you, sir." But the words were like bile to her.

She knew what was happening. It was a test. If she was seen to offer less than her best effort toward the destruction of the ersatz *Millennium Falcon*, they'd know she was not trustworthy.

Well, she'd show them something. She'd hit the *Falsehood* again and again.

"*MILLENNIUM FALCON*," came the woman's voice, "this is the former Wraith Two. Prepare to die." The source of the transmission, the lead TIE interceptor, opened fire.

The voice was Lara's. Donos stiffened. He'd been tracking

the incoming TIEs, aiming at the lead starfighter, but now he let his aim drift off her.

Green laser fire streamed from the interceptor. It was the only one of the four TIEs to fire. The first few linked bursts missed, then Lara began connecting, and the *Falsehood* rocked under the impact of her hits.

The first pair of TIEs roared past the *Falsehood* and immediately looped around for a second pass. The second pair came on, and a new voice crackled across the comm waves. "I believe I address General Solo. You can spare the lives of your crew by surrendering now."

Donos had heard that voice before, at the *Implacable* fight. Baron Soontir Fel. He twisted to look up the access tube at Wedge. His commander had some sort of personal relationship with Fel, doubtless something that had come about during the brief time Fel served with Rogue Squadron, though Donos didn't know what it was. And sure enough, Wedge had stiffened in his seat, his aim faltering.

Donos almost smiled. It was good to know that he wasn't the only one caught off guard by the forces confronting them.

Then came another voice over the comlink. Han Solo's.

Solo's voice said, "Baron Fel. They still say you're the best Imp pilot since Darth Vader. When you were a Rogue, I didn't want to hurt your feelings, but now I can tell you, I flew against him—and you're not fit to shine his helmet."

"We'll never know," Fel said. "I'm certainly pilot enough to put an end to *you*." He and his wingman came on, firing, with twenty TIE interceptors in their wake.

DONOS'S AIM WAS thrown off as the *Falsehood* suddenly began spinning along its bow-to-stern axis. He recognized the maneuver's intent, to change the sight profile of the

Falsehood so incoming attackers would have an irregular target.

Fel and his wingman blasted by, their laser fire hitting the bow and forward mandibles. The ship's lights dimmed as its shields strained to hold up under the assaults. Donos's return fire missed both TIEs, but he was able to swing back in line and tag the second interceptor of the next pair. His shots chewed through a solar wing array and sent the interceptor spinning off into the blackness of space. On his sensor screen, the second interceptor vanished; streaks of debris exploded away from its last position, then faded.

And more TIEs came on as, in the distance, the bow of the Dreadnaught grew larger and larger.

SQUEAKY WATCHED WITH fascination as the universe spun crazily before him. He switched back to his normal voice. "I say. If I were human, I imagine I'd be throwing up all over your control panels."

Chewbacca turned and grumbled something.

Squeaky turned to look in amazement at the Wookiee— what he could see of Chewbacca, anyway, through the holes in the absurd, oversized mask Squeaky was wearing. "Why, that's the nicest thing you've ever said to me. Did I really sound like him?"

Chewbacca grumbled an assent.

Squeaky sat back, suddenly delighted. All the work he'd done with General Solo, recording his voice, analyzing and parsing appropriate phrases and recurrent remarks, might have paid off. It had not only fooled Baron Fel, it had finally gained him Chewbacca's admiration.

The *Falsehood* rocked, accompanied by noises of hardware and systems leaping from their wall brackets and crashing around against the walls, as it sustained more incoming fire. "Chewbacca, can't we do all this without the participation of enemy forces?"

The Wookiee spared a moment to glare at him.

"What did I say?"

THE LAST OF the TIEs finished their first pass. Behind the *Falsehood*, they began looping around for a second run. The squadron of TIE fighters that had escorted them out of the planet's atmosphere was on an approach back toward the planet, doubtless ordered away so the *Reprisal* and the interceptors could have all the glory arising from the *Millennium Falcon*'s destruction. Donos watched his sensor board with concern. The *Falsehood* had been lucky to survive one run through that gauntlet.

First to return would be Lara and her wingman. They were only seconds from optimal firing range. "Commander?" Donos said. "Opinions about Lara?"

"When we do the breakaway move," Wedge said, "when we vector away from the Dreadnaught's bow, she may overshoot us. Try for one of her wings. Disable instead of kill."

The next voice was Squeaky's. "If you'll pardon me, sirs, I think you should let Flight Officer Notsil continue shooting us."

Laser fire from Lara's interceptor and her wingmate's began pouring down on the *Falsehood* again. Out of the corner of his eye, Donos saw a hydrospanner rocketing down the access tube toward him. He tried twisting up and out of the way; it slammed into his rib cage instead of his head, and he grunted from the sudden pain.

"What?" Wedge's voice suggested the frown Donos could easily imagine him wearing. "Squeaky, have you shaken loose your logic circuits?"

"No, sir. It's rather complicated. It will take too long to explain. Just trust me." The droid's voice was surprisingly confident. "This is something I know about. What? Oh. Chewbacca says thirty seconds to release-and-turn."

Donos twisted and swept his arc of fire across Lara's TIE, but didn't begin firing until his crosshairs were just past her wing. His series of blasts flashed between her and her wingman, then one grazed the second TIE. It jumped up, gaining relative altitude, and was suddenly out of sight.

Then it was a bright, expanding ball as Wedge's shot hulled it.

ON THE BRIDGE of *Iron Fist*, Zsinj and Melvar watched with interest the holocomm broadcast from the bow of the *Reprisal*. It showed the *Millennium Falcon*'s suicidal charge, the horde of TIE interceptors converging upon the Corellian freighter.

"Come on, come on," Zsinj breathed. "Bring in *Mon Remonda*. You'll die if you don't."

"TEN SECONDS TO BREAKAWAY," Squeaky said. "Nine . . . Eight . . ."

Chewbacca rumbled at him.

"You want me to do the jettison? Very well." Squeaky's metal hands sought out the large switch that had been bonded to the main console earlier today. "Four . . . Three . . ."

Chewbacca ceased the freighter's spinning motion. The *Falsehood* shuddered as a vicious shot from Fel's interceptor slammed into its top hull.

"One . . ." Squeaky threw the switch.

ALL ALONG THE STARBOARD side of the *Falsehood*, seals holding the new extension, the mock-up that made the ship better resemble a YT-2400 freighter, opened with little flashes of explosive charges. The extension drifted half a meter from the *Falsehood*'s hull.

Chewbacca yanked the controls hard to port. The freighter's inertial compensators shrieked as they tried to accommodate the nearly ninety-degree maneuver. TIE interceptors, their pilots caught momentarily off guard by the surprise move, overshot the *Falsehood*. The jettisoned portion of the ship continued on, laser-straight, toward the bow of the *Reprisal*.

Squeaky said, "Flight Officer Konnair, you are free to detach when ready."

LARA AND FEL looped back quickly, getting back into position behind the *Falsehood*. They continued their erratic, side-to-side motion, which made it all but impossible for the ship's gunners to target them.

Lara heard Fel report, "There's something attached to the *Falcon* where that piece of debris just detached. It's—oh."

Lara saw the "something" break free of the *Falsehood*. It was an A-wing fighter. It drifted free of the freighter with the puff of small explosive bolts detonating; then its engines lit off and it vectored away at the kind of speed only an A-wing could manage.

"Don't be distracted, Petothel," Fel said. "Stay with the primary target."

"Don't worry about me," she said, and opened up again on the *Falsehood*.

Fel's wingman veered away in pursuit of the A-wing.

ON THE BRIDGE of the *Reprisal,* the captain and crew watched the *Falsehood*'s movements.

"He's vectoring to sweep around us," the weapons operator reported. "He'll probably return to his primary course when he's clear of our guns."

"Order the TIEs to herd him back in toward our side," said the captain, a burly man who could not return to his home on Coruscant until Rebels like Han Solo were purged from the galaxy. "We can't keep Fel from firing on her, but maybe we can steal the kill. What's the status of that debris?"

"On a collision course with us," the sensor specialist said. "But its speed and tonnage are insufficient to do us harm. Our shields will repel it."

"Very well," the captain said.

LARA AND FEL continued to pour laser fire into the *False-hood*'s stern, all the while dodging with the mad speed and maneuverability of which only TIE interceptors were capable. The remaining TIEs swept out ahead of the *Falsehood*, forming up in her path, dictating a run through their gauntlet or a turn—either toward space, along the Dreadnaught's flank, or back toward the planet.

But Dorset Konnair in her A-wing flashed along behind the line of TIEs, firing her blaster cannons continuously, vaping two of the TIEs before she emerged from the other side. Fel's wingman pursued her, firing at maximum range, unable to overtake the starfighter.

Donos kept up ineffectual fire at Lara whenever she was under his sights, while trying with all his skill to tag Fel whenever that pilot came within view. He had no more success hitting the pilot he wanted to kill than he did the one he wanted to miss. And shot after shot from the pursuing TIEs rocked the *Falsehood*, sounding alarms as shields threatened to fail.

Chewbacca veered back toward the escape course short of the gauntlet of TIEs. His maneuver left them too close to the Dreadnaught; the *Falsehood* would be running under the guns of the *Reprisal*. Donos shook his head and stayed focused on his more immediate problems. If the *Reprisal* hit them, he'd be dead before he felt anything.

ZSINJ WATCHED THE CORELLIAN freighter's run. He rapped his knuckles against a bulkhead, trying to bleed his nervousness away with activity. "Why isn't *Mon Remonda* jumping in?" he said. "Petothel said that these *Millennium Falcon* missions had cruiser support."

Melvar said, "Maybe she was wrong. Or they changed tactics."

"No, it makes sense. He just isn't calling in his cruiser. Why isn't the *Reprisal* dealing with that debris?"

Melvar glanced at the data feed from the Dreadnaught. "It's not real ship's construction. Too light. Their shields will handle it."

Zsinj glanced away from the transmitted view from the *Reprisal*'s bridge to the data feed. Cold suspicion clawed at him. "Contact the *Reprisal*! Tell them to blow that debris *now*!"

THE TUMBLING PIECE of space junk that had been attached to the *Falsehood* made contact with the *Reprisal*'s bow shields.

Inside, a sensor attuned to sudden shocks and gravitational variances registered impact. It triggered the large cache of explosives fastened within the debris's hull.

The bomb, originally intended for a drop onto one of Zsinj's production facilities on the surface of Comkin Five, exploded with far more force than the Dreadnaught's shields could withstand.

A BRIGHT GLOW washed over the *Falsehood* from the side. Donos glanced away from Lara's TIE interceptor to look.

The entire bow of the *Reprisal* seemed to be awash in bright light and flame.

His comm unit crackled. Squeaky said, "We have good news to report. The Wraiths are incoming."

SQUEAKY TURNED OFF the comm mike and glared at Chewbacca. "You didn't tell me it was a bomb."

Chewbacca rumbled a reply.

"No, now *is* the time to talk about it. You've made me a participant in this fight! I've actually done damage to other beings! I'm not allowed to do that. I don't know if I can cope."

FACE BROUGHT THE SEVEN X-wings of Wraith Squadron, including Kell in Donos's snubfighter, around the *Reprisal's* stern along its starboard side, putting them on the same side of the conflict as the *Falsehood* and her pursuit. The X-wings were already in attack position, their S-foils spread and locked. "Fire One," he said.

Fourteen proton torpedoes launched toward the mass of enemy TIEs. As close as the Wraiths were to their targets, the torpedoes crossed the intervening distance almost immediately. As tightly packed as the TIEs were, when those on the leading edge were able to veer out of the way and break a torpedo's targeting lock, the TIEs behind them were not. Ten kills registered on Face's sensor screen, then the TIE force was spreading, scattering, breaking by twos and preparing to engage the Wraiths.

"That won't work twice," Face said. "Change Target Two to the Dreadnaught's bow. Fire Two." Fourteen more proton torpedoes leaped away. Face saw detonations all around the *Reprisal's* bow, couldn't determine if they were penetrating the damaged Dreadnaught's shields. "Break and engage by pairs."

ON THE BRIDGE of *Mon Remonda,* Han Solo sat in his command chair, his stomach threatening to knot ever tighter, while he watched the holocomm broadcast from the *Falsehood.* The sensor-display portion of the broadcast showed the *Falsehood* on her outbound flight and all the vehicles around her.

At the moment, only two TIE starfighters assailed the *Falsehood.* The Dreadnaught was not firing, its command crew obviously thrown into disarray by the detonation of the bomb.

"They're going to escape, Zsinj," he said, his words intended for no one's ears but his own. "You can't have that. Jump in. Bring *Iron Fist* in. Come on, Zsinj."

"SIR," SQUEAKY SAID, "do we tell the Wraiths about Lara?"

Wedge hesitated. If they broadcast an encrypted message telling the Wraiths that one of the TIEs was Lara and she was conceivably an ally, the message would eventually be broken. A voice signal like that simply offered too much data. "Tag her as a friendly on the sensor board and transmit only that information, and only as data," he said. That might do it— a tiny data update was much less likely to be intercepted by the enemy or decoded.

"Yes, sir."

"ME UP, YOU DOWN," Kell said.

"We're your wing," Runt responded.

They aimed straight for the *Millennium Falsehood,* Kell

approaching above the level of the freighter's top hull, Runt beneath her keel, both firing at the TIEs pursuing the freighter.

Kell kept his fire a little high so no slight deviation in his progress would bring his lasers down onto the *Falsehood*. But his target's erratic motion brought it up toward his field of fire . . .

And then, on his targeting computer, his target changed color from red to blue. Kell swore, took his finger from the trigger, and the *Falsehood* and its pursuit blasted past underneath him. He began as tight a turn as was possible to come up behind the *Falsehood* again. Below him, Runt was doing the same.

THE *FALSEHOOD* ROCKED more violently than before and suddenly air was howling through the freighter. Wedge's ears popped as the air pressure changed.

Squeaky's voice, for once, contained alarm. "We are breached! Shields are down on the keel!"

"Chewbacca, roll her!" Wedge shouted.

Outside his viewport, the universe rotated 180 degrees. Fel was abruptly in his gunsights instead of Lara. He opened fire on Fel. "Donos, lock down that hull breach. Chewie, keep our good shields between us and Fel. Maybe Lara won't vape us."

What a thing to have to count on. Squeaky's assurance that they shouldn't destroy Lara—and now, with the *Falsehood*'s unprotected keel exposed to her guns, she could vape them with no effort.

LARA SAW THE *FALSEHOOD* ROTATE, exposing its belly, and her sensors showed its shields there were gone.

She could fire, or she could reveal herself to Zsinj to be a traitor to his cause.

Or she could—

She deliberately twitched the pilot's yoke a little too hard and her maneuver carried her forward, right into the *Falsehood*'s keel. Suddenly she was spinning out of control, and there was an ominous cracking noise as a jagged line appeared on her viewport.

"Petothel?" It was Fel's voice. "Petothel, are you hurt?"

She didn't answer.

ZSINJ WATCHED, his mouth slack and expression disbelieving, as the holocomm display from the *Reprisal* continued.

The bridge view was gone, of course. It had vanished when the bridge was destroyed. But sensor data continued to pour in.

The *Reprisal* was breaking up. The initial explosion had breached her hull, smashed her bow shields, and temporarily deprived her of effective command. The proton torpedoes that followed had inflicted massive structural damage on the old Dreadnaught.

Now she continuously vented atmosphere into space, her crumpling bulkheads preventing airtight doors from sealing. Her captain had sent her into a turn just before the bomb's impact, doubtless to track the *Millennium Falcon* with her guns, and the stress of the maneuver was cracking the mighty old ship open like a nut.

Zsinj sagged against the bulkhead. "I can't kill him. I can't kill Han Solo. I don't know the formula. I don't have the plan."

Melvar, in his ear, said, "The One Eighty-first is disconnected. I've ordered them to break away from the attacking force. But we can send in another capital ship and get them coordinated again."

"No. Throw good money after bad? Besides, Solo will be in hyperspace before another ship can get into proper position. This assault is over."

Melvar saluted and moved over to look down into the crew pit, where his starfighter director was. "Send the starfighters down to a planetary base." His voice was heavy with regret.

Zsinj knew that regret.

He knew frustration, too. Nothing was working. Nothing was working.

THE TIEs WERE still swarming, but abruptly they were swarming in another direction, back toward the planet.

With no TIE fighters close enough to see in the cockpit viewport, Squeaky dispensed with the human-face mask he wore. It served merely to conceal the gold tone of his face and was only effective against distant or fast-moving observers. At Wedge's direction he returned to his Han Solo voice and activated the comm unit. "Wraiths, form up, prepare for hyperspace. Polearm Seven, it's time for you to return to dock with the *Falcon*."

"Coming in, General."

Wedge leaned in over Squeaky's shoulder. "Now say, 'Good shooting out there.'"

"Doesn't she know she shot well?"

Wedge glowered. "Just do it."

"Good shooting out there, Konnair."

"Thank you, General."

Dorset Konnair's A-wing sidled in toward the *Falsehood*'s starboard. Delicately, she maneuvered it alongside the docking station temporarily installed where one of the freighter's escape pods should be. A moment later, Squeaky felt the thump of contact. "All ready," he said, in his own voice.

"Go back and help Donos patch that leak, would you?"

"If I must. One minute a general, the next minute a sheet-metal worker."

Wedge smiled at him. "That's life in the armed forces."

———

"PETOTHEL, COME IN."

Lara stirred, trying to convey with body language that she was dazed. She stared out the forward viewport. Fel's TIE interceptor cruised there, mere meters from her. It seemed to be spinning, though she knew that it was her own interceptor that was rolling. "What? I, what?"

"Are you injured? We can bring in a shuttle with a tractor to get you out of there."

"No, I'm good to fly." That was the pilot's automatic response, whether Imperial or New Republic, whether truth or self-delusion. She sat upright. "Did—did we get him?"

"Almost," Fel said. "Come along, you're my wing." He vectored away and moved planetward, away from the burning wreckage of the *Reprisal,* only a few kilometers away.

She'd spent her time "unconscious" productively. The datapad that had transmitted its unusual commands to her laser weaponry was now back in a pocket. She'd hammered her helmeted head against the side of the cockpit until it really was sore, until she was almost as dizzy as she claimed to be—she'd need the telltale physical signs of injury when she got back to *Iron Fist.*

She'd done it. She couldn't keep a smile off her face as she followed in Baron Fel's wake.

CAPTAIN ONOMA STOOD before Solo. "We have found the position *Iron Fist* held throughout the engagement. A wing-pair from *Mon Delindo* detected her a few minutes ago."

Solo came upright. "Alert Rogue and Nova Squadrons, tell them to stand ready. Communicate with *Mon Delindo.* We'll converge on *Iron Fist*'s position—"

"Sir, *Iron Fist* has already jumped out of system."

Solo sagged into his chair. "Abandoning his pilots? Not even bothering to pick up survivors off the *Reprisal*?"

Onoma nodded in the awkward Mon Calamari fashion. "Doubtless he's relying on planetary forces for rescue, and will send a freighter back for his TIE squadrons. He's gone, sir."

Solo offered him a disbelieving shake of the head. "He just won't come in close enough to a system for its mass shadow to delay his departure. He's that spooked."

"You should be honored, General. You're what's 'spooking' him."

"Failures don't get honored, Captain." He shook his head, looked away from the captain. "I have to think about this."

THE CREW OF the *Millennium Falsehood*—two Corellian men, a Wookiee, and a 3PO droid in a general's uniform—descended the loading ramp more hastily than usual, as though they expected the battered craft to burst into flame, and turned to look at the freighter.

She had new laser scoring all over her hull. Smoke drifted from beneath the keel and rose to the hangar's ceiling.

"Not bad," Wedge said. "I've flown worse."

Squeaky said, "You are joking, I hope, sir."

Wedge turned his attention to the droid. "And now that we have a moment or two, Squeaky, would you mind telling me why you said we should allow Lara Notsil to blow holes in our hull?"

"Well, I thought she was trying to tell us something."

Wedge blinked. Then he turned to the Wookiee. "Chewbacca, go ahead. Pull his legs off and hit him with them."

"Wait!" Squeaky threw up his arms as if to ward off the blows to come. "Let me explain."

And he did.

GENERAL SOLO, Captain Onoma, and Wedge were already in the briefing room when Donos arrived. Within a minute, they were joined by Shalla and Face.

"This meeting concerns Lara Notsil," Wedge said. "Each of you is here for a different purpose. General Solo and Captain Onoma are here because this pertains to mission planning. Shalla, because of your knowledge of Imperial Intelligence techniques . . . and mentalities. Donos, because of your familiarity with Lara. Face, because of your training as an actor; we assume that you can recognize your own kind."

Face managed a smile. "From time to time," he said.

Wedge said, "Earlier today, the *Falsehood* was fired upon by Lara Notsil, who was acting as a TIE interceptor pilot for Zsinj's forces. Squeaky, acting as communications officer, noticed that every time she hit us with laser fire, our comm unit stored fragments of a transmission."

Donos frowned. "Her attacks were also transmissions?"

"That's right. She had apparently rigged one of her laser cannons to pulse in the fashion of a line-of-sight laser communicator. She had also, according to what we can determine, reduced the strength of her lasers somewhat—else we would have suffered more damage than we did."

Shalla said, "This is sort of what Donos did with his laser rifle at Halmad." Above that world, needing to trigger an explosive device but prevented from doing so by comm jamming, Donos had modified the output of his laser sniper rifle to transmit the detonation signal.

Wedge nodded. "That may have been what gave her the idea. Here's the message. It's voice only." He reached over to the terminal keyboard beside the conference table and pressed a button.

First, a hiss suggesting a low-quality recording, then Lara's voice emerged from the air around them. "This is Lara Not-sil, transmitting to Wraith Squadron and *Mon Remonda*."

Donos tensed. Knowing that the message was from her hadn't prepared him for actually hearing her voice; he felt almost as though he'd been physically struck. Then he became aware of Shalla's gaze on him. Face's, too. They were evaluating him, his reaction.

Once, he would have washed all expression away from his face, giving them nothing to read. But he didn't care about that anymore. It hurt to hear Lara. It didn't matter if they could see the bleakness of his expression. He closed his eyes to listen more carefully.

"I was the one who suggested to the warlord that he'd encounter you at Comkin Five. If you did show up there, I hope it's because it's part of your mission plan, that you were hoping to engage him. I told him you might also appear at Vahaba. You might want to keep that on your schedule. You should be able to engage him there as well."

Donos opened his eyes to glance at Solo and Wedge. They were exchanging a look, and Solo shook his head, a trace of confusion to his expression.

"I'm working on a plan now whereby I might be able to transmit you *Iron Fist*'s location, just as we did with the Parasite plan." That mission, in which Wraith Squadron had planted a program in the computer of a new Super Star Destroyer, *Razor's Kiss*, had led to the new ship automatically sending its location to Solo's fleet. Ultimately, it had resulted in the ship's destruction. "If I die, the plan might be able to continue in my absence, so don't just give up on it if someone manages to shoot me down. Attached to this message is a data package showing what I've done, what conclusions I've reached. I hope you can use them.

"Please tell the Wraiths that I'm holding faith with them." There was a long pause, the distinct sound of Lara swallowing with difficulty. "The rest of this message is for Myn Donos."

Wedge tapped a key on the terminal and her voice cut off. He looked apologetically at Donos. "I'm sorry. I've heard it already, and it does pertain to her state of mind. We're all going to have to hear it."

Donos nodded, not trusting himself to speak.

Wedge tapped the key again.

A little background hiss returned to the air, but Lara didn't speak for several seconds. Then, "Myn, it's not likely that we'll ever see each other again. So I wanted to take this opportunity to say good-bye. Well, more than that. I wanted to explain. About what I did.

"I was fighting a war, the way I'd been trained, and that involved infiltrating the enemy and getting their secrets back to my superiors, or sabotaging the data the enemy possessed. There was never a time I saw a file labeled 'How to Destroy Talon Squadron' and thought to myself, 'Oh, that's what I want to do.' To me, it was just data about occupied territories and interplanetary borders.

"Then I infiltrated Wraith Squadron, just a ploy to make myself more valuable to prospective employers, and things started happening. All the furniture that made up the way I'd thought and felt about things all my life started coming loose in my head. Nowadays it slides around and breaks into pieces and I have no idea what parts of it are real and what aren't." There was a waver to her voice now, a suggestion she was having trouble keeping it under control. "It hurts, and a lot of the time I don't know who I am anymore.

"But I know what I have to do. Whoever I am, I'm staying here, like a vibroblade right next to Zsinj's vitals, and when the right time comes I'm going to stab him deep. That'll probably be the last thing I do.

"I don't have any friends here, except one droid, and I don't have any where you are, or anywhere else in the galaxy, so when I'm gone there isn't going to be anyone to remember me kindly. So I was just sort of hoping you wouldn't hate me anymore. I really can't stand thinking that's the only way I'll be remembered."

There was a long silence, the sound of a sniffle. Her voice finally returned, quieter than it had been. "I wish I'd been someone else. To give you that chance you wanted.

"Lara Notsil out."

Donos felt his eyes burning. He put his hand over them. He felt tears under his fingers.

They were silent a long moment. Then Wedge, regret in his voice, said, "All right. Opinions. Shalla?"

Shalla cleared her throat. "Tough call. At a certain level, I think Corran Horn was right. Mentally and emotionally, Lara's not all together. But she seems to be sticking to her plan, to her perception that Zsinj is the enemy. And if I read her words right, she's resigned herself to death in this effort. That makes it more likely that her words can be trusted.

"Add to that the very interesting way she transmitted data. It was complicated, it was unreliable. It was a desperation measure. If she really was an agent of Zsinj's, she could have just shot us a tight-beam transmission from her interceptor's comm system. We would have known that there was very little chance of such a message being detected. The approach she actually used suggests to me that she's afraid that her interceptor's comm system is tapped, recording, something, and she wanted to get around whatever measures had been taken that way."

"All right. Face?"

"She's a pretty good actress," Face said. "In her line of work, she'd have to be. But there was a lot of what seemed like very genuine strain in her voice. I'd lean toward the side of her telling the truth."

"Donos?"

Decorum demanded that he look at them when he answered. To do that, he'd have to put his hand down. If he did that, they'd see his tears. They'd know he wasn't in control of himself. They'd know—

Well, to hell with what they knew, with what they thought. He slammed his hand down on the tabletop. Shalla and Solo jumped. He looked around the table, defying all to say anything about the tears on his cheeks. "She was telling the truth," he said.

"I need a little more than that," Wedge said. "Your reasons?"

"That final bit . . . if she's luring us into a trap for Zsinj, what was that last bit for? To make me feel bad? What good would that do?" He took a deep, shuddery breath. "If she had wanted to manipulate me, to make me come in on her side, she'd have said, 'If I get out of this alive, I'll come back to stand trial.' That gives me everything, puts everything on me. If I just want justice, I win—she stands trial. If I want *her*, I win—I stand beside her at her trial, and I can dream that she'll get off light. That's the way to swing me over, but she didn't do that. She just said good-bye."

Wedge nodded. "All right. There you go, General. Three opinions, all in the same direction, for different reasons."

Solo asked, "Why did she think Vahaba would be on our list?"

"I looked at the data file she'd appended to the audio," Wedge said. "She had done a good job of calculating the criteria we were using, except that she thought that the planets our false Han Solo would be visiting would all be former trading partners with, or recipients of regular trade goods from, Alderaan."

Solo leaned back. "That makes sense. It does. One of the factors we used was choosing worlds that produced certain types of matériel that are valuable in times of war and times of peace. That would correspond to a certain degree to the types of goods Alderaan was importing after it banned all its weapons. Can you run the numbers on our projections again, substituting trade with Alderaan for what we had?"

Wedge gave him a smile. "Already did. And guess which

system, discounting the ones we've already visited, jumps to the top of the list? Vahaba."

"Vahaba." Solo smiled. "If we can get the *Falsehood* repaired fast enough, we can dangle it like bait for Zsinj again. All right, Nelprin, Donos, thanks for coming. Loran, I need you for a moment more."

Donos rose, offered a salute, and was the first one out the door.

WHEN THE THREE pilots were gone, Solo turned to Wedge. "If Zsinj wouldn't come in at Kidriff to get me, he won't come in anywhere. He's just too conservative. Protecting *Iron Fist* all the way. So if we can't get *Iron Fist* close enough to a gravity well to trap it for a while, we need to bring a gravity well to *Iron Fist*."

Wedge frowned. "Meaning what? An Interdictor cruiser?" Those vessels, uncommon even in the Imperial fleet where they were most prevalent, possessed gravity-well generators that, when activated, could keep all vessels within range from entering hyperspace.

"That's right."

"Does Fleet Command have one available for you?"

"No," Solo said. He turned to Face. "That's where you come in."

"Uh-oh," Face said.

"I'm going to set up an appointment between you and your Imperial admiral buddy. I want you to go ask him for an Interdictor."

Face said, "Begging your pardon, sir, but you're crazy enough to be a Wraith."

Solo grinned. "Until you've crewed with me for a few years, kid, you have no idea what 'crazy' means."

14

TONIN DECIDED THAT it might be a good thing to be the King of the Droids.

He was now a mighty leader, in command of hundreds of utility droids aboard *Iron Fist*.

He had modified many of them, with magnetic treads replacing their wheels, so that they might maneuver on the outer hull of the vessel. They clustered at the engines and the hypercomm antennae, using their internal tools to chew and splice their way into external system ports and accesses.

More moved within *Iron Fist* at Tonin's commands. Some were in the engine compartments. Others had spliced into the computer data cables. One was now in the security system that monitored Lara's quarters; it fed modified recordings of her to the observers, so she could do whatever she pleased in her quarters while they saw only footage of her sleeping. Others dragged cables and dataports through the walls, giving Lara access to more and more secure portions of the ship and the computer archives.

Even so, half of the utility droids Tonin commanded confined themselves to ordinary ship's functions . . . for Tonin had to make sure the ship's central computer didn't notice a sudden drop in the utility droid population. If droid MSE-6-P303K spent its day doing Tonin's bidding, droid MSE-6-E629L would spend half its day doing the duties assigned by the ship's computer, then would visit one of the special interfaces Tonin had had installed at points in the ship, assume the identity of MSE-6-P303K, and spend the other half of its day doing that droid's duties.

So far, the ship's main computer hadn't noticed. This was, Tonin reflected, because Tonin was so much better at this task than the ship's computer was. Perhaps the ship's computer considered maintenance of a fleet of MSE-6 droids beneath its dignity.

The droid-guard in the corridor transmitted a warning to Tonin; it indicated someone was approaching Lara's door. Tonin decoupled himself from Lara's terminal and rolled hastily into her closet. But when the door opened, it was Lara herself who entered, looking tired and even dazed—but not hurt or unhappy, so far as Tonin could read human emotions. "Good morning, Tonin."

He beeped a greeting at her, then returned to his post at the terminal and extended his scomp-link once more into its data port. To the terminal's screen, he transmitted, YOU WERE GONE FOR A LONG TIME.

"I'm sorry. I had to go on a mission. I think I got a communication through to *Mon Remonda*, though." She sat on her bed, pulled her boots off, and lay down. "I also gave myself a mild concussion and got personally congratulated by General Melvar for 'tenacity and courage in pursuit of the enemy.'"

THE CONCUSSION WAS PROBABLY A BAD IDEA.

"Don't be so sure." She gave him a little smile. "What have you been up to?"

WE HAVE HOLOCOMM ACCESS WHENEVER YOU NEED IT, BUT IF YOU USE IT, THEY WILL DETECT IT VERY QUICKLY. AND MY DROIDS FOUND AN UNMAPPED SECTION OF THE SHIP.

"Show me."

Tonin accessed this morning's most interesting recording and transmitted it to the terminal's screen.

It was a very low view, as was to be expected due to the MSE-6's tiny size, of a bank of rectangular viewports seen from an adjoining corridor. Beyond the viewports were chambers that were obviously medical wards. One was an operating theater. Another held cages filled with sapient and near-sapient life-forms: Ewoks, rodentlike Ranats, Bilars with their stuffed-doll features but lacking the carefree expressions of most of their kind, a pink Ortolan with its trunklike nose pressed against the front bars of its cage, meter-long Chadra-Fan with their furry faces and gigantic ears, and more.

She sat up, her tiredness apparently forgotten for the moment. "Is this everything you have on this chamber?"

YES, FOR NOW.

"We need more. Get a holocam droid into that chamber, assign it there permanently. And get a droid with a computer link in behind the walls, see what sort of data we can intercept. This is really important."

IT WILL BE DONE.

"Now, I've got to sleep." She flopped back onto the bed. "Concussions are no fun."

DON'T DO THAT ANYMORE.

ADMIRAL ROGRISS FROZE with his wineglass halfway to his lips. "You want what?"

Face smiled. "Surely you have one available."

Rogriss set his glass down with a thump. "Available to me, yes. I can't make it available to you."

"Even to destroy Zsinj?"

"Even then. Factor in the likelihood that *Iron Fist* will destroy her. Factor in the likelihood that you Rebels will destroy her—accidents *do* happen. Then append the certainty that you'll take the credit for Zsinj's destruction regardless. I become a failure who, at worst, collaborated with the enemy and, at best, lost an Interdictor cruiser. No, no, no."

"Well, we can do a lot of things to keep this from happening," Face said. "First, we'll assign two of our own Imperial

Star Destroyers to protect your Interdictor. Second, if you inform only the most trusted members of the Interdictor's bridge crew that they're temporarily working with the New Republic, the majority of the crewmen will never figure it out—they'll see our Star Destroyers out of their ports and presume that they're Imperial. Later, you can say that the Interdictor blundered into a fight between the New Republic and Zsinj and was able to get in the killing blow while everyone else was figuring out whom to shoot."

"What will you give me?"

Face frowned. "How's that again?"

"If I do this, I'll be giving you an Interdictor, even temporarily. Will you give me, say, a Mon Calamari cruiser for one of *my* missions?"

"I'll give you a framed and autographed holo of Face Loran, Boy Actor."

Rogriss brightened. "Excellent! I can trade it for a framed and autographed holo of Tetran Cowall. I always preferred his holodramas anyway."

Face seized his chest over his heart. "A good shot, Admiral. I concede the duel." Then he gave the admiral his most frank and evaluative stare. "Realistically, you're not giving us anything. You're joining us on a mission of mutual interest. If we succeed, we both win. If you lose your Interdictor, you can be assured we'll have lost both Imperial Star Destroyers assigned to protect it . . . and many more ships besides. I guess it boils down to the question of what's more important—accomplishing your Zsinj mission because it's good for the Empire or because it's good for Admiral Rogriss."

The admiral touched his own chest, an echo of Face's gesture. "You shoot well yourself." He looked away, at the white bulkhead wall, and was silent for several long seconds. "I'll do it," he said.

"I'm glad."

"We must have a rendezvous point." The admiral held up his wineglass.

Face touched it with his own. "Good to be collaborating with you, Admiral."

LARA COULD ALMOST feel the stare of Tonin's holocam eye on her. The R2 had been very solicitous since her return from the Comkin mission. Worse, it seemed to sense the way her spirits lowered as she reviewed the data they continued to receive from the secret chamber on *Iron Fist.*

It was awful stuff. She didn't get into the worst of it in the summary she recorded for *Mon Remonda.* The attached data file would give the New Republic the most gruesome details.

"Project Chubar is what they call the techniques used to raise the intelligence of sapient and near-sapient beings. The name derives from a character in a series of children's holos about a bilar, a cute mammalian creature, who is a clever pet of a young girl. The holos used animated graphics instead of actors. It's a twisted sort of touch that Face Loran supplied the voice for Chubar. Maybe you ought not tell him that one of his roles was the inspiration for the name of the project. Anyway, Chubar involves chemical treatments and a teaching regimen to bring a humanoid's mental functions up to those of human average—sometimes higher. In the case of creatures that are already intelligent—for instance, Ewoks— the process enhances mental traits that bring its *type* of intelligence more in line with a human's. Less reliance on sensory data and more on analysis, for instance.

"Project Minefield derived from Chubar. It involves a second, and much faster-acting, set of chemical treatments that affect the victim's mind on a much shorter-term basis. While the chemicals are at their maximum effect, Zsinj's agents can implant a delusion and a mission in the victim's mind. The delusion is usually that some awful situation is in effect and can't be stopped until the mission is accomplished.

"Both the delusion and the mission are associated with a trigger, usually a code phrase. Until the phrase is used, the victim is unaware of what has been done to him . . . in theory. Some of the doctor's annotations indicate that the victims sometimes suspect that something is wrong. But when the phrase is used, the mission pops to the top and becomes the victim's number one priority. Um, this conditioning wears off after a while. The length of time it remains viable varies from species to species, but seldom exceeds one standard year."

She scrolled through screens of data on her terminal. "The code phrase can have a variable in it. Let's say the mission is 'Kidnap someone' and the trigger phrase is 'I need a new speeder, someone broke mine.' You'd tell the brainwashed agent, 'I need a new speeder, Elassar Targon broke mine,' and the victim would interpret that as 'Kidnap Elassar Targon.' It's a fairly versatile setup." She skimmed through more screens of data. "So far, the treatment only works on mammalian species.

"Project Funeral is Zsinj's major operation using the Minefield technique. Our brainstorming session pretty much nailed its purpose and intent—fomenting suspicion between the humans and nonhumans of the New Republic. Addenda to the files suggest that the project has recently been suspended, pending a new direction or a shutdown. In other words, it's been stopped dead, at least temporarily.

"I'm going to do what I can for the test subjects on *Iron Fist*. I'll end their suffering, one way or another.

"End Session Three." She switched off the recording and leaned back in her chair.

She felt strange. Growing up on Coruscant, raised in the planet's long-standing traditions concerning other species, she'd always believed in the basic superiority of humans. Oh, it wasn't necessarily wrong to have affection for a member of another species—a household servant, or a reliable merchant who knew his role in life—but Coruscant was a world for and made by humans. Imperial doctrine solidified these traditions into something like duracrete.

Then, as an infiltrator in the Rebel navy and, later, Wraith Squadron, she'd run again and again into evidence suggesting that these traditions simply made no sense. With Wraith Squadron, her long-standing assumption of superiority over even the nonhumans she'd liked simply wilted away.

And now, with only a droid—held by the Empire in even lower esteem than nonhumans—for a friend, longing to return to a society full of what she'd once considered aliens, she once again knew that the Gara Petothel that had been her childhood identity was dead. Dead and unmourned.

And the nonhumans in their cages deep in *Iron Fist*'s belly were beginning to haunt her dreams.

Words popped up on her screen. ARE YOU SAD?

"No," she lied. "Just tired. But it's time to get back to work." She leaned forward again. "What's our situation with the hyperdrive?"

WE HAVE UNITS IN PLACE ALL OVER THE ENGINES. THEY CAN BEGIN THEIR SABOTAGE AT ANY TIME. BUT THERE ARE NOT YET ENOUGH IN CRITICAL POSITIONS FOR US TO BE CERTAIN THAT THEY CAN DISABLE THE HYPERDRIVE.

"Keep pouring on resources," she said. "We have to be able to bring those engines down when we want to.

"Let's see here . . . even though we have some access to the ship's computers, we can't afford to play around with them too much. We'll be detected. Zsinj's slicers aren't bad. So I've been thinking about the most efficient way to give Solo's force an advantage in any direct confrontation with Zsinj's fleet. To me, that suggests messing with *Iron Fist*'s strategic coordination of Zsinj's fleet. We might be able to flag friendly ships as enemies, temporarily, and enemies as friendly. Can we proceed that way?"

YES.

"Chance of being detected?"

VERY LOW, IN OUR INITIAL PHASE OF MANIPULATING THE PROGRAMMING. ONCE THE PROGRAM IS ACTIVATED, DETECTION CHANCE IS NINETY-NINE PERCENT IN THE FIRST SECOND OF OPERATION, WITH ODDS INCREASING EACH ADDITIONAL SECOND. PROBABLE DURATION OF PROGRAM ONCE IT IS RUNNING IS ABOUT TWELVE SECONDS.

"Not good enough. How about something to lower the ship's shields?"

PROBABILITY OF SUCH A THING SURVIVING EVEN IN LATENT FORM FOR MORE THAN A FEW MOMENTS IS VERY LOW. THE MAIN COMPUTER'S SECURITY MEASURES LOOK FOR PROBLEMS THAT CATASTROPHIC.

"So most forms of self-destruct are not even worth looking into."

THAT IS CORRECT.

"Well, then what—" She stopped as a new idea occurred to her. "Ooh."

THE DOCUMENT ON Wedge's screen was labeled "Routine Examination," but Wedge knew it to be anything but. It was a fitness report, the accumulated conclusions of *Mon Remonda*'s most experienced medics and analysts.

About Myn Donos.

The review board had been unable to confirm or deny that the torpedo launch was an accidental discharge. That was a break in his favor.

However, the medics collectively pronounced him borderline. One medic said it was a certainty that he'd lose control again; the trauma from the loss of his squadron and his conflicting feelings concerning Lara Notsil made it inevitable.

The others disagreed, but indicated that his stress levels made him a less than ideal candidate for missions.

It was the sort of data-based torpedo that could sink a career. All Wedge had to do was accept their conclusions, scrub Donos permanently from the active flight list, and the problem he represented would go away forever.

But one party hadn't voted yet, and that was Wedge's gut instinct.

A knock sounded on his door. "Come," he said.

Donos entered, saluted. "Reporting as ordered, sir." His expression was somber, but was not the rigid mask Wedge remembered from most of their earlier interviews.

"Have a seat."

Donos complied, then quirked a smile. "Shall I take off my boot, sir?"

"Not this time. Lieutenant, I've asked you in here to find out what role you'd like to play in the Vahaba mission."

"If I could do anything I wanted?"

"That's right."

"I'd be back in my X-wing. That's where I feel I belong."

"And if that were denied you?"

"I'd like to be put in command of the *Millennium Falsehood*."

Wedge leaned back. Donos's comment had taken him momentarily off guard, though he believed he'd kept his surprise from his face. "That has been my role."

"I expect you'd rather be back in *your* X-wing, sir."

"I don't recall inviting you to attempt mind reading, Donos."

Donos's expression became more serious. "No, sir. But we've flown in the same squadron. Learning to anticipate the reactions of your squadmates—emotional ones as well as physical reflexes—is a survival trait. Maybe you find it a gross insult for me to make predictions this way, sir, but I'd say you wanted to get back in your X-wing cockpit and were doing these *Falsehood* runs because of duty. Because you're most qualified—second, perhaps, to General Solo. If I can't fly my own snubfighter, I'd be happy to free you up to fly yours."

"Very generous of you. What if you couldn't pilot at all?"

"Then I'd volunteer for a gunnery position on the *Falsehood*."

"And in any of these three roles, what would you do about Lara Notsil?"

Donos hesitated, and his expression went from somber to melancholy. "I'd follow orders, sir."

"What orders would you prefer?"

"Let her go."

"And if you were ordered to fire on her?"

"I'd do it. I've sworn an oath to the New Republic. To hold its needs above my own."

"And if you killed her? What would you do then?"

"I don't know, sir." Donos's eyes lost focus as they stared off into the distance—perhaps to some future. His expression suggested that this future was not appealing to him. "I don't know who I'd *be* then, sir."

"Fair enough." Wedge regarded the lieutenant for a moment.

This wasn't the Donos he'd met several months before. Not a man whose every worry, every crisis was kept bottled up inside.

Wedge typed a few words into his terminal and sent the file on to the ship's central computer. "Donos, for your information, you were right. I'd rather be in an X-wing, and for the upcoming and future engagements I plan to be. And so will you. I'm certifying you fit to fly. You'll be back with the Wraiths at Vahaba."

Donos's eyes opened wide. "Thank you, sir."

"Thank me after you've performed your duties to my satisfaction. That's when I'll know I haven't made a mistake. Dismissed."

———

VAHABA WAS A RED giant circled by numerous planets. At some time in the past, a celestial catastrophe had destroyed the largest of those worlds and scattered its remains in a thin ring around the sun. The asteroids were spread across such an enormous distance that the Vahaba Asteroid Belt was not a hazard to navigation; any capital ship could blast through it at full acceleration with minimal worry about collision with one of the belt's misshapen stony satellites.

Not that *Mon Remonda* was close enough for her handlers to feel even that minimal worry. To Han Solo's eye, Vahaba was a distant red dot, and none of the system's planets was visible to the naked eye. Solo's fleet hung in space so far out that no set of Imperial sensors within the planetary system would pick them up. Meanwhile, pairs of X-wings off *Mon Remonda* and his fleet's other cruisers scoured the system.

And found nothing.

He resisted the urge to gripe, to drum on his chair arm, to ask once more if there were any updates. Or to tell the new sensor officer to quit looking at him. He'd felt the woman's curious gaze on him ever since *Stellar Web* joined his fleet.

To the bridge crew, *Stellar Web* was an unknown, tagged Contact M-317. It hovered some considerable distance from the rest of the fleet, far out of the range of the most capable visual enhancer. Messages from Contact M-317 were supposed to be sent directly to Solo, and the communications officer was under direct orders not to monitor, not to record them.

Solo and a few others knew the distant ship to be an Imperial *Interdictor*-class cruiser, the new flagship of Admiral Rogriss. But it would be best for that information not to spread.

"New contact, sir." The sensor officer's quiet words nearly jolted Solo out of his seat.

"Let me see," Solo said, and brought up his own chair's terminal screen.

It lit up with a wobbly visual image. Distant ships, forming up slowly into an attack group. Solo nodded. Two Star Destroyers, one *Imperial*-class, one *Victory*-class. Two Dreadnaughts. One smaller ship, a featureless needle at this distance; Solo couldn't recognize it.

"Standard for a Zsinj group," Solo said. "The question is, is this all he's deploying to Vahaba, or is it just part of his fleet?" He raised his voice. "What's the source of this recording?"

"A wingpair from Corsair Squadron, off *Mon Karren*," said the comm officer. "They recorded this, using only visual sensors so they'd be harder to spot. Then one of the pair returned with the data while the other stayed out there to monitor."

"Where is this?"

"At the approximate orbit of the outermost planet, on the approach from Halmad."

"Reinforce the X-wings monitoring this group with another pair. As our reconnaissance units come in for refueling, assign half of them to concentrate on the orbit of the outermost planet, on the direct-line approaches from other surrounding stars."

"Yes, sir."

Solo settled back. His heart was pounding just a little faster.

"SICK OF IT YET?" Face asked his temporary wingman.

"We are growing absolutely sick of it, Face," said Runt. The need for hyperdrive-equipped reconnaissance pairs had placed him with Face for this mission.

The starfield outside their cockpits was brilliant, unchanging. They cruised at sublight speeds at what would be considered the boundary of the Vahaba system.

"Good." Face changed the timbre of his voice, dropping it a register, making it smooth, insidious. " 'Please don't insult my intelligence. Please don't tell me you don't know what I'm talking about.' " He forced a falsetto. " 'I don't, I really don't. Please put down the blaster. You're frightening me.' " He dropped into the lower register again. " 'Fright is the least of what you will suffer.' "

"Are we wrong?" Runt asked. "Or is this as terrible as we think? The writing is awful. You are not improving on it."

"Sometimes you rise above your material, sometimes you don't. I had to learn this when I was seven. It has never left me." He dropped his voice again. " 'Now, tell me where the map is, or I—' "

"New contact, course thirteen degrees, down eighty-two." Runt's voice was suddenly crisp, professional.

"Roll for visual inspection, kill forward thrust, kill cockpit lights, passive sensors only."

"Acknowledged, One."

Face rolled his X-wing upside down. It would have been an unsettling experience in a vessel not equipped with an inertial compensator, but to his perspective it appeared only that the universe rotated around him. He shut down most of his vehicle systems and visually scanned the area of space Runt had indicated.

Nothing; the target was too far away. He brought up the visual enhancer on his sensor board and directed it toward the target area.

A minute's worth of careful panning and searching yielded the target: a group of four ships in close formation. The smallest of them was too tiny to identify by class, but the other three were not. Three Star Destroyers, one of them an ancient *Victory*-class, one an *Imperial*-class, and the other—

"We have her," Face said. "*Iron Fist*. Give me a minute while I calculate range, Six."

"Yes, sir."

Face ran numbers through his navigational computer and compared them with what he knew about the likely sensor ranges of Imperial capital ships. "All right," he said. "Six, I want you to run ahead at one-third acceleration for ten minutes, then set your course to *Mon Remonda*'s station and transit back there. You were recording, weren't you?"

"Yes, sir! Wait, let us check. Yes, we have it."

"Good. Go."

THE NEWS HIT *Mon Remonda*'s bridge like a concussion missile. Solo came up out of his chair, began issuing orders. Captain Onoma did the same. Often their words overlapped one another.

"Recall all starfighters in close range," Solo said. "Launch our hyperdrive-equipped shuttles to the regions we sent recon units to and have them transmit the new coordinates."

"Battle stations," Onoma said. "All spacetight doors to be closed in three minutes."

"Transmit our course to Contact M-317," Solo said. "Dispatch *Skyhook* and *Crynyd* to form up with M-317. They're to shadow her at all times, protect her at all costs, not to interfere with her operations."

"Bring our course to one-oh-six-point-two-two-four, elevation thirty-six-point-oh-nine-nine. Transmit same to fleet."

"Tell the *Falsehood* crew to stand down and go to their secondary mission parameters; we won't need them as bait."

A low, unsettling rumble filled the bridge. Solo felt the hair on his arms and the back of his neck rise. He swung around to see Chewbacca standing in the doorway, his expression happy, uttering the jubilant hunting call. "That's right, Chewie," he said. "It's our best shot yet."

15

L ARA WAS NEARLY jolted out of her seat by the high pitch and panic in the voice of the sensor officer, three seats down from her in the crew pit. "Contact, contact, a drop out of hyperspace, I read four, five, seven vessels cruiser size or better, total fleet size thirteen vessels. They're already deploying starfighters."

Boots clattered on the command walkway overhead and Lara saw Zsinj, General Melvar, and Captain Vellar, the stern-faced man who would have been master of *Iron Fist* had not Zsinj chosen the vessel as his flagship, running forward, toward the main bow viewports. Zsinj skidded to a sudden stop halfway there and Melvar nearly crashed into him. It was obvious that Zsinj could see the enemy with the naked eye—they were *close.*

Lara rolled her chair back to get a look at the sensor officer's terminal screen. It was filled with red blips, outnumbering Zsinj's group more than three to one.

"Return to original course," Zsinj shouted. His face was red. "Prepare for hyperspace. Signal the group. Inform Groups Two and Three. Tell them our situation and instruct them to stand by to jump to the abort rendezvous locations."

"Yes, sir."

Lara rolled back into place and nudged the technician next to her, an Intelligence operative dedicated to analyzing patterns in comm traffic. "Why is he running?" she asked. "They outnumber us, but they couldn't possibly destroy us before the rest of our fleet jumps in."

The analyst gave her a look of scorn. "Zsinj's doctrine," he said. "No matter what the odds look like, if the enemy has chosen the battleground, he has more resources than we're aware of. It becomes imperative to choose a new battlefield, one the enemy can't have prepared. Don't mistake that for cowardice."

"I never would have, sir." She returned her attention to her terminal, then typed a command, sixteen characters of gibberish, into her keyboard, and sent the command.

Somewhere under the floor beneath her, a utility droid that was spliced into the data cables should be intercepting the command, interpreting it, then switching the terminal over from its analysis duties to a direct connection with her quarters—a connection the ship's computer was not set up to monitor.

HELLO, KIRNEY.

She donned a set of goggles and plugged it into the terminal. "Hello, Tonin," she whispered. "Are we set to disable the hyperdrive?"

His next transmission showed up on her goggles. YES. BUT FROM THE MOMENT YOU ISSUE THE COMMAND, IT WILL TAKE A FEW MINUTES TO TAKE EFFECT.

"Understood. On my command, we pin him in place and make our run for it. Three, two, one—"

"Sir, we're in a gravity well," the sensor operator shouted.

"Hold it, Tonin."

Zsinj leaned down to look into the crew pit. "We're not even near—damn. Sensors, identify the Interdictor. Captain Vellar, that's our primary target. Dispatch *Red Gauntlet* and *Serpent's Smile* to annihilate that nuisance. Keep *Blood Gutter* in tight to us. Communications, new message for Groups Two and Three. Send them our current position—update it constantly. Tell them to hold in readiness to jump to our position on my order. If we're not able to jump out of here before we're likely to be disabled, we'll just have to bring the fleet in here and fight on Solo's preferred playground."

"I'm disconnecting, Tonin. We may not have to reveal ourselves yet." She typed and sent the countercommand, restoring the terminal to its proper function, and got back to work.

WEDGE LED HIS group in a wide loop around *Skyhook*, *Crynyd*, and *Stellar Web*, the lead ships of Solo's fleet; around *Red Gauntlet* and *Serpent's Smile*, the Star Destroyers coming in to eliminate the Interdictor; and then straight in toward the retreating *Iron Fist*.

Wedge was lead fighter in the lead squadron of twenty-four squadrons of fighters—every fighter in Solo's fleet except those from the *Skyhook* and *Crynyd*, which were charged with the defense of *Stellar Web*. Several of the X-wing squadrons were light, with pilots still scattered across the solar system, awaiting word that the battle had materialized, but the group was still imposing, the largest force he'd led in quite a while.

"Rogue Leader, this is *Mon Remonda*. Still no sign of starfighter deployment from your target."

"Thanks, *Mon Remonda*. X-wings, set your S-foils to attack position. All fighters, arm your weapons." Wedge looped around so he was lined up more perfectly with *Iron Fist*'s long axis. The lack of starfighters didn't surprise him; Zsinj was hoping to make a jump to hyperspace and didn't want to lose time and pilots by deploying his TIEs and then summoning them back in. But that decision was about to cost him.

Ahead, the Super Star Destroyer's turbolasers and other weapons flared into life. Space around the group was suddenly bright with laser flares and the ball-shaped detonation of concussion missiles.

"Leader to group: make a trench." Wedge threw more

power to acceleration and Rogue Squadron leaped out ahead. The X-wing squad to his starboard, the Gauntlets off the *Allegiance*, dropped back and sideslipped in directly behind. The Y-wing squad to his port, Lightning Squadron off *Battle Dog*, slid in just as neatly behind them.

In a matter of seconds, the broad wing of starfighters became a single concentrated line.

Wedge brought them down low over *Iron Fist*'s stern and fired down at the Star Destroyer's top hull, his lasers striking into but being dissipated by the great ship's shields, his proton torpedoes detonating on impact with those defensive screens rather than against the hull itself. Still, every shot he took battered away at shield integrity and drained badly needed energy resources . . . and more than two hundred fighters strung behind him were doing exactly the same thing. He veered from side to side, varying his altitude as he came, and turbocannon fire was so dense his cockpit interior was constantly illuminated by its brightness.

Then *Iron Fist* dropped away beneath him. He'd run the gauntlet. Tycho was still tucked in beside him, and his sensor board read all Rogues still accounted for. "At the end of your run," he said, "break by squadrons and make further passes at your discretion."

ZSINJ KNEW FROM the way *Iron Fist* rattled that some of those detonations were taking place at the hull, not above it. The beeps and wails of damage reports began to sound. A near-constant line of starfighters flashed forward past the bridge viewports.

"What was that?" he asked of no one, then leaned over the edge of the command walkway. "Petothel! What is he doing?"

His new analyst looked up. "He's concentrating fire on your centerline, since you don't have a starfighter screen out to prevent such a move. But he won't do it on his second run. He knows you'll concentrate your gunnery crew's attention on the centerline now, so he'll break his group up for more standard strafing runs. Don't be fooled."

"I asked for your analysis, not your advice," Zsinj said, and was surprised by the snap in his voice. He turned to Melvar. "Prepare for them to come back by way of the bow the same way. Alert the gunners on top and below for a repeat of the same tactic."

Melvar looked uncertain. "Yes, sir."

On the sensor screens, the deadly line of starfighters emerged from its strafing run off *Iron Fist*'s bow, then broke up into individual squadrons and looped back toward the ship, a broad cloud of enemies.

LARA ALLOWED HERSELF a small smirk of triumph. She'd thought that if she phrased her reply a certain way, suggesting that Wedge Antilles could outthink the warlord, Zsinj would respond with pride instead of with his tactical ability. And she'd been right. It didn't make much of a difference in this situation; the gunnery crews were now receiving corrections, being told to abandon the previous orders. But Zsinj's response meant she might be able to manipulate him again. If only she could persuade him to abandon his group, leave them behind. Then, wherever he emerged, she could shut down his hyperdrive and summon Solo's fleet for the kill.

She sat upright. Wait a second. Maybe she *could* get Zsinj to abandon his fleet. It wouldn't take persuasion, either. Just a minor course correction.

She switched her terminal over to direct communication with Tonin and plugged her goggles back in. "Has *Iron Fist* already transmitted its jump course to the rest of the fleet?" she asked.

YES.

"Can you enter a course correction? I don't mean enter it as a new course—they'd notice that. I mean, like an automated minor correction, as the nav computer continues to process new data?"

YES.

"Is there a star within range of the kind of variation you can enter?"

YES. SELAGGIS. JUST WITHIN ZSINJ-CONTROLLED SPACE. A FEW LIGHT-YEARS AWAY. A YELLOW STAR, SEVEN WORLDS.

"Never mind the almanac data. Correct *Iron Fist*'s jump course so that the distance is unchanged but the destination is on the far side of a direct line through Selaggis's sun."

COLLISION DETECTION IN THE NAVIGATIONAL SOFTWARE WILL PREVENT IT.

"Oh." She sagged.

UNLESS I DELETE SELAGGIS FROM THE STARMAP.

"Do it!"

DONE. WE ARE NOW BOUND FOR SELAGGIS.

"Tonin, you are wonderful. Kirney out."

Perfect. Either *Iron Fist* would remain here, trapped by the Interdictor, until Solo destroyed it, or it would jump to Selaggis, where Solo's fleet could finish it off.

She didn't switch back to normal terminal functions. Instead, she lifted her goggles and glanced right and left, making sure that the analysts on either side of her were fully occupied with their tasks. Then she began recording.

ZSINJ WATCHED IN pained fascination as the battle unfolded.

Red Gauntlet, the *Imperial*-class Star Destroyer, and *Serpent's Smile,* the *Victory*-class, had now dropped behind far enough to engage the Interdictor cruiser and her two escorts. His forces were somewhat overmatched; the Interdictor's screen consisted of two *Imperial*-class Star Destroyers, and they had their starfighters deployed to offer additional damage to Zsinj's ships.

But *Red Gauntlet* and *Serpent's Smile* didn't have to destroy the enemy. They merely had to make one ship driver flinch.

They had to do it quickly, too. Zsinj took in the broader range of the sensor data available to him. *Mon Remonda,* two more Mon Cal cruisers, another Imperial Star Destroyer, two frigates, and a swarm of smaller ships were converging on *Iron Fist.*

Already swarming with Rebel starfighters—Zsinj could see the tiny flashes of their lasers and torpedoes in the long-distance visual feed—his vessels dropped within range of the enemy capital ships' guns. Brilliant streams of light lit up between them.

Red Gauntlet began a stately turn to starboard, bringing her main batteries to bear on the enemy ships. Her flank offered more firepower than the bows of all three Rebel vessels—and more target area, too. Zsinj bit his lip. "Bring up damage and diagnostics holos for *Gauntlet* and *Smile,*" he said.

"Yes, sir." A starboard viewport was replaced by the giant-sized holoprojection of a data screen. It showed both his ships with shields intact, minor damage accumulating throughout their systems, especially on the older *Serpent's Smile.*

But that ship had a canny captain who was a fine pilot. As *Red Gauntlet* rained destructive—and distracting—fire down on the enemies, *Serpent's Smile* rotated ninety degrees on her long axis to narrow her approach profile and sideslipped between the Rebel Star Destroyers.

As they advanced, the Rebel ships unloaded only a portion of the full might of their flank batteries against *Serpent's Smile*—any miss might continue on to hit the other Rebel ship. And, though *Smile* had only a few stem guns to bring to bear against the Interdictor, she had one other weapon—her considerable mass, which was decelerating right in the Interdictor's path.

"Flinch," Zsinj said. All the Interdictor had to do was veer away from the collision. Then *Iron Fist* and, ultimately, all the ships in Zsinj's group could get enough distance from the Interdictor to jump into hyperspace.

The Interdictor came on, her own guns now firing on *Serpent's Smile.*

"Flinch, damn you," Zsinj said.

Melvar said, "We've identified the Interdictor. She's *Stellar Web.*"

"*Stellar Web?* Nonsense." Zsinj shook his head. "That's an Imperial craft. Captained by Barr Moutil. He doesn't have the nerve to do what that captain's doing."

"You were the one who said the Rebels and the Imperials were cooperating against you," Melvar reminded him. "And *Stellar Web* has been observed to be part of Admiral Rogriss's task force."

"Rogriss." Zsinj took a look at the sensor board. *Stellar Web* still came on, straight at the *Victory*-class destroyer decelerating into its path. "If he's transferred his flag to the Interdictor . . . he has more nerve, better timing than my man. My captain will flinch first. We may have to summon the other groups and fight this one out. On *their* chosen battlefield."

The communications officer called up, "Communications lost with *Serpent's Smile.*"

Zsinj scowled down at him. "Nonsense. We still have data feeds."

"Sorry, sir. I meant bridge communications."

Zsinj looked at the enhanced view of the battle zone. The top hull of *Serpent's Smile* was afire, with much of the flame concentrated around the command tower. Increasingly, the old destroyer looked like something a giant beast had chewed upon.

"We're getting communications from their auxiliary bridge. They're requesting orders."

Zsinj felt a sense of loss as he realized what needed to be done. "Tell them to lock down their current course, launch all starfighters, and abandon ship."

"They say they can save her, sir."

"Do as I ordered." Zsinj turned to Melvar. "It's a heavy loss. But now they can't flinch."

Melvar nodded.

SOLO WATCHED AS the stern of *Serpent's Smile* slid ever closer to the bow of the oncoming *Stellar Web*. He was unconscious of the fact that he was rocking forward and back in his seat. Games of head-to-head between capital ships tended to result in disaster for both participants, and disaster was almost upon the two ships he watched.

"They're going to hit," Onoma said. "They cannot avoid it now."

Stellar Web finally vectored, her bow turning slowly away from the oncoming destroyer wreckage. Solo waited for the inevitable collision between ships, but *Serpent's Smile* seemed to slow as it approached the Interdictor. *Stellar Web* shot away from the destroyer, her course taking her dangerously close to *Crynyd*, then vectored away from that vessel as well. Suddenly she was headed out to space, away from the surviving Imperial Star Destroyers.

"How did she do that?" Onoma said.

"I'm not sure," Solo said. "But if I were driving a dragship in that situation, I'd reverse the gravity-well generators so they pushed instead of pulled. That would give me extra propulsion to bounce away from any mass in the area. Must have wreaked havoc with the ship's artificial gravity, though. She can't be set up to do such a thing normally." He couldn't keep dull disappointment out of his voice. *Stellar Web*'s course was now at an angle to *Iron Fist*'s. Distance increased between the two ships. "Weapons, how soon before we overtake *Iron Fist*?"

"They'll be within firing range in thirty-eight seconds," the weapons officer said. "Within effective damage range in a minute ten."

"Sensors, how soon, assuming optimal piloting by *Stellar Web*, before *Iron Fist* is out of her projected mass shadow?"

"Two minutes fifteen, sir."

"Weapons, ready your guns."

WEDGE BROUGHT THE ROGUES around for another pass. Casualties had been high in his group owing to the sustained effort against *Iron Fist*; of the Rogues, Hobbie had been hit by an ion cannon and his snubfighter was out of combat, though he was undamaged, and Asyr Sei'lar had been forced to punch out when turbolaser damage sent her X-wing into a fatal spin toward *Iron Fist*'s hull. A shuttle off *Mon Karren* was now endeavoring to pick her up. Losses had been even more severe among many other squadrons, especially the slower-moving Y-wings and the Cloakshape fighter squadron off *Battle Dog*.

But *Iron Fist* was starting to look bad, portions of her deck gouting flame. *Mon Remonda* reported *Serpent's Smile* destroyed, and *Red Gauntlet* sustaining heavy damage from the two *Imperial*-class Star Destroyers she faced.

"Rogues, stay on her bow," Wedge ordered. "Solo's group is coming up off her stern and we don't want to get caught in the crossfire." He rolled toward the Super Star Destroyer, evened out his shields, and opened fire once more.

His lasers plowed into *Iron Fist*'s shields and through—he

saw hull plates explode out under the pressure of the atmosphere they'd once contained. As he looped around from this side-to-side strafing run, he saw the guns of *Mon Remonda, Mon Karren,* and *Mon Delindo* chewing away at *Iron Fist*'s stern, the destroyer's batteries returning fire against the Mon Cal cruisers.

Then *Iron Fist* became a single streak of light leaping out into space. A moment later, the destroyer was gone. Only the battered-looking cruiser that had been hugging her belly remained, and a second later it disappeared as well.

Wedge set his jaw. This wasn't the sort of victory they needed. "Rogues, form up. Let's assess remaining threats."

But the flaming wreckage that was *Serpent's Smile* was no threat, and neither *Red Gauntlet* nor the three ships around her—*Crynyd, Skyhook,* or *Stellar Web*—was firing. Zsinj's other destroyer had surrendered.

"I CAN'T BEAT HIM," Solo said. His voice was duller than before, even to his own ears. He couldn't seem to muster the energy even to pretend to be enthusiastic. "We've lost."

Captain Onoma regarded him steadily; the Mon Calamari's eyes were wide, evaluative. "We have reduced him."

"He'll swell up again. And there we'll be, locked in this struggle forever." He heaved a sigh. "All right. Recall the starfighters. Assemble the group. Secure *Red Gauntlet* and put a crew aboard her. Maybe we can draft her against Zsinj until Fleet Command decides to reallocate her."

"Yes, General."

The communications officer said, "Message from Contact M-317."

"Put it through."

Admiral Rogriss's face came up on Solo's private screen. He looked unshaken, undismayed by the events of the last few minutes. "General Solo."

"Admiral. Let me compliment you on your flying."

"Thank you. I think we're done here, however. A shame."
The admiral shrugged. "It was a trap that could have succeeded."

Solo nodded. "Let me ask you. Would you do it again?"

Rogriss froze. After a moment, he gave a slight nod. "I
imagine I would. You have my frequency."

"I do. Good luck . . . against the warlord, anyway."

Rogriss laughed. Then his image vanished from the screen.
A moment later, *Stellar Web* made the jump into hyperspace
and was gone.

Solo sat, alone with his thoughts, his crew choosing not to
disturb him.

In the murmur of their voices, he could pick up details of
their status. How many pilots lost. How many starfighters
temporarily out of combat, how many permanently. Damage
tallies. Reports on reconnaissance pilots finally rejoining the
group.

Then his communications officer said, "Sir, we're receiving
holocomm traffic."

"That will be Zsinj," Solo said. "Calling to brag."

"No, sir."

LONG BEFORE SHE was supposed to, *Iron Fist* dropped out of
hyperspace. Directly ahead, though at a sufficient distance
that they were in no danger, was a yellow sun.

Zsinj leaned over to bellow down at his navigator. "What
is this?"

"A star, sir," the navigator said, then wilted as he realized
how unnecessary the statement was. "Name unknown. It's
not on my charts."

"*Not on your charts?*" The words escaped Zsinj in a bellow. "Just how incompetent are you? How far did we travel?"

"Less than eight light-years, sir."

Zsinj felt himself gaping like a fish. *"There are no un-known systems eight light-years from Vahaba!"* He turned to Melvar, dropped the volume of his voice to a whisper. "Are there?"

"Well, if we knew," the general said, "they wouldn't be unknown. But to answer the question more appropriately, no yellow sun like this could exist eight light-years from Vahaba without the people of Vahaba knowing—and so it would be on our star charts."

Zsinj returned his attention to the navigator. "Well, turn us around, get us out of this gravity well and into hyperspace, and get us to our rendezvous point." He didn't bother to keep anger out of his voice.

"Sir?" Another voice, the officer in charge of engineering. "New damage reports. We're experiencing a progressive failure in our hyperdrive system."

Zsinj felt his gut turn cold. "Define 'progressive failure.'"

"Primary subsystems are shut down and secondary systems and optional reroutes are failing. But it's not instantaneous. It's spreading, like a disease."

"How long before the system is inoperable?"

"One minute, maybe two."

"Navigation, how long before we can make our next jump?"

The navigator looked up and slowly shook his head.

"Fix it," Zsinj said. "Now. Now. Now."

"We have a holocomm message," called the communications officer.

"Directed to whom?" Zsinj asked.

"I don't know, sir. It's not to us. It's *from* us."

"I didn't authorize—Oh, Melvar, we're in trouble. Communications, put that message up where I can see it."

The holoprojected status board was replaced by a face— that of Gara Petothel. She had goggles pushed up on her forehead and was leaning in close to the holocam. Her expression was somber. The view behind her was of the back wall of the crew pit. Zsinj looked down at her seat in the pit; it was empty.

"General Solo," the woman said. "If everything has gone correctly, *Iron Fist* is now in the Selaggis system with her hyperdrive inoperable. Other portions of Zsinj's fleet are continuing on to their rendezvous points and won't be able to get to him for a little while—minutes in some cases, hours in others. I recommend you come by and take a look. Oh, bring your fleet, too. Lara Notsil out." The image faded.

Zsinj stood there a moment, his mind a blank. For the first time in years, he couldn't think of anything to say. He did notice the deadly quiet that had fallen on the bridge.

Finally, he turned to Melvar. "Dispatch Security. Have her found and brought to the interrogation chamber." He took a deep breath. "I intend for her death to be so horrible that it will give *me* nightmares."

Melvar nodded and brought out his comlink.

Zsinj addressed the navigator. "We're at Selaggis. Selaggis is normally on our charts. What does that suggest to you?"

"Our charts have been tampered with, sir. I'm already restoring them from our archives."

"Very good. You just saved your own life."

Zsinj turned his attention to Captain Vellar. "How soon can we reassemble the fleet here?"

"If they've already launched for the rendezvous points," the man said, "about six hours for the other units of Group One, four for Group Two, two and a half for Group Three. But, sir, Groups Two and Three had no urgent reason to leave Vahaba. If they've lingered, they're only minutes away."

"Communications! Direct a holocomm signal to any remaining units at Vahaba. Bring them here." Zsinj returned his attention to Vellar. "Bring in *Second Death*. We may actually have to use her in her primary role. Bring in any stray vessels under my command in this region. Bring in any pirate or mercenary forces we've used in the past. Hire any vessel of any sort operating in or near this system. Find a good spot in this system for us to hide until our reinforcements arrive or our hyperdrive is fixed." He took a deep breath to calm himself. "And prepare all our starfighters to launch. We're in for a fight."

AT A HALF TROT, Lara followed the tiny utility droid down the busy corridor, and Ensign Gatterweld followed her. "Should you be doing this?" Gatterweld asked. "Aren't you supposed to be on station?"

"No, I'm not," she said. "I'm tending to an emergency."

"What's with the droid?"

"It knows where to go."

The droid pulled over to stop beneath a utility access hatch. Lara typed numbers into the keyboard beside it. "If this weren't authorized, would I be able to open this?" The hatch offered up a clank of confirmation and swung open. Beyond, in the narrow access shaft, waited another utility droid. A broad box was strapped to its top.

"I suppose not. Where are we going?"

Lara reached in, opened the box partway, and fumbled within it. Her hand rested first upon a trigger housing. She grabbed the weapon's grip and switched the weapon over from blast to stun settings. "I'm going to go get killed. If you're not smart, you will, too." She reached back with her free hand to give him a shove, rocking him back on his heels, then she turned and shot him.

The stun beam caught him in his midsection. He fell backward, hitting the corridor's metal flooring with a clang. Passersby—officers, crewmen, pilots rushing toward their launch bays—stared in momentary surprise, and some lunged toward her.

She stepped into the access shaft and yanked the hatch closed. The hammering of fists sounded against the hatch.

Lara pulled the empty package from the utility droid's back and discarded it. Then she tapped the droid three times.

It turned obligingly and headed off into the shaft, Lara close behind it.

"BUT CAN WE BELIEVE HER?" Solo asked.

Captain Onoma gave him a shrug. "Your analysis team believed her before, and our engagement here at Vahaba confirmed the data she gave us."

"True. But it could still be a plan to draw us into some trap Zsinj has set up at Selaggis. Trusting her could mean the end of the fleet." Solo sat back, frustrated, struggling with conflicting impulses.

"Sir," the comm officer said, "we have more holocomm traffic. A recorded message, not a live transmission."

Solo sat up. "From Notsil again?"

"No, sir. From some sort of automated router in the Halmad system. It didn't come straight from there, though. The route data says it went to a holocomm relay satellite in New Republic space first, then Coruscant, then to a high-security fleet satellite, then to us. It's eyes-only for Commander Antilles or Captain Loran."

Solo frowned. "That's odd. And Halmad is so close the timing can't be coincidence. Captain, is either Wedge or Loran back on board?"

Onoma nodded. "Both are."

"Get them up to the closest conference room, right now."

SOLO MET THE TWO pilots in the conference room. As soon as the door was shut, he said, "Bring up the message."

The room's comm terminal responded in what sounded like a recorded female voice. "State your name and rank for verification purposes."

Wedge looked at the general, who nodded, and said, "Wedge Antilles, Commander, New Republic Starfighter Command."

"Thank you."

The room's holoprojector activated and a hologram swam into focus in the center of the conference table. It showed Warlord Zsinj against a neutral gray background. "General Kargin and the Hawk-bats, greetings," the warlord said.

"It's a recording," Solo said. "You're not compromised."

"I have a proposition for you," the warlord continued. "It's my hope that you're still stationed out of the Halmad system, because if you are, I can offer you a considerable sum to join me on a sort of impromptu exercise. If you're available, please transit immediately to the Selaggis system— practically your next-door neighbor. However, our window of opportunity is very narrow—in a very few hours from this message's time stamp, it will close. I hope to see you soon." With a confident smile, the warlord closed down the transmission and his holo image faded.

"Notsil was telling the truth," Solo said. "Zsinj is trapped at Selaggis." His expression transformed from tiredness and premature age to his familiar cocky appearance.

"And he's desperate for troops," Face said. "He's calling in the Hawk-bats and probably every pirate he's dealt with within a few light-years. We've got him."

"Do you want to go in as the Hawk-bats?" Solo asked.

Face shook his head. "We'd have to put on the makeup, repaint some of the interceptors. Call it half an hour to an hour's delay. And all it would get us is proximity to *Iron Fist* in a half dozen TIEs."

"Where do I know the name Selaggis from?" Wedge asked.

"Another Zsinj strike zone," Solo said. "One of the first I looked at after I assumed command of this task force. One of the moons of Selaggis Six was colonized. I guess Zsinj decided to make a lesson of someone colonizing on his border without his permission. *Iron Fist* wiped out the whole colony. I think it would be very appropriate if he were wiped out in the same system."

"Right."

"Get back to your squadrons," Solo said. "We'll jump immediately." He raced from the room, showing haste inappropriate for a general.

Wedge and Face headed back for their hangar at a trot. "Shalla is going to be so relieved," Face said.

"How so?"

"Her assault on Netbers back in the Saffalore complex. She's been beating herself up for a while, wondering whether she should have risked all our lives to keep the Wraith Squadron and Hawk-bats link a secret. Now she gets to know she was right."

16

"*SECOND DEATH* is on station," announced *Iron Fist*'s communications officer.

"Very well," Zsinj said.

"Sir."

Zsinj turned at the sound of Vellar's voice. "Captain. What is it? You're almost smiling."

Vellar did in fact smile. "I got through to the *Chains of Justice*. Group Three had not yet entered hyperspace at Vahaba. The entire Group Three is en route to us now."

Zsinj beamed at him. "We might not only survive—we may have just won this engagement, Captain. Thank you."

MON REMONDA and the New Republic fleet dropped out of hyperspace well within the Selaggis system.

"Contact," announced the sensor operator. "Multiple contacts moving well ahead of us. Their course takes them toward Selaggis Six."

"Show me," Solo said.

The holoimage brought up to hang before Solo's chair jerked and flickered, the result of the extreme visual enhancement needed to offer any detail at this range. It showed a gradually lengthening line of ships headed toward a distinct yellow-orange world. The closest ships, those at the rear of the formation, were two Star Destroyers—one Imperial, one Victory—and a smaller vessel. Like *Carrack*-class cruisers, the small ship looked like a thick bar with thickened areas fore and aft, but Solo recognized it as a *Lancer*-class frigate. Smaller than Carracks, the Lancers were configured to repel starfighter squadrons. Stretching out ahead of these vessels were two Dreadnaughts and, in front, a smaller craft that would have been difficult to identify if seen from an above angle, where it would look like a simple triangle. But *Mon Remonda*'s position was slightly below the flight path of the outbound ships, and from this perspective Solo could see the teardrop-shaped command pod hanging from the bow, the boxy starfighter bay depending from the stern. It was a *Quasar Fire*-class starfighter transport. Solo had one in his own fleet.

Solo ran the numbers through his head. It was a habit he'd gotten into as a general; the Corellian habit of ignoring odds until one crashed right into them was inappropriate for an officer who had lives depending on his decisions.

"If they join up with *Iron Fist,* they will outgun us," Captain Onoma said, confirming Solo's calculations.

"But not by an impossible amount," Solo said. "We'll just have to be better than they are."

The world the enemy forces approached, Solo knew, was a gas giant, a beautiful yellow-orange thing whose atmosphere was characterized by constant storm activity. The storms unceasingly changed the planet's patterns of swirls and lines of color, so that each new day offered variations in the worldscape. It must have been an ever-changing work of art for the colonists on one of the world's moons. Selaggis Six also had a heavy debris ring thought to have been another moon at one time.

Solo nodded. "Selaggis Six is the perfect place for Zsinj to make a stand. He can use the terrain to his advantage. An asteroid ring to hide in, a planetary atmosphere he might even be able to bring *Iron Fist* into for cover. That's our destination, Captain. Follow that group."

———

LEAVING TONIN BEHIND, Lara stepped out of the turbolift onto a deck of *Iron Fist* that wasn't supposed to exist.

She'd only seen it through holocam recordings taken by utility droids. It didn't seem quite as cavernous from a human perspective.

Ahead was a long, dimly lit corridor. To the right was a bank of viewports showing more brightly lit chambers.

The first chamber she passed was the one she thought of as the zoo. In it were a couple of monitoring consoles and an entire wall of metal and transparisteel cages, stacked three high, the upper ones accessed by a sort of portable turbolift—a metal floor in an open-air upright frame. Most of the cages still seemed to be full. Two human men were seated at a desk, one typing away on a large terminal. Neither noticed Lara. She wasn't surprised; inside the more brightly lit room, the transparisteel of the viewport would be very reflective. If they did see her, all they'd see was a naval officer walking at a slow, measured rate.

It was making her crazy, having to pace herself now that she was within sight of humans and holocams again—though Tonin's measures should have rendered those holocams ineffective. She wanted to dash down to the end and do her business. But she couldn't afford to attract attention, not now.

The next chamber was a surgical theater. The operating table featured an inordinate number of straps and fasteners of varying sizes. There were also injectors on robot arms, monitor screens, tools she couldn't recognize. She suppressed a shudder. Then, the office. Within it, another two men, medical technicians. One looked up as she passed, squinted, and shaded his eyes to see her through the partial reflection.

She rounded the turn to the right and punched the combination Tonin had given her into the door keypad there. The door slid open.

The two technicians, dark-haired men of ordinary appearance, their features so similar they were probably brothers, glanced at each other and their expressions brightened. "A new liaison officer?" asked one.

"That's right." Lara entered and shut the door.

"Would you *please*—" said the first.

"Please please please," said the second.

"Tell us what's going on with the ship?"

"We were in a battle, weren't we?" said the second. "I could feel the vibrations even down here."

"I felt them first."

Lara looked between them. "You two, and the men in the containment chamber, are the most vomitously despicable creatures I think I've ever met."

The two men looked at each other. "You haven't even gotten to know us yet," said the first.

From where she'd tucked it into her belt at her back, she drew her blaster. Both men flinched. "Take me to the containment chamber," she said. "Or I'll kill you."

In moments she was in the largest chamber, four prisoners standing splayed against one blank wall, while she examined the cages at ground level.

Inside the nearest was an Ewok. "Do you understand Basic?" she asked.

It nodded, its motion quick and very human. Its eyes looked like those of an Ewok but possessed an understanding that was unsettling.

"I'm going to free you and get you off this ship. So you can go home or live where you please. Would you like that?"

It nodded.

One of the medics said, "Zsinj will kill you for this."

"No, he's going to kill me for several other things." The lock on the cage was simple, mechanical; she lifted it and the Ewok emerged. The creature looked at the medics and uttered a low, rolling growl.

Then, to Lara's discomfiture, it spoke, its voice rising and falling in a singsong that did not belong to any Basic dialect she'd ever heard. "I will kill them."

"No," she said. "You will go to each cage. Ask each prisoner if it will refrain from attacking me if it is freed. Tell it that I will get them all off this ship. Then free the ones who agree."

The Ewok looked up at her, so obviously considering her command and his other options that Lara could almost see a strategic program running behind his eyes. Then he shrugged like a human and moved to the next cage.

OUT THE FORWARD VIEWPORT, Zsinj could see little but tumbling asteroids and brilliant flashes of light as *Iron Fist*'s forward guns blasted the largest of them.

The communications officer said, "The shuttles report our explosives packages being planted on schedule."

"Good."

"And *Chains of Justice* reports sensor contact with Solo's fleet, sir."

"Very well."

"And we have a report from the chief engineer."

"Hold on." Zsinj stepped back to his hologram pod in the security foyer directly behind the bridge. "Send it to me here."

The face and torso of the chief engineer, whose light build and scrupulous cleanliness belied his profession, swam into focus in the air. "Sir, we've identified the trouble. The engineering compartments are swarming with, well, saboteur droids."

Zsinj gave him a look to suggest the man shouldn't make jokes. "Would you like to try again?"

"Standard MSE-6 utility droids, sir. They've gone mad or been reprogrammed. With their internal tools, they're opening access hatches, chewing their way into wire clusters, sending false data, dragging chips out of their housings. All in the hyperdrive systems."

The absurdity of what the man was saying hit Zsinj and he almost snorted. "And what are you doing about this?"

"We're, uh, kicking the things to pieces with our boots, Warlord. Between the primary and redundant systems, we're restoring the system to functionality. But when we jump, we'll need to make it a careful one; there won't be any backup systems in case of component failure."

"Understood. How long?"

"Pessimistically, an hour. Optimistically, somewhat less. I don't know how much less."

"As much less as possible, if you please. Out." The image faded.

Zsinj turned to Melvar. "Very clever. I wish our analysts had anticipated such an approach to sabotage. We need thinkers like her in my organization, General."

"Are we not going to kill her, then?"

"I said thinkers *like* her. But loyal ones. Her fate will serve to reinforce that loyalty."

THE STARFIGHTERS OF Solo's fleet finished forming up, then broke off by task.

Wedge's task force included four X-wing squadrons, one A-wing, and the Wraiths. They turned toward Selaggis Six and leaped forward, drifting a little out from the path taken by Zsinj's group, their intent to pass it by and reach the planet first. Other groups of starfighters would head straight for the Star Destroyers at the rear of the formation, hoping to get some early licks in, while still others remained on station with Solo's fleet as a defensive screen.

"Group, this is Leader. When we reach the ring, we'll break by squads to our assigned task. Rogue and Wraith Squadrons will head counter-spinward and spread out the width of the ring for reconnaissance. Corsair and High Flight Squadrons will do the same spinward. Polearm and Shadow Squadrons will break by wingpairs and do recon runs on the moons. First pilot to spot *Iron Fist* gets an extra three-day leave."

IRON FIST'S COMMUNICATIONS officer announced, "*Chains of Justice* reports starfighter launch and deployment from *Mon Remonda*. X-wings incoming. Y-wings remaining behind as a screen."

Zsinj smiled. "Launch all our squadrons, except the One Eighty-first and the experimentals." He turned to Melvar. "While they send their fastest fighters looking for us, we can concentrate ours on them. *Mon Remonda* is in for the beating she deserves."

"INCOMING STARFIGHTER SQUADRONS from Selaggis Six," the sensor operator said.

Solo nodded. "Bring the Y-wings up front. Let them think that's all we have. Array the rest behind *Mon Remonda*." He had four squadrons of Y-wings, two each from *Mon Karren* and *Mon Delindo*, plus two more Y-wing squadrons and a Cloakshape squad off the *Battle Dog*.

The Y-wings were good at hammering large targets, and rugged enough to sustain a lot of damage from enemy starfighters. But they weren't fast or nimble enough to keep TIE fighters from bypassing them and hitting a target like *Mon Remonda*.

However, the last ship in Solo's formation, the Imperial Star Destroyer *Skyhook*, after its capture from the Empire, never had its complement of Imperial fighters replaced by the New Republic's ubiquitous Y-wings. Instead, it retained its original complement of six TIE fighter squadrons, crewed mostly by former Imperial pilots who'd joined the Alliance over the years.

The approaching force, nine squadrons of TIE fighters and interceptors, came on in a spread pattern toward *Mon Remonda*, ignoring the other ships in Solo's group. Several kilometers out from *Mon Remonda*, as they reached maximum firing range from the Y-wing squadrons, they opened up with a salvo of lasers, then broke around the Y-wing force in four groups, leaving the slower New Republic starfighters to turn awkwardly in their wake.

"Open mass fire," Solo said. "Forward guns only. Prepare to drop them at my command. Bring up the TIEs."

The cruiser's forward turbolaser batteries and ion cannons flashed into life, and Solo could feel vibrations in the heels of his boots as wave after wave of destructive energy poured out toward the enemy. On his sensor board, the cluster of TIEs waiting to *Mon Remonda*'s stern, colored blue to indicate their friendly status, suddenly leaped into motion, half moving up over the cruiser, half under her hull.

Off the cruiser's bow, the incoming TIEs began reaching effective fire range. The cruiser throbbed and vibrated as her shields absorbed concentrated laser fire from a hundred starfighters.

The friendly TIEs reached *Mon Remonda*'s midway point. Solo said, "Cease mass fire. Begin individual defensive fire by sensor only—with friendly TIEs out there, they can't rely on visuals. Good luck to the pilots." Then, all he could do was wait and watch.

He saw a collective waver along the line of enemy TIEs as their pilots, momentarily freed from the distraction of the turbolaser barrage, recognized that the incoming TIEs were not friendly. Some looped back the way they'd come. Two red dots vanished instantly, destroyed by incoming fire from the pursuing Y-wings. Then the clouds of red and blue targets became hopelessly intermixed.

The turbolasers opened up again, their fire more intermittent, their gunners firing more discriminately now that friendly and enemy forces were in such close proximity.

Far ahead, Solo's X-wing reconnaissance squadrons should be reaching the ring of Selaggis Six about now. "Come on, guys," he breathed. "Get me what I need, fast."

"GROUP LEADER, this is Polearm One. I have the *Iron Fist*." Captain Todra Mayn, once of Commenor, now a Starfleet Command lifer, had only to glance out her port viewport to see the mighty vessel. "I'm flying parallel to the center of the interior rim of the debris ring. *Iron Fist* is about forty kilometers deep in the ring. She seems to be blasting herself a channel parallel to the edge. It's the turbolaser flashes that let me spot her."

"Polearm One, Group Leader. Good work. Stay in position and we'll form up on you."

IRON FIST DIDN'T alter course in the minutes it took Wedge to form up his group of six squadrons. "Group, Leader. Any guesses as to her intent?"

"Leader, this is Shadow One. This sort of ring includes particles much finer and closer than we see in normal asteroid fields. Most of them won't worry a shielded Star Destroyer. But even finger-sized bits can wreck an X-wing at high speeds. I think he's giving himself a second set of shields here."

"Good point," Wedge said. "But space around the larger asteroids should be a little clearer—their gravity will have drawn in some of the proximate particles. We'll take it slow going in and move from asteroid to asteroid until we're close, an island-hopping approach. Break by squads, each squad choosing its own approach." He suited action to words by heeling over to starboard, descending relative to *Iron Fist*'s orientation, along the inner rim of the debris field. Rogue Squadron formed up behind him.

Entering the debris field was like flying into an odd sandstorm. The asteroid debris was mostly small, and was sufficiently well spaced so that only the larger asteroids interfered with vision. But every few seconds, forward shields would light up with the impact from a tiny asteroid, or Wedge would hear a metallic clank as something hit his hull. His diagnostics continued to register full atmospheric pressure, though.

He set his course from large asteroid to large asteroid. Some of them were the size of small moons, the others merely as large as good-sized houses.

His comm unit crackled. "Group Leader, this is Wraith One. Wraith Squadron in position to begin assault run."

"Wraith One, Leader. Good flying. Stand by until all squadrons are in position."

"Acknowledged."

Rogue Squadron finished a half orbit around one of the larger asteroids and suddenly *Iron Fist* was in full view again—less than a kilometer below. Other than the bow guns being used to clear a path for her, the ship's weapons were not active. A few large asteroids floated between the Rogues and their target, partially obscuring Wedge's view.

"Maintain this orbit," Wedge said. "Rogue Squadron in position."

"Shadow Squadron in position."

"Corsair Squadron in position."

A minute later, the remaining units had reported in.

At the end of another quick orbit, Wedge said, "Leader to group. Set S-foils to attack position. Begin your assault runs." He looped away from his orbital path and dove toward the Super Star Destroyer.

As WRAITH SQUADRON formed up to begin its assault run, Donos suddenly felt uncertain. More than that, he felt awash in unreality.

He'd been here before. He knew he had.

The last time he'd felt this way—above a moon circling the third planet of solar system M2398—he'd witnessed the destruction of his astromech, Shiner. Then the sense of unreality had claimed him and he'd found himself back in the ambush at Gravan Seven, the one that had cost him his squad . . . and his sanity.

It was happening again—

He clamped down on his feeling of desperation. But neither Gravan Seven nor M2398 had had an asteroid field. Neither resembled the space around him. What was here that threatened to send him back into a state of collapse?

"BREAK OFF, BREAK OFF! It's an ambush!"

Wedge grimaced. The voice was that of Donos. Wedge had been wrong. The pilot's mind had snapped back to the Gravan system ambush yet again.

"Group Leader, this is Wraith Three." Donos's voice was in control again. "Please order an abort on the assault run. *This is an ambush.*"

"Group, abort. Pull back and regroup." Wedge hauled back on his yoke, veering away from *Iron Fist.* "Wraith Three, this better be good."

Abruptly the Star Destroyer's gun batteries went active, pouring laser blasts into the asteroid field all around it. Wedge could see bright flashes as dozens of asteroids detonated. Comm traffic told the story of the other pilots' conditions. "This is High Flight Three. I'm hit by debris. Experiencing engine shutdown." "Shadow Twelve is gone, repeat, is gone! He ran right into a chunk of asteroid."

"Wraith Three, that's two casualties and all we did was break off," Wedge said. "You'd better have a good reason." Well out of range of *Iron Fist*'s guns, he put Rogue Squadron into orbit around another planetoid.

"Yes, sir. I thought I was going crazy for a minute. I distinctly remembered going through this exact raid once before. I hadn't, really—it was a simulator run back when I was first getting pilot training with the Alliance."

"Go ahead."

"The sim was based on a story, a lesson from one of my instructors. He'd been a Y-wing pilot. His unit encountered an old *Victory*-class Star Destroyer in a debris field like this one. Took the same kind of approach in, island-hopping from big asteroid to big asteroid to minimize damage from debris. When they got close enough, the destroyer opened up— shooting the asteroids they were nearest. The rock debris superheated and exploded like bombs. It was a disaster for the Y-wing unit. I ran through the simulation of it several times. It was a nightmare."

Wedge thought about it. Their target's barrage had seemed to hit a lot of the asteroids near his starfighters. "Which *Victory*-class Star Destroyer was it?"

"*Iron Fist*, sir. The original one. Zsinj's first command."

"Good work, Wraith Three. Group, we have a new plan. Squads who feel up to it can still approach laterally, but stay away from any asteroid large enough for them to target and blow up—say, anything half the size of your vehicle or larger. The rest, drop down into *Iron Fist*'s wake, into the path they've already cleared out for us, and strafe her stern. Resume your assault runs." He heeled his X-wing over, choosing a path between asteroids, and began another run, Rogue Squadron following close behind.

———

Deep in the automated processes of *Iron Fist*'s main computer, a watchdog program, recently activated, detected the fact that the ship's laser batteries had recently fired on targets in a nondrill fashion. A timer associated with the program started up, counting down from three minutes.

Zsinj offered up a heavy sigh. "The starfighter trap appears to have failed," he told Melvar. "Bring back our own starfighters from *Mon Remonda*. We'll need them."

"They suffered substantial losses before they understood what they were facing there," the general said. "It'll be even worse when they have to disengage and run home."

"I know." Dispirited, the warlord looked down at his feet, a neutral image that could bring him no bad news. "I'm getting tired, Melvar. Making mistakes. Not anticipating my opponents' moves the way I should. And I'm going to have to sacrifice more if I'm to win this engagement. I'm pouring credits on this problem instead of solving it with ingenuity." He looked up at his general. "Bring them back."

The four medics lay with their limbs tied, their mouths gagged, as Lara assembled the humanoids she'd freed. There were two pachydermal Ortolans, three Ewoks, male and female Gamorreans, three bilars looking like large children's toys, two knee-high Ranats with suspicious eyes and frequently bared incisors, one huge, white-furred Talz with four pain-racked eyes, and five waist-high Chadra-Fan whose ears flicked back and forth between listening to Lara's words and to the struggles of the medics.

"We can get you out on escape pods," Lara said. "Unless— can any of you pilot a shuttle?"

One of the humanoids raised a paw.

The Ewok.

Lara stared at him. "You're kidding."

"No," he said. "Doctors put me in sim-u-la-tors. See if Kolot can learn to fly."

"And you can."

"Yes."

"Kolot, you can't even reach all the controls."

"Warlord had mechanics make me pros-the-tics. For hands and feet—"

"Stop it!" The words emerged from Lara as a shout and she buried her face in her hands. "I know this joke already."

"Joke?"

After a moment, she uncovered her face and knelt before the Ewok to look at him from his own altitude. "Kolot, we're the same thing, you and I. We're both lies that eventually became the truth."

The Ewok shook his head, not comprehending.

"Don't worry. You'll understand someday. Let's go."

Tonin was still in the turbolift, his scomp-link inserted into the lift controls. He uttered a relieved whistle when he saw Lara returning safely.

She counted heads as her rescuees entered the turbolift and came up two short. "Where are the Gamorreans?"

She saw them now, down at the end of the corridor, coming toward her at a trot. As they got closer she could see something different about them.

Blood. It was splashed across their chests and dripped from their tusks.

She looked at the viewport into the zoo. She couldn't see much of the containment chamber, certainly couldn't see where she had left the bound medics, but she could see the splash of blood across the inside of the near corner of the viewport.

She looked at the Gamorreans and could think of nothing to say. How could she protest their actions, not knowing what was happening behind their eyes, not knowing what the medics had subjected them to? As they entered the turbolift, they regarded her steadily, with no hint of regret or apology in their eyes.

Her voice emerged in a whisper. "Let's go."

ZSINJ'S FLEET MOVED out over the broad portion of Selaggis's debris ring, then turned back toward Solo's. Two of the ships, the antistarfighter frigate and the bulk cruiser acting as a TIE carrier, continued on toward the inner edge of the ring. The stream of TIE fighters fleeing *Mon Remonda* and the starfighters pursuing them caught up with the two smaller ships, passed them by, then dove into the debris ring.

"That's where they're making their stand," Solo said. "All right. Bring up *Allegiance, Crynyd, Tedevium, Etherhawk,* and *Ession Strike* to engage and hold Zsinj's fleet. The rest of our fleet will bounce around them and head on straight for *Iron Fist.* Except *Warder*—keep the medical frigate out of the engagement zone."

Solo's two *Imperial*-class Star Destroyers, one of the frigates, his *Marauder*-class corvette, and his Corellian blockade runner surged ahead, a spearpoint aimed at Zsinj's fleet. Solo waited until they were well ahead, then directed the navigator to enter the angled course that would take the three Mon Cal cruisers, remaining Star Destroyer, and *Quasar Fire* carrier toward Zsinj himself.

WITHIN *IRON FIST*'s computer system, the three-minute countdown ended.

The program looked for and found the fleet diagnostic data being piped to the ship's bridge—damage analysis from each ship in Zsinj's fleet. It was already assembled in a convenient package to be displayed as a holoimage for Zsinj's use.

The program took the package and encrypted it under a Wraith Squadron communications scheme. Then it checked *Iron Fist*'s threat board, identified the distant target *Mon Remonda* as the chief designated threat, and broadcast the package to that cruiser as an ordinary data stream.

"COMM TRANSMISSION FROM *Iron Fist*, sir."

"Chewie, your favorite correspondent is calling you again."

"No, sir," the comm officer said. "It's a data stream." His voice indicated confusion. "It's diagnostic data, sir. For all the ships in Zsinj's fleet. It's being broadcast under a recent Wraith Squadron encryption on New Republic frequencies."

Solo looked up at his comm officer, then glanced at Captain Onoma, who regarded him with one eye turned back toward him. "That would be Notsil again," Solo said. "Probably. Are all our ships getting this data?"

"No, sir."

"Send it to all our ships. They're to use the data until I say otherwise."

"Yes, sir."

Solo allowed himself a smile.

ZSINJ'S COMLINK BEEPED. He brought it up. "Yes?"

"Sir, Engineering. We have the hyperdrive functional again."

Zsinj checked his chrono. "Thirty-eight minutes. Excellent. Continue with repairs. Perhaps you can get some of the redundant systems functional and improve the odds that we'll survive a hyperspace leap."

"Already on it, sir."

Zsinj pocketed the device. "Put him down for extra leave time and a raise in pay. I approve of efficiency."

Melvar nodded, but did not look at the warlord. His attention was fixed on the holo showing the damage *Iron Fist* had sustained and was continuing to suffer. The primary projection showed a series of wire-frame renderings of the destroyer as shown from above; blinking red zones indicated damaged areas. A secondary list indicated system failures. "We have a radiation leak on Deck Four."

Zsinj grimaced. "I see six radiation leaks." There was a tremendous bang from overhead and the bridge lights momentarily dimmed as a nearby torpedo strike momentarily overloaded some ship's systems. "Ah. Seven, now. Deck Four is the least of our troubles."

"Yes, sir. Still, I want to check it out personally. On a hunch." The general bowed and headed back toward the bridge exit.

Zsinj followed him but stopped at one of the secondary communications consoles in the security foyer. He leaned over the shoulder of the man there.

The officer didn't turn, but said, "Our TIEs have returned to *Iron Fist*. Now making an attack on the squadrons assaulting us."

"Good. Is any of the units assaulting us now confirmed as Rogue Squadron?"

The man nodded. "Yes, sir. Eighty-three percent probability. We haven't cracked their current transmission scramble code, but based on performance we still get a better than fifty percent probability that Antilles is leading them."

"Excellent." Zsinj pulled out his comlink again. "Zsinj to Baron Fel."

"Fel here."

"Prepare to launch. Don't worry about defending *Iron Fist*. We'll give you a course that will take you within visual range of Rogue Squadron, then you can head out to an engagement zone of your own choosing. Do whatever it takes to draw them away—far away."

"And then?"

"I'll send a support squadron a couple of minutes later. Between your pilots, your special systems, and this support, you should be able to kill Antilles. Please do so."

"Warlord, it will be a pleasure."

Zsinj pocketed the device and moved slowly back up to his preferred station on the command walkway. It was time, almost time to decide. The next few minutes would show him whether Solo's fleet or his own would prevail in this battle. In the latter case, he would send Solo yelping back to Rebel space . . . or, best of all, kill him. In the former, he would have to destroy *Iron Fist*.

Temporarily, at least.

SOLO'S STAR DESTROYER group closed with Zsinj's force. Even at this range, Solo could see the needles of laser light flash between ships engaged in that action.

His sensor operator kept data on the status of all his ships projected as holos up on one of the bridge viewports. But now those images were smaller than usual, joined by similar data being broadcast from *Iron Fist*.

Solo saw red areas creeping through the engine compartments of the data screen labeled *Flash Fire*. The captains of his own ships *Tedevium* and *Etherhawk* began concentrating their fire on the stern of the Dreadnaught and the redness spread even faster.

That engagement was visible through his starboard viewport. Ahead was the glorious color pattern that was Selaggis Six. Below was the debris field that, from a distance, was just a ring, an attractive ornament for the planet.

"We're above *Iron Fist* now," the navigator said.

"Very well," Solo said. "Make your course straight for *Iron Fist*. Bow shields to maximum. Sensors, relay data to gunners on all asteroids in our path that could conceivably harm us. All other ships in the group are to line up behind *Mon Remonda*. We're going to drill a hole straight to *Iron Fist,* and we're going in fast. "

WEDGE AND TYCHO whipped across a massive stone ridge on a city-sized asteroid; the instant they knew the pursuing TIEs had lost sight of them, they decelerated.

Their pursuers came around at full speed, hugging the asteroid's surface more closely than they had, and overshot the two X-wings. Wedge fired, saw his twin-linked lasers hammer the side of his target. The TIE, not penetrated, struggled to return to its original course, but the blast had sent it tumbling too close to the asteroid surface. It veered straight into a hill-sized projection and detonated.

Wedge glanced at Tycho, then at his sensor board. His wingman was intact; the other TIE was a ball of orange-and-yellow gases half a kilometer back. The other starfighters of his group were holding up well in spite of the sudden arrival of several TIE fighter squads—and not all the new arrivals were enemies. Some were friendlies off *Skyhook*.

Wedge looped back around toward *Iron Fist* for another strafing run—or another head-to-head with TIEs.

A new cloud of TIEs, two squads of interceptors, rose from the destroyer's belly and veered off into the asteroid field. All wore red horizontal stripes on their solar wing arrays.

Wedge checked their course. It took the interceptors away from *Iron Fist,* away from Solo's engagement, toward Selaggis Six's once-occupied moon.

"Leader, Two. I don't like the sight of that."

"Me either, Two." He switched his comm unit to the group frequency. "Group, this is Leader. Polearm One, take command of the group. Rogues, Wraiths, form up on me. We have something to check out."

———

Lara pushed open the access hatch just a few centimeters and peered out into the corridor beyond. It was empty, echoing with a radiation alarm, flashing with the red lights appropriate to such a dangerous condition. Opposite the hatch was the door into the hangar bay she wanted.

She stepped out and helped haul Tonin over the hatch lip. "Give us a minute to get the door open," she told the nonhumans crowded into the access shaft. "Then look both ways to make sure no one is coming, and join us."

They nodded, a little excited but confident, like a roomful of businessfolk just before an important meeting. She was left with the unsettling impression that she was leading a horde of humans dressed up for no particular reason in humanoid suits.

The hangar door opened to their approach. She breathed a sigh of relief; she and Tonin wouldn't have to run a lengthy bypass on the door controls. She toggled the control so the door would remain open for the humanoids following; despite their human-level, or genius-level, intelligence, they might still be startled by the suddenness with which ship's doors tended to shoot up into their housings.

Within the hangar, only three vehicles remained: Lara's X-wing, a *Lambda*-class shuttle, and a larger shuttle of similar design, an Imperial landing craft. "We'll give them the landing craft," she told Tonin. "I'll get it prepped for launch. You still have the file on my X-wing?"

Tonin tweetled an affirmative.

"Open it up, disable all transponder systems, and disengage whatever else the file says they've done to it. I don't want them to be able to detonate it remotely."

"They won't need to." The voice, cultured and self-assured, came from behind her, from the hangar corner nearest the door.

She whirled. General Melvar stood there, a blaster pistol in his hand, and Ensign Gatterweld, looking surly and betrayed, held a blaster rifle at the ready beside him. Both men moved toward her.

"You had to come back here for your souvenir X-wing," Melvar said. "Perhaps your only mistake in a skillful escape attempt. I knew your arrival was pending when you or your droid falsified the radiation leak for this deck."

Lara saw shadows congregating behind the two men, at the door into the bay. She raised her hands. "That's why the hangar doors were not secured. You were waiting for me."

"Correct."

"Will you be killing me now?"

"No. That's the warlord's prerogative." Melvar looked sad, and Lara had the unsettling feeling that the emotion was genuine. "I do wish you'd been faithful. You could have helped the warlord lock down this quadrant of the galaxy. He's generous with those he respects. You could have owned a world."

"I wish I had something witty to say to you," she told him. "But the thought of helping Zsinj is turning my stomach."

The humanoids moved forward, a nonhuman mob, the sounds of their passage masked by the alarm sounding in the corridor.

"I think—" Melvar stopped, his eyes darting right, where one of the Gamorreans had just moved up within his peripheral vision.

He turned, brought the blaster around. The other Gamorrean, the female, grabbed his forearm and slammed him to the hangar's metal floor. Gatterweld spun, panic on his face—

And then the nonhumans were all over the two men, pounding them, raking claws across their faces, biting at limbs and heads and torsos.

"Stop it!" Lara yelled.

The humanoids looked up at her.

"Just bind them. Leave them. They'll die when *Iron Fist* is destroyed."

They looked at each other, then rose from the downed men.

IN MINUTES, she and Tonin had the two vehicles ready for departure. She fitted a ladder to the side of her X-wing. "You're sure you can fly this thing."

The Ewok, standing at the base of the shuttle's boarding ramp, nodded. He carried the objects he'd brought with him from the hidden medical facility—four prosthetic extensions, two with articulated hands at the ends, two with long-toed feet.

Tonin rolled up to her and whistled a question.

She didn't have to know the musical speech of droids to understand. "No, Tonin. You're going with them. You have to broadcast all that data I recorded about Zsinj's projects. The medical data."

He whistled again, more urgently, shrilly, a complicated message.

She drew her goggles from her pack, put them on, plugged the trailing wire into Tonin's side.

WHERE ARE YOU GOING?

"I'm going to rejoin my unit."

YOU SAID THEY HATED YOU. THEY WILL BE YOUR ENE-MIES. THE WARLORD'S FORCES ARE YOUR ENEMIES. YOU'LL DIE IF YOU DO THIS.

"Maybe," she said. "Probably."

DON'T.

She stared down into his holocam eye, and suddenly found it, and Tonin's stance, to be as expressive as any human mannerism. "Oh, Tonin. I have to. I have to do this to be who I decided I want to be. Do you understand?"

No. You've already reprogrammed yourself. That's enough.

"I wish it were. But an intention isn't anything unless you carry it out." She knelt, wrapped her arms around the droid, gave him a squeeze she knew he could not feel.

You will tell us if you need help. We will help.

"I have my comlink," she said. "I'll tell you." Tears blurred her vision for the first time in days. She rose, pulled her goggles free of Tonin's jack, and hurriedly climbed up into her cockpit, unable to face the droid again.

Tonin wheetled one last, sad sound and rolled toward the landing craft.

17

Oɴ Wᴇᴅɢᴇ's sᴇɴsᴏʀ ʙᴏᴀʀᴅ, the interceptors of the 181st had a commanding lead; they were already entering the atmosphere of the moon, once home to Selaggis's colony.

Four friendly starfighters trailed the 181st, not losing ground to them—Kell, Elassar, Shalla, and Janson, flying four of Wraith Squadron's own TIE interceptors. The X-wings of Rogue and Wraith Squadrons trailed by a distance that increased with every minute.

"Wraith Five to Leader. They're descending toward the west coast of the primary continent. I think that's where the colony used to be. Atmospheric conditions not helpful. Heavy rain, heavy winds."

"Acknowledged, Five. Do not engage. Continue to update us on their progress. Transmit us your sensor data." Wedge suppressed a curse. He preferred the X-wing to every other starfighter ever made, for its nearly ideal balance of ruggedness, speed, and firepower, but sometimes—such as now—he devoutly wished for more speed.

"They're banking toward a set of ruins—the colony, I guess. No sign of life in the ruins—they're strafing! There has to be a living target down there, Leader. Permission to engage."

Wedge closed his eyes. He'd already confirmed that there was no native comm traffic from Selcaron. *Mon Remonda*'s records had reported no survivors from Zsinj's barrage of five months ago. And yet Zsinj was dedicating his best pilot, his best-trained starfighter unit, to pound those ruins flatter.

It had to be a trap. Had to be. But if it wasn't . . .

The New Republic wasn't here to protect itself, but to protect innocents. There might be colony survivors down there. It was that simple.

He opened his eyes again. One second had clicked by on his console chrono. "Permission granted."

KELL BANKED AND DOVE toward one of two rearmost pairs of interceptors. It was difficult to see them; the sky was overcast, and fierce winds blew sheeting rain almost horizontally across his path. His heart hammered—in his throat, it felt like—and he knew that he might at any moment introduce his lunch to the inside of his helmet.

The old fear. It had paralyzed him at the *Implacable* fight. In the months since, it had never entirely left him. It might never leave him.

It made him feel like hell. He decided to take it out on the enemy.

The rearmost interceptor of the wingpair he'd targeted chittered for a split second in his targeting brackets, then broke to starboard. Its wingmate made a sudden deceleration, seeming to blast backward past Kell's port side, preparatory to setting up for an attack on him—

It exploded, vanishing from his sensor screen. "Good shot, Nine." He banked tighter, trying to stay inside his target's turn radius, but the enemy interceptor's maneuver was sharper than any Kell had ever made. A moment later the interceptor came up behind him, a quarter klick back. Kell heard his sensor system howl with the confirmation of his enemy's targeting lock on him.

He dove toward the ground—a two-tone surface, gray seas to his port, brown soil to starboard, the wreckage of prefabricated dome buildings where the two colors met. Lasers flashed above him, visible through his top viewport. He angled over toward the sea, dropping almost straight toward the shoreline.

As the range meter dropped, he felt wind kicking him to port. He struggled with the piloting yoke, heard the howl of his sensors again, and juked to throw off his pursuer's aim. He was kicked to port again, and from the sensor's unmusical complaints, this time it had to have been from a laser graze rather than atmospheric conditions.

At a mere couple of hundred meters from the ocean's surface he fired his lasers and hauled back on the yoke. The lasers hit the water's surface, boiling it, sending up a column of steam. He flashed through it, actually felt the drag of the mist as his interceptor hit the column, and banked to port, a maneuver so fast and tight his vision began to gray out.

His pursuer emerged from the column of steam, not banking instantly—its pilot had to be taking a moment to find Kell.

That was the moment he needed. He held his turn, struggled against the centrifugal forces trying to slam him into the starboard side of his cockpit, and came around behind his enemy. The TIE vibrated in his targeting brackets and he fired.

The TIE exploded spectacularly, transformed into the biggest fireball Kell had ever seen yielded by an interceptor's detonation, a hundred-meter-diameter ball of destruction. Kell climbed to stay above the rising cloud of smoke and flame, then shook his head to try to clear his vision. "Two down," he said. "Twenty-two to go."

"Twenty." That was Janson's voice. "But they're changing tactics."

Kell looped around, back toward the ruined town, and Elassar fell in beside him.

Ahead, the interceptors of the 181st continued with their low-level strafing runs against the ruins. They seemed to have no particular target; their aim seemed to be the transformation of the entire set of ruins into smaller rubble and dust.

Kell saw Janson and Elassar come in from the east, aiming for a pair of interceptors near the ruins' border. Their targets shied away toward the colony center; two more turned in the direction of Janson and Elassar for a head-to-head. Janson and Elassar banked toward the newcomers, but those targets, too, looped away as a third pair maneuvered to engage the Wraiths.

It was a deadly game of keep-away, fliers of the 181st turning to engage the Wraiths just long enough to get their attention, then breaking away to return to their strafing. As Kell and Elassar neared shore, two interceptors turned toward them.

"If they come at us," Kell said, "standard head-to-head. If they bank away, don't follow."

"Acknowledged," Elassar said.

Their enemies banked away well before they were in targeting range. A new pair angled in from the north, timing their approach so they'd hit Kell and Elassar from the side if the Wraiths continued their straight-line approach.

"Up," Kell said, and drew back on his yoke. His interceptor rose at a dizzying pace. "I don't get it. They're playing defensively."

"They're waiting," Janson said. "For the rest of the Rogues and Wraiths."

ZSINJ WATCHED IN mounting disbelief as his fleet's damage displays grew ever redder. "Melvar," he said.

Captain Vellar looked over from his position on the command walkway. "He's not back from his errand. Did his errand involve a shuttle launch? We have a landing craft taking off from the personal-vehicles bay. It seems to be in pursuit of an X-wing."

Zsinj shook his head, unconcerned. "Never mind that. Vellar, are they that good? Oh, Sithspit, we just lost *Venom*." Red flashes crossed and crisscrossed the display of the *Victory*-class Star Destroyer like a flash fire.

"They seem to be, sir," the captain said. There was tension in his voice, but his expression was unwavering. "*Mon Remonda* is almost in position to engage us."

"Your opinion?"

The captain gave the sensor holoprojections a long look. "Our group isn't going to defeat their secondary group. They're being pounded to pieces. Solo's main group, which is almost unhurt, is going to hit us in just a minute. We're damaged, and we don't know the extent to which we may have been further sabotaged. Eventually Solo's secondary group will reinforce the main group." He turned a regretful face to Zsinj. "Sir, we're not going to win this fight."

"All ahead full," Zsinj said. "Get us out of the debris field. Set your course for *Second Death*'s position. Bring in all starfighters from all ships—except the 181st and their support—to harass Solo's group."

"Sir, that will accelerate the damage the rest of our group is taking."

"You don't think I know that?" Zsinj couldn't keep the venom out of his tone. "As soon as we're free of the debris ring, issue orders for the ships that survive to flee at their discretion." He felt something sharp in his chest, a pain that had everything to do with the sudden loss of his reputation for infallibility on the battlefield.

ROGUE SQUADRON AND Wraith Squadron broke through the high cloud over into a dark world lashed by rains. They dove toward the colony ruins, breaking by wingpairs, each pair of pilots seeking out prey—starfighters that were frailer but far faster than theirs. They saw the enemy interceptors scatter by pairs, each trying to find an advantageous angle to repel the X-wings' assaults.

Wedge tried to pick out by eye which of the enemies was Baron Fel. He needn't have bothered. A pair of interceptors rose straight toward him and Tycho.

"Fel, is that you?"

"Antilles," came the familiar voice. "So good to see you at last. Again at last."

"*Iron Fist* isn't doing so well. You can save yourself some trouble by surrendering."

The interceptors came on straight at them. The range meter dropped below two kilometers and the interceptors fired. Wedge sideslipped, sending his X-wing into a defensive dance, and pressed his own laser's trigger.

Then the TIEs were past, roaring back the way Wedge and Tycho had come. Oddly, they didn't immediately loop around to gain an advantageous position on the X-wings' tails. They continued their run eastward, then looped around south, headed once again toward the coastline.

Wedge and Tycho turned to pursue. The maneuver was made a little more difficult by a ferocious crosswind that threatened to drive them eastward. "Fel, let's not do this. You've been a Rogue. I really don't want to kill you."

"Why ever not, Wedge? I don't share any such sentiment about you."

Wedge gritted his teeth. *Because you haven't yet told me where my sister is. Tell me that, and I may lose all compunction about vaping you where you fly.*

KELL AND ELASSAR veered in opposite directions, the Devaronian to rejoin Face, his regular wingman. Kell swung around and came up behind Runt's X-wing.

"Welcome back," Runt said.

"Good to be home. Let's get 'em."

They turned toward a new pair of interceptors. The 181st seemed to have abandoned their defensive, scurrying tactics; now they seemed eager for runs against the Rogues and Wraiths. A pair veered toward Kell and Runt, accelerating.

Kell dropped behind Runt, constantly adjusting his position to keep the X-wing between him and the oncoming interceptors. As the range closed to nearly two kilometers, he popped up above Runt for a snap shot against the rear interceptor, then dropped below his wingman for sustained fire against the lead TIE. Incoming laser fire hammered against Runt's forward shields, diffusing to a pastel green as it failed to penetrate.

Kell's sustained fire finally tracked on the ball of the interceptor. He saw the green of his own lasers stitch the fuselage. There was no visible change to the interceptor's exterior, but the lead enemy dropped on a ballistic course toward the ground below. His wingman veered off at an angle seemingly impossible even for a TIE and headed back toward the colony center.

HE'S RUNNING AWAY," Onoma said.

Beyond the forward viewport, they could see wave after wave of TIE fighters making suicidal runs against *Mon Remonda*. Three had already come within tens of meters of crashing into the cruiser's side; only brilliant gunnery by the turbolaser handlers had prevented collisions. Solo's TIEs were helping, but they were outnumbered by the enemy force, which had been bolstered by squadrons diverted from the other engagement zone.

And Zsinj's choice of a battlefield was proving to be a good one for the warlord. Solo's Y-wings, tough as they were, weren't nimble enough to handle the debris field at dogfighting speeds—report after report came in of pilot loss because of an injudicious turn into the path of an asteroid. Between the speed *Mon Remonda* had to make to catch up to the destroyer and the necessity of diverting most of the gun batteries to anti-starfighter use, the cruiser didn't have enough laser power to clear the path ahead entirely of asteroids; every few moments, stones, some the size of R2 units and some the size of X-wings, would hammer into the cruiser's shields or penetrate and crash into her hull.

Though *Mon Karren* and *Mon Delindo* followed in *Mon Remonda*'s wake, Solo knew they had to be suffering worse. Their shields and hull were not up to *Mon Remonda*'s specs.

"We're in range," said the sensor officer.

"Bow batteries, open fire on *Iron Fist*." Solo breathed a sigh of relief. At last they were in contact.

The topside stern of the destroyer lit up under *Mon Remonda*'s barrage. But *Iron Fist*'s own batteries opened fire and suddenly space before the forward viewport was bright with laser flashes.

Mon Remonda shuddered under impacts against her shields.

AHEAD, FEL AND HIS wingman lost speed. Wedge and Tycho rapidly overtook them. In a moment, Wedge could see them again, two dots that grew into interceptors blurred by rain and distance. There was only ocean beneath them, shore a mere kilometer or two off to starboard.

One of the interceptors dropped behind the other, losing ground rapidly, but maintaining the high-speed side-to-side maneuvering that was so effective at throwing off a pursuer's aim. Wedge and Tycho squeezed off ranging shots.

Then the interceptor decelerated further, right into Wedge's path. Reflex took over, twitching his yoke to port so that he veered out of its path.

Tycho veered in skillful mimicry of Wedge's move—right into the interceptor's path.

It should not have been a problem. At their relative speeds and courses, no collision was possible; he should have been well clear of the interceptor. But the decelerating vehicle exploded into a brilliant ball of fire and debris—and Tycho's X-wing flew straight through the heart of the detonation.

Tycho emerged from the explosion, his X-wing trailing smoke, its S-foils shuddering. He rapidly lost ground on Wedge.

"One to Two, come in."

There was no answer. Tycho banked to starboard, back toward land.

"Tycho, come in. Are you all right?"

His comm unit hissed, then words, partial words, emerged. ". . . failure . . . hold her . . . repulsorlifts out . . ."

As Wedge watched, Tycho's starboard lower S-foil began to shake more ferociously, then to crumple under air friction. Ahead, the other TIE interceptor began to loop around for a head-to-head.

"Tycho, don't try to hold her together. She's a wreck. Get over land and punch out. Do you understand?"

". . . land . . . understood."

The other interceptor roared toward them.

Toward Tycho.

Wedge accelerated forward past his wingman, laser-straight at the interceptor. "Is that Fel again, or did we get lucky?"

"No luck for you, Wedge. This is your last engagement zone."

The interceptor drifted up, firing. Wedge hit his trigger, saw his lasers pass harmlessly beneath the TIE.

Fel's lasers didn't miss. They chewed into the nose of Tycho's X-wing. Fel shot past and began to bank again.

Wedge saw Tycho's snubfighter shudder and begin to disintegrate at the nose. The cockpit's cowling popped up and a moment later Tycho ejected, still half a kilometer short of the shore.

"Group, this is Leader. I need extravehicular pilot rescue at this position. Mark it and get someone here." Wedge wrestled his X-wing around to confront Fel once more.

But the nimbler interceptor settled into position behind him, its lasers opening up, bracketing Wedge.

Wedge set his teeth and flew southward, clearing his head of distractions, letting the sensor board and targeting brackets become extra eyes.

Fel settled in on his tail and would not be shaken free. But the onetime Rogue had no more luck firing than Wedge did shaking him; burst after burst of laser fire flashed to the left, the right, beneath the X-wing as Wedge used every trick he knew to make the man miss.

Another violent crosswind hit Wedge. He didn't struggle against it; he let it propel him toward shore, a sudden movement that caught Fel off guard. Then Fel, too, crossed into the wind and was pushed eastward, farther even than Wedge had been.

Wedge felt his spine stiffen. That was it. The interceptors were lighter than X-wings, with much broader cross sections—

He resumed his original course and waited until another crosswind hit him. As it propelled him shoreward, he wrenched his yoke that way, turning in the direction he was being shoved, and saw out his starboard viewport as Fel was victimized by the same wind. The interceptor rolled eastward, momentarily out of control.

Wedge maintained his loop, was pressed hard into his pilot's couch as he came around . . .

And then, for a brief moment, his targeting brackets went green around Fel's interceptor. Wedge fired and saw the red flashes of his lasers score the squint's engines.

Fel's interceptor dropped, half out of control, and he banked toward shore. Wedge followed, alert for a trick. But Fel continued to lose altitude at a dangerous rate and hit the ground in a skidding, rolling, half-controlled crash that constituted the worst landing Wedge had seen in years.

He circled the downed interceptor and angled in to land.

CORRAN HORN DOVE toward his target interceptor, trying to bring his targeting brackets to bear over it, hoping for a maximum-distance shot—these enemies were more maneuverable than even he was used to. His target continued sideslipping, dancing around, avoiding the target lock—

He blinked. There was something fundamentally wrong with his target. Something that turned his gut cold.

It wasn't his pilot's skills telling him this. It was the other, his slowly improving ability with the Force . . .

"Group, this is Rogue Nine. Be advised. My current target is not a living being. Repeat, not living. I think it's a droid ship." He finally got a green flicker on his brackets and fired.

His lasers hit the interceptor's fuselage. The squint detonated with far more force than was appropriate for a vehicle with twin ion engines. The blast was powerful enough to engulf his target's wingman fifty meters behind the explosion. That interceptor emerged from the fireball spinning, flaming, out of control, and smashed through the already-ruined dome of one of the colony buildings. It exploded, too, but in a fashion that was subdued by comparison.

"Group, Wraith Eight." Piggy's voice, jarring and mechanical. "I am an idiot. This is why the wingman of each pair at the *Razor's Kiss* fight behaved in such a similar fashion. They have droid pilots. And they are packed with explosives. A moment while I calculate."

Corran looped back toward the fight and Ooryl, his wingman, stayed tight with him.

Piggy's voice came back a moment later. "Observation suggests that each wingpair is one human pilot, one droid. In free flight, the droid falls back to wingman position. The droid units' maneuverability increases as your range to them decreases. Their performance suggests they are enjoying computerized coordination. They must be transmitting sensor data to the ship handling coordination. Who is the Rogues' communications specialist?"

"That's me. Rogue Seven."

"With the permission of the Wraith and Rogue leaders, I offer a plan."

Corran Horn's voice came back instantly. "Go ahead, Wraith Eight."

Face's followed a moment later. "Let's hear it."

"Rogue Seven and Wraith Six use their comm gear to jam transmissions in the area for thirty seconds. In that time, we'll either enjoy dramatic improvement in our ability to handle the enemy . . . or we're no worse off than before."

"Wraith One authorizes," Face said.

"Rogue Nine says go," Horn said.

Mon Remonda dropped into the channel Iron Fist had already blasted through the debris field and began gaining on the Super Star Destroyer. Still close enough for long-range fire, the Mon Cal cruiser continued blasting away at Iron Fist's stern, despite the distraction of TIE fighters making constant assaults against Mon Remonda's bow and bridge.

"Gaining," Solo said. "Gaining."

"Detonation ahead!" said the sensor officer.

"Iron Fist?"

"No," she said. "To starboard of her course. Something on the far side of that planetoid she's passing."

Solo brought up his visual enhancers to focus on the area she described. She was correct: asteroids opposite a two-kilometer-long hunk of rock were illuminated by some sort of sustained explosion taking place just on the far surface of the larger asteroid.

Whatever its cause, the explosion was propulsion as well as detonation. The two-kilometer rock began moving slowly toward the channel left in *Iron Fist*'s wake.

"Navigator?" Solo asked.

The Mon Calamari navigation officer turned an eye toward him. "It will partially block the channel. We must destroy it or pass it by."

"Weapons?"

His weapons officer shook his head. "Too big for our guns to dismantle before we get there."

Solo offered up a rich curse he'd learned on the back streets of Corellia. "Navigator, divert our course around it. Through the debris. Alert the rest of our group what's happening. Zsinj has set up at least one asteroid, maybe more, with explosives or thrusters to move it in our path. Stay alert."

Mon Remonda began a slow maneuver, veering to starboard inside the path of the asteroid. As the bow of the cruiser entered the uncleared portion of the debris field, Solo heard ominous clankings and felt trembling under his heels.

Red lights flashed across more portions of *Mon Remonda*'s diagnostics display.

The numbers on the gauge showing the distance between *Mon Remonda* and *Iron Fist* slowed their rapid descent. The numbers stopped and then began climbing.

Mon Remonda was falling behind.

LARA'S SENSOR BOARD had shown the Rogues and Wraiths descending into Selcaron's atmosphere, and the ten strange TIEs she pursued did likewise. She entered the moon's atmosphere at the angle necessary to keep air friction from burning her alive, then set her S-foils to attack position.

When she broke through the cloud cover she could see, ahead and below, the unusual fighters split up by pairs, most heading to the main engagement, four vectoring to the south.

Her sensor board said Rogue One, Rogue Two, and one unfriendly lay in that direction. Then it updated and only Rogue One and the unfriendly were left.

She looped around to the south and dropped nearly to the surface of the water.

JANSON HIT HIS trigger and the distant TIE interceptor detonated in a brilliant flash, leaving behind one of the hundred-meter-diameter fireballs the Rogues and Wraiths were coming to expect. The jamming technique had been a spectacular success—this unit of droids and humans had been trained to function under coordination and fell to pieces without that benefit. In the first thirty seconds, the Rogues and Wraiths had reduced the number of interceptors by half. Then they sustained a one-minute jamming period . . . and the last of the interceptors had now fallen to Janson.

The communications jamming fell away. "Group, Wraith Eight. We have incoming traffic descending from high altitude from the east-northeast."

Janson veered in that direction and climbed. Yes, there were more starfighters coming in.

He gave them a second look. "What in the world are those?"

WEDGE SWUNG HIS legs over the lip of his cockpit and slid with reckless haste to the ground. He drew his blaster and moved at a full run across the sand toward Baron Fel.

Fel, evidently injured, was crawling at a good pace away from his smoking interceptor. Fel was not in a traditional TIE fighter pilot's gear; the black jumpsuit was standard, but the red featureless mask, gloves, and boots, and the poisonous yellow piping on those accouterments were pure Raptor uniform.

Wedge reached him and prodded his boot with his toe. Fel rolled over on his back. His right leg did not turn the way it should have; Wedge could see it was badly broken beneath the knee.

Wedge aimed his blaster. "Mind answering a few questions?"

"Not at all." Fel's voice was muffled. He reached up to pull his helmet free.

Wedge blinked. The man under his gun had Fel's height and build, but his blond hair and homely features were not Fel's. "Who are you?"

The man offered him a pained smile. "My name is Tetran Cowall."

"I know that name." Wedge frowned. "Some sort of actor. Face Loran doesn't think much of you."

"That's because he is my inferior in every way," the man said. His voice did not resemble Fel's. It was higher in pitch, though melodious.

"You used computer voice enhancement to sound like Fel."

"Very good."

"Where is Fel?"

The man shrugged. "You should know. You had him last. Where was he when you last saw him?" He gave Wedge a smirk. "Really, we have no idea."

"So this was all a ploy." Wedge felt sudden exhaustion begin to eat at him. All these months, hoping that this man would have some word of his sister . . . and this man turned out to be the wrong one. "Why?"

Cowall slowly put his hands behind his head, a posture of relaxation and contentment that was belied by the sweat on his face and the odd angle at which his right leg lay. "Well, you, actually. Scuttlebutt had it that Fel had deserted you and that you'd taken it rather personally. Had arranged for him to be looked for since then. The warlord decided that his reappearance would be a mystery you just had to solve. He put together a new One Eighty-first. Half with human pilots, half with flying bombs that could sidle up next to you and detonate—making hash of the famous Wedge Antilles despite your overly vaunted skills."

"So your only job was to lure me out and kill me."

Cowall smiled. "And it worked."

"Not exactly."

Cowall pointed eastward. Wedge sidestepped to be sure he could keep the actor under his gun while he looked.

In the distance, two or three kilometers off, TIE fighters, their outlines unusual, were looping around from east to south, obviously intending to turn northward near or at the shoreline.

"TIE Raptors," Cowall said. "New design, nice to fly. They'll be on us in a few seconds. And you can't get into the air by then. You're dead, Wedge Antilles."

For a quarter second, Wedge debated shooting the man, then sheathed the blaster and made a sprint for his X-wing. He heard the actor laugh behind him.

Cowall was right, of course. He could hear the distant shriek of the TIEs. They'd be in firing position about the time he was sliding into his cockpit.

He reached his X-wing, leaped up to swing himself in, dropped into his chair.

There were three incoming TIEs, and they were of a type he'd never seen before. They had the standard TIE ball cockpit, but lacked wing pylons. Instead, four trapezoidal wings, smaller than half the size of a regular TIE fighter's wings, protruded from the cockpit at even intervals. They rolled to port to line up along the straight section of beach and came on, their engines shrill, a second from firing.

Then Wedge saw something blue flash over his head from behind and the center TIE exploded. The other two broke left and right, momentarily abandoning their run.

Wedge finished shutting his canopy and got his X-wing up on repulsorlifts. He had his S-foils locked into attack position before he'd drifted ten meters forward.

Another X-wing flashed by mere meters overhead. It was painted in the darker gray of Wraith Squadron and had no astromech. Wedge put power to acceleration and checked his sensor board. The X-wing wasn't returning a transponder signal.

The X-wing looped in pursuit of one of the alien-looking TIEs, climbing in its wake. Wedge turned in the direction of the other, coaxing his X-wing up to speed. "Lara, is that you?"

"Sorry I was late." She was banking hard, trying to get her X-wing around at an angle that could fire on her target. "Had to hit one of these weird TIEs that was trying to strafe a downed Rogue."

"Tycho—is he—"

"He's under cover now. Hopping mad, I think."

"When you come around north, you may get crosswinds. He'll get them worse. They may blow him back across your path. Hold tight." Wedge turned after his target TIE Raptor, saw that the unusual vehicle was now looping around to get behind Lara. "I owe you one," he said.

"I owe *you*," she said. "I—there!"

The Raptor pilot hit a bad patch of crosswind and was tumbled eastward. Lara fired, her lasers creasing the rear of the TIE.

A plume of smoke emerged from her target. The starfighter dropped tumbling into the sea, hitting with enough force to turn anything within it into something resembling jelly.

But the last Raptor dropped in behind Lara and began

stitching her rear with laser fire. Wedge put all discretionary energy into acceleration, hurtling toward the engagement.

The TIE Raptor fired again. This was no laser—a concussion missile detonated just below Lara's X-wing. Wedge saw her stern leap up, and then the X-wing was tumbling, unaerodynamic, slinging components in all directions as it dropped.

"Punch out, punch out," Wedge said, but had no time to watch. He turned after the TIE Raptor.

That pilot tried an immediate roll to port, diving toward the water, a frantic effort to shake Wedge from his tail. Wedge flicked his targeting brackets back and forth but was unable to get a lock.

So he fired directly over the TIE Raptor's hull, immediately above its top viewport.

The pilot dodged out of reflex.

Straight down.

The leading edges of its odd wings dipped into the surf. The TIE rolled forward, its wings breaking free and being flung into the air with more speed and violence than anything coming off Lara's X-wing.

Wedge looped around, looking for Lara.

He found her X-wing fifty meters offshore. It was a twisted, broken thing, slowly rolling over from its belly onto its side.

He cruised over it at a slow rate of speed, running on repulsorlifts, and looked into the cockpit. Then he shook his head and banked back toward Tycho and the colony.

"ON MY COMMAND," Piggy said, "Wraith Nine and Ten, begin straight-line flight but maintain evasive maneuvering. Rogue Three and Four, climb at a thirty-degree angle, target their pursuit, and fire. Ready . . . now."

Two kilometers below him, Shalla and Janson discontinued their efforts to get around behind the unusual TIEs pursuing them. They accelerated into straightforward flight toward the west. Their pursuit accelerated, swinging into firing position behind them.

A kilometer below that, Pedna Scotian and Hobbie Klivian rose toward the engagement now passing above them. Piggy could tell the exact moment they acquired targeting locks: both pursuing TIEs suddenly wobbled in flight as their pilots were alerted to the danger they were in.

But it was too late. Both Rogues fired. Hobbie's lasers sheared through the lower portion of one TIE's forward viewport and continued cycling against that target. A moment later, Piggy saw his lasers emerge from above the TIE's engines. The TIE hurtled forward ballistically for half a kilometer, then detonated.

Scotian's lasers missed the second TIE. It veered abruptly upward. Shalla and Janson looped around in tight maneuvers and gave pursuit.

Piggy turned away from that engagement, looked again at the swirling colored dots on his sensor board. Flight vectors, acceleration rates, probabilities ran through his mind like unregulated data streams. He saw the blip designated Rogue One returning. That would begin to figure into his calculations in two minutes. He saw another blip, yellow for unknown, descend from low lunar orbit toward Wedge's earlier engagement zone. He dismissed it. It wouldn't factor into his equations until it came closer to his current engagement zone.

His comm system lit up, indicating reception of a recorded message. He glanced at the data portion of the screen. It was a lengthy message, flagged as low priority, going to all vehicles on New Republic frequencies. He dismissed it from his mind.

Numbers and formulae clicked into place in his mind. "Wraith Seven, two targets will be crossing over your space from the east in six-point-four seconds." Dia, her fuzial thrust engines malfunctioning, was now running on repulsorlifts only; Face had directed her to stay under cover, and she now hovered within a half-ruined colony dome, able to swivel her guns toward any one of three large holes in the dome. "Wraith Five, please make your course due east and come up to full speed. You should pull two of the new intruders . . . yes, you have." Kell veered as Piggy had requested, momentarily abandoning his slower-moving wingman, and both new TIEs that had been lining up for a run on Wraiths Five and Six opted to pursue him. Kell blasted across Dia's position and the lead TIE pursuing him was suddenly illuminated from the dome, painted and then penetrated by Dia's lasers. It rolled, a deceptively pretty corkscrew, and then hit rubble that had once been a duracrete street.

Piggy started to speak again, then saw Kell's TIE interceptor vector back at a sharp angle toward Runt's position. Kell and Runt closed on each other as though they planned a head-to-head, but when Runt fired, it was Kell's pursuit he hit. The unusual TIE fired, too, its concussion missile flashing past Kell and hitting a ruined wall, before Runt's lasers punched through the TIE's hull. It became, to Piggy's eye, a tiny, pretty ball of red, yellow, and orange.

Piggy sat back and nodded to himself, satisfied. He loved math.

"WE'RE IN OPEN SPACE, WARLORD," the captain announced.

Zsinj offered him a tight, unhappy smile. "Make your course directly toward *Second Death*. Instruct *Second Death* to deploy the Nightcloak in a channel long enough for us to make a hyperspace jump from. And to finish this masquerade, I'm going to have to stand by in a shuttle. The fleet is in your capable hands."

"Yes, sir."

In his shuttle bay, Zsinj and his pilot found his personal shuttle unharmed, but Melvar and Gatterweld were there in much less intact condition. Both men were tied, bleeding, unconscious.

He clucked over them but didn't delay. Time was pressing. He called in a medical team as he and his pilot prepared the shuttle for flight.

"*IRON FIST* IS OUTBOUND," Onoma said. "And as much as the debris field is delaying us, we're not going to be able to catch her."

Solo looked at the damage diagnostics projections, which showed an ever-mounting damage total for *Iron Fist*. "Keep the starfighters on her. There's a chance they can crack her open before she can jump. See, concentrate there on the forward top shield projector and the starboard engines. Both systems are faltering like mad. Her hyperdrive is damaged, too. There's got to be a chance it will fail when activated."

Mon Remonda's own damage totals were mounting, too. Numerous asteroid impacts had reduced her shields, battered her bow hull in several places, even vented atmosphere from portions of the bow near the keel. And *Iron Fist*'s starfighter screen had been insane in its prosecution of *Mon Remonda*.

But suddenly the enemy starfighters were running, fleeing in the wake of *Iron Fist*.

Solo sat, his muscles knotting, uncertainty burning at his gut. It didn't matter that he and his force had just destroyed or captured the rest of Zsinj's group. It didn't matter that they'd survived each trap Zsinj had set, each ploy he had initiated. Nor did it matter that they'd sent *Iron Fist* fleeing for the second time in the mighty destroyer's career.

The only thing that mattered, the only acceptable outcome, was *Iron Fist*'s capture or destruction.

More data crawled across his personal screen. Rogue Squadron and Wraith Squadron were returning from Selcaron. They were requesting shuttles for pilot rescue and enemy pilot capture. Rogue One was among the pilots re-turning. Solo breathed a sigh of relief. He had few enough friends. Win or lose, he didn't want to lose any more in this engagement.

TETENGO NOOR, POLEARM NINE, finished another pass across *Iron Fist*. He'd dumped more laser fire across the great ship's bow. Turbolasers and ion cannons had failed to touch his A-wing. Now he banked around for another run. His wingman was dead; most of the friendly starfighters within sight were Y-wings and even TIE fighters.

Selaggis Six was growing small behind him and his target. But *Mon Remonda* was coming on strong. His home was chasing him. He got lined up for another run and dove toward the destroyer, his lasers stitching destruction across her hull.

Halfway across, he sensed something wrong to his port, toward the ship's bow. He glanced that way, saw nothing beyond the bow.

Nothing. No stars. No starfighters. Blackness, an immense sea of blackness. It so jarred him that he ceased fire, ceased maneuvering until a near miss from an *Iron Fist* turbolaser jolted him out of his surprise.

Iron Fist's bow entered the darkness and disappeared. The blackness rolled across the ship's hull and swallowed Tetengo Noor.

All the stars disappeared, but he could still see *Iron Fist*'s lights, still see the glows of fire from friendly and enemy starfighters. He shook off his apprehension and banked for another run at his colossal enemy. "Polearm Nine to *Mon Remonda*. Something odd is going on here."

He heard nothing but the alarmed comm chatter of other pilots near him.

Sensor data was strange. It showed new blips where none had been a moment ago. There were now two capital ships in his near vicinity. *Iron Fist,* immediately to his stern, and something about a third of *Iron Fist*'s size—still larger than any Imperial Star Destroyer—well below Zsinj's flagship. In addition, there were four stationary objects arrayed in a square back the way he'd come, and four more, similarly arrayed, kilometers ahead along *Iron Fist*'s outbound course.

He looped around to get a look at the new capital ship. "Polearm Nine to *Mon Remonda,* come in. I think *Iron Fist* has additional support up here."

Only static answered him.

ZSINJ STAYED ON his comlink while his pilot did the work. His shuttle lifted off, moved smoothly out into the eerie darkness now surrounding *Iron Fist,* and headed off at a course perpendicular to the Super Star Destroyer's.

"Captain Vellar, report."

"Thirty seconds to hyperspace entry. I've transmitted the countdown to *Second Death.*"

"*Second Death,* report."

"Yes, warlord. Our detonation is linked to the countdown. Countdown plus two seconds. We've already abandoned ship. Our crew is on the landing craft and we've launched."

"Well, get clear of here or you'll be nothing but a dim memory and a pension bonus." Zsinj turned to his pilot. "That stands for us, too."

The taciturn pilot nodded and brought the shuttle up to speed. A few moments later, the stars returned as though they'd been switched back on by some cosmic being.

Zsinj checked his sensors. There was nothing behind him, no trace of *Iron Fist, Second Death,* or the starfighters battling around them.

———

"No, no, no," Solo said. "She can't have jumped. We'd have seen the sensor signs of hyperspace entry."

The sensor officer offered him a face full of confusion. "No, sir. But she's gone. It's strange. Several minutes ago, we thought we detected a ship out there at that position; her sensor echo wasn't anything we could identify, and she vanished almost immediately. Now *Iron Fist* goes out there and vanishes, too—and all the starfighters on her, ours and theirs. We're not even getting comm traffic from them. We do have an odd visual."

"Bring it up."

The visual enhancer brought up a hologram of— nothingness. A black square blotting out the stars directly ahead of *Mon Remonda,* on the exact path *Iron Fist* took, many kilometers ahead. Three shuttles were outbound from the anomaly. Several Y-wings from *Mon Remonda* approached it at cautious speeds.

"What is that?"

The sensor operator shook her head. "It's not on any sensors but visual. It's not like anything I've ever seen."

CAPTAIN VELLAR STARED out the forward viewport and tried to keep all emotion out of his face.

It was hard. He had to focus all that energy on his task.

He was a soldier. He always did his duty.

This time, his duty, as defined by the warlord, demanded that he be party to the murder of dozens of his own pilots.

"Captain," called the comm officer, "the starfighter group leader is asking if it's time to bring the TIEs in."

"Tell him one minute," Vellar said. "Then we'll open up the bay and transmit approach channels where they won't be chopped to pieces by our own batteries."

"Yes, sir."

A moment later, another officer called, "Ten seconds to hyperspace."

"Very well." Vellar closed his eyes. He would not bear the sight of the eyes of the bridge crew. They knew why all the pilots were being sacrificed—so *Iron Fist* would not be delayed in her jump to safety. So the intermixed wreckage of friendly and enemy starfighters would convince Han Solo that *Iron Fist* and her starfighter screen were destroyed.

TETENGO NOOR BROUGHT in his A-wing close to the misshapen capital ship.

It was not illuminated and was firing no weapons. He switched on forward lights as he cruised over it.

He saw an engine pod, a bridge pod, a long spar connecting them, and three kilometers of vehicle wreckage between bow and stern.

One piece of wreckage was instantly recognizable. The triangular point of a Star Destroyer's bow. On it were painted the words IRON FIST.

Apprehension seized him—not fear for himself, but fear for his mission, his fleet's mission. He turned back toward *Mon Remonda* and accelerated.

Behind him, the utter blackness became pure, burning brightness. For a moment, as it swept forward across him, he thought he felt heat.

As SOLO AND HIS bridge crew watched, flame gouted out from the center of the blackness, then spread to engulf it entirely. The approaching Y-wings veered away. Metal debris, brilliantly glowing, hurtled from the center of the explosion. In moments, the bright ball of explosive gas faded—and the blackness, too, was gone, the stars beyond it restored.

The sensor operator blinked. "We had signs of a hyper-space entry just before the explosion, sir."

"Find out," Solo said. "Find out if it was *Iron Fist* or that phantom ship."

"Yes, sir."

A moment later, the communications officer rocked back in his chair as if slapped. He turned to Solo. "Sir, I have a transmission from one of our Y-wings. The pilot thinks you ought to see this right away."

"Put it up."

The enhanced starfield wavered. The stars changed, and much of the view was replaced by a tumbling piece of debris, an enormous triangle of metal trailing cables and metal spars. Portions of the debris still glowed from the heat of the explosion.

Painted on the side of the triangle, rotating into and out of sight as the debris spun, were the words IRON FIST.

Captain Onoma joined him. "That is her bow."

"Yes." Solo let out a breath and felt five months of pressure and frustration begin to leave him. If he could breathe like that for a while, expelling the nightmare of this command one lung-ful at a time, he could someday become a real human again.

He moved back to his control chair and sat heavily. All across the bridge, officers began applauding, offering hand-shakes, exchanging embraces.

"Comm, let me address the fleet."

"Ready, sir."

"This is General Solo. *Iron Fist* is destroyed. We'll tell you more as we know more." He gestured for the comm officer to cease the transmission. "Sensors, Communications, what about our pilots who were close to her?"

The sensor officer shook her head. "They were awfully near to the explosion. Unless they move under their own power, we won't be able to distinguish them from debris."

"I have a transmission from a Y-wing pilot," the comm officer said. "He's injured, coming in on one engine. He was just emerging from the darkness field when *Iron Fist* blew. He was pretty disoriented while he was in the darkness field. He saw a second capital ship on sensors; it must have been the one that made hyperspace. He thinks most of our starfighters are gone, sir."

Solo closed his eyes.

Maybe, just maybe, those were the last beings he would ever have to order to their deaths.

"Incoming message, sir. From one of those outbound shuttles. He says it's Warlord Zsinj."

"Of course," Solo murmured. "He wouldn't stay aboard *Iron Fist* and let himself be blown up. Not even if I asked him nicely." He raised his head. "Chewie, you took the last one. Come join me for this one."

Chewbacca moved in to stand behind Solo. "Put it on," Solo said.

Zsinj's image, against the background of a Lambda shuttle cockpit, appeared both on Solo's private screen and as a holoprojection over the bridge's main viewport.

There was no humor remaining to Zsinj's expression. Sweat darkened parts of his white uniform. His mustachios drooped in what might have been, under other circumstances, a comical fashion. "I've signaled you to offer congratulations," the warlord said. His voice was low, pained. "You realize you have cost me very dearly."

Han summoned up the energy to give him a mocking smile. "I don't have much to offer you in compensation. Maybe I could let you kiss my Wookiee."

Chewbacca grumbled, a noise of dissent.

The color rose in Zsinj's face and he spoke again—words Solo did not know, each few syllables sounding different in character and pitch than the ones before. The rant went on for nearly a minute, and Solo was glad they routinely recorded bridge communications—he wanted one of the 3PO units to translate this multilingual composition of profanity for him. One blast in the Rodian language he understood quite well; it described Han Solo's chemical composition in a fashion that would make any Rodian's blood boil.

Then Zsinj sagged, all energy seemingly having fled him. "General," he said, "we will meet again."

"I'm sure we will." Solo lost his smile. "Zsinj, I'm not a rich man. Not really an ambitious man. Maybe you should take that into account. It means that you can never cost me as much as I've cost you. Never."

Zsinj regarded him soberly for a moment. Then his holo-image faded.

"Shuttle's made the launch to hyperspace," reported the sensor operator.

Solo nodded. Then he looked up at Chewbacca. "We got him. He's not dead, but his fleet is a shambles and his financial empire is coming to pieces. He may never recover."

Chewie rumbled a reply.

"No, I never really would have asked you to kiss him."

WITH THE COLORS of hyperspace flowing past the forward viewport, sign of safety that was finally his, Zsinj turned to his pilot. "What did you think of my performance?"

The man looked at him blankly. "I suppose it was pretty good, sir."

"You obviously have no appreciation of the theater, dear boy. Oh, well. In a few minutes, we'll rendezvous with *Iron Fist* and head on to Rancor Base, where you won't be called upon to provide artistic criticism you're not qualified to offer." He heaved a sigh.

18

DR. GAST LAY on her bed in the tiny chamber that was her cell, bored, and watched the same holodrama for the third time in as many days. It was called *High Winds,* and told the story of performing wire-walkers, madmen who stretched fibra-ropes between the skyscrapers of Coruscant and then tried to walk across for the entertainment of others. It was a tragedy, of course; any such account, made by Imperial holomakers, of such nontraditional and independent behavior always ended in sadness and death.

There was a murmur of voices from outside, her guard talking to someone, and then there was a knock at her door.

She paused the holo. Actor Tetran Cowall froze in midslip, his plunge to death delayed for a few moments, his expression wide-eyed and hopeless. "Come in," she said.

Nawara Ven entered, stared at her impassively. "You'll launch tomorrow in the shuttle *Narra* for Coruscant. Nobody wants you to arrive with Solo's fleet." He tossed a packet tied together with cord at her feet. "Your new identity," he said. "Maharg Tulis, home decorator from Alderaan. It will stand up to any scrutiny, New Republic or Imperial."

She didn't reach for the packet. "That's an ugly name."

"To accompany an ugly spirit."

"And my money?"

"I'll give you one more chance on the money. Tell me you don't want it, that you're donating it back to the New Republic cause to save lives. That could be your very first step in returning from what you've become."

"I'll take the money, thanks."

"As you wish. I won't ever again try to protect you from yourself." He offered her a toothy smile. "We have to send out a holocomm request for your money. How would you prefer your credits—New Republic or Imperial?"

"Imperial, of course. What did you think?"

"Imperial it is. As soon as they arrive, you'll be off to Coruscant."

"I need a bodyguard! I'll be carrying half a million credits. It wouldn't do to let me be robbed. That would reflect badly on your New Republic."

The Twi'lek nodded. "You're absolutely right. I'll be your bodyguard until we get to Coruscant. Once we're there, you can hire one to your liking and book your own passage to whatever world you like."

"Well . . . I suppose you'll do."

Ven took a step back and shut the door.

Gast grabbed the identity packet, plucked the string free, and examined the documents, shoving the datacards in her terminal one by one. An identity card. A falsified personal history—born on Alderaan, a traveler among Outer Rim worlds since her home planet's destruction eight years before. A permit permitting her to carry a large sum of money, up to a half million New Republic credits or the equivalent. Memberships in various decorators' guilds—Imperial, New Republic, various unaligned planets.

She sat back, satisfied. One or two more days, and she'd be rid of Zsinj, rid of the Rebels, rid of this whole business forever.

WEDGE LOOKED OVER the fighter pilots of *Mon Remonda*. The Rogues and Wraiths were present in nearly full strength;

he had lost only one pilot from those squadrons yesterday, and had lost her only temporarily. A few survivors from Polearm and Nova Squadrons, pilots who had been knocked out of battle minutes before *Iron Fist* detonated, were also present.

This was the last time the four squadrons were ever likely to be assembled this way. The pilots stared at him, their expressions tired, solemn, battered, triumphant.

In spite of the high casualty toll, it had been a successful engagement. *Iron Fist* was gone.

"We'll start with pilot updates," he said. "Sadly, all the Nova and Polearm pilots missing at the site of *Iron Fist*'s last stand remain listed as missing in action and presumed dead. But our injured Rogue, Asyr Sei'lar, is out of danger, and the medics say she will suffer no permanent effects of her exposure.

"Most of the Rogues and Wraiths received a communication from an unknown craft as we were departing Selcaron. It turned out to be a lengthy message and data package from Lara Notsil, recorded before her death. It included many details about Zsinj's brainwashing project that should allow Intelligence to dismantle Zsinj's operation on Coruscant. We probably won't have to worry again about the kind of circumstances that led to the deaths of Tai'dira and Nuro Tualin." He spared a glance at Horn and Tyria. Both had been sobered by the mention of the pilots they'd been forced to kill, but Wedge could see no uncertainty in their expressions. Horn had always known whom to blame for his squadmate's death. Tyria had apparently begun to understand the same thing.

"Many commendations will be resulting from our recent actions," Wedge continued. "We'll get to them later. I think I first ought to let you know that Fleet Command and Starfighter Command seem to be in agreement—that you all have seen enough carrier duty for a while. Squadron transfers are in order and will be coming through in the next day or two. Rogue Squadron can expect to see some planet-based duty, at least for a while. Polearm and Nova Squadrons will be returning to Coruscant so they can be rebuilt."

Face's hand shot up. "And the Wraiths? We're still on *Mon Remonda*?"

"Not exactly. For you, I have good news, bad news, and news you'll have to interpret for yourselves. Face, I'm obliged to inform you that your captaincy has stuck. It's Captain Loran from now on."

The pilots closest to Face treated him to backslaps. Dia tickled him, causing him to shy away from her until he could pin her hands. He turned back to Wedge, his expression serious. "And the good news?"

"The *bad* news is that as of today, Wraith Squadron has been decommissioned as an X-wing unit."

Face released Dia's hands and dropped back in his seat, looking as stunned as if Kell had just side-kicked him in the head. "*What?* Sir?"

Wedge heard intakes of breath from several pilots, not just from Wraiths. "It's not quite what it sounds like. It seems you've done too good a job, accomplishing a broad set of objectives, few of which have anything to do with the perceived strengths of an X-wing unit. You've made quite an impression on General Cracken, the head of Intelligence. As of now, Wraith Squadron has been recommissioned as an Intelligence unit. Commandos, insurgents, pilots—it will do whatever the situation warrants. With, unfortunately, less celebrity than even the little an X-wing unit typically receives." He offered them an expression of apology. "Obviously, the government won't just yank you out of Starfighter Command and give you like presents to another branch of the service. But all you have to do is say yes and your transfer to the new Wraith

Squadron will be accepted instantly—and with thanks. General Cracken offers his personal wishes that you do accept transfer, and that you stay together as a team."

"I'm coming back to Rogue Squadron," said Janson. "That was the deal."

Wedge smiled at him. "Wes, the Wraiths don't want you anyway."

"That's right," Elassar said. "You're unlucky."

Dia said, "I hate how serious he is all the time."

Runt said, "We don't like the way he chews his food."

Shalla said, "But we'll miss his rear end."

Janson grinned as he took it, and accepted handshakes from the Wraiths and Rogues around him.

"Those Wraiths who do not intend to accept General Cracken's offer can tell me more privately than Wes here," Wedge said. "And regardless of where you choose to go, drop by the pilots' lounge this evening for one last drink together. You can celebrate where you've been and where you're going.

"Now, for those commendations. Flight Officer Dorset Konnair, step forward . . ."

FACE LEANED AGAINST the pilot lounge bar and felt the brandy ease its way down his throat, warming him from within.

There was also warmth from without. The lounge was filled with pilots and friends—and tonight, with the mechanics, other technical staffers, and astromechs that had supported the starfighter squadrons. The heat of so many bodies raised the temperature in the lounge to a level no Mon Calamari would want to bear for long.

It was the end. Tomorrow, his profession would be different, and his surroundings would be changed, and so much of what he'd known for so long would be left behind.

"How is the voting running?" Wedge asked him.

"We'll be staying together," Face said. "Not everybody has talked to me yet, but most of the Wraiths will be Intelligence Wraiths tomorrow."

Wedge nodded. "I think that's the right choice. I thought the New Republic needed a unit like the Wraiths. Now others have bought in as well."

"Does that mean Admiral Ackbar has let you off the hook? You don't have to accept the generalship?"

Wedge smiled. "I had a congratulatory message from him this morning. 'Even I wanted you to win,' he said. 'How could I vote against a starfighter unit proving its worth?' "

"Good point."

Donos moved through the crowd to stand before them. He extended his hand to Face.

Face took it. "You've already congratulated me."

"And now I'm leaving you."

"Staying with Starfighter Command?"

"Yes. Flying is what I want to do." Donos gave a helpless shrug.

Face grinned. "And staying with X-wings, too?"

"I hope so. I put in my request for transfer to any X-wing unit with openings."

"Ah," Wedge said. "I forgot to mention. Your approval for transfer came in earlier today. You have a new unit."

"Really? Which one?"

"Rogue Squadron."

Donos took a half-step back. "You're kidding."

"No, no, no." Wedge shook his head. "Kidding sounds like this. 'The next candidate's name is Kettch, and he's an Ewok.' See the difference?"

Donos's mouth worked for a moment. Finally he said, "Thank you, sir."

"You're welcome. Go talk to your new squadmates. Maybe you could manage to be a little less distant with them than you were with the old ones."

Donos managed a smile. "Yes, I guess I could use the practice."

THE DESCENT TO Coruscant's surface was uneventful, but Dr. Gast, seeing the former Imperial throneworld for the first time in years, was thrilled by every moment, by every glimpse the shuttle's viewports afforded her of the world's soaring buildings and rain-filled skies.

Nawara Ven, beside her—far too close for her peace of mind, but that, too, would soon change—obviously did not share her enthusiasm for the world's attractions. He sat ignoring her, stonily facing forward throughout the landing. And that, too, gave her a little thrill of victory: to discommode the subhuman who had offered her so much grief was simply lovely.

An hour later, she and the Twi'lek neared the head of the customs entry line. It was one of many such lines in a cavernous hall that was broken, mazelike, by transparisteel barriers designed to keep arrivals from entering Coruscant unexamined and untaxed.

"Where do you go from here?" Ven asked her.

"I'm not fool enough to tell you," she said. "You can be sure it's somewhere well away from Rebel space. Somewhere far from bad-smelling, bad-tempered Twi'leks. Somewhere orderly, where the cutting edge of medical research is admired and respected."

Ven nodded sagely. "Well, then, I know exactly where you're going."

"No, you don't."

"I'll bet you half a million credits I can name the planet."

She offered him a scowl. Then the man ahead of her in line moved past the customs station. She swung her two bags atop the examination table.

The customs worker, an aging human man, quickly ran a

scanner across her bags, then opened the first and probed through the few garments and personal possessions that made up most of what she retained of her former life.

Then he opened her other bag and froze. He looked up at her, astonishment in his eyes. "What's this?"

"Money." She handed him a datacard. "Here's my financial record. It constitutes authorization to travel with a large sum such as this."

"It's not the *sum*." His look suggested that she was a victim of sun-madness. "These are Imperial credits."

"Yes, of course."

"And bringing them into Coruscant is an act of smuggling." His hands shoved the currency around in her bag.

Nawara Ven leaned in close. "Actually, by Coruscant law, bringing in that many Imperial credits can only be for purposes of sedition. That's a far more serious charge than merely smuggling. You'll be spending at least a lifetime in prison on Coruscant."

The customs official snapped his fingers and waved. Security officers approached.

Gast turned on Ven. "You set me up."

He looked down at her impassively. "No, I let you do exactly as you wanted. I also saved your life. I'd say I've treated you rather well."

She spat at him. A gooey mass hit his cheek and clung there.

He brought out a handkerchief of fine cloth, wiped the sputum away, and discarded it, as though the substance were poison, ruining the cloth forevermore.

Then strong hands gripped Dr. Gast's arms and she was yanked away.

HAN SOLO AND WEDGE ANTILLES sat in the cockpit of the *Millennium Falsehood,* their feet up on the control boards.

All lights in the ship and in the bay were off, including the strip around the magcon field, so they had an unimpeded view of the colorful swirl of hyperspace beyond.

"What are you going to do with her?" Wedge asked.

"Hmmm?" Solo stirred, his train of thought broken. "Do with who?"

"With the *Falsehood*."

"Well, technically, I can't do anything with her," Solo said. "She belongs to the New Republic. But if they listen to me—which they will—I'll recommend they put her up in a museum. As a near replica of the *Falcon*. That way nobody is ever likely to bother me anymore about donating the old girl."

"Which old girl?"

"You know what I mean."

The comm unit crackled into life, startling both men. "Bridge to General Solo."

Solo thumbed the system to two-way transmission. "Solo here."

"Communications here, sir. We have a situation."

"Go ahead."

"A while back you ordered my station to run all incoming messages through a voice-analysis program. So you could be notified immediately if Lara Notsil contacted you again."

"That's right."

"No one thought to end the program after her death. Well, just before we made our last jump, we received a recorded message. Let me patch it through to you, sir."

"Hold on." Solo activated the bridge lights and powered up the *Falsehood*'s cockpit terminal screen. "Ready to receive."

The terminal glowed into life. A data screen popped up, announcing the details of the message's origin and route before arriving on *Mon Remonda*. Its origin was Corellia; it was originally transmitted one day before; its intended recipient was Myn Donos, New Republic Starfighter Command. The data shrank and moved over into the left margin, to be replaced by a full-holo message.

The woman it showed had long red hair artfully draped in a braid over her shoulder. She was rather delicate of features, with an uncertain smile on her lips. "Hello, Myn," she said. "It's been a while since we've seen each other."

Solo and Wedge looked at each other. "That's Lara Notsil," Solo said.

Wedge glanced over at the data stream. "No, it's someone named Kirney Slane."

"You're not even surprised." Solo glared at him, suspicion on his face.

"I'm back on Corellia now," the redhead said, "after a few years of knocking around the galaxy."

"Years?" Solo asked. "More like a few days."

"Pretty good Corellian accent," Wedge said.

"I don't believe this," Solo said.

"And I know, after the way we parted company, you may not want to see me again. But I had to find out if there was any sort of chance for us. I think I'm finally ready and able to give it a try again." There was hope in the woman's expression, and acceptance. "I'll be here, at the address given in the message header, for the next few weeks. I'm trying to drum up traffic for my new shuttle business. I have a ship, a *Sentinel*-class landing craft I obtained used. I have a copilot you really need to meet and an astromech you already know. Contact me, visit me—do whatever you feel you have to. I'll accept whatever you decide."

The screen faded.

"Stand by, Communications." Solo shut off the cockpit microphone and gave Wedge an accusing look. "You said, when you overflew her X-wing, that you saw no sign she'd ejected."

"That's right." Wedge stretched lazily. "There was no automated comm signal indicating an ejection."

"Of course, that could have been damaged in combat, or she could have disabled it."

"Sure, sure. Anyway, as the X-wing was rolling over and sinking as I flew over her, I couldn't see whether the pilot's chair was still in there."

"Commander Square Corners himself, showing a streak of duplicity. Lying by omission. I can't believe it."

"Maybe, ultimately, I believe in happy endings," Wedge said. "I can hope for them, anyway. Besides, with Wraith Squadron on one side of me and Han Solo on the other, how can I keep from being infected with duplicity?"

"Good point." Solo considered. "She could come back. What she did as an Imperial agent is nothing compared to what she did *for* us."

Wedge shook his head. "I think the way you do, but the law doesn't. In her false identity, she swore an oath to the New Republic, then transmitted classified data to the Empire during a time of war. That's treason. The only legal outcome for her would be the death sentence. Regardless of what she did for us. Regardless of the fact that she's not remotely the same person who served the Empire and Admiral Trigit."

"You're right." Solo reactivated the comm unit. "Communications, you have a false reading. The sender's vocal similarity to Lara Notsil is a coincidence. She's dead. Understood?"

"Uh, sir, our correlation is something like ninety-nine-point-nine-nine-seven—"

"Tell you what. I'll send Chewbacca up there and have him explain to you what I just said."

"No, sir, not necessary. I understand."

"Forward the message to Lieutenant Donos and then erase all other ship's copies of the message. Nothing goes into archives. Understood?"

"Fully, sir."

"Solo out." He rose. "Come on, we've got an hour before arrival at Coruscant. I'll buy you a drink."

"I'll let you."

As they walked down the *Falsehood*'s loading ramp, Solo threw an arm over Wedge's shoulders. "Corellian to Corellian, you know what the great thing about being a general is?"

"No, what?"

"In lots of circumstances, you can pretty much do whatever you want." With his free hand, Solo reached over and gave Wedge's hair a thorough mussing.

Wedge batted his hand away. "Hey, stop it."

"No. I don't have to. Hey, you should try this general thing. You'd like it."

"I don't think so."

"I'm going to send a message to Ackbar and tell him just what a natural you are for that rank."

"General, I'm warning you . . ."

ACKNOWLEDGMENTS

Thanks go to . . .

Bruce Harlick, Kevin Jennings, Beth Loubet, Matt Pinsonneault, Susan Pinsonneault, Bob Quinlan, Roxanne Quinlan, Luray Richmond, and Sean Summers, my "Eagle-Eyes," whose efforts to intercept my errors of thought and deed keep me from looking quite as foolish as I otherwise might.

All the *Star Wars* fiction authors from whose work I have been able to draw details, most especially Michael A. Stackpole and Timothy Zahn.

Drew Campbell, Troy Denning, Shane Johnson, Paul Murphy, Stephen J. Sansweet, Peter Schweighofer, Jen Seiden, Bill Slavicsek, Bill Smith, Curtis Smith, Eric S. Trautmann, and Dan Wallace, for the invaluable resources they have written.

David Pipgras, for the Wraith Squadron unit patch.

The netizens of alt.fan.wedge, for their support and commentary.

Sue Rostoni and Lucy Autrey Wilson of Lucas Licensing, for their help.

Denis Loubet, Mark and Luray Richmond, my roommates, for occasionally reminding me to eat, sleep, and breathe.

THE STAR WARS LEGENDS NOVELS TIMELINE

BEFORE THE REPUBLIC
37,000–25,000 YEARS BEFORE STAR WARS: A NEW HOPE

c. 25,793 YEARS BEFORE STAR WARS: A NEW HOPE

Dawn of the Jedi: Into the Void

OLD REPUBLIC
5,000–67 YEARS BEFORE STAR WARS: A NEW HOPE

Lost Tribe of the Sith: The Collected
Stories

3,954 YEARS BEFORE STAR WARS: A NEW HOPE

The Old Republic: Revan

3,650 YEARS BEFORE STAR WARS: A NEW HOPE

The Old Republic: Deceived
Red Harvest
The Old Republic: Fatal Alliance
The Old Republic: Annihilation

1,032 YEARS BEFORE STAR WARS: A NEW HOPE

Knight Errant
Darth Bane: Path of Destruction
Darth Bane: Rule of Two
Darth Bane: Dynasty of Evil

RISE OF THE EMPIRE
67–0 YEARS BEFORE STAR WARS: A NEW HOPE

67 YEARS BEFORE STAR WARS: A NEW HOPE

Darth Plagueis

33 YEARS BEFORE STAR WARS: A NEW HOPE

Cloak of Deception
Darth Maul: Shadow Hunter
Maul: Lockdown

32 YEARS BEFORE STAR WARS: A NEW HOPE

STAR WARS: EPISODE I
THE PHANTOM MENACE

Rogue Planet
Outbound Flight
The Approaching Storm

22 YEARS BEFORE STAR WARS: A NEW HOPE

STAR WARS: EPISODE II
ATTACK OF THE CLONES

22–19 YEARS BEFORE STAR WARS: A NEW HOPE

STAR WARS: THE CLONE
WARS

The Clone Wars: Wild Space
The Clone Wars: No Prisoners

Clone Wars Gambit
  Stealth
  Siege

Republic Commando
  Hard Contact
  Triple Zero
  True Colors
  Order 66

Shatterpoint
The Cestus Deception
MedStar I: Battle Surgeons
MedStar II: Jedi Healer
Jedi Trial
Yoda: Dark Rendezvous
Labyrinth of Evil

19 YEARS BEFORE STAR WARS: A NEW HOPE

STAR WARS: EPISODE III
REVENGE OF THE SITH

Kenobi
Dark Lord: The Rise of Darth Vader
Imperial Commando 501st

Coruscant Nights
  Jedi Twilight
  Street of Shadows
  Patterns of Force
The Last Jedi

10 YEARS BEFORE STAR WARS: A NEW HOPE

The Han Solo Trilogy
  The Paradise Snare
  The Hutt Gambit
  Rebel Dawn

The Adventures of Lando Calrissian
The Force Unleashed
The Han Solo Adventures
Death Troopers
The Force Unleashed II

THE STAR WARS LEGENDS NOVELS TIMELINE

 REBELLION
0–5 YEARS AFTER
STAR WARS: A NEW HOPE

 NEW REPUBLIC
5–25 YEARS AFTER
STAR WARS: A NEW HOPE

Death Star
Shadow Games

 0

> **STAR WARS: EPISODE IV**
> ***A NEW HOPE***

Tales from the Mos Eisley Cantina
Tales from the Empire
Tales from the New Republic
Scoundrels
Allegiance
Choices of One
Honor Among Thieves
Galaxies: The Ruins of Dantooine
Splinter of the Mind's Eye
Razor's Edge

3 YEARS AFTER *STAR WARS: A NEW HOPE*

> **STAR WARS: EPISODE V**
> ***THE EMPIRE STRIKES BACK***

Tales of the Bounty Hunters
Shadows of the Empire

4 YEARS AFTER *STAR WARS: A NEW HOPE*

> **STAR WARS: EPISODE VI**
> ***THE RETURN OF THE JEDI***

Tales from Jabba's Palace

The Bounty Hunter Wars
 The Mandalorian Armor
 Slave Ship
 Hard Merchandise

The Truce at Bakura
Luke Skywalker and the Shadows of
 Mindor

X-Wing
 Rogue Squadron
 Wedge's Gamble
 The Krytos Trap
 The Bacta War
 Wraith Squadron
 Iron Fist
 Solo Command

The Courtship of Princess Leia
Tatooine Ghost

The Thrawn Trilogy
 Heir to the Empire
 Dark Force Rising
 The Last Command

X-Wing: Isard's Revenge

The Jedi Academy Trilogy
 Jedi Search
 Dark Apprentice
 Champions of the Force

I, Jedi
Children of the Jedi
Darksaber
Planet of Twilight
X-Wing: Starfighters of Adumar
The Crystal Star

The Black Fleet Crisis Trilogy
 Before the Storm
 Shield of Lies
 Tyrant's Test

The New Rebellion

The Corellian Trilogy
 Ambush at Corellia
 Assault at Selonia
 Showdown at Centerpoint

The Hand of Thrawn Duology
 Specter of the Past
 Vision of the Future

Scourge
Survivor's Quest

NEW JEDI ORDER
25–40 YEARS AFTER
STAR WARS: A NEW HOPE

The New Jedi Order
Vector Prime
Dark Tide I: Onslaught
Dark Tide II: Ruin
Agents of Chaos I: Hero's Trial
Agents of Chaos II: Jedi Eclipse
Balance Point
Edge of Victory I: Conquest
Edge of Victory II: Rebirth
Star by Star
Dark Journey
Enemy Lines I: Rebel Dream
Enemy Lines II: Rebel Stand
Traitor
Destiny's Way
Force Heretic I: Remnant
Force Heretic II: Refugee
Force Heretic III: Reunion
The Final Prophecy
The Unifying Force

35 YEARS AFTER *STAR WARS: A NEW HOPE*

The Dark Nest Trilogy
The Joiner King
The Unseen Queen
The Swarm War

LEGACY
40+ YEARS AFTER
STAR WARS: A NEW HOPE

Legacy of the Force
Betrayal
Bloodlines
Tempest
Exile
Sacrifice
Inferno
Fury
Revelation
Invincible

Crosscurrent
Riptide
Millennium Falcon

43 YEARS AFTER *STAR WARS: A NEW HOPE*

Fate of the Jedi
Outcast
Omen
Abyss
Backlash
Allies
Vortex
Conviction
Ascension
Apocalypse

X-Wing: Mercy Kill

45 YEARS AFTER *STAR WARS: A NEW HOPE*

Crucible

ABOUT THE AUTHOR

AARON ALLSTON was the *New York Times* bestselling author of thirteen *Star Wars* novels as well as the Doc Sidhe novels, which combine 1930s-style hero-pulp fiction with Celtic myth. In addition to being a writer, he was a game designer, and in 2006 he was inducted into the Academy of Adventure Gaming Arts and Design Hall of Fame. Allston died in 2014.

Read on for an excerpt from

ALPHABET SQUADRON

———

BY ALEXANDER FREED

CHAPTER 1

SITUATIONAL AWARENESS

I

"I WAS EIGHTEEN KILOMETERS above sea level when they caught me," she said.

The droid measured her heart rate from across the room (sixty-two beats per minute, seven above her baseline) and stored her voiceprint for post-session analysis. It performed a cursory optical scan and noted the scrapes on her lips and forehead; the sling supporting her right arm. She had begun to regain muscle mass, though she remained—the droid permitted itself a poetic flourish—*frail*.

"You remember the precise altitude?" the droid asked. For this interaction it had chosen a masculine voice, bass and hollow. The sound projected from a speaker on the underside of its spherical black chassis.

"I have an extremely good memory."

The droid oriented the red lens of its photoreceptor as if to stare. "So do I."

The woman met its gaze. The droid readjusted the lens.

This is the story she told.

EIGHTEEN KILOMETERS ABOVE the surface of the planet Nacronis, Yrica Quell fled for her life.

The siltstorm raged outside her starfighter, blue and yellow mud roiling against the faceted viewport. A burst of wind lifted the ship's port-side wing, nearly sending her into a spin; she adjusted her repulsors with her gloved left hand while the right urged a rattling lever into position. The ship leveled out, and the comforting howl of its twin ion engines rose to a screech as six million stony granules entered the exhaust. Quell winced as she bounced in her harness, listening to her vessel's agony.

Emerald light shot past the viewport, incinerating ribbons of airborne mud. She increased her thrust and plunged deeper into the storm, ignoring the engines' scream.

Her scanner showed three marks rapidly closing from behind—two fewer than she'd hoped for. She moved a hand to the comm, recalibrated her frequency, and called out two names: "Tonas? Barath?" When no one answered, she recalibrated again and tried, "This is TIE pilot Yrica Quell to Nacronis ground control." But Tonas and Barath were surely dead, and the locals were jammed, out of range, or ardently inclined to ignore her.

Another volley of emerald particle bolts sizzled past her ship. Quell maintained her vector. She was a fine defensive pilot, but only the storm could keep her alive now. She had to trust to the wind and the blinding mud to throw off her enemy's aim.

Her comm sounded at last. "Lieutenant Quell?"

She leaned forward, straining at her harness, trying to peer through the storm as her teeth chattered and her hips knocked against her seat. A ribbon of blue silt streaked by and she glimpsed, beyond it, a flash of white light: lightning ahead and twenty degrees to port.

"Lieutenant Quell? Please acknowledge."

She considered her options. She could head toward the lightning—toward the storm's center, where the winds would be strongest. There she could try to locate an updraft. Reduce her thrust, overcharge her repulsors, and let the draft and the repulsors' antigravity toss her ship high while her pursuers passed below. If she didn't black out, if she didn't become disoriented, she could dip back down and re-engage her enemy from behind, eliminating one, maybe two before they realized where she'd gone.

"You are hereby ordered to reduce speed, eject, and await pickup, detention, and court-martial."

She couldn't imagine that the man on the other end of the comm would fall for such a maneuver. More likely she'd be shot down while she spun helplessly through the sky.

Of course, she'd also be shot if she ejected. Major Soran Keize was a good man, an *admirable* man, but she knew there would be no court-martial.

She changed course toward the lightning and pitched her ship incrementally downward. Toward the ground, she reminded herself—ground, like atmosphere and gravity, was a challenge she normally flew without. Another flash of emerald suggested her foes were getting closer, likely attempting to catch her in their crossfire.

She let the wind guide her. She couldn't outfly Major Keize, but she was at least as good as his squadron mates. She'd flown with Shana, seen Tong's flight stats, and Quell deserved her fate if she couldn't match them both. She dived through a ribbon of yellow silt that left her momentarily blind, then reduced her repulsor output until the TIE fighter's aerodynamics took over and sent it veering at a sharp angle. Quell might find atmospheric flight challenging, but her opponents would find an enemy jerked about by gravity positively confounding. The next volley of particle blasts was just a glimmer in her peripheral vision.

They would be back on her soon. A thunderclap loud enough to resonate in her bones reassured her she was near the storm's center. She wondered, startled by the thought, if she should say something to the major before the end—make some last plea or acknowledgment of their years together—then blotted the idea from her mind. She'd made her decision.

She looked through her streaked cockpit at the swirling vortex of colors. She accelerated as hard as the TIE would allow, checked her instruments through the pain in her skull and the glimmering spots in front of her eyes, counted to five, then tilted her fighter an additional fifty degrees toward the ground.

After that, two events occurred nearly simultaneously. Somehow she was aware of them both.

As Quell's fighter rushed toward the surface of Nacronis, her three pursuers—already accelerating to match Quell's speed—flew directly toward the storm center. Two of the enemy TIEs, according to her scanner, attempted to break away. They were caught by the gale and, as they decelerated, swept into each other. Both were immediately destroyed in the collision.

The third pilot attempted to navigate the gauntlet of lightning and silt. He fared better, but his starfighter wasn't equal to his skill. Something went wrong—Quell guessed that silt particles had crept into seams in the TIE's armor, or that a lightning strike had shorted the fighter's systems—and Major Soran Keize, too, disappeared from her scanner. The ace of the 204th Imperial Fighter Wing was dead.

At the same time her pursuers met their end, Quell attempted to break out of her dive. She saw nothing of the world outside her cockpit, nothing beyond her instruments, and her body felt leaden as she operated the TIE's controls. She'd managed to level out the ship when she heard a deafening crash and felt her seat heave beneath her. She realized half a second later that the bottom of her starboard wing had struck the mire of Nacronis's surface and was dragging through the silt. Half a second after that, she lost total control of her vessel and made the mistake of reaching for the ejector switch with her right hand.

The TIE fighter halted abruptly and she was thrown at the now-cracked viewport. The safety harness caught her extended right arm and snapped her brittle bones as the straps cut into her body. Her face smashed against the inside of her flight helmet. Agony and nausea followed. She heard nothing but an unidentifiable dull roar. She blacked out and woke almost immediately—swiftly enough to savor the still-fresh pain.

Quell had an extremely good memory, but she didn't remember cutting herself free of the safety harness or clambering out of the cockpit hatch. She didn't remember whether she'd vomited when she'd removed her helmet. She remembered, vaguely, the smell of burning circuits and her own sweat—but that was all, until she sat on top of her broken craft amid a multicolored marsh and looked up at the sky.

She couldn't tell if it was night or day. The swirling, iridescent storm looked like an oily whirlpool, blotting out sun or stars or both. It churned and grew, visibly expanding moment by moment. Glimmering above the white lightning, faint and high, were the orange lights of atmospheric explosions: the payloads of other TIE fighters.

The explosions would stoke the storm, Quell knew—stoke and feed it, and others like it, until storms tore through every city on Nacronis. The silt would flay towers and citadels to their steel bones. Children would choke on mud flooding the streets. All because an order had been given, and only Quell and Tonas and Barath had bothered to defy it.

This was what her Empire had become in the days after Endor. She saw it now, but she was too late to save Nacronis.

"YOU WERE FORTUNATE to survive," the droid said when Yrica Quell finished her story.

"The TIE gave me somewhere to shelter. The open marshland wasn't hit as hard as the main settlements."

"I don't doubt it. My observation stands. Do you *feel* fortunate, Lieutenant Quell?"

She wrinkled her nose. Her eyes flickered from the spherical droid to the corrugated metal walls of the repurposed shipping container where they met.

"Why shouldn't I?" she asked. "I'm alive. And I've been assigned a charming therapist."

The droid hesitated, ran the statement through multiple analysis programs, and was pleasantly surprised to conclude that its patient's hostility was omnidirectional, counterproductive, and obnoxious, but in no way aimed at the droid. Creating a rapport remained possible. It was, in fact, a priority—albeit not the droid's *only* priority.

"Let's resume tomorrow," the droid said, "and talk more about what happened between your crash and your discovery by the emergency crew."

Quell grunted and rose, raising the hood of her poncho before taking the single step needed to reach the shipping container's door. She paused there and looked from the droid's photoreceptor to the injector syringe attached to its manipulator.

"Do people try to hurt you," she asked, "when they see an Imperial torture droid waiting to treat them?"

This time, her voice suggested an admixture of hostility and curiosity.

"I see very few patients," the droid answered. That fact was dangerously close to qualifying as classified intelligence, but the droid deemed the risk of breach acceptably low next to the benefits of earning Quell's trust.

Quell only grunted again and departed.

The droid reviewed the recorded conversation seventeen times. It focused on the woman's biofeedback throughout, but it didn't neglect more conventional verbal analysis. Quell's story, it decided, was largely consistent with the testimony of a traumatized Imperial defector.

Nonetheless, the droid was certain she was lying.

II

Traitor's Remorse was a frost-bitten shantytown of an outpost. Once a nameless rebel base built to harbor a handful of desperate insurgents, it had evolved into a sprawling maze of improvised shelters, security fencing, and duracrete bunkers housing twelve thousand would-be defectors from the crumbling Galactic Empire. Under an ashen sky, former Imperial military personnel suffered debriefings and scrutiny and medical examinations as they waited for the nascent rebel government—the so-called New Republic—to determine their fate.

Most of the defectors occupied the outpost only in passing. They were infantry and engineers, com-scan officers and admirals' aides. Designated *low risk* and *high value,* they received an offer of leniency and redeployment within a week, then shipped out to crew captured Star Destroyers or to join orbital minesweeper teams. Meanwhile, those less fortunate— the defectors designated *high risk* and *low value* by whatever New Republic interviewer they'd annoyed—were stuck trying to prove themselves reliable, loyal, and of sound moral character without going mad from tedium.

Yrica Quell occupied the latter category. She didn't think the name *Traitor's Remorse* was funny, but after a month she couldn't think of one better.

On a foggy afternoon, Quell jogged down the gravel path running from her housing unit to the landing pads. She kept her pace slow to reduce the throbbing in her shoulder and minimize the bounce of her sling, rapidly transitioning from chilled to overheated to clammy with cold sweat. She shouldn't have been running at all in her condition. (She hadn't needed to heal naturally from a broken bone since she'd been twelve years old, but medical bacta was in short supply for ex-Imperials.) She ran anyway. Her routine was the only thing keeping her sane.

Once, she would have cleared her mind by flying. That wasn't an option now.

Certainly her therapist wasn't doing much good. The reprogrammed IT-O torture droid seemed more interested in examining and reexamining her last flight than in helping her adapt to her circumstances. There was nothing *useful* about the images of Nacronis the droid had dredged up in her mind—siltstorms tearing through settlements, explosions in the sky. Nothing that would serve her or the New Republic. Yet until the droid was satisfied, it seemed she wouldn't be allowed to move on.

She approached a checkpoint and turned off the gravel path ten meters before the entrance to the landing zone, running alongside the fence surrounding the tarmac. Brittle cyan grass crunched satisfyingly under her boots. One of the sentries threw her a wave, and she returned a curt nod. This, too, was part of her routine.

She kept running, past the informal junk swap and the communications tower. Two hundred meters down the tarmac fence she drew to a stop, adjusted her sling, smoothed back her sweat-slicked hair—the blond locks longer and sloppier than she was used to, irritating her nape—and listened to a howl mixed with a high-pitched whine far above. She craned her neck, squinting into the gray light, and looked to the blotch in the sky.

Right on time. In all the chaos of a civil war, in one obscure corner of the galaxy, the rebels somehow kept their daily transport on schedule. Maybe the New Republic had a chance after all.

The GR-75 was an aging beast of a starship, slow to maneuver and bulky even for its class, but Quell felt a pang as the tapered vessel descended, washing her with exhaust and radiant heat. Somewhere aboard a pilot calculated landing vectors and calibrated instruments for atmospheric pressure. A pilot who—if only when flying without passengers or cargo—surely accelerated past her ship's recommended limits and tested herself against the resulting g forces. Quell's fingers played along an invisible set of controls. Then she clenched her fists shut.

Give me a shuttle, she thought. *An airspeeder. Even a flight simulator.*

The GR-75 tapped the tarmac hard enough to jolt the ground. Quell watched through the fence as one of the outpost sentries performed a cursory inspection of the ship's hull before signaling for the boarding ramp to lower. A tentacled New Republic officer was the first passenger to disembark. The officer passed a datapad to the sentry, and the march of new arrivals began.

After the officer, they were nearly all human. That was the most obvious clue to their origins—the Empire had been, as the propaganda said, built on the labor of galactic humanity. The passengers were mostly young, but not without exception. Mostly clean-cut, though a few were untidy. They looked across the tarmac with trepidation. To a person, they had attempted to rid themselves of identifying gear—even the ones still in Imperial uniforms had stripped away all symbols and regalia. Quell suspected some carried their insignia badges anyway, secreted in pockets or sleeves. She'd encountered more than one set of rank plaques at the junk swap.

She identified the ex-stormtroopers by their boots—too sturdy and well fitted to abandon, their white synth-leather caked in grime and turned the yellow of a bad tooth. Quell gave the stormtroopers a perfunctory glance and removed them from her mental checklist. The officers were given away by their bearing, and she scanned their features, searching her memory for matches and finding none. (*I have an extremely good memory,* she'd told the droid, and it was true.) She felt a vague satisfaction at identifying a combat medic by her Academy ring, but otherwise noticed nothing remarkable.

All of them were bastards, she knew. The new arrivals got worse every day.

When Quell had arrived a month ago, Traitor's Remorse had already been crowded with the first wave of deserters who'd abandoned their posts after the Battle of Endor. Some had come out of bravery, others out of cowardice, but Quell respected their foresight: They'd understood that the Emperor who'd built an interstellar civilization and governed for two decades was dead, and that his Empire wouldn't endure without him. That without an heir, the Empire's sins (and they were many—the most zealous loyalty officer couldn't believe otherwise) would corrupt and destroy what remained. That the impossible victory that the Rebel Alliance had achieved—the assassination of the Emperor aboard his own massive battle station—was worth embracing wholeheartedly.

Quell hadn't been part of that first wave. Instead she'd come during the second.

The days after the Emperor's death had been chaotic. The massive uprisings on thousands of planets—along with proving that the rebels had been right all along about public sentiment toward the Empire—made it clear that there would be no return to the old ways, no swift restoration of familiar rule. Yet a strategy, of sorts, soon emerged inside the remains of the Imperial military. Fleets across known space took part in Operation Cinder: the leveling of civilizations on Nacronis and Vardos, Candovant and Commenor, and more besides. Planets both loyal and in open revolt. Planets rich in resources and planets that possessed nothing but faded glory. They were bombed and gassed and flooded, their own weather patterns and geology turned against them. Nacronis was ravaged by siltstorms. Tectonic devices shattered the crust of Senthrodys.

The Empire tried to destroy them all. Not to deny the New Republic access to vital territories. Not to thwart insurrections. Not as part of any meaningful plan to secure the Empire. The surviving admirals had said it was for *all* those reasons, yet not one was fully satisfactory. Maybe Operation Cinder had been conducted out of some sort of perceived necessity, but it was fueled by rage and it would do nothing—it was obvious, *beyond* obvious—to slow the Empire's disintegration.

Cinder had been a turning point. Loyal soldiers who had executed whole planets at the Emperor's behest had seen billions of lives snuffed out for no strategic gain and known that the moral calculus had changed. Imperial heroes unable to stomach the slaughter had turned on their superiors. Naboo, the Emperor's own homeworld, had been saved from genocide with the aid of Imperial Special Forces commandos. They had come to a shared realization: It was one thing to fight a losing battle, and another to disregard the cost.

That had been the second wave of desertions and defections.

Which meant anyone who'd stayed afterward had made a conscious choice to forget the cost. To forget the fact that preserving the Empire as it had been was a lost cause. To fight on anyway, consequences be damned.

Every day after Operation Cinder, the pointlessness of the carnage became clearer. Every day, those remaining inside the Empire were tested anew. So far as Quell was concerned, the men and women aboard the GR-75 transport had failed *too many* tests to deserve sympathy or redemption. The ones who came tomorrow would be worse still.

A voice penetrated her thoughts like a needle into skin. "See anyone you like?"

A man in a rumpled coat picked his way toward Quell, looking between her and the grass as if afraid he might step on a mine or a glass shard. He would have appeared human—

wiry black hair flecked with gray, brown skin shades darker than Quell's own tawny hue, a skinny physique lost under his garments—if it hadn't been for the two wormy stalks protruding from his skull. She identified the species: Balosar.

"Not really," she said. She hadn't seen him before—hadn't noticed him arrive on a transport, nor stood in line with him for rations. He wasn't in uniform, but he surely wasn't a defector. She added: "No rule about standing on this side of the fence."

"Stand where you want," the man replied. He stopped three paces away and squinted in the direction of the transport. The new arrivals continued their march, each exchanging a few words with the sentry before heading for processing. "Who *are* you watching for? You come here every day. Are you expecting friends? A lover? Rescue?"

"We're free to go, aren't we? Why would I need rescue?"

It was a half-truth, and Quell was curious how the man would react. Officially, the residents of Traitor's Remorse could leave at any time. But taking flight would guarantee the New Republic's ire, and who knew what sort of grudge the rebel government would hold? Anyone not in line for a pardon was risking a perilous future.

The man simply shrugged. "I'm glad to hear you say that. Not everyone feels the same way." His voice flattened. "Answer the question, please? Who are you watching for?"

Quell heard the entitlement. The man had authority, or wanted her to think he did. She didn't look at him, and found her answer in the march of defectors. "You see the one with the scars?" She lifted one finger—barely a gesture—in the direction of a bulky man in a leather vest. Rough red marks ran from his neck to the undersides of his ears.

"I do," the Balosar said, though his attention was entirely on Quell.

"I've seen scars like that. Surgical augmentations. My guess is he was a candidate for one of the elite stormtrooper divisions—death troopers, maybe—but his body couldn't take the mods."

"Supposing that's true, it's very likely in his file. Why are you watching him?"

Quell whirled to face the man. She kept her voice level, excised the frustration. If he was with the New Republic, she needed him. "You've got a man with that past, who stayed with the Empire as long as he did—you think he's good recruiting material? You want him wandering around the outpost, free and clear?"

The Balosar's lips twitched, and he smiled in realization. "You're looking out for us. That's generous, but we won the war; we can manage our own security." He extended a hand. "Caern Adan. Alliance—excuse me. *New Republic* Intelligence."

Quell took the hand. In all her interviews since arriving, she'd never met a New Republic spy. If he'd been Imperial Intelligence, she might have been terrified, but terror seemed premature.

The man's grip was weak until she squeezed. Then it became a pinch. "Yrica Quell," she said. "Former lieutenant, 204th Fighter Wing. At your mercy."

"The 204th was never known for its *mercy*, though, was it?" He looked like he was about to laugh, but he never did. "'Shadow Wing,' your people called it. Quite a name, up there with *Death Star*. Sightings all over prior to Endor, at Blacktar Cyst and Mennar-Daye, slaughtering rebels and keeping the hyperlanes safe . . . did you happen to fly at Mimban?"

The litany of names struck like blows. She didn't flinch. He had come prepared and he had come for her. "Before my time," she said.

"Too bad. It's a story I'd love to hear. Some of my colleagues didn't notice you all until—well, until Nacronis—but we both know you were spectacular for years. If Grand General Loring had appreciated you more, if Vader had paid more attention to the starfighter corps, you'd probably have been at Endor yourselves. Maybe kept the poor Emperor alive."

"Maybe so."

Adan waited for more. His smile wilted but didn't disappear. Finally he went on. "That's all past. Since Operation Cinder, though, Shadow Wing keeps popping up. Nine sightings in just over two weeks, tearing apart convoys, bombing outposts . . . even took out one of our star cruisers."

Another blow, aimed with more care than before. He might have been lying about Shadow Wing, but it sounded possible. Even plausible. Again, she didn't flinch, though she felt her injuries throb in time with her pulse.

"Nine sightings in two weeks," Quell said. "It's been a month since Nacronis."

Adan nodded brusquely, scanned the ground as if searching for a place to sit, then shifted his weight from foot to foot. "Which is why I'm here. Dozens of the Empire's finest pilots disappear at a time like this? They're not hiding out awaiting orders; they're running silent."

She didn't look at the trail of defectors still emerging onto the tarmac. She didn't even meet Adan's gaze. She was focused on the words, turning them over in her head. "You have a theory?" she asked.

"I have a plan," Adan said. "I'm assembling a working group to study the situation. Experts who can analyze the data and predict the enemy's next move. Maybe do some investigative legwork."

She fixed the words in her mind: *I'm assembling a working group.*

She cut the resistance from her voice like a tumor. Cautiously, she answered: "I was hoping for a military position. Somewhere I could fly."

Adan's smile was rejuvenated. "I'm sure you were, but

we've seen your file. The Shadow Wing pilot who couldn't save Nacronis? No high-level clearance, no access to classified intelligence or special expertise—just a solid track record of shooting rebels. You're not anyone's favorite candidate for recruitment."

So work for New Republic Intelligence, Quell heard, though he didn't say the words. *Sit at a console and help us hunt your friends. Maybe you'll even get a pardon out of it.*

What Adan uttered aloud was: "Consider it. If I decide I want you, I'll find you—and I expect you to have an answer ready."

FOR A MONTH, Yrica Quell had waited to prove herself. To show that she had abandoned the 204th Fighter Wing for a reason. To show that she could offer the New Republic a talent it lacked, bringing Imperial rigor and discipline to its starfighter corps.

She had waited to take part in the war's end. To fly again. She had waited to do something *decent* for once, the way she'd wanted to long ago.

She wasn't certain Caern Adan was offering any of what she wanted. Maybe she hadn't earned it.

Traitor's Remorse turned cold at night. The gently numbing chill of the day turned to wind that whipped Quell's poncho around her hips and forced her to keep her good hand on the brim of her hood. She pushed against the gale as she trudged between stacked containers-turned-houses, under swinging electrical cables, and into the shelter of a bunker dug out of a low hillside.

The wind's roar faded within, replaced by laughter and conversation. As her eyes adjusted to the dim light, Quell saw two dozen figures seated on crates and on the dirt floor. They were playing cards and dice; swapping old tales and showing old scars. They should have been drinking, but there was nothing worth drinking in Traitor's Remorse. (There was harder contraband for those with a taste for ryll or death sticks, but no one was fool enough to indulge where the New Republic watched.)

Quell had come to the Warren to trade. She had no friends in Traitor's Remorse—passing acquaintances, an old man with whom she shared her supper rations, but no friends— yet seniority had its privileges. She'd been at the outpost as long as anyone, and she knew which New Republic officers were forgiving and which held "special" grudges. She knew where to buy an extra meal and who claimed to be able to smuggle out messages. She could swap rumors for rumors, and the people who might know about Caern Adan would give her a measure of attention.

She passed deeper into the bunker, down a hallway and past a young logistics consultant brokering the exchange of military casualty lists. She nodded to an engineer who'd helped her repair a faulty heater, but the man was fixated on a diagram he'd sketched on the floor. She saw none of the regulars she sought, and she was nearly ready to move on when she spotted the stormtrooper.

The surgical augmentation scars on his neck seemed to burn in the flickering electric light. He turned a hydrospanner over in his hands as if it were a weapon. If he was the sort to join the death troopers, maybe he'd used one as a bludgeon before.

Quell wasn't a fighter by nature. She'd never gotten into a pointless scrap in her Academy days and only once been in a fistfight as a teenager. She was military, true, but she was a *pilot* first—shooting things was the least of her duties. Nonetheless, she approached the man unafraid of what might come next. *Why'd you finally jump ship?* she planned to say.

And if he gave the wrong answer? If he took a swing at her? After a day of feeling small and frustrated and helpless, maybe a fight was what she needed.

She never got to say a word.

She felt the rumble first. The ground bucked and she swallowed a lungful of dust before the thunder even registered. The screaming that followed was strangely muffled, and she realized she'd gone deaf. She was blind, too, but that was the dust again—pale white clouds that stung her nostrils and scattered the dim illumination.

I'm hit, she thought, and knew it to be a lie. She was fine. She wasn't sure about the rest of the Warren.

One part of her brain calmly reconstructed what had happened as she stumbled forward. There had been a bomb—nothing big, maybe a jury-rigged plasma grenade. Someone had planted it in another room, or carried it inside and triggered the detonator. Someone like one of the new defectors who'd arrived on the GR-75, determined to make an example of those who betrayed the Empire. She pieced the story together easily because it had happened twice before. This was the closest she'd been to a blast.

Her foot crushed something soft—an arm covered in blood and scraps of leather. Leaning forward, she was desperately relieved to see it was attached to a body. The stormtrooper. The death trooper candidate. She knelt beside him and wrapped her good arm around his burly chest, allowing him to scale her and stand.

He was a bastard, she reminded herself as they lurched toward the exit. But then, so was everyone at Traitor's Remorse.

They struggled forward step by step, coughing up grime and navigating by the muted shouting. Eventually Quell felt the weight of the stormtrooper disappear and realized another person had lifted him away. She could almost hear again. Someone—perhaps the same person who had taken the stormtrooper—asked about her health. She choked out a reply and stepped out of the Warren and into the artificial glow of the shantytown.

No one prevented her from pushing forward through the perimeter of ex-Imperial onlookers and tense New Republic security officers. No one cared enough to try. She briefly considered going back, but she was dizzy and half deaf and could see the dust on her breath. She'd just get in the way of the rescue team.

But she realized as she coughed and spat that she had the answer she'd come for.

She wasn't sure Caern Adan would give her an opportunity to fly, or to prove herself, or to do anything decent. But the bombing had reminded her that those things were luxuries.

She had to find a way out of Traitor's Remorse. Any chance was worth taking.

III

CAERN ADAN STRETCHED an elastic band between thumb and forefinger, let loose, and watched the band soar across the supply closet that served as his office. It deformed in flight, missing IT-O by ten centimeters and puncturing the cone of azure particles emitted by the droid's holoprojector. The humanoid figure standing within the cone pixelated and flickered into nonexistence.

"You're aggravated," the droid said, unhelpfully.

"I'm attempting to get something actionable out of you," Caern answered.

"Actionable intelligence is your area, not mine."

IT-O adjusted its holoprojector—a gift Caern had installed in the droid many months earlier—and the figure re-formed, magnified a dozen times over. Yrica Quell stared lifelessly over her jutting nose out of creaseless, bloodshot eyes. There was a fragility to her that went beyond the obvious cuts on her lips and scalp—a sort of glasslike sharpness, equally likely to injure or shatter. Imperial arrogance ground down and humbled.

Caern studied the image and sighed. "Suppose you're right," he said. "She's lying. What exactly is she lying about? Or—" He silenced the droid with a slash of his hand. "—give me this: What do we think is *true*?"

IT-O floated like a toy boat in a slow current. "She has suffered trauma," it said.

Caern resisted the urge to interject: *Haven't we all?*

"Physically, of course," the droid went on, "but she's struggling to process recent events. She's isolated. Simultaneously hypervigilant and unfocused."

"Vague," Caern said. "Ever consider telling fortunes for a living?"

"Building a rapport requires time. Without a rapport, I can be of little use to my patient or to you."

It was an old argument, and Caern was eager to move past it. "Her background checks out, so far as we can tell. We can't confirm operational details, but she was definitely part of Shadow Wing." He rose and moved his hand to the door's control panel. "Any reason to think she's a spy? Could the whole *defector* story be a ruse?"

"If she's a spy, she's not an especially good one, given how suspicious we are of her already."

"Maybe the Empire is fresh out of competent spies." Caern tapped the panel and stepped into the hallway. "Come on. We need air."

They moved through the corridors of the bunker, past makeshift processing stations and communications rigs. One of the military interviewers mumbled a greeting at Caern, and Caern muttered back. IT-O received glowers from several officers and was ignored by others. The torture droid was divisive at the best of times.

Once outside, Caern pulled his coat around him. He felt a distant buzz—some sort of cutting rig slicing through rock—and retracted his antennapalps into his skull to reduce the bothersome sensation. The source appeared to be a fenced-off section of the outpost over the next hill. He waved IT-O along, tromping through grass and dirt until he saw the ruins of the bombed bunker. A dozen New Republic workers clustered about the entrance, dragging equipment and stone and bodies into the midmorning light.

"You know what this is?" he asked IT-O, nodding in the direction of the rubble.

"Something symbolic of whatever argument you intend to make?"

Caern scoffed. He brought his sleeve to his upper lip as his nose dripped from the cold. "It's an intelligence failure. Yes, it's symbolic. It was also predictable and preventable. It's the fourth bombing we've had here."

"We are in agreement," IT-O said. "It was indeed preventable."

"But no one else sees it. We've got an outpost full of ground-pounders and flyboys who think *security* means 'shoot down anyone who finds the *secret base*.' But the bases aren't *secret* anymore and we've got too many problems to shoot."

In truth, it was worse than that. The problem was leadership. The New Republic was a military organization—no matter what Chancellor Mothma said, its roots in the insurgent Rebel Alliance ran deep—and it only understood military solutions. He didn't need to reiterate that point to IT-O, and instead said: "Intelligence will hold the New Republic together, or the New Republic won't hold at all. No one up top seems to realize that. No one seems to care, no matter how many bombs are planted."

"There are those in government who care about the dead. You know this."

"About the dead? Maybe. But not about what's killing them."

"We're talking about a government that's barely had time to form," IT-O said. "To attribute any philosophy of national security to the New Republic is, at this stage, premature."

"Maybe," Caern repeated. He glanced at the droid, wondering (as he often did) whether IT-O was manipulating him, nudging him toward a conclusion he might not otherwise reach. But the droid's crimson photoreceptor gave no hints. "Regardless, New Republic Intelligence is underfunded and understaffed. But if someone did something *right* for a change . . ."

"You believe that an intelligence operation to dismantle the 204th Fighter Wing would force New Republic leadership to reexamine its priorities."

"Shouldn't it?" Caern turned his back on the rubble and dust. "Shadow Wing was trouble before the Battle of Endor, but back then we were more scared of another Death Star battle station than Imperial fighter pilots. Now they're making precision strikes. We lost all hands aboard the *Huntsman* and the *Kalpana*. I'm sure the 204th was involved in the raid on Beauchen. Exclude the Operation Cinder genocides and they're still responsible for the deaths of thousands." He swept his arms to indicate the broken bunker. "This is what the Empire looks like, now: fewer planet-killing superweapons, more murderous fanatics."

"Counterterrorism being an intelligence specialty."

"Exactly!" Caern clapped his hands together. "If an intelligence working group were to neutralize Shadow Wing, it would prove everything I've been saying. The threat and the solution."

"And once New Republic leadership agrees that Imperial splinter groups are best countered by intelligence officers, do you imagine that would justify a massive resource allotment to the working group that neutralized Shadow Wing? Along with said working group's supervisor?"

Caern shrugged. "Why not? It's better for everyone."

The droid's repulsors whined as its spherical body navigated past Caern, descending a meter down the hillside in the direction of the rubble. "Is this about defeating an enemy of the New Republic? Or about seizing power in a time of political instability?"

"Why not both?" Caern failed to hide his irritation. He wanted to repeat himself: *It's better for everyone.* And it was—Shadow Wing's threat was real and ongoing, and if neutralizing it led to greater intelligence resources and his own personal elevation, that would lead to fewer bombings and fewer Operation Cinders. Running a government and defending a populace weren't the same as assassinating an emperor; the sooner the New Republic realized that, the better.

He forced himself to draw a breath and regroup. "The real question," he said, "is this: Is Yrica Quell the person I need?"

The droid didn't move. Caern recognized IT-O's deep concentration as it ran dozens of scenarios and dredged through a thousand years of medical texts for an answer. The silence calmed Caern. However much of an annoyance IT-O could be, Caern found the droid's willingness to *work*—to sort facts and make the best call possible, no matter how ferociously they'd argued—comforting.

"No," IT-O said. "I don't believe she is."

He visibly flinched as frustration reignited in his chest. He turned his eyes to the column of smoke rising intermittently from the rubble. She had been there, he knew—Quell had been spotted pulling someone from the wreckage—and he tried to picture her wounded, brittle form caked in dust and blood.

She was a liar. A woman who'd committed who-knew-*what* crimes during her time with the 204th. A woman who'd seen the Empire crumble and now claimed to have a conscience. Caern had seen her kind before. He never forgave them, and sooner or later they all reverted to type.

But he could handle that.

He needed her, whatever IT-O claimed.

"Call our friend," Caern said. "The working group convenes tomorrow."

ABOUT THE TYPE

This book was set in Sabon, a typeface designed by the well-known German typographer Jan Tschichold (1902–74). Sabon's design is based upon the original letter forms of sixteenth-century French type designer Claude Garamond and was created specifically to be used for three sources: foundry type for hand composition, Linotype, and Monotype. Tschichold named his typeface for the famous Frankfurt typefounder Jacques Sabon (c. 1520–80).

A long time ago in a galaxy far, far away. . . .

STAR WARS

Join up! Subscribe to our newsletter at ReadStarWars.com or find us on social.

𝕏 **@StarWarsByRHW**

⬡ **@StarWarsByRHW**

f **StarWarsByRHW**